Praise for Robert Jordan and The Wheel of Time®

"His huge, ambitious Wheel of Time series helped redefine the genre." —George R. R. Martin, internationally bestselling author of *A Game of Thrones*

"Anyone who's writing epic secondary world fantasy knows Robert Jordan isn't just a part of the landscape, he's a monolith within the landscape." —Patrick Rothfuss, internationally bestselling author of The Kingkiller Chronicle

"*The Eye of the World* was a turning point in my life. I read, I enjoyed. (Then continued on to write my larger fantasy novels.)" —Robin Hobb, *New York Times* bestselling author of The Farseer Trilogy

"Robert Jordan's work has been a formative influence and an inspiration for a generation of fantasy writers." —Brent Weeks, *New York Times* bestselling author of *The Way of Shadows*

"Jordan has come to dominate the world Tolkien began to reveal." —*The New York Times*

"One of fantasy's most acclaimed series." —*USA Today*

"Robert Jordan was a giant of fiction whose words helped a whole generation of fantasy writers, including myself, find our true voices. I thanked him then, but I didn't thank him enough." —Peter V. Brett, internationally bestselling author of The Demon Cycle

The Wheel of Time®

By Robert Jordan

By Robert Jordan and Brandon Sanderson

By Robert Jordan and Teresa Patterson

By Robert Jordan, Harriet McDougal, Alan Romanczuk, and Maria Simons

NEW
SPRING:
THE NOVEL

ROBERT JORDAN

A TOM DOHERTY ASSOCIATES BOOK
NEW YORK

This is a work of fiction. All of the characters, organizations, and events portrayed in this novel are either products of the author's imagination or are used fictitiously.

NEW SPRING: THE NOVEL

Copyright © 2004 by Bandersnatch Group, Inc.

The phrase "The Wheel of Time" and the snake-wheel symbol are trademarks of Bandersnatch Group, Inc.

Maps by Ellisa Mitchell
Interior illustrations by Matthew C. Nielsen and Ellisa Mitchell

A Tor Book
Published by Tom Doherty Associates
120 Broadway
New York, NY 10271

www.tor-forge.com

Tor® is a registered trademark of Macmillan Publishing Group, LLC.

ISBN 978-1-250-25263-0

Our books may be purchased in bulk for promotional, educational, or business use. Please contact your local bookseller or the Macmillan Corporate and Premium Sales Department at 1-800-221-7945, extension 5442, or by email at MacmillanSpecialMarkets@macmillan.com.

First Edition: 2004
First Premium Mass Market Edition: 2020

Printed in the United States of America

0 9 8 7 6 5 4 3 2 1

For Harriet
Now and forever

Contents

New Spring:
The Novel

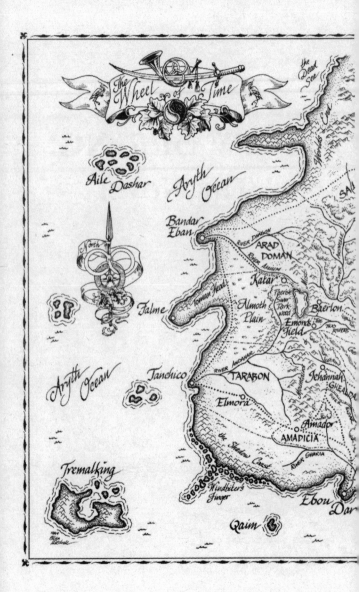

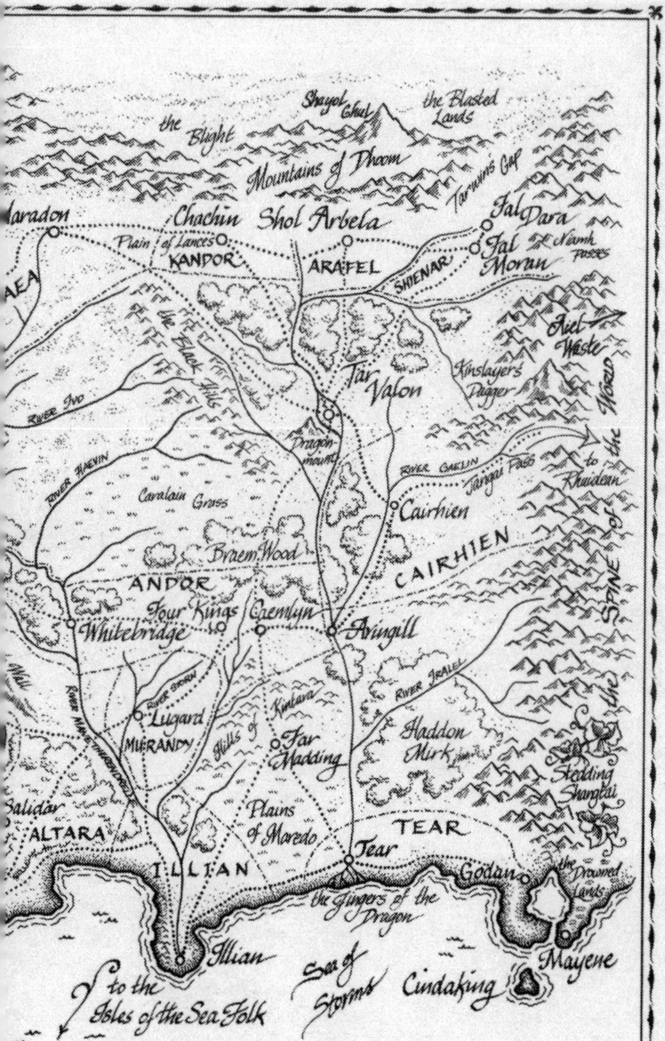

Shayol Ghul
the Blasted Lands
the Blight
Mountains of Dhoom
Tarwin's Gap
Fal Dara
Fal Moran
Niamh Passes
Chachin
Shol Arbela
Plain of Lances
KANDOR
ARAFEL
SHIENAR
Aiel Waste
Kinslayer's Dagger
the Black Hills
Tar Valon
River Ivo
Dragonmount
River Haevin
River Gaelin
Jangai Pass
to Rhuidean
Caralain Grass
Cairhien
CAIRHIEN
Braem Wood
ANDOR
Four Kings
Chemlyn
Aringill
Whitebridge
SPINE of the WORLD
River Storn
River Iralell
Lugard
Hills of Kintara
MURANDY
Far Madding
Haddon Mirk
Stedding Shangtai
Salidar
ALTARA
Plains of Maredo
TEAR
Tear
ILLIAN
Godan
the Drowned Lands
the Fingers of the Dragon
Illian
Mayene
Sea of Storms
Cindaking
to the Isles of the Sea Folk

CHAPTER

I

The Hook

A cold wind gusted through the night, across the snow-covered land where men had been killing one another for the past three days. The air was crisp, if not so icy as Lan expected for this time of year. It was still cold enough for his steel breastplate to carry the chill through his coat, and his breath to mist in front of his face when the wind did not whip it away. The blackness in the sky was just beginning to fade, the thousands of stars like the thick-scattered dust of diamonds slowly dimming. The fat sickle of the moon hung low, giving barely light to make out the silhouettes of the men guarding the fireless camp in the sprawling copse of oak and leatherleaf. Fires would have given them away to the Aiel. He had fought the Aiel long before this war began, on the Shienaran marches, a matter of duty to friends. Aiel-men were bad enough in daylight. Facing them in the night was as close to staking your life on the toss of a coin as made no difference. Of course, sometimes they found you without fires.

Resting a gauntleted hand on his sword in its scabbard, he pulled his cloak back around himself and continued his round of the sentries through calf-deep snow. It was an ancient sword, made with the One Power before the Break-ing of the World, during the War of the Shadow, when the Dark One had touched the world for a time. Only legends remained of that Age, except perhaps for what the Aes Sedai might know, yet the blade was hard fact. It could not be broken and never needed sharpening. The hilt had been re-placed countless times over the long centuries, but not even tarnish could touch the blade. Once, it had been the sword of Malkieri kings.

The next sentry he came to, a short stocky fellow in a long dark cloak, was leaning back against the trunk of a heavy-limbed oak, his head slumped on his chest. Lan touched the sentry's shoulder, and the man jerked upright, almost dropping the horn-and-sinew horsebow gripped in his gloved hands. The hood of his cloak slid back, revealing his conical steel helmet for an instant before he hastily pulled the cowl up again. In the pale moonlight, Lan could not make out the man's face behind the vertical bars of his faceguard, but he knew him. Lan's own helmet was open, in the style of dead Malkier, supporting a steel crescent moon above his forehead.

"I wasn't sleeping, my Lord," the fellow said quickly. "Just resting a moment." A copper-skinned Domani, he sounded embarrassed, and rightly so. This was not his first battle, or even his first war.

"An Aiel would have wakened you by slitting your throat or putting a spear through your heart, Basram," Lan said in a quiet voice. Men listened closer to calm tones than to the loudest shouts, so long as firmness and certainty accompanied the calm. "Maybe it would be better without the temptation of the tree so near." He refrained from adding that even if the Aiel did not kill him, the man risked frostbite standing in one place too long. Basram knew that. Winters were nearly as cold in Arad Doman as in the Borderlands.

Mumbling an apology, the Domani respectfully touched his helmet and moved three paces out from the tree. He held himself erect, now, and peered into the darkness. He shifted his feet, too, guarding against blackened toes. Rumor said Aes Sedai were offering Healing, closer to the river, injuries and sickness gone as if they had never been, but without that, amputation was the usual way to stop a man losing his feet to black-rot, and maybe his legs as well. In any case, it was best to avoid becoming involved with Aes Sedai more than absolutely necessary. Years later you could find one of them had tied strings to you just in case she might have need. Aes Sedai thought far ahead, and seldom seemed to care who they used in their schemes or how. That was one reason Lan avoided them.

How long would Basram's renewed alertness last? Lan

wished he had the answer, but there was no point in taking the Domani to task further. All of the men he commanded were bone-weary. Likely every man in the army of the grandly named Great Coalition—sometimes it was called the Grand Coalition, or the Grand Alliance, or half a dozen other things, some worse than uncomplimentary—likely every last man was near exhaustion. A battle was hot work, snow or no snow, and tiring. Muscles could knot from tension even when they had the chance to stop for a time, and the last few days had offered small chance to stop very long.

The camp held well over three hundred men, a full quarter of them on guard at any given time—against Aiel, Lan wanted as many eyes as he could manage—and before he had gone another two hundred paces, he had had to wake three more, one asleep on his feet without any support at all. Jaim's head was up, and his eyes open. That was a trick some soldiers learned, especially old soldiers like Jaim. Cutting off the gray-bearded man's protests that he could not have been asleep, not standing up straight, Lan promised to let Jaim's friends know if he found him sleeping again.

Jaim's mouth hung open for a moment; then he swallowed hard. "Won't happen again, my Lord. The Light sear my soul if it does!" He sounded sincere to his bones. Some men would have been afraid that their friends would drub them senseless for putting the rest in danger, but given the company Jaim kept, more likely he dreaded the humiliation of having been caught.

As Lan walked on, he found himself chuckling. He seldom laughed, and it was a fool thing to laugh over, but laughter was better than worrying over what he could not change, such as weary men drowsing on guard. As well worry about death. What could not be changed must be endured.

Abruptly, he stopped and raised his voice. "Bukama, why are you sneaking about? You've been following me since I woke." A startled grunt came from behind him. Doubtless Bukama had thought he was being silent, and in truth, very few men would have heard the faint crunching of his boots in the snow, yet he should have known Lan would. After all, he had been one of Lan's teachers, and one of the first lessons had been to be aware of his surroundings at all times, even in his sleep. Not an easy lesson for a boy to learn, but only the dead could afford oblivion. The oblivious soon became the dead, in the Blight beyond the Borderlands.

"I've been watching your back," Bukama announced gruffly, striding up to join him. "One of these black-veiled Aiel Darkfriends could sneak in and cut *your* throat for all the care you're taking. Have you forgotten everything I taught you?" Bluff and broad, Bukama was almost as tall as he, taller than most men, and wearing a Malkieri helmet without a crest, though he had the right to one. He had more concern for his duties than his rights, which was proper, but Lan wished he would not spurn his rights so completely.

When the nation of Malkier died, twenty men had been given the task of carrying the infant Lan Mandragoran to safety. Only five had survived that journey, to raise Lan from the cradle and train him, and Bukama was the last left alive. His hair was solid gray now, worn cut at the shoulder as tradition required, but his back was straight, his arms hard, his blue eyes clear and keen. Tradition infused Bukama. A thin braided leather cord held his hair back, resting in the permanent groove across his forehead it had made over the years. Few men still wore the *hadori*. Lan did. He would die wearing it, and go into the ground wearing that and nothing else. If there was anyone to bury him where he died. He glanced north, toward his distant home. Most people would have thought it a strange place to call home, but he had felt the pull of it ever since he came south.

"I remembered enough to hear you," he replied. There was too little light to make out Bukama's weathered face, yet he knew it wore a glower. He could not recall seeing any other expression from his friend and teacher even when he spoke praise. Bukama was steel clothed in flesh. Steel his will, duty his soul. "Do you still believe the Aiel are pledged to the Dark One?"

The other man made a sign to ward off evil, as if Lan had spoken the Dark One's true name. Shai'tan. They had both seen the misfortune that followed speaking that name aloud, and Bukama was one of those who believed that merely thinking it drew the Dark One's attention. *The Dark One and all the Forsaken are bound in Shayol Ghul,* Lan recited the catechism in his head, *bound by the Creator at the moment of creation. May we shelter safe beneath the*

Light, in the Creator's hand. He did not believe thinking that name was enough, but better safe than sorry when it came to the Shadow.

"If they aren't, then why are we here?" Bukama said sourly. And surprisingly. He liked to grumble, but always about inconsequential things or prospects for the future. Never the present.

"I gave my word to stay until the end," Lan replied mildly.

Bukama scrubbed at his nose. His grunt might have been abashed this time. It was hard to be sure. Another of his lessons had been that a man's word must be as good as an oath sworn beneath the Light or it was no good at all.

The Aiel had indeed seemed like a horde of Darkfriends when they suddenly spilled across the immense mountain range called the Spine of the World. They had burned the great city of Cairhien, ravaged the nation of Cairhien, and, in the two years since, had fought through Tear and then Andor before reaching these killing fields, outside the huge island city of Tar Valon. In all the years since the nations of the present day had been carved out of Artur Hawkwing's empire, the Aiel had never before left the desert called the Waste. They might have invaded before that; no one could be sure, except maybe the Aes Sedai in Tar Valon, but, as so often with the women of the White Tower, they were not saying. What Aes Sedai knew, they held close, and doled out by dribbles and drops when and if they chose. In the world outside of Tar Valon, though, many men had claimed to see a pattern. A thousand years had passed between the Breaking of the World and the Trolloc Wars, or so most historians said. Those wars had destroyed the nations that existed then, and no one doubted that the Dark One's hand had been behind them, imprisoned or not, as surely as it had been behind the War of the Shadow, and the Breaking, and the end of the Age of Legends. A thousand years from the Trolloc Wars until Hawkwing built an empire and that, too, was destroyed, after his death, in the War of the Hundred Years. Some historians said they saw the Dark One's hand in that war, too. And now, close enough to a thousand years after Hawkwing's empire died, the Aiel came, burning and killing. It *had* to be a pattern. Surely the Dark One must have directed them. Lan would never have come south if he had not believed that. He no longer did. But he had given his word.

He wriggled his toes in his turned-down boots. Whether or not it was as cold as he was used to, iciness burrowed into your feet if you stood too long in one place in snow. "Let's walk," he said. "I don't doubt I'll have to wake a dozen more men if not two." And make another round to wake others.

Before they could take a step, however, a sound brought them up short, and alert: the sound of a horse walking in the snow. Lan's hand drifted to his sword hilt, half consciously easing the blade in its sheath. A faint rasp of steel on leather came from Bukama doing the same. Neither feared an attack; Aiel rode only at great need, and reluctantly even then. But a lone horseman at this hour had to be a messenger, and messengers rarely brought good news, these days. Especially not in the night.

Horse and rider materialized out of the darkness following a lean man afoot, one of the sentries by the horsebow he carried. The horse had the arched neck of good Tairen bloodstock, and the rider was plainly from Tear as well. For one thing, the scent of roses came ahead of him on the wind, from the oils glistening on his pointed beard, and only Tairens were fool enough to wear scent, as if the Aiel had no noses. Besides, no one else wore those helmets with a high ridge across the top and a rim that cast the man's narrow face in shadow. A single short white plume on the helmet marked him an officer, an odd choice for a messenger, albeit an officer of low rank. He huddled in his high-cantled saddle and held his dark cloak tightly around him. He seemed to be shivering. Tear lay far to the south. On the coast of Tear, it never snowed so much as a single flake. Lan had never quite believed that, whatever he had read, until he had seen it for himself.

"Here he is, my Lord," the sentry said in a hoarse voice. A grizzled Saldaean named Rakim, he had received that voice a year back, along with a ragged scar that he liked to show off when drinking, from an Aiel arrow in the throat. Rakim considered himself lucky to be alive, and he was. Unfortunately, he also believed that having cheated death once, he would continue to do so. He took chances, and even when not drinking, he boasted about his luck, a fool thing to do. There was no point to taunting fate.

"Lord Mandragoran?" The rider drew rein in front of Lan

and Bukama. Remaining in his saddle, he eyed them uncertainly, no doubt because their armor was unadorned, their coats and cloaks plain wool and somewhat worn. A little embroidery was a fine thing, but some southern men decked themselves out like tapestries. Likely under his cloak the Tairen wore a gilded breastplate and a silk satin coat striped in his house colors. His high boots were certainly embroidered in scrollwork that shone in the moonlight with the glitter of silver. In any case, the man went on with barely a pause for breath. "The Light burn my soul, I was sure you were the closest, but I was beginning to think I'd never find you. Lord Emares is following about five or six hundred Aiel with six hundred of his armsmen." He shook his head slightly. "Odd thing is, they're heading east. Away from the river. At any rate, the snow slows them as much as it does us, and Lord Emares thinks if you can place an anvil on that ridgeline they call the Hook, he can take them from behind with a hammer. Lord Emares doubts they can reach it before first light."

Lan's mouth tightened. Some of these southlanders had peculiar notions of polite behavior. Not dismounting before he spoke, not naming himself. As a guest, he should have named himself first. Now Lan could not without sounding boastful. The fellow had failed even to offer his lord's compliments or good wishes. And he seemed to think they did not know that east would be away from the River Erinin. Perhaps that was just carelessness in speech, but the rest was rudeness. Bukama had not moved, yet Lan laid a hand on his sword-arm anyway. His oldest friend could be touchy.

The Hook lay a good league from the camp, and the night was failing, but he nodded. "Inform Lord Emares that I will be there by first light," he told the horseman. The name Emares was unfamiliar, but the army was so large, near two hundred thousand men representing more than a dozen nations, plus Tower Guards from Tar Valon and even a contingent of the Children of the Light, that it was impossible to know above a handful of names. "Bukama, rouse the men."

Bukama grunted, savagely this time, and with a gesture for Rakim to follow, stalked away into the camp, his voice rising as he went. "Wake and saddle! We ride! Wake and saddle!"

"Ride hard," the nameless Tairen said with at least a hint of command in his voice. "Lord Emares would regret riding against those Aiel without an anvil in place." He seemed to be implying that Lan would regret this Emares' regretting.

Lan formed the image of a flame in his mind and fed emotion into it, not anger alone but everything, every scrap, until it seemed that he floated in emptiness. After years of practice, achieving *ko'di,* the oneness, needed less than a heartbeat. Thought and his own body grew distant, but in this state he became one with the ground beneath his feet, one with the night, with the sword he would not use on this mannerless fool. "I said that I would be there," he said levelly. "What I say, I do." He no longer wished to know the man's name.

The Tairen offered him a curt bow from his saddle, turned his horse, and booted the animal to a quick trot.

Lan held the *ko'di* a moment longer to be sure his emotions were firmly under control. It was beyond unwise to enter battle angry. Anger narrowed the vision and made for foolish choices. How had that fellow managed to stay alive this long? In the Borderlands, he would have sparked a dozen duels in a day. Only when Lan was sure that he was calm, almost as cool as if he were still wrapped in the oneness, did he turn. Summoning the Tairen's shadowed face brought no anger with it. Good.

By the time he reached the center of the camp among the trees, it would have seemed a kicked ant-heap to most men. To one who knew, it was ordered activity, and almost silent. No wasted motion or breath. There were no tents to be struck, since pack animals would have been an encumbrance when it came to fighting. Some men were already on their horses, breastplates buckled in place, helmets on their heads, and in their hands lances tipped with a foot or more of steel. Nearly all of the rest were tightening saddle girths or fastening leather-cased horsebows and full quivers behind the tall cantles of their saddles. The slow had died in the first year fighting the Aiel. Most now were Saldaeans and Kandori, the rest Domani. Some Malkieri had come south, but Lan would not lead them, not even here. Bukama rode with him, but he did not follow.

Bukama met him carrying a lance and leading his yellow roan gelding, Sun Lance, followed by a beardless youth named Caniedrin, who was carefully leading Lan's Cat

Dancer. The bay stallion was only half-trained, but Caniedrin was well advised to take care. Even a half-trained warhorse was a formidable weapon. Of course, the Kandori was not as innocent as his fresh face suggested. An efficient and experienced soldier, an archer of rare skill, he was a cheerful killer who often laughed while he fought. He was smiling now, at the prospect of fighting to come. Cat Dancer tossed his head, also impatient.

Whatever Caniedrin's experience, Lan checked Cat Dancer's saddle girths carefully before taking the reins. A loose girth could kill as quickly as a spear-thrust.

"I told them what we're about this morning," Bukama muttered after Caniedrin had headed off to his own mount, "but with these Aiel, an anvil can turn into a pincushion if the hammer is slow in coming." He never grumbled in front of the men, just to Lan.

"And the hammer can become a pincushion if it strikes with no anvil in place," Lan replied, swinging into the saddle. The sky was plainly gray now. Still a dark gray, but only a scattered handful of stars remained. "We will have to ride hard to reach the Hook before first light." He raised his voice. "Mount!"

Ride hard they did, cantering half a mile, then trotting, then leading the animals by the reins at a fast walk before mounting to begin over. In stories, men galloped for ten miles, twenty, but even without snow, to gallop the whole four or five miles would have lamed half the horses and winded the rest long before reaching the Hook. The silence of the fading night was broken only by the crunch of hooves or boots in the snow crust, the creak of saddle leather, and sometimes the muttered curses of men who caught a toe on a hidden stone. No one wasted breath on complaints or talk. They had all done this often, and men and horses hit an easy rhythm that covered ground quickly.

The land around Tar Valon was rolling plain for the most part, dotted with widely spaced copses and thickets, few large, but all thick with darkness. Large or small, Lan eyed those clumps of trees carefully as he led his men past, and he kept the column well away. Aiel were very good at using whatever cover they could find, places where most men would be sure a dog could not hide, and very good at springing ambushes. Nothing stirred, though. For all his eyes could see, the band he led could have been the only living men in the world. The hoot of an owl was the only sound he heard that they did not make.

The sky in the east was a much paler gray by the time the low ridge called the Hook came into sight. Well under a mile in length, the treeless crest rose little more than forty feet above the surrounding ground, but any elevation gave some advantage in defense. The name came from the way the northern end curved back toward the south, a feature plainly visible as he arranged his men in a long line along the top of the ridge to either side of him. The light was definitely growing. To the west, he thought he could make out the pale bulk of the White Tower itself, rising in the center of Tar Valon some three leagues distant.

The Tower was the tallest structure in the known world, yet it was overshadowed by the bulk of the lone mountain that rose out of the plains beyond the city, on the other side of the river. That was clear enough when there was any light at all. In the deepest night, you could see it blocking the stars. Dragonmount would have been a giant in the Spine of the World, but there on the plain, it was monstrous, piercing the clouds and rising taller. Higher above the clouds than most mountains were below, its broken peak always emitted a streamer of smoke. A symbol of hope and despair. A mountain of prophecy. Glancing at it, Bukama made another sign against evil. No one wanted that prophecy fulfilled. But it would be, of course, one day.

From the ridgeline, gently rolling ground ran more than a mile to the west, to one of the larger thickets, half a league wide. Three trampled paths crisscrossed the snow between, where large numbers of horses or men afoot had passed. Without going closer, it was impossible to say who had made them, Aiel or men of the so-called Coalition, only that they had been made since the snowfall stopped, late two days ago.

There was no sign of Aiel yet, but if they had not changed direction, which was always possible, they could appear out of those trees any moment. Without waiting for Lan's order, men drove their lances point-down into the ground beneath the snow, where they could be snatched up again easily at need. Uncasing their horsebows, they pulled arrows from their quivers and nocked them, but did not draw. Only newlings thought they could hold a drawn bow for long. Lan alone carried no bow. His duty was to direct the fight, not to select targets. The bow was the preferred weapon against the Aiel, though many southlanders disdained it. Emares and his Tairens would ride straight into the Aiel with their lances and swords. There were times when that was the only way, but it was foolish to lose men needlessly, before you must, and as surely as peaches were poison, you did lose men in close quarters with Aiel.

He had no fear that the Aiel would turn aside on seeing them. They were not wild fighters, no matter what some said; they refused battle when the odds were too great. But six hundred Aiel would see the numbers as just right; they would be facing fewer than four hundred, although placed on the high ground. They would rush forward to attack and be met with a hail of arrows. A good horsebow could kill a man at three hundred paces and wound at four, if the man drawing it had the skill. That was a long corridor of steel for the Aiel to run. Unfortunately, they carried bows made of horn-and-sinew, too, just as effective as the horsebows. The worst would be if the Aiel stood and exchanged arrows; both sides would lose men however quickly Emares arrived. Best would be if the Aiel decided to close; a running man could not shoot a bow with any accuracy. At least, it would be best if Emares was not behind time. Then the Aiel might try for the flanks, especially if they knew they were being followed, and that would kick open the hornets' nest. Either way, when Emares struck them from the rear, Lan would gather the lances and ride down.

In essence, that was the hammer and anvil. One force to hold the Aiel in place until the other struck it, then both closing in. A simple tactic, but effective; most effective tactics were simple. Even the pigheaded Cairhienin had learned to use it. A good many Altarans and Murandians had died because they refused to learn.

Grayness welled into light. The sun would be peeking over the horizon behind them soon, silhouetting them on the ridge. The wind gusted, catching Lan's cloak, but he assumed the *ko'di* once more and ignored the cold. He could hear Bukama and the other men near him breathing. Along the line, horses stamped their hooves impatiently in the snow. A hawk quartered above the open ground, hunting along the edge of the wide thicket.

Suddenly the hawk wheeled away and a column of Aiel appeared, coming out of the trees at a quick trot, twenty men abreast. The snow did not appear to hamper them to any great degree. Lifting their knees high, they moved as quickly as most men would have on cleared ground. Lan pulled his looking glass from the leather case tied to his saddle. It was a good glass, Cairhienin made, and when he pressed the brass-bound tube to his eyes, the Aiel, still a mile off, seemed to leap closer. They were tall men, many as tall as he and some taller, wearing coats and breeches in shades of brown and gray that stood out against the snow. Each had a cloth wrapped around his head, and a dark veil hiding his face to the eyes. Some might be women—Aiel women sometimes fought alongside the men—but most would be men. Each carried a short spear tipped in one hand, with a round, bull-hide buckler and several more spears clutched in the other. Their bows were in cases on their backs. They could do deadly work with those spears. And their bows.

The Aiel would have had to be blind to miss the horsemen waiting on them, but they came on without a pause, their column a thick serpent sliding out of the trees toward the ridge. Far to the west a trumpet sounded, thin with distance, and then another; to be that faint, they had to be near to the river, or even on the other side. The Aiel kept coming. A third trumpet called, far off, and a fourth, a fifth, more. Among the Aiel, heads swung, looking back. Was it the trumpets drew their attention, or did they know Emares was following?

The Aiel continued to issue from the trees. Someone had miscounted badly, or else more Aiel had joined the first party. Over a thousand were clear of the trees, now, and still more came. Fifteen hundred, and more behind. He slid the looking glass back into its case.

"Embrace death," Bukama muttered, sounding like cold steel, and Lan heard other Borderlanders echo the words. He merely thought them; it was enough. Death came for every man eventually, and seldom where or when he expected. Of course, some men died in their beds, but from boyhood Lan had known he would not.

Calmly, he looked left and right along the line of his men. The Saldaeans and Kandori were standing firm, of course, but he was pleased to see that none of the Domani showed any signs of edginess, either. No one looked over a shoulder for a path to run. Not that he expected any less after two years fighting alongside them, but he always had more trust of men from the Borderlands than elsewhere. Bordermen knew that sometimes hard choices had to be made. It was in their bones.

The last of the Aiel cleared the trees, easily two thousand of them, a number that changed everything, and nothing. Two thousand Aiel were enough to overrun his men and still deal with Emares, unless the Dark One's own luck was with them. The thought of withdrawing never arose. If Emares struck without the anvil in place, the Tairens would be slaughtered, but if he could hold until Emares arrived, then both hammer and anvil might be able to draw clear. Besides, he had given his word. Still, he did not mean to die here to no purpose, nor to have his men die to none. If Emares failed to arrive by the time the Aiel came inside two hundred paces, he would wheel his company off the ridge and try to ride around the Aiel to join the Tairen. Sliding his sword from its scabbard, he held it loosely at his side. It was just a sword now, with nothing about it to catch the eye or set it out. It would never again be anything except a sword. But it held his past, and his future. The trumpets to the west were sounding almost continuously.

Abruptly, one of the Aiel in the front of the column raised his spear overhead, holding it up for the length of three strides. When he brought it down, the column came to a halt. A good five hundred paces separated them from the ridgeline, well beyond bowshot. Why under the Light? As soon as they were halted, the rear half of the column turned to face the way they had come. Were they simply being cautious? Safer to assume they knew about Emares.

Drawing out his looking glass again, left-handed, he studied the Aiel. Men in the front rank were shading their eyes with their spear-hands, studying the horsemen on the ridge. It made no sense. At best they would be able to make out dark shapes against the sunrise, perhaps the crest on a helmet. No more than that. The Aielmen seemed to be talking to each other. One of the men in the lead suddenly raised his hand overhead, holding a spear, and others did the same. Lan lowered his looking glass. All of the Aiel were facing forward, now, and every one held a spear raised high. He had never seen anything like this before.

As one, the spears came down, and the Aiel shouted a single word that boomed clearly across the space between, drowning the trumpets' distant calls. "*Aan'allein!*"

Lan exchanged wondering glances with Bukama. That was the Old Tongue, the language that had been spoken in the Age of Legends, and in the centuries before the Trolloc Wars. The best translation Lan could come up with was One Man Alone. But what did it *mean*? Why would the Aiel shout such a thing?

"They're moving," Bukama muttered, and the Aiel were.

But not toward the ridge. Turning northward, the column of veiled Aiel quickly reached a trot again and, once the head of it was well beyond the end of the ridge, began to angle eastward once more. Madness piled on madness. This was no flanking maneuver, not on only one side.

"Maybe they're going back to the Waste," Caniedrin called. He sounded disappointed. Other voices scoffed him loudly. The general view was that the Aiel would never leave until they were all killed.

"Do we follow?" Bukama asked quietly.

After a moment, Lan shook his head. "We will find Lord Emares and talk—politely—concerning hammers and anvils," he said. He wanted to find out what all those trumpets were about, too. This day was beginning strangely, and he had the feeling there would be more oddities before it was done.

CHAPTER
2

A Wish Fulfilled

Despite a fire blazing on the green marble hearth, the Amyrlin's sitting room was cold enough to make Moiraine shiver, and only a tight jaw kept her teeth from chattering. Of course, it also stopped her from yawning, which would never have done, half a night's sleep or not. The colorful winter tapestries hanging on the walls, bright scenes of spring and garden parks, ought to have had a coating of frost, and icicles should have been hanging from the scroll-carved cornices. For one thing, the fireplace lay on the other side of the room from her, and its warmth did not extend far. For another, the tall glassed casements behind her, filling the arched windows that let onto the balcony overlooking the Amyrlin's private garden, did not fit as well as they might, and they leaked cold around the edges. Whenever the wind gusted outside, an icy breeze hit her back and cut through her woolen dress. Another struck her closest friend, as well, but for all that Siuan was Tairen, she would not have let it show if she were freezing to death. The Sun Palace in Cairhien, where Moiraine had done most of her growing up, had often been as cold in winter, yet there she had never been forced to stand in drafts. The chill seeped from the marble floor tiles through the flowered Illianer carpet and Moiraine's slippers, too. The golden Great Serpent ring on her left hand, the snake biting its own tail that symbolized eternity and continuity and an initiate's bond to the Tower, felt like a band of ice. When the Amyrlin told an Accepted to stand over there and not bother her, however, the Accepted stood where the Amyrlin pointed and tried not to let her notice any shivers. Worse than the cold, really, was the heavy smell of acrid smoke that even the heavy drafts could not dispel. It was not the smoke of chimneys, but of burned villages around Tar Valon.

Concentration on the cold kept her from fretting over the smoke. And the battle. The sky outside the windows held the gray of early morning, now. Soon, the fighting would begin again, if it had not already. She wanted to know how the battle was going. She had a *right* to know. Her uncle had started this war. She certainly did not excuse the Aiel in the slightest for the destruction they had brought to Cairhien, city and nation, but she knew where the ultimate blame lay. Since the Aiel arrived, though, Accepted had been confined to the Tower grounds as strictly as novices. The world outside the walls might as well have ceased to exist.

Reports came at regular intervals from Azil Mareed, High Captain of the Tower Guard, but the contents were not shared with anyone except full sisters, if with them. Questions about the fighting addressed to Aes Sedai earned admonitions to concentrate on your studies. As though the largest battle fought since Artur Hawkwing's time, and practically under her nose, was a mere distraction! Moiraine knew she could not be involved in any meaningful way—not in any way, really—yet she wanted to be, if only by knowing what was happening. That might be illogical, but then, she had never thought she was going to join the White Ajah once she gained the shawl.

The two silk-gowned women in shades of blue, seated on opposite sides of the small writing table on one side of the room, gave no sign that they were aware of the smoke or the cold, though they were almost as far from the fireplace as she. Of course, they were Aes Sedai, with ageless faces, and for the smoke, they had certainly seen the aftermath of more battles than any general. They could remain serenity made flesh if a thousand villages burned right in front of them. No one became Aes Sedai without learning to control her emotions at need, inwardly and outwardly. Tamra and Gitara did not seem tired, though they had taken only catnaps since the fighting began. That was why they had Accepted in attendance all night, in case they wanted errands run or someone brought to them. As for the cold, neither cold nor heat touched sisters the way it did other people. They always appeared unaware of either. Moiraine had tried to work out how that was done; every Accepted tried sooner or later. However it was worked, it did not involve the One Power, or she would have been able to see the weaves, or at least feel them.

Tamra was more than simply Aes Sedai, she was the Amyrlin Seat, the ruler over all Aes Sedai. She had been raised from the Blue, but of course the long stole draped on her shoulders was striped in the colors of the seven Ajahs, to show that the Amyrlin was of all Ajahs and none. Over the history of the Tower, some Amyrlins had taken that more literally than others. Tamra's skirts were slashed with all seven colors, though that was not required. No Ajah could feel itself advantaged or disadvantaged with her. Beyond the Tower, when Tamra Ospenya spoke, kings and queens listened, whether they had Aes Sedai advisors or hated the White Tower. That was the power of an Amyrlin Seat. They might not take her advice or obey her instructions, but they listened, and politely. Even the High Lords of Tear and the Lord Captain Commander of the Children of the Light did that much. Her long hair, lightly streaked with gray and caught in a jeweled silver net, framed a square, determined face. She usually got her way with rulers, but she did not take her power lightly, or use it indiscriminately, either outside the Tower or inside. Tamra was fair and just, which were not always the same thing, and she was often kind. Moiraine admired her greatly.

The other woman, Tamra's Keeper of the Chronicles, was a different matter altogether. Perhaps the second most powerful woman in the Tower, and certainly at least equal to the Sitters, Gitara Moroso was always just, and usually fair, but kindness never seemed to occur to her. She was also flamboyant enough for a Green or a Yellow. Tall and close to voluptuous, she wore a wide necklace of firedrops, earrings with rubies the size of pigeon's eggs, and three jeweled rings beside her Great Serpent ring. Her dress was a deeper blue than Tamra's and brocaded, and the Keeper's stole on her shoulders—blue, since she also had been raised from the Blue—was nearly wide enough to be called a shawl. Moiraine had heard that Gitara still considered herself a Blue, which would be shocking if true. The width of her stole certainly spoke in favor of the whispers; that was a matter of personal choice.

As with all Aes Sedai, once they had worked long enough with the One Power, it was impossible to put an age to Gitara's face. At a glance, you might think she was no more than twenty-five, perhaps less, then a second glance would say a youthful forty-five or fifty and still just short of great beauty, while a third changed it all again. That smooth, ageless face was the mark of Aes Sedai, to those who knew. To those who did not know, and many did not, her hair would have added to the confusion. Caught with carved ivory combs, it was white as snow. By whispered rumor, she was over three hundred years old, very old even for an Aes Sedai. Speaking of a sister's age was extremely rude. Even another sister would be given a penance for it; a novice or Accepted would find herself sent to the Mistress of Novices for a switching. But surely thinking about it did not count.

Something else placed Gitara out of the ordinary. She had the Foretelling sometimes, the Talent of speaking what was still in the future.

That was a very rare Talent, and came to her only occasionally, but gossip—the Accepted's quarters overflowed with tittle-tattle—gossip said that Gitara had had more than one Foretelling in the last few months. Some claimed that the reason the armies outside the city had been in place when the Aiel came was one of Gitara's Foretellings. No one among the Accepted knew for certain, of course. Maybe some of the other sisters did. Maybe. Even when the fact that Gitara had had a Foretelling was common knowledge, sometimes no one other than Tamra learned what it had been. It was foolish to hope to be present when Gitara had a Foretelling, yet Moiraine had hoped. But in the four hours since she and Siuan had replaced Temaile and Brendas in attendance on the Amyrlin, Gitara had only sat there writing a letter.

It suddenly hit her that close on four hours was a very long time to spend on one letter. And Gitara had not covered half of one sheet of paper yet. She was sitting there with her pen suspended above the cream-colored page. As if Moiraine thinking of it had somehow reached her, Gitara glanced at the pen and made a small sound of irritation, then swirled the steel nib in a small red-glazed bowl of alcohol to clean away dried ink, clearly not for the first time. The liquid in the bowl was as black as that in the silver-capped ink jar of cut glass on the table. A gilt-edged leather folder full of papers lay open in front of Tamra, and she appeared to be studying them intently, yet Moiraine could not remember seeing the Amyrlin turn over a single sheet. The two Aes Sedai's faces were images of cool calm, but plainly they were worried, and that made her worried, too. She bit at her lower lip in furious thought, then had to stop when a yawn threatened. The biting, not the thinking.

It had to be something to make them worry today in particular. She had seen Tamra in the corridors yesterday, and if there had ever been a woman bubbling with confidence, it had been she. So. The battle that had been raging for the last three days. If Gitara really had Foretold the battle, if she really had had other Foretellings, what else might they have been? Guessing would do no good, but reasoning might. The Aiel crossing the bridges and breaking into the city? Impossible. In three thousand years, while nations rose and fell and even Hawkwing's empire was swept away in fire and chaos, no army had managed to breach Tar Valon's walls or break down its gates, and quite a few had tried over that time. Perhaps the battle turning to disaster in some other way? Or something needed to avoid disaster? Tamra and Gitara were the only two Aes Sedai actually in the Tower at that moment, unless some had returned in the night. There had been talk of injured soldiers in such numbers that all sisters with the smallest ability at Healing were needed, but no one had said straight out that that was where they were going. Aes Sedai could not lie, yet they often spoke obliquely, and they were not above misdirection. Sisters also could use the Power as a weapon if they or their Warders were in danger. No Aes Sedai had taken part in a battle since the Trolloc Wars, when they faced Shadowspawn and armies of Darkfriends, but perhaps Gitara had Foretold disaster unless Aes Sedai joined. But why wait until the third day? Could a Foretelling be that detailed? Maybe if the sisters had entered the battle earlier, *that* would have caused. . . .

Out of the corner of her eye, Moiraine saw Siuan smiling at her. That smile turned Siuan's face from handsome to pretty and made her clear blue eyes twinkle. Nearly a hand taller than Moiraine—Moiraine had gotten over the irritation she had once felt at being shorter than nearly all the women around her, but she could never help noticing height—taller and almost as fair-skinned as she, Siuan wore her formal Accepted's dress with an air of assurance that Moiraine had never quite mastered. The high-necked dresses were the purest white except for the bands at hem and cuffs that copied the Amyrlin's seven-colored stole. She could not understand how so many sisters of the White Ajah could bear to wear white all the time, as if they were forever in mourning. For her, the hardest thing about being a novice had been dressing in plain white day after day. The hardest aside from learning to control her temper, anyway. That still dropped her in hot water now and then, but not so often as during her first year.

"We'll find out when we find out," Siuan whispered with a quick glance at Tamra and Gitara. Neither moved an inch. Gitara's pen was held over the letter again, the ink drying.

Moiraine could not help smiling back. Siuan had that gift, making her smile when she wanted to frown and laugh when she wanted to weep. The smile turned into a yawn, and she looked hastily to see whether the Amyrlin or the Keeper had noticed. They were still absorbed in their own thoughts. When she turned back, Siuan had a hand over her own mouth and was glaring at her over it. Which almost set her giggling.

It had surprised her at first, she and Siuan becoming friends, but among novices and Accepted, the closest friends always seemed to be very much alike or very different. In some things she and Siuan were alike. They were both orphans; their mothers had died while they were young, their fathers since they left home. And both had been born with the spark, which was uncommon. They would have begun channeling the Power eventually whether or not they had tried to learn how; not every woman could learn, by any means.

That was where the differences began, before they arrived in Tar Valon, and it was not just that Siuan had been born poor and she wealthy. In Cairhien, Aes Sedai were respected, and Moiraine had been given a grand dance in the Sun Palace to celebrate her departure for the Tower. In Tear, channeling was outlawed, and Aes Sedai were not popular. Siuan had been bundled onto a ship bound upriver for Tar Valon the very day a sister discovered she could learn to channel. There were so many differences, though none mattered between them. Among other things, Siuan had come to the Tower in full control of her temper, she was quick with puzzles, which Moiraine was not, she could not abide horses, which Moiraine loved, and she learned at a rate that left Moiraine dazed.

Oh, not about channeling the One Power. They had been entered in the novice book on the same day, and moved almost in lockstep with the Power, even to passing for Accepted on the same day. Moiraine, though, had received the education expected of a noblewoman, everything from history to the Old Tongue, which she spoke and read well enough that she had been excused classes in it. The daughter of a Tairen fisherman, Siuan arrived barely able to read or do more than the simplest arithmetic, but she had soaked her lessons in like sand soaking up water. She *taught* the Old Tongue to novices, now. At least the beginning classes.

Siuan Sanche was held up to novices as an example of what they should aspire to. Well, both of them were. Only one other woman had ever finished novice training in just three years. Elaida a'Roihan, a detestable woman, had completed her time as Accepted in three years, too, also a record, and it seemed at least possible that they might match that, as well. Moiraine was all too aware of her own shortcomings, but she thought that Siuan would make a perfect Aes Sedai.

She opened her mouth to whisper that patience was for stones, but wind rattled the casements, and another blast of freezing air hit her. She might as well have been standing in her shift for all the protection her dress gave. Instead of whispering, she gasped, loudly.

Tamra turned her head toward the windows, yet not because of Moiraine. The sound of distant trumpets suddenly was floating on the wind, dozens of them. No, hundreds. To be heard here inside the Tower, there would have to be hundreds. And the sound was continuous, call rolling over call. Whatever the cause, it must be urgent. The Amyrlin closed the folder lying before her with a slap.

"Go see if there's news from the battlefield, Moiraine." Tamra spoke almost normally, but her voice held an unidentifiable edge, a sharpness. "Siuan, make some tea. Quickly, child."

Moiraine blinked. The Amyrlin *was* worried. But there was only one thing to do.

"It will be as you say, Mother," she and Siuan said together without hesitation, offering deep curtsies, and turned for the door to the anteroom, beside the fireplace. The gold-chased silver teapot sat on a ropework tray on a table near that door, along with a tea canister, a honey jar, a small pitcher of milk, and a large pitcher of water, all in worked silver. A second tray held cups made of delicate green Sea Folk porcelain. Moiraine felt a faint tingle as Siuan opened herself to the Source and embraced *saidar,* the female half of the Power; a glow surrounded her, though it would be visible only to another woman who could channel. Normally, channeling to do chores was forbidden, yet the Amyrlin had said quickly. Siuan was already preparing a thin thread of Fire to bring the tea water to a boil. Neither Tamra nor Gitara spoke a word to stop her.

The anteroom to the Amyrlin's apartments was not large, since it was only meant to hold a few visitors until they could be announced. Delegations came to the Amyrlin in one of the audience halls or in her study next door, not her private chambers. Backed by the sitting-room fireplace, the anteroom was almost warm. There was only one chair, simply carved but large, yet despite its weight, the chair had been dragged closer to one of the gilded stand-lamps, so Elin Warrel, the slender novice on duty, would have better light to read. Facing away from the sitting-room door and intent on her wood-bound book, she did not hear Moiraine cross the fringed carpet.

Elin should have felt her presence long before she was close enough to peer over the child's shoulder. Not really a child, since she had been seven years a novice and had come to the Tower at eighteen, but a novice was referred to as a child no matter her age. For that matter, Aes Sedai called Accepted "child," too. Moiraine had been able to feel the child's ability to channel soon after entering the room. Elin certainly should have been able to sense hers from this near. One woman who could channel could never sneak up on another if the second was paying attention.

Peering over Elin's shoulder, she recognized the book instantly. *Hearts of Flame,* a collection of love stories. The Tower Library was the largest in the known world, containing copies of almost every book that had ever been printed, but this was unsuitable for a novice. Accepted were granted a little leeway—by that time, you knew that you would watch a husband age and die, and your children and grandchildren and great-grandchildren, while you changed not at all—but novices were quietly discouraged from thinking about men or love, and kept away from men entirely. It would never do for a novice to try running away to get married or, worse, to get herself with child. Novice training was purposefully hard—if you were going to break, better it happened as a novice than as a sister. Being Aes Sedai was truly hard—and adding a child to it would only make matters beyond difficult.

"You should find more appropriate reading, Elin," Moiraine said levelly. "And pay more attention to your duties."

Before Moiraine finished speaking, Elin leaped to her feet with a startled gasp, the book tumbling to the floor, and whirled around. She was not tall for an Andoran, but Moiraine still had to look up to meet her eyes. When she saw Moiraine, she heaved a small sigh of relief. Very small. To novices, Accepted were only a tiny step below Aes Sedai. Elin spread her plain white skirts in a hasty curtsy. "No one could have come in without my seeing, Moiraine. Merean Sedai said I could read." She tilted her head to one side, toying with the wide white ribbon that held her hair. Everything novices wore was white, even their thin leather slippers. "Why's that book inappropriate, Moiraine?" She was three years the elder, but the Great Serpent ring and banded skirts marked a fount of knowledge in novice eyes. Unfortunately, there were subjects Moraine felt uncomfortable talking about with just anyone. There was such a thing as decorum.

Picking up the volume, she handed it to the novice. "The Librarians would be very put out if you returned one of their books in damaged condition." She felt a measure of satisfaction at that. It was the sort of reply a full sister might have given when she did not want to answer the question. Accepted practiced the Aes Sedai way of speaking against the day they gained the shawl, but the only ones to practice on safely were the novices. Some tried it with the servants, for a little while, but that only got them laughed at. Servants knew very well that in Aes Sedai eyes, Accepted were not a small step below the sisters but a small step above the novices.

As hoped for, Elin anxiously began examining the book for damage, and Moiraine went on before the novice could come back to her embarrassing question. "Have there been any messages from the field of battle, child?"

Elin's eyes widened indignantly. "You know I'd have brought it in right away if there'd been any message, Moiraine. You know I would."

She did know. Tamra had known, too. But while the Keeper or a Sitter might point out that the Amyrlin had given a foolish order—at least, she thought they might—an Accepted could only obey. For that matter, novices were not supposed to point out that an Accepted had asked a foolish question. "Is that the proper way to answer, Elin?"

"No, Moiraine," Elin said contritely, bobbing another curtsy. "There hasn't been any message the whole time I've been here." Her head tilted again. "Did Gitara Sedai have a Foretelling?"

"Go back to your reading, child." As soon as the words were out of her mouth, Moiraine knew they were wrong, contradicting what she had said before. It was too late for a recovery, now, though. Turning quickly, and hoping that Elin had not noticed the blush suddenly heating her face, she glided out of the anteroom with as much dignity as she could muster. Well, the Mistress of Novices had told the child she could read, and the Librarians had let her take the book, if one of the Accepted had not loaned it to her. But Moiraine did hate sounding like a fool.

A faint trickle of steam was rising from the teapot's spout and more from the water pitcher when Moiraine reentered the sitting room and closed the door. The glow of *saidar* no longer shone around Siuan. Water boiled very quickly when the One Power was used; the trick was to keep it all from flashing to steam. Siuan had filled two of the green cups and was stirring honey into one. The other was milky.

Siuan pushed the cup she had been stirring toward Moiraine. "Gitara's," she said softly. And then in a whisper, with a grimace, "She likes enough honey to turn it to syrup. She told me not to be stingy!" The porcelain was just barely too hot on Moiraine's fingertips, but it should be cooled to exactly the right point by the time she crossed the room to the writing table where Gitara still sat, now drumming her fingers on the tabletop impatiently. The polished blackwood clock on the mantel over the fireplace chimed First Rise. The trumpets were still calling. They seemed to sound frantic, though Moiraine knew that was only imagination.

Tamra was standing at the windows, peering out at a sky that was growing brighter by the moment. She continued to stare out after Siuan had curtsied and proffered her cup, then finally turned and saw Moiraine. Instead of taking the tea, she said, "What news, Moiraine? You know better than to delay." Oh, she *was* on edge, to speak so. She had to know Moiraine would have spoken immediately if there had been anything.

Moiraine was just offering Gitara her own cup, but before she could reply, the Keeper jerked to her feet, bumping the table so hard that the ink jar overturned, spreading a pool of black across the tabletop. Trembling, she stood with her arms rigid at her sides and stared over the top of Moiraine's head, wide-eyed with terror. It *was* terror, plain and simple.

"He is born again!" Gitara cried. "I feel him! The Dragon takes his first breath on the slope of Dragonmount! He is coming! He is coming! Light help us! Light help the world! He lies in the snow and cries like the thunder! He burns like the sun!"

With the last word, she gasped, a tiny sound, and fell forward into Moiraine's arms. Moiraine dropped the teacup to try to catch her, but the truth of it was that the larger woman bore both of them to the carpet. It was all Moiraine could do to end up on her knees holding the Keeper rather then lying beneath her.

In an instant, Tamra was there, kneeling careless of the ink trickling from the table. The light of *saidar* already surrounded her, and she already had a weave prepared of Spirit, Air and Water. Gripping Gitara's head between her hands, she let the weave sink into the still form. But delving, used to check health, did not turn to Healing. Looking helplessly into Gitara's staring eyes, Moiraine knew why not. She had hoped there was some tiny fragment of life left, something that Tamra could work with. Healing could cure any sickness, mend any injury. But you could not Heal death. The pool of ink on the table had spread to ruin whatever the Keeper had been writing. It was very odd, what you noticed at a time like this.

"Not now, Gitara," Tamra breathed softly. She sounded weary to the bone. "Not now, when I need you most."

Slowly, her eyes came up to meet Moiraine's, and Moiraine started back on her knees. It was said Tamra's stare could make a stone move, and at that moment, Moiraine believed. The Amyrlin shifted her gaze to Siuan, still standing in front of the windows. Siuan had both hands pressed to her mouth, and the teacup she had been carrying lay on the carpet at her feet. She gave a jerk under that gaze, too.

Moiraine's eye found the cup she had been carrying. *A good thing the cups did not break,* she thought. *Sea Folk porcelain is quite expensive.* Oh, the mind did play odd tricks when you wanted to avoid thinking about something.

"You are both intelligent," Tamra said finally. "And not deaf, unfortunately. You know what Gitara just Foretold." There was just enough question in that for both of them to nod and say that they did. Tamra sighed as if she had been wishing for a different response.

Taking Gitara out of Moiraine's arms, the Amyrlin eased her down to the carpet and smoothed her hair. After a moment, she pulled the wide blue stole from Gitara's shoulders, folded it carefully, and laid it over the Keeper's face.

"With your permission, Mother," Siuan said in a husky voice, "I'll send Elin to fetch the Keeper's serving woman to do what's needful."

"Stay!" Tamra barked. That iron-hard gaze studied them both. "You will tell no one about this, not for any reason. If necessary, lie. Even to a sister. Gitara died without speaking. Do you understand me?"

Moiraine nodded jerkily, and was aware of Siuan doing the same. They were not Aes Sedai, yet—they still could lie, and some did occasionally, for all their efforts to behave like full sisters—but she had never been expected to be *ordered* to, especially not to Aes Sedai, and never by the Amyrlin Seat.

"Good," Tamra said tiredly. "Send—the novice on duty is named Elin?—send Elin in to me. I'll tell her where to find Gitara's woman." And make sure that Elin had heard nothing through the closed door, obviously. Otherwise, the task would have been Siuan's or Moiraine's. "When the girl comes in, the two of you may go. And remember! Not a word! Not one!" The emphasis only drove home the peculiarity. An order from the Amyrlin Seat was to be obeyed as if on oath. There was no need to emphasize anything.

I wished to hear a Foretelling, Moiraine thought as she made her final curtsy before leaving, *and what I received was a Foretelling of doom.* Now, she wished very much that she had been more careful of what she wished for.

CHAPTER
3

Practice

The wide corridor outside the Amyrlin's apartments was as cold as her sitting room had been, and full of drafts. Some were strong enough to ripple one or another of the long, heavy tapestries on the white marble walls. Atop the gilded stand-lamps between the bright wall hangings, the flames flickered, nearly blown out. The novices would be at their breakfast at this hour, and likely most of the other Accepted, too. For the moment, the hallways were empty save for Siuan and Moiraine. They walked along the blue runner, half the width of the corridor, taking advantage of the small protection the carpet gave from the chill of the floor tiles, a repeating pattern in the colors of all seven Ajahs. Moiraine was too stunned to speak. The faint sound of the trumpets still sounding barely registered on her.

They turned the corner into a hallway where the floor tiles were white, the runner green. To their right, another wide, tapestry-hung corridor lined with stand-lamps spiraled gently upward, toward the Ajahs' quarters, the visible portion floored in blue and yellow, with a runner patterned in gray and brown and red. Inside each Ajah's quarters, the Ajah's own color predominated, and some others might be missing altogether, but in the communal areas of the Tower, the colors of all the Ajahs were used in equal proportion. Irrelevant thoughts drifted through her head. Why equal, when some Ajahs were larger than others? Had they once been the same size? How could that have been achieved? A newly raised Aes Sedai chose her Ajah freely. Yet each Ajah had quarters of the same size. Irrelevant thoughts were better than. . . .

"Do you want breakfast?" Siuan said.

Moiraine gave a small start of surprise. Breakfast? "I could not swallow a bite, Siuan."

The other woman shrugged. "I have no appetite myself. I just thought I'd keep you company if you wanted something."

"I am going back to my room and try to get a little sleep, if I can settle myself. I have a novice class in two hours." And likely more classes to teach today, if the sisters did not start returning soon. Novices could not miss classes for little things like battles or. . . . She did not want to think about the "or." She would miss lessons, too, if the Aes Sedai failed to return. Accepted studied on their own for the most part, but she had a private class scheduled with Meilyn Sedai, and another with Larelle Sedai.

"Sleep would be wasting time we don't have," Siuan said firmly. "We'll practice for the testing. We might have almost a month, but it could be tomorrow just as easily."

"We cannot be sure we *will* be tested any time soon. Merean just said she thought we were close."

Siuan snorted. Loudly. While she was still a novice the sisters had cleaned up her language, which had been strongly redolent of the docks and often rough with it, but they still had not managed to smooth away all the edges of her. Which was just as well. Rough edges were a part of Siuan. "When Merean says someone is close, she tests within the month, and you know it, Moiraine. We'll practice."

Moiraine sighed. She did not really believe she could sleep, not now, but she doubted she could concentrate very well, either. Practice took concentration. "Oh, all right, Siuan."

The second surprise, after their friendship, had been the realization that between them, the fisherman's daughter led and the noblewoman followed. Of course, rank in the outside world carried no rights inside the Tower. There had been two daughters of beggars who rose to be Amyrlin Seat, as well as daughters of merchants and farmers and craftsfolk, including three daughters of cobblers, but only one daughter of a ruler. Besides, Moiraine had been taught to judge people's capabilities long before she left home. In the Sun Palace especially, you began learning that as soon as you were old enough to walk. Siuan had been born to lead. It felt surprisingly natural to follow where Siuan led.

"I wager you will be in the Hall of the Tower by the time you have worn the shawl a hundred years, and Amyrlin before fifty more," she said, not for the first time. It brought the same reaction it always did.

"Don't ill-wish me," Siuan said with a scowl. "I intend to see the world. Maybe parts of it no other sister has seen. I used to watch the ships sail into Tear full of silk and ivory from Shara, and I'd wonder if any of the crew had had the nerve to sneak outside the trade ports. I would have." Her face matched Tamra's for determination. "Once, my father took his boat all the way downriver to the Sea of Storms, and I could hardly pull on the nets for staring south, wondering what lay beyond the horizon. I'll see it, one day. And the Aryth Ocean. Who knows what lies west of the Aryth Ocean? Strange lands with strange customs. Maybe cities as great as Tar Valon, and mountains higher than the Spine of the World. Just think of it, Moiraine. Just think!"

Moiraine suppressed a smile. Siuan was so fierce about her intended adventures, though she would never call them that. Adventures were what took place in stories and books, not in life, as Siuan would point out to anyone who used the word. Without a doubt, though, once she had the shawl, she would be off like an arrow leaving the bow. And then they might see one another twice in ten years if not longer. That brought a pang of sadness, but she did not doubt that her own predictions would come true, as well. It did not take Foretelling. No; that was thinking in the wrong direction.

As they turned another corner and walked past a narrow marble staircase leading down, Siuan's scowl faded, and she began studying Moiraine in sidelong glances. The floor tiles here were a vivid green, the runner deep yellow, and the white walls were plain and bare. The stand-lamps were not gilded in this part of the Tower, which was used more by servants than sisters.

"You're trying to change the subject, aren't you," Siuan said abruptly.

"Which subject?" Moiraine asked, half laughing. "Practice or breakfast?"

"You know what subject, Moiraine. What do you think about it?"

The bubble of laugher vanished. There was no need to ask what "it" was. Exactly the thing that she did *not* want to think about. *He is born again.* She could hear Gitara's voice in her head. *The Dragon takes his first breath....* Her shiver had nothing to do with the cold this time.

For more than three thousand years the world had waited on the Prophecies of the Dragon to be fulfilled, fearing them, yet knowing they told of the world's only hope. And now a boychild was about to be born—very soon, perhaps, by the way Gitara had spoken—to bring those Prophecies to a conclusion. He would be born on the slopes of Dragonmount, reborn where it was said the man he had once been had died. Three thousand years ago and more, the Dark One had almost broken free into the world of humankind and brought on the War of the Shadow, which had ended only with the Breaking of the World. Everything had been destroyed, the very face of the earth changed, humanity reduced to ragged refugees. Centuries passed before the simple struggle for survival gave way to building cities and nations once more. That infant's birth meant the Dark One would break free again, for the child would be born to face the Dark One in Tarmon Gai'don, the Last Battle. On him rested the fate of the world. The Prophecies said he was the only chance. They did not say he would win.

Maybe worse than the thought of his defeat, though, was the fact that he would channel *saidin,* the male half of the One Power. Moiraine did not shiver at that; she shuddered. *Saidin* bore the Dark One's taint. Men still tried to channel from time to time. Some actually managed to teach themselves, and survived learning without a teacher, no easy feat. Among women, only one in four survived trying to learn on their own. Some of those men caused wars, usually false Dragons, men who claimed to be the Dragon Reborn, while others attempted to hide in ordinary lives, but unless they were caught and brought to Tar Valon to be gentled—cut off from the Power forever—every one of them went mad. That could take years, or just months, yet it was inevitable. Madmen who could tap into the One Power that turned the Wheel of Time and drove the universe. The histories were full of the horrors men like that had done. And the Prophecies said that the Dragon Reborn would bring a new Breaking of the World. Would his victory be any better than a victory by the Dark One? Yes; yes, it must be. Even the Breaking had left people alive to rebuild, eventually. The

Dark One would leave only a charnel house. And in any case, prophecies did not turn aside for the wishes of Accepted. Not for the prayers of nations.

"What I think is that the Amyrlin told us not to talk about it," she said.

Siuan shook her head. "She told us not to tell anyone else. Since we already know, it must be all right for us to talk about it between us." She cut off as a stout serving woman with the white Flame of Tar Valon on her breast appeared around a corner just ahead of them.

As the round woman walked past, she peered down her long nose at them suspiciously. Perhaps they looked guilty. Male servants often turned a blind eye to what Accepted, and even novices, got up to; perhaps they wanted no more involvement with Aes Sedai than their jobs entailed. Female servants, on the other hand, kept as close a watch as the sisters themselves.

"As long as we're careful," Siuan breathed, once the liveried woman was beyond earshot. However certain she was that talking between themselves was all right, she seemed content to say no more until they reached the Accepted's quarters, in the Tower's western wing.

There, stone-railed galleries in a hollow well surrounded a small garden, three levels below. The garden was only a handful of evergreen bushes poking through the snow at this time of year. An Accepted who put her feet too far wrong might find herself clearing away that snow with a shovel— the sisters were great believers that physical labor built character—but no one had gotten into that much trouble lately. Resting her hands on the railing, Moiraine peered up at the bright winter-morning sky, past the six silent rows of galleries above. Her breath made a white mist in front of her face. The trumpets were more audible here than in the hallways, the stink of smoke stronger in the air.

There were rooms for over a hundred Accepted in this well, and the same in a second well, too. Perhaps the numbers would not have come to mind now except for Gitara's Foretelling, yet she had thought about them before. They were etched in her brain as if with acid. Space for above two hundred Accepted, but the second well had been shut up since time out of memory for any living Aes Sedai, and barely more than sixty of these rooms were occupied. The novices' quarters also had two wells, with rooms for almost four hundred girls, but one of those was long closed, too, and the other held under a hundred. She had read that once novices and Accepted had both been housed two to a room. Once, half the girls who were entered in the novice book had been tested for the ring; fewer than twenty of the current novices would be allowed to. The Tower had been built to house three thousand sisters, but only four hundred and twenty-three were in residence at the moment, with perhaps twice as many more scattered across the nations. Numbers that still burned like acid. No Aes Sedai would say it aloud, and she would never dare say it where a sister might hear, but the White Tower was failing. The Tower was failing, and the Last Battle was coming.

"You worry too much," Siuan said gently. "My father used to say, 'Change what you can if it needs changing, but learn to live with what you can't change.' You'll only get a sick stomach, otherwise. That was me, not my father." With another snort, she gave an overdone shiver and wrapped her arms around herself. "Can we get inside now? I'm freezing. My room is closest. Come on."

Moiraine nodded. The Tower taught its students to live with what they could not change, too. But some things were important enough to try even if you were sure to fail. That had been one of *her* lessons as a child.

Accepted's rooms were identical, except in detail, slightly wider at the back than at the door, with plain wall panels of dark wood. None of the furnishings were fine, or indeed anything a sister would have tolerated. There was a small, square Taraboner rug woven in faded blue and green stripes on Siuan's floor, and the mirrored washstand in the corner held a chipped white pitcher sitting in the washbasin. Accepted were required to make do unless something actually broke, and if it broke, they had best have a good explanation why. The small table, with three leather-bound books stacked on it, and the two ladder-back chairs could have come from a penniless farmer's house, but Siuan's slept-in bed with its tumbled blankets was wide, like something from a moderately prosperous farmhouse. A small wardrobe completed the furnishings. Nothing was carved or ornamented in any way. When Moiraine had moved from the small, stark room of a novice, she had felt as if she were moving into a palace, though the chamber was half the size of any room in her apartments in the Sun Palace. Best of all, at the moment, was the fireplace of dressed gray stone. Today, any room with a fireplace would seem a palace, if she could stand near it.

Siuan hastily moved three pieces of split wood to the fireirons on the hearth—the woodbox was almost empty; serving men brought Aes Sedai their firewood, but Accepted had to carry theirs up themselves—then grunted when she discovered that her efforts at banking the coals of last night's fire had failed. No doubt in a hurry to reach the Amyrlin's chambers, she had not covered them with ashes well enough to stop them from burning out. A frown creased her forehead for a moment, and then Moiraine felt that small tingle again as the light of *saidar* briefly surrounded the other woman. Any woman who could channel could feel another wielding the Power if she was close enough, but the tingle was unusual. Women who spent a lot of time together in their training sometimes felt it, but the sensation was supposed to fade away over time. Hers and Siuan's never had. Sometimes Moiraine thought it was a sign of how close their friendship was. When the glow winked out, the short lengths of log were burning merrily.

Moiraine said nothing, but Siuan gave her a look as if she had delivered a speech. "I was too cold to wait, Moiraine," she said defensively. "Besides, you must remember Akarrin's lecture two weeks ago. 'You must know the rules to the letter,'" she quoted, "'and live with them before you can know which rules you may break and when.' That says right out that sometimes you can break the rules."

Akarrin, a slender Brown with quick eyes to catch who was not following her, had been lecturing about being Aes Sedai, not Accepted, but Moiraine held her tongue. Siuan had not needed the lecture to think about breaking rules. Oh, she never broke the major strictures—she never tried to run away or was disrespectful to a sister or anything of that sort, and she would never think of stealing—but she had had a liking for pranks from the start. Well, Moiraine did, too. Most Accepted did, at least now and then, and some novices, as well. Playing jokes was a way to relieve the strain of constant study with few freedays. Accepted had no chores beyond those necessary to keep themselves and their rooms tidy, unless they got into trouble at least, but they were expected to work hard at their studies, harder than novices dreamed of. Some relief was needed, or you would crack like an egg dropped on stone.

Nothing she and Siuan had done was malicious, of course. Washing a hated Accepted's shift with itchoak did not count. Elaida had made their first year as novices a misery, setting standards for them that no one could have met, yet insisting they be met. The second year, after she gained the shawl, had been worse until she left the Tower. Most of their pranks had been much more benign, though even the most innocent could bring swift punishment, especially if the target was an Aes Sedai. Their major triumph had been filling the largest fountain in the Water Garden with fat green trout one night the previous summer. Major in part because of the difficulty, and in part because they had escaped discovery. A few sisters had directed suspicious looks at them, but luckily no one could prove they had done it. Luckily, asking them whether they had was simply not done with Accepted. Putting trout in the fountain might not have brought a visit to the Mistress of Novices' study, but leaving the Tower grounds without permission in order to buy them—and worse, at night!—surely would have. Moiraine hoped that Siuan was not building up to a prank with this talk of breaking rules. She herself was too tired; they were bound to be caught.

"Will you go first, or shall I?" she asked. Maybe the practice would take Siuan's mind off getting into trouble.

"You need the practice more. We'll concentrate on you this morning. And this afternoon. And tonight."

Moiraine grimaced, but it was true. The test for the shawl consisted of creating one hundred different weaves perfectly and in a precise order while under great stress. And it was necessary to display complete calm the entire time. Exactly what that stress would be, they did not know, except that attempts would be made to distract them, and to break their composure. For practice, they provided the distractions for each other, and Siuan was very good at throwing her off at the worst moment or provoking her temper. Too much temper, and you could not hold on to *saidar* at all; even after her six years of work at it, her channeling required at least a degree of calm. Siuan could seldom *be* unsettled, and her temper was held with an iron grip.

Embracing the True Source, Moiraine let *saidar* fill her. Not as much of it as she could hold, but enough for practicing. Channeling was tiring work, and the more of the Power you channeled, the worse. Even that tiny amount spread through her, filling her with joy and life, with exultation. The wonder of it was near to torment. When she had first embraced *saidar,* she had not known whether to weep or laugh. She immediately felt the urge to draw more, and forced the desire down. All of her senses were clearer, sharper, with the Power in her. She thought she could almost hear Siuan's heart beating. She could feel the currents of air moving against her face and hands, and the colors banding her friend's dress were more vivid, the white of the wool whiter. She could make out tiny cracks in the wall panels that she could not have seen without putting her nose against the wall, lacking the Power that suffused her totally. It was exhilarating. She felt . . . more alive. Part of her wished she could hold *saidar* every waking moment, but that was strictly prohibited. That desire could lead to drawing more and more, until eventually you drew more than you could handle. And that either killed you, or else burned the ability to channel out of you. Losing this . . . bliss . . . would be much worse than death.

Siuan took one of the chairs, and the glow enveloped her. Moiraine could not see the light around herself, of course. Weaving a ward against eavesdropping around the inside of the room, flat against walls and floor and ceiling, Siuan tied it off so she did not have to maintain it. Holding two weaves at once was more than twice as taxing as one, three more than twice as wearing as two. Beyond that, difficult no longer sufficed as a description, though it could be done. She motioned for Moiraine to turn her back.

With a frown for the ward, Moiraine complied. It would be easy to avoid distraction if she could see the weaves Siuan was preparing for her. But why ward against eavesdropping? Someone with an ear pressed to the door would hear nothing if she screamed at the top of her lungs. Surely Siuan would not do anything to make her scream. No. It had to be the first part of trying to unsettle her, by making her wonder over it. She felt Siuan handling flows, Earth and Air, then Fire, Water and Spirit, then Earth and Spirit, always changing. Without looking, there was no way to tell whether the other woman was creating a weave or just trying another diversion. Taking a deep breath, she concentrated on utter calm.

Most of the weaves in the test were extremely complex, and had been designed solely for the test. Oddly, none required any gestures, which a good many weaves did. The motion was not really part of the weave, except that if you did not make it, the weave did not work. Supposedly, the gestures set certain pathways in your mind. The lack of gestures made it seem possible that you might lack the use of your hands during at least part of the test, and that sounded ominous. Another oddity was that none of those incredibly intricate weaves actually *did* anything, and even done incorrectly, they would not produce anything dangerous. Not too dangerous, anyway. That was a very real possibility with a number of weaves. Some of the simplest could prove disastrous, done just a little off. Women had died in the testing, but obviously not from bungling a weave. Still, a mistake with the first could yield a deafening thunderclap.

She channeled very thin flows of Air, weaving them just so. This was a fairly simple weave, but you could not force *saidar* no matter how small the threads. The Power was like a vast river, flowing inexorably onward; try to force it, and you would be swept away like a twig on the River Erinin. You had to use its overwhelming strength to guide it as you wanted. In any case, size was not specified, and small was less work And the noise would be smaller if Siuan managed to. . . .

"Moiraine, do you think the Reds will be able to make themselves leave him alone?"

Moiraine gave a jerk even before the weave she was making produced a boom like a kettledrum. Any sister was expected to deal with a man who could channel if she encountered one, but Reds concentrated on hunting them down. Siuan meant the boychild. That explained the ward. And maybe the talk of breaking rules. Maybe Siuan was not so sure as she pretended that Tamra would not care if they discussed the child between themselves. Moiraine glared over her shoulder.

"Don't stop," Siuan said calmly. She was still channeling, but not doing anything beyond handling the flows. "You really do need practice if you fumbled that one. Well, do you? About the Reds?"

This time, the weave produced a silver-blue disc the size of a small coin that dropped into Moiraine's outstretched hand. The shape was not specified, either, another oddity, but discs and balls were easiest. Woven of Air yet hard as steel, it felt slightly cold. She released the weave, and the "coin" vanished, leaving only a residue of the Power that would soon fade away as well.

The next weave was one of the complex and useless sort, requiring all of the Five Powers, but Moiraine answered as she wove it. She *could* talk and channel at the same time, after all. Air and Fire so, and Earth thus. Spirit, then Air once more. She wove without stopping. For some reason, you could not hold these weaves only partly done for very long or they collapsed into something else entirely. Spirit again, then Fire and Earth together. "They will have twenty years to learn how. Or nearly so, at worst. At best, they will have longer." Girls sometimes, if rarely, began channeling as young as twelve or thirteen, if they were born with the spark, but even with the spark boys never did before eighteen or nineteen, unless they tried to learn how, and in some men the spark did not come out until they were as old as thirty. Air again, then Spirit and Water, all placed precisely. "Besides, he will be the Dragon Reborn. Even the Reds will have to see that he cannot be gentled until after he fights the Last Battle." A grim fate, to save the world if he could, then for reward be cut off from this wonder. Prophecy was not known for mercy any more than for yielding to prayers. Earth again, then Fire, then more Air. The thing was beginning to look like the most hopeless knot in the world.

"Will that be enough? I've heard some Reds don't try all that hard to take those poor men alive."

She had heard that, too, but it was only a rumor. And a violation of Tower law. A sister could be birched for it, and likely exiled to a secluded farm to think on her crime for a time. It should be counted as murder, but given what those men would do unrestrained, she could almost see why it was not. More Spirit laid down, and Earth threaded through. Invisible fingers seemed to run up her sides to her armpits. She was ticklish, as Siuan knew well, but the other woman would need to do better than that. She barely flinched. "As someone told me not long ago, learn to live with what you cannot change," she said wryly. "The Wheel of Time weaves as the Wheel wills, and Ajahs do what they do." More Air, and Fire like so, followed by Water, Earth *and* Spirit. Then all five at once. Light, what a ghastly tangle! And not done yet.

"What I think," Siuan began, and the door banged open, letting in a surge of freezing air that swept away all the warmth of the fire. With *saidar* filling her, her awareness heightened, Moiraine felt suddenly covered with a coat of ice from head to toe.

The door also let in Myrelle Berengari, an Accepted from Altara who had earned the ring in the same year as they. Olive-skinned and beautiful, and almost as tall as Siuan, Myrelle was gregarious and also mercurial, with a boisterous sense of humor and a temper even worse than Moiraine's when she let it go. The two of them had begun with heated words as novices that got them both switched and had somehow found themselves friends. Oh, not so close as Siuan and she, but still friends, the only reason she did not snap at the other Accepted for walking in without knocking. Not that they would have heard if she had pounded, with the ward set. Not that *that* mattered. There was the principle of the thing!

"How long before the Last Battle, do you think?" Myrelle asked, shutting the door. She took in the half-completed weave in front of Moiraine and the ward around the room, and a grin appeared on her lips. "Practicing for the test, I see. Have you been making her squeal, Siuan? I can help, if you like. I know a sure way to make her squeal like a piglet caught in a net."

Moiraine hurriedly let the weave dissipate before it could collapse and exchanged confused looks with Siuan. How could Myrelle know?

"I did not squeal like . . . in the way you said," she said primly, playing for time. Most Accepted's pranks were aimed at other Accepted, and Myrelle's numbers almost matched hers and Siuan's. That particular one had involved ice in the depths of summer heat, when even shade felt like an oven. But she had not sounded *anything* like a piglet!

"What do you mean, Myrelle?" Siuan asked cautiously.

"Why, the Aiel, of course. What else could I mean?"

Moiraine exchanged another look with Siuan, of chagrin this time. A number of sisters claimed that various passages in the Prophecies of the Dragon referred to the Aiel. Of course, just as many said they did not. At the beginning of the war, there had been rather animated discussions about the matter. They would have been called shouting arguments if the women involved had not been Aes Sedai. But with what they knew now, all of that had slipped right out of Moiraine's head, and plainly out of Siuan's, as well. Keeping their knowledge hidden was going to take constant vigilance.

"The pair of you have a secret, don't you?" Myrelle said. "I don't know anybody for having secrets like you two. Well, don't think I'll ask, because I won't." By her expression, she was dying to ask.

"It isn't ours to tell," Siuan replied, and Moiraine's eyebrows climbed before she could control her face. What was Siuan up to? Was she trying to play *Daes Dae'mar*? Moiraine had tried to teach her how the Game of Houses worked. In Cairhien, even servants and farmers knew how to maneuver for advantage and deflect others from their own plans and secrets. In Cairhien, nobles and commoners alike lived by *Daes Dae'mar,* more so than anywhere else, and the Game was played everywhere, even in lands where everyone denied it. For all Moiraine's efforts, though, Siuan had never shown much facility. She was just too straightforward. "But you can help me with Moiraine," the woman went on, even more surprisingly. Their practice was always just the two of them. "She knows my tricks too well by now."

Laughing, Myrelle rubbed her hands together gleefully and took the second chair, the light of the Power springing up around her.

Grimly, Moiraine turned her back again and took up the second weave, but Siuan said, "From the beginning, Moiraine. You know better. You have to have the order fixed in your head so firmly that *nothing* can make you fumble it."

With a small sigh, Moiraine produced the silver-blue coin of Air once more, then moved on.

Siuan was right, in a way, about her knowing Siuan's tricks. Siuan liked to use tickles at the worst possible mo-

ment, sudden pokes in unpleasant places, embarrassing ca-
resses, and startling noises right beside her ear. That and
saying the most shocking things she could think of, and she
had a vivid imagination even after the sisters' work with her
language. Knowing the other woman's tricks did not make
it any easier to hold on to complete composure, though. She
had to start over twice because of Siuan. Myrelle was worse.
She liked ice. Ice was easy to make, a matter of using Water
and Fire to draw it out of the air. But Moiraine would like
to see how Myrelle managed to make it materialize *inside*
her dress, in the worst places. Myrelle also channeled flows
to make sly pinches and sharp flicks as if Moiraine had
been snapped with a switch, and sometimes a solid blow
across her bottom like the fall of a strap. They were real
pinches and real blows; the bruises they left were real, too.
Once, Myrelle lifted her a foot off the ground with ropes
of Air—she was certain it was her; Siuan had never done
anything like this—and slowly rotated her head down and
feet pointed toward the ceiling so her skirts fell down over
her head. Heart pounding and close to frantic, she pushed
her skirts up from in front of her face with her hands. It was
not modesty; she had to keep weaving. You could hold a
weave without seeing it, but you could not weave, and if this
particular bundle of the Five Powers collapsed, it would
give her a painful shock, as though she had scuffled her feet
across a carpet and then touched a piece of iron, only three
times as bad and felt all over. She managed to complete that
one successfully, but all in all, Myrelle broke her concentration *four* times!

She felt a growing irritation over that, but with herself,
not Myrelle. One thing every Accepted agreed on was that
whatever the sisters did to you in the test would be worse
than anything your friends could think of. And if they *were*
your friends, they would do the worst they could think of,
short of actual harm, to help you prepare. Light, if Myrelle
and Siuan could make her fail six times in so short a time,
what hope did she have in the actual test? But she kept on
with unbending determination. She would pass, and on her
first try. She would!

She was making that second weave yet again when the
door opened once more, and she let the flows vanish, reluctantly let go of *saidar* altogether. There was always a

reluctance to let go. Life seemed to drain away along with the Power; the world became drab. But she would not have had time to finish in any case before her novice class. Accepted were not allowed clocks, which were too expensive for most to afford in any event, and the gongs that sounded the hour were not always audible inside the Tower, so it was best if you developed a keen sense of time. Accepted were no more permitted to be late than novices were.

The woman who stood holding the door open was not a friend. Taller than Siuan, Tarna Feir was from the north of Altara, close to Andor, but her pale yellow hair was not her only difference from Myrelle. Accepted were not allowed to be arrogant, yet one look into those cold blue eyes told you that she was. She possessed no sense of humor, either, and as far as anyone knew, she had never played a joke on anyone. Tarna had gained the ring a year before Siuan and Moiraine, after nine years as a novice, and she had had few friends as a novice and few now. She did not seem to notice the lack. A *very* different woman from Myrelle.

"I should have expected to find you two together," she said coolly. There never seemed to be any heat in her. "I can't understand why you don't just move into the same room. Are you joining Siuan's coterie now, Myrelle?" All said matter-of-factly, yet Myrelle's eyes began to flash. The glow had vanished from Siuan, but Myrelle still held the Power. Moiraine hoped she was not rash enough to use it.

"Go away, Tarna," Siuan said with a quick dismissive gesture. "We're busy. And close the door." Tarna did not move.

"I have to hurry to make my novice class," Moiraine said, to Siuan. Tarna, she ignored. "They are just learning how to make a ball of fire, and if I am not there, one of them is sure to try it anyway." Novices were forbidden to channel or even embrace the Source without a sister or one of the Accepted looking over their shoulders, but they did anyway, given half a chance. New girls never really believed the dangers involved, while the older were always sure they knew how to avoid those dangers.

"The novices have been given a freeday," Tarna said, "so no classes today." Being dismissed and ignored did not disconcert her a bit. Nothing did. No doubt Tarna would pass for the shawl on her first try with ease. "The Accepted are summoned to the Oval Lecture Hall. The Amyrlin is going to address us. One other thing you should know. Gitara Moroso died just a few hours ago."

The light surrounding Myrelle winked out. "So that's the secret you were keeping!" she exclaimed. Her eyes flashed hotter than they had for Tarna.

"I told you it wasn't ours to share," Siuan replied. An Aes Sedai answer if ever there was one. It was enough to make Myrelle nod agreement, however reluctantly. And that nod *was* reluctant. Her eyes did not lose their heat. Moiraine expected that she and Siuan might soon have surprising encounters with ice.

Still holding the door open—was the woman immune to the cold, like a sister?—Tarna studied Moiraine and then Siuan. "That's right; you two would have been in attendance. What happened? All the rest of us have heard is that she died."

"I was handing her a cup of tea when she gasped and fell dead in my arms," Moiraine replied. And that was an even better Aes Sedai answer than Siuan's, every word true while avoiding the whole truth.

To her surprise, an expression of sadness crossed Tarna's face. It was fleeting, but it had been there. Tarna *never* showed emotion. She was carved from stone. "Gitara Sedai was a great woman," she murmured. "She will be badly missed."

"Why is the Amyrlin going to speak to us?" Moiraine asked. Plainly Gitara's death had already been announced, and by custom, her funeral would be tomorrow, so there was no need to announce that. Surely Tamra did not mean to tell the *Accepted* about the Foretelling?

"I don't know," Tarna replied, all coolness once more. "But I shouldn't have stood here talking. Everyone else was told to leave breakfast immediately. If we run, we can just make it before the Amyrlin arrives."

Accepted were required to maintain a certain amount of dignity, preparation for the day they reached the shawl. They certainly were never supposed to run unless ordered to. But run they did, Tarna as hard as the rest of them, hiking their skirts to their knees and ignoring the startled looks of liveried servants in the corridors. Aes Sedai did not keep the Amyrlin Seat waiting. Accepted never even *thought* of it.

The Oval Lecture Hall, with its wide scrollwork crown running beneath a gently domed ceiling painted with sky and white clouds, was seldom used. Moiraine and the others were the last of the Accepted to arrive, yet the rows of polished wooden benches were less than a quarter filled. The babble of voices, Accepted offering suggestions of why the Amyrlin would address them, seemed to emphasize how few they were compared to what the chamber had been built to hold. Moiraine put dwindling numbers firmly out of her head. Maybe, if the sisters. . . . No. She would *not* brood.

Thankfully, the dais at the front of the hall was still empty. She and Siuan found places at the back of the crowd, and Tarna sat beside them, but clearly not with them. The woman wore aloofness like a cloak. Myrelle, still in a huff over not being told about Gitara, stalked around to the other end of the row. Half the women in the room seemed to be talking, all on top of one another. It was nearly impossible to make out what anyone in particular was saying, and the little Moiraine did hear was utter nonsense. *All* of them to be tested for the shawl? *Immediately?* Aledrin must have brain fever to be spouting such drivel. Well, she *was* excitable. Brendas was even worse. Normally sensible, she was claiming they were all to be sent home because Gitara had Foretold the end of the White Tower, or maybe of the world, before she died. Likely by noon there would be a dozen tales about Gitara having a Foretelling if there were not more than that already—rumors grew in the Accepted's quarters like roses in a hothouse—but Moiraine still did not like hearing one. To keep their secret, she was going to have to spin the truth like a top, at least for the next few days. She hoped she was up to it.

"Does anybody know anything," Siuan asked the Accepted next to her, a slim, very dark woman with straight black hair hanging to her waist and a scattering of black tattoos on her hands, "or is it all just wind?"

Zemaille regarded her soberly for a moment before saying, "Wind, I think." Zemaille always took her time. For that matter, she was always sober and thoughtful. Very likely, she would choose Brown when she was raised. Or perhaps White.

She was a rarity in the Tower, one of the Sea Folk, the Atha'an Miere. There were only four Sea Folk Aes Sedai, all

Browns, and two of them were almost as old as Gitara had been. Atha'an Miere girls never came to the Tower unless they manifested the spark or managed to begin learning on their own. In either case, a delegation of Sea Folk delivered the girl, then left as soon as they could. The Atha'an Miere disliked being very long away from salt water, and the nearest sea to Tar Valon lay four hundred leagues to the south.

Zemaille, though, seemed to want to forget her origins. At least, she would never talk about the Sea Folk unless pressed by an Aes Sedai. And she was diligent, intently focused on earning the shawl from her first day, so Moiraine had heard, though she was not quick to learn. Not slower than most, just not quick. She had been Accepted for eight years, now, and ten years a novice before that, and Moiraine had seen her fumble a weave time after time before suddenly setting it so perfectly that you wondered why she had failed before. But then, everyone progressed at her own pace, and the Tower never pushed harder than you could go.

A tall Accepted on the row in front of them, Aisling Noon, twisted around. She was almost bouncing on the bench with excitement. "It's the Foretelling, I say. Gitara had a Foretelling before she died, and the Amyrlin is going to tell us what it was. You two had the duty this morning, didn't you? You were with her when she died. What did she say?"

Siuan stiffened, and Moiraine opened her mouth to lie, but Tarna saved her. "Moiraine told me Gitara didn't have a Foretelling, Aisling. We'll find out what the Amyrlin wants to tell us when she arrives." Her voice was cool, as always, but not cutting. Aisling blushed furiously anyway.

She was another rarity for the Tower, one of the Tuatha'an, the Tinkers. The Tuatha'an lived in garishly painted wagons, traveling from village to village, and like the Sea Folk, they wanted no self-taught wilders among them. If a band discovered the spark coming out in one of their girls, they turned their train of wagons and headed for Tar Valon as fast as their horses could move. Verin, a stout Brown who was even shorter than Moiraine, said that Tinker girls never tried to find their way to channeling on their own, that they did not want to channel or become Aes Sedai. It must be so, since Verin had said it, yet Aisling applied herself with just as much determination as Zemaille, and with more success. She had earned the ring in five years, in the same year as Moraine and Siuan, and Moiraine thought she might test for the shawl in another year, perhaps less.

One of the doors at the back of the dais opened, and Tamra glided out, still in the blue dress she had worn the night before, the Amyrlin's stole draped around her neck. Moiraine was one of the first to see her, the first to rise, but in moments everyone was on her feet and silent. It seemed strange to see the Amyrlin by herself. Always when Tamra was seen in the corridors, she was accompanied by at least a few Aes Sedai, whether ordinary sisters presenting petitions or Sitters in the Hall of the Tower discussing some matter that was before the Hall. She looked weary, to Moiraine. Oh, her back was straight, and her expression said she could walk through a wall if she took it in mind, but something about her eyes spoke of tiredness that had little to do with missing sleep.

"In thanksgiving for the continued safety of Tar Valon," she said, her voice carrying easily to everyone, "I have decided the Tower will give a bounty of one hundred crowns in gold to every woman in the city who bore a child between the day the first soldiers arrived and the day the threat is ended. It is being announced on the streets even as I speak."

Everyone knew better than to make a sound while the Amyrlin was speaking, yet that brought a few murmurs, including one from Siuan. Actually, hers was more of a grunt. She had never seen ten gold crowns in one place, much less a hundred. A hundred would buy a very large farm, or who knew how many fishing boats.

Ignoring the break in the proprieties, Tamra continued without a pause. "As some of you may already know, an army is always accompanied by camp followers, sometimes more camp followers than there are soldiers. Many of these are craftsfolk an army needs, the armorers and fletchers, the blacksmiths and farriers and wagonwrights, but among them are soldiers' wives and other women. Since the army provided the shield to Tar Valon, I have decided to extend the bounty to those women also."

Moiraine realized she was biting at her lower lip, and made herself stop. It was a habit she was trying to break. There was certainly no point to letting anyone who saw you know that you were thinking furiously. At least now they knew what Tamra was after. She must believe the boychild really would be born soon. But why under the Light tell Accepted?

"That threat might continue for some time," Tamra said, "though I have reports this morning that the Aiel may be retreating, yet the situation appears safe enough to begin collecting names, at least in the camps closest to the city. To be fair to those women, we must begin as soon as possible, before any of them leave. Some will, if the Aiel really are going. Many of the soldiers will follow the Aiel, soon to be joined by their camp followers, and other soldiers will return to their homes. No sisters have returned to the Tower yet, so I am sending all of you to begin taking names. Since, inevitably, some women will slip away before you find them, you also will ask after those who gave birth and can't be found. Write down everything that might help locate them. Who the father is, from what town or village, what country, everything. You will each be accompanied by four Tower Guards to make sure no one troubles you."

Moiraine almost choked trying to keep silent. Astonished gasps rose from women less successful than she. It was rare enough for Accepted to be allowed to leave the city, but without a *sister*? That was unheard of!

With a small, indulgent smile, Tamra paused to let order restore itself. She plainly knew she had startled them out of their wits. She also apparently heard something that Moiraine did not catch. As silence fell again, the Amyrlin said, "If I hear that someone has used the Power to defend herself, Alanna, that someone will sit very tenderly after a visit to the Mistress of Novices."

A few of the Accepted were still unsettled enough to giggle, and one or two laughed aloud. Alanna was a shy woman at heart, but she worked hard at being fierce. She told anyone who would listen that she wanted to belong to the Green, the Battle Ajah, and have a dozen Warders. Only Greens bonded more than a single Warder. None had *that* many Warders, of course, but that was Alanna, always exaggerating.

Tamra slapped her palms together, quieting gigglers and laughers alike at a stroke. There were limits to her indulgence. "You will all take great care, and heed the soldiers escorting you." There were no smiles, now. Her voice was firm. The Amyrlin Seat brooked no nonsense from rulers; she certainly would not from Accepted. "The Aiel are not the only danger outside Tar Valon's walls. Some may think you are Aes Sedai, and you may let them so long as you aren't foolish enough to claim that you are." That deepened the stillness; claiming to be Aes Sedai when you were not violated a Tower law that was enforced strictly, even against women who were not initiates of the Tower. "But there are ruffians who will see only a youthful woman's face. Easy prey, they might think, if not for your escort. Better to remove temptation and avoid the problem altogether. And don't forget that there are Children of the Light in the army. A Whitecloak will know an Accepted's dress when he sees one, and if he can safely put an arrow through her back, it will please him as much as if she were Aes Sedai."

It hardly seemed possible the room could grow any quieter, yet it did. Moiraine thought she could have heard people breathing, except that no one seemed to *be* breathing. When an Aes Sedai went out into the world and vanished, as sometimes happened, the first thought was always the Whitecloaks. The Children called Aes Sedai Darkfriends and claimed that touching the One Power was blasphemy punishable by death, a sentence they were all too willing to carry out. No one could understand why they had come to help defend Tar Valon. No one among the Accepted, at least.

The Amyrlin ran her eyes slowly along the rows. At last she gave a nod, satisfied that her warning had sunk in. "Horses are being saddled for you at the West Stable. There will be food for midday in the saddlebags, and everything else you will need. Now, return to your rooms, put on stout shoes, and fetch your cloaks. It will be a long day for you, and cold. Go in the Light." It was a dismissal, and they offered curtsies almost as one, but as they began moving toward the door to the corridor, she added, as though it had just occurred to her, "Oh, yes." The words jerked everyone to a halt. "When you record the woman's name, also put down the infant's name and sex, the day he or she was born, and exactly where. The Tower's records must be complete in this matter. You may go." Just as though what she had left till last was not the most important thing. That was how Aes Sedai hid things in plain sight. Some said Aes Sedai had invented the Game of Houses.

Moiraine could not help exchanging excited glances with Siuan. Siuan absolutely hated anything that smacked of clerical work, but she wore a wide grin. They were going to help find the Dragon Reborn. Just his name, of course, and his mother's name, but it was as near to an adventure as Accepted could dare to hope for.

Chapter
4

Leaving the Tower

Moiraine's room was little different from Siuan's. Her small square table, with four books lying on it, and the two cushionless straight-backed chairs could have come from the same farmhouse that had provided Siuan's. Her bed was narrower, her Illianer carpet round and flowered, and darned in several places, while on her washstand, it was the basin that had taken a blow sometime in the past. The mirror had a crack in one corner. Apart from that, they could have been the same room. She did not bother with starting a fire. She had banked her coals more carefully than Siuan, but there was no time to so much as take the edge off the room's chill.

Reaching into the back of her wardrobe, slightly larger than Siuan's but just as plain, she brought out a stout pair of shoes that made her grimace. Ugly things, made of leather much thicker than her slippers. The laces could have done to mend a saddle. But the shoes would keep her feet dry in the snow, and her slippers would not. Adding a pair of woolen stockings, she sat on the edge of her unmade bed to pull them on over those she was already wearing. For a moment, she considered donning a second shift, as well. However cold it was inside the Tower, it would be colder where she was going. But time was short. And besides, she did not want to take off her dress in that icy air. Surely recording names would be done in some sort of shelter, with a fire or a brazier for warmth. Of course it would. Most people in the camps likely would take them for sisters, just as Tamra had suggested.

Next out of the wardrobe came a narrow, worked leather belt with silver buckle and a plain scabbard holding a slim, silver-mounted dagger, its blade a little longer than her hand. She had not worn that since arriving in the Tower, and it felt awkward at first, hanging at her waist. Perhaps she was forbidden to use the Power to defend herself, but the dagger would do nicely, if need be. Transferring her belt pouch from the white leather belt she had laid on the bed, she thought for a moment. It was all very well for Tamra to say that everything they needed would be waiting, but depending on someone else, even the Amyrlin Seat, to provide *everything* was unwise. She tucked her ivory comb and ivory-handled hairbrush into a leather scrip. No matter how urgent the need to gather names, she doubted that any Accepted who let herself go untidy for long would escape sharp words at best. Her good riding gloves, dark blue leather with just a touch of embroidery on the back, followed, plus a small sewing kit in a carved blackwood box, a ball of stout twine, two pairs of spare stockings in case those she was wearing got wet, several kerchiefs in various sizes, and a number of other items that might be useful, including a little knife that folded, for trimming quill pens, in the event that was what they found themselves using. Sisters would never be forced to put up with such an inconvenience, but they were not sisters.

Hanging the scrip from one shoulder, she gathered her cloak, with its banded hem and another band bordering the hood, and rushed out just in time to see Meidani and Brendas go scurrying through the doorway that led off the gallery, cloaks flaring behind them. Siuan was waiting impatiently, a scrip on her shoulder, too, beneath her cloak, and her blue eyes sparkling with excitement. She was not alone in being caught up in the moment. On the other side of the gallery, Katerine Alruddin popped out of her room, demanding at the top of her lungs that Carlinya return her sewing kit, then darted back inside without waiting for an answer.

"Alanna, Pritalle, can one of you lend me a pair of clean stockings?" someone called from below.

"I loaned you a pair yesterday, Edesina," came a reply from above.

Doors banged throughout the well as women rushed out to shout for Temaile or Desandre, Coladara or Atuan or a score of others to return this or that borrowed item or lend something. Had a sister been present, the cacophony would put them all in the soup kettle to their necks, on a hot fire.

"What kept you, Moiraine?" Siuan said breathlessly. "Come on before we're left behind." She set off at a rapid stride, as though she really expected the Guardsmen to be gone if they did not hurry. There was no chance of that, of course, but Moiraine did not dawdle. She was not about to drag her feet at a chance to leave the city. Especially not at this chance.

Outside, the sun was still well short of halfway to its noonday peak. Thickening dark gray clouds rolled across the sky. They might have more snowfall today. That would not make the task ahead any easier. The walk *was* easy, since the wide, graveled path through the trees that led to the West Stable, beyond the Tower wing that held the Accepted's quarters, had been cleared. Not for the convenience of the Accepted, of course; most of the sisters kept their horses in the West Stable, and workmen shoveled that path clean two or three times a day if necessary.

The stable itself was three sprawling stories of gray stone, larger than the main stables of the Sun Palace, the wide stone-paved stableyard in front of it almost filled by a crowd of rough-coated grooms and saddled horses and helmeted Tower Guards who wore gray steel breastplates over nearly black coats and equally dark cloaks worked with the white teardrop of the Flame of Tar Valon. Seven-striped tabards over the breastplates marked out bannermen and the lone officer. Brendas and Meidani were climbing into their saddles, and half a dozen other Accepted, cloaked and hooded in a strung-out line, were already riding toward the Sunset Gate surrounded by their Guards. Moiraine felt a moment of irritation that so many had beaten her and Siuan down. Had they packed nothing, to be so quick? But they did not know what they really were looking for. That buoyed her spirits again.

Pushing through the crowd, she found her bay mare, the reins held by a lanky groom with a disapproving expression on her narrow face. Very likely she frowned on an Accepted having her own horse. Few did—most could not afford to keep a horse, and besides, opportunities to ride anywhere outside the Tower grounds were rare—but Moiraine had purchased Arrow to celebrate attaining the ring. An act of ostentation that she suspected had nearly earned her a trip to Merean's study. She did not regret the purchase, even so. The mare was not tall, since she despised looking like a child, which she did on tall animals, yet Arrow could keep running long after larger horses had tired out. A fast mount was good, but a mount with endurance was better. Arrow was both. And she could jump fences that few other horses would even try. Finding that out *had* earned a visit to the Mistress of Novices. Sisters took a dim view of Accepted risking a broken neck. A very dim view.

The groom tried to hand her the reins, but she hung the scrip from the saddle's tall pommel by its strap, then unbuckled the flaps of the saddlebags. One side held a cloth-wrapped parcel that proved to contain half a loaf of dark bread, dried apricots in oiled paper, and a large piece of pale yellow cheese. More than she could eat by herself, but some of the others had larger appetites. The other side bulged with a polished wooden lapdesk, complete with a thick sheaf of good paper and two good steel-nibbed pens inside.

No need for the penknife, she thought ruefully, careful to keep her face smooth. She did not intend to let the groom see her look abashed. At least she had been prepared.

The lapdesk also held a tightly stoppered ink jar of heavy glass. Much to the groom's undisguised amusement, she checked to make sure it *was* tightly stoppered. Well, the woman could snicker all she wanted, not bothering to hide it behind a hand, but she would not have had to deal with the mess if the ink leaked out over everything. Sometimes Moiraine thought it a pity the servants did not see Accepted the way novices did.

The groom made a derisory bow as she finally took the reins, and bent to offer cupped hands for a mounting step, another mocking gesture, but Moiraine disdained the help. Donning her snug riding gloves, she swung easily up into the saddle. Let the woman snicker at that! She had been put on her first pony—on a lead, to be sure—as soon as she was old enough to walk without someone holding her hand, and had been given her first real horse at ten. Unfortunately, Accepted's dresses did not have skirts divided for riding, and the necessity of pushing her skirts down, vainly trying to cover her legs, spoiled the dignity of the moment somewhat. It was the cold that concerned her, not modesty. Well, partly modesty. She noticed some of the Guardsmen studying her stockinged legs, bare almost to the knee, and blushed furiously. Attempting to ignore the men, she looked for Siuan.

She had wanted to buy Siuan a horse in celebration, too,

and now she wished she had not let Siuan talk her out of it. Siuan could have used whatever practice she might then have had. She scrambled onto her mount, a stout gray gelding, so awkwardly that the placid-seeming animal twisted his head around to look at her in consternation. She nearly fell off trying to get her other foot into the stirrup. That done, she gripped her reins so tightly that her dark gray gloves strained over her knuckles, her face set in a grim expression, as if prepared for an onerous test she might fail. For her, it was. Siuan could ride; she was just very bad at it. Some of the men stared at her half-exposed legs, too, but she appeared not to notice. Of course, if she had, it would not have flustered her. According to her, working a fishing boat meant tying your skirts up, and exhibiting your legs well *above* the knee!

As soon as they were both mounted, a slim young underlieutenant, his helmet marked by a short white plume, told off eight Guardsmen for the escort. He was quite pretty, really, behind the face-bars of his helmet, but any Tower Guard knew better than to smile at Accepted, and he barely looked at her and Siuan before turning away. Not that she wanted him to smile, or to smile back—she was no brainless novice—but she would have enjoyed looking at him a while longer.

The leader of the escort was not pretty. A tall, grizzled bannerman with a permanent scowl who curtly introduced himself in a deep, gravelly voice as Steler formed his soldiers in a loose ring around the pair of them and turned his rangy roan gelding toward the Sunset Gate without another word. The Guardsmen heeled their mounts after him, and Siuan and she found themselves being herded along. Herded! She held on to calmness with an effort. It was good practice. Siuan seemed not to think she needed any practice.

"We are supposed to go to the west bank," she called, glowering at Steler's back. He did not answer. Thumping her heels against the gray's plump flanks, she pushed up beside the man, almost sliding out of her saddle in the process. "Did you hear me? We are to go to the west bank."

The bannerman sighed loudly, and finally turned his head to look at Siuan. "I was told to take you to the west bank. . . ." He paused as if thinking of what title to use in addressing her. Guardsmen seldom had reason to speak to Accepted. Nothing occurred to him, apparently, because when he went on, it was without honorifics and in a firmer tone. "Now, if one of you gets herself bruised, I'm going to hear about it, and I don't want to hear about it, so you stay inside the ring, hear? Well, go on, now. Or we'll stop right here until you do."

Clenching her jaw, Siuan fell back beside Moiraine.

With a quick glance to make sure none of the soldiers was close enough to overhear, Moiraine whispered, "You cannot think we will actually be the ones, Siuan." She hoped for it, true, but this was real life, not a gleeman's tale. "He might not even be born, yet."

"As much chance us as anyone else," Siuan muttered. "More, since we know what we're really looking for." She had not stopped scowling at the bannerman. "When I bond a Warder, the first thing I'll make sure of is that he does what he's told."

"You are thinking of bonding Steler?" Moiraine asked in an innocent voice. Siuan's stare was such a blend of astonishment and horror that she nearly laughed. But Siuan nearly fell off her horse again, too, and she could not laugh at that.

Once past the iron-strapped Sunset Gate, with the gilded setting suns that gave it its name set high in the thick timbers, it quickly became apparent that they were angling southwest through the stone-paved streets, toward the Alindaer Gate. There were any number of water gates to the city, where small boats could enter, and of course Northharbor and Southharbor for riverships, but only six bridge gates. The Alindaer Gate was the most southerly of the three to the west, and not a good omen for coming near to Dragonmount, but Moiraine did not think Steler would let himself be turned. *Live with what you cannot change,* she told herself sourly. Siuan must be ready to chew nails.

Siuan was silently studying Steler's back, though. Not glaring any longer, but studying, the way she did with the puzzles she loved so much, the maddening intricate sort, with pieces fitted together so it seemed they could never come apart. Only, they always did come apart eventually, for Siuan. The word puzzles, too, and the number puzzles. Siuan saw patterns where no one else could. She was so absorbed with the bannerman that she actually rode with some ease, if not skill. At least she did not seem ready to topple off at every other step.

Perhaps she would figure out a way to turn him, but Moiraine gave herself over to enjoying the ride through the city. It was not as if even Accepted were allowed outside the Tower grounds every day, after all, and Tar Valon was the largest city, the grandest city, in the known world. In the whole world, surely. The island was nearly ten miles long, and except for public parks and private gardens—and the Ogier Grove, of course—the city covered every square foot of it.

The streets they rode along were wide and long since cleared of snow, and all seemed full to overflowing with people, mostly afoot, though sedan chairs and closed litters wove through the crowd. In that press, walking was faster than riding, and only the proudest and most stubborn—a Tairen noblewoman, stiff-necked in a tall lace collar, with her entourage of servants and guards, a cluster of sober-eyed Kandori merchants with silver chains across their chests, several knots of brightly coated Murandian dandies with curled mustaches who should have been out in the fighting—were mounted. Or those with a long way to go, she amended, making another futile effort at covering her legs and frowning at a tilt-eyed Saldaean, a tradesman or craftsman by his plain woolen coat, who was ogling them much too openly. Light! Men never seemed to understand, or care, when a woman wished to be looked at and when not. In any case, Steler and his soldiers managed to clear a path ahead of them with their mere presence. No one wanted to impede the way of eight armed and armored Tower Guards. It had to be that which opened the crush of people. She doubted that anyone in the crowd would know that a banded dress indicated an initiate of the White Tower. People who came to Tar Valon stayed clear of the Tower unless they had business there.

Every country seemed to be represented in that crowd. The world comes to Tar Valon, so the saying went. Taraboner men from the far west, wearing veils that covered their faces to the eyes, and were transparent enough to show their thick mustaches clearly, rubbed shoulders with sailors, leather-skinned and barefoot even in this cold, from the riverships that plied the Erinin. A Borderman in plate-and-mail passed them riding in the other direction, a stone-faced Shienaran with his crested helmet hanging from his saddle and his head shaved except for a topknot. He was certainly a messenger headed for the Tower, and Moiraine briefly considered stopping him. But he would not reveal his message to her, and she would have had to force her way through Steler's Guardsmen. Light, she hated not knowing!

There were dark-clad Cairhienin, easy to pick out because they were shorter and paler than nearly everyone else, Altaran men in heavily embroidered coats, Altaran women clutching their cloaks, bright red or green or yellow, to shield what their low-cut dresses exposed to the icy air, Tairens in broad-striped coats or lace-trimmed dresses, and plainly garbed Andorans who strode along as though they not only knew exactly where they were going but intended to reach there as soon as possible. Andorans always focused on one matter at a time; they were stubborn people, over-proud, and they lacked imagination. Half a dozen copper-skinned Domani women in fancifully worked cloaks—doubtless merchants; most Domani women seen abroad were—stood buying meat pies from a pushbarrow, and nearby, an Arafellin wearing a coat with red-slashed sleeves, his black hair dangling down his back in two braids decorated with silver bells, was waving his arms and arguing with a stolid Illianer who appeared more interested in wrapping his vividly striped cloak around his bulk. She even glimpsed a charcoal-skinned fellow who might have been one of the Sea Folk, though some Tairens were as dark. His hands were hidden in his frayed cloak as he scuttled away in the throng, so she could not see whether they were tattooed.

So many people made a din just by their normal talking, but wagons and carts added to it with the squeak of poorly greased axles, the clatter of hooves and the grate of steel-rimmed wheels on the paving stones. The carters and wagon drivers shouted for people to give way, which they did reluctantly, and hawkers cried ribbons or needles or roasted nuts or a dozen things more from barrows and trays. Despite the cold, jugglers and tumblers were performing on some street corners, men and women with caps laid out to collect coins were playing flute or pipes or harp, and shopkeepers standing in front of their shops called out the superiority of their goods over any others. Streetcleaners with their brooms and shovels and barrows cleaned away what the horses left behind, and any other trash as well, shouting, "Make way for clean shoes! Make way if you want clean shoes!" It was so . . . normal. No one appeared to notice the heavy smell of sour smoke that hung in the air. A battle outside Tar Valon could not alter what went on inside Tar Valon's walls. Perhaps even a war could not. But you could see as much in Cairhien, if not in quite the same numbers or quite as much variety. It was Tar Valon itself that made the city unlike any other.

The White Tower rose from the center of the city, a thick bone-white shaft climbing almost a hundred spans into the sky and visible for miles. It was the first thing anyone approaching the city saw, long before they could make out the city itself. The heart of Aes Sedai power, that alone was sufficient to mark Tar Valon apart, but other, smaller towers rose throughout the city. Not simply spires, but spirals and fluted towers, some close enough together to be linked by bridges a hundred feet in the air, or two hundred, or higher. Even the topless towers of Cairhien did not come close to matching them. Every square had its fountain or monument in the center, or a huge statue, some atop plinths as much as fifty paces tall, but the buildings themselves were grander than most monuments in other cities. Around the palatial homes of wealthy merchants and bankers, with their domes and spires and colonnaded walks, crowded shops and inns, taverns and stables, apartment buildings and the homes of ordinary folk, yet even they were ornamented with carvings and friezes fit for palaces. A fair number could have passed for palaces. Nearly all were Ogier built, and Ogier built for beauty. More wondrous still were the structures dotted through the city, half a dozen in sight on every street, where the Ogier masons had been given a free hand. A three-story banking house suggested a flight of golden marble birds taking wing, while the Kandori merchants' guild hall seemed to represent horses running in surf, or perhaps surf turning into horses, and a very large inn called The Blue Cat strongly resembled exactly that, a blue cat curled up to sleep. The Great Fish Market, the largest in the city, seemed to *be* a school of huge fish, green and red and blue and striped. Other cities boasted of Ogier-built buildings, but nothing like what Tar Valon possessed.

Scaffolding surrounded one of the Ogier-made structures, obscuring its form so that all she could make out was green and white stone and the fact that it seemed all curves, and

Ogier stonemasons moved on the wooden platforms, some hoisting large pieces of white stone on a long wooden crane that stuck out over the street. Even Ogier work needed mending now and then, and no human mason could duplicate their craft. They were not often seen, though. One of them was standing in the street, at the foot of the broad ladder leading up to the first platform, in a long dark coat that flared out above his boot tops, with a thick roll of paper under one arm. Plans, no doubt. He could have been taken for human, if you squinted. And ignored the fact that his huge eyes were on a level with Moiraine's as she drew abreast of him. That and the long, tufted ears that stuck up through his hair, a nose nearly as wide as his face, and a mouth that all but cut that face in two. His eyebrows dangled onto his cheeks like mustaches. She offered him a formal bow from her saddle, and he returned it with equal gravity, stroking the narrow beard that hung down his chest. But his ears twitched, and she thought she saw a grin as he turned to begin climbing the ladder. Any Ogier who came to Tar Valon would know an Accepted's dress when he saw one.

Flushing, she glanced from the corner of her eye to see whether Siuan had seen, but the other woman was still studying Steler. She might not even have noticed the Ogier. Siuan could become very engrossed in her puzzles, but to miss seeing an *Ogier*?

Nearly an hour after leaving the Tower, they reached the Alindaer Gate, wide enough for five or six wagons abreast to pass uncrowded and flanked by tall towers with crenellated tops. There were towers all along the city's high white walls, thrusting out into the river, but none so tall or strong as the bridge towers. The huge, bronze-strapped gates stood wide open, yet Guardsmen atop the gate towers were keeping watch, ready to order them winched shut, and two dozen more at the side of the road, carrying halberds, kept an eye on the very few who passed by. She and Siuan and their escort drew those eyes like iron filings to magnets. Or rather, the banded dresses did. No one said anything about Accepted leaving the city, though, which suggested that another party had gone out of this gate already. Unlike the bustling streets, the gate had no traffic. All who had wanted to seek the safety of Tar Valon's walls were long since inside, and despite the apparent normality inside the walls, no one seemed to think it safe to depart just yet. One of the Guardsmen on the roadside, a wide-shouldered bannerman, nodded to Steler, who nodded back without stopping.

As their horses' hooves rang on the bridge, she felt her breath catch. The bridges themselves were marvels, constructed with the aid of the Power, stone lacework arching nearly a mile to solid ground beyond the marshy riverbank, unsupported that whole way and high enough at the center for the largest rivership to sail beneath. That was not what struck her, though. She was out of the city. The sisters impressed deeply on every novice that so much as setting foot on the bridges constituted an attempt to run away, which was the worst crime a novice could commit short of murder. The same held true for Accepted; they just did not need to be reminded. And she was out of the city, as free as if she already wore the shawl. She glanced at the soldiers around her. Well, nearly as free.

At the highest point of the bridge, more than fifty paces above the river, Steler abruptly drew rein. Was he mad enough to pause for the view of Dragonmount rising in the distance, its broken peak emitting a ribbon of smoke? In her euphoria, she had forgotten the cold, but a strong breeze slicing down the Alindrelle Erinin, slicing right through her cloak, reminded her quickly enough. The stench of charred wood seemed particularly strong on that wind. The trumpets had stopped, she realized. Somehow, the silence seemed as ominous as their calling had been.

Then she saw the cluster of horsemen at the foot of the bridge, nine or ten of them, staring at the city walls. Why the trumpets had gone silent no longer seemed so worrisome. The riders' burnished breastplates and helmets shone like silver, and they all wore long white cloaks, spread across their mounts' cruppers. Embracing the Source filled her with life and joy, but more importantly at the moment, it sharpened her sight. As she had suspected, a flaring golden sun was embroidered on the left breast of each of those cloaks. Children of the Light. And they dared to block traffic on one of Tar Valon's bridges? Well, there was only her and Siuan and the Guardsmen, but the principle was the same. The fact that it was Siuan and her and Tower Guards made it worse, in truth. That made it intolerable.

"Bannerman Steler," she said loudly, "Whitecloaks must

not be allowed to think they can intimidate initiates of the Tower. Or Tower Guards. We ride forward." The fool man did not so much as glance around at her from his study of the Whitecloaks. Perhaps if she gave him a little rap on top of his head with a small flow of Air. . . .

"Moiraine!" Siuan's whisper was low, but managed a sharp edge.

She looked at her friend in surprise. Siuan wore a scowl. How had the other woman known? She had not begun to weave! Still, Siuan was right. Some things were just not allowed. Guiltily, she released *saidar,* and sighed as all of that joyous exultation drained away. Shivering, she pulled her cloak tighter. As if that would do any good.

At last the Whitecloaks turned and rode back into the village. Alindaer was a very large village, practically a town, with brick houses of two or even three stories roofed in blue tiles, where they showed through the snow, and its own inns and shops and markets. The blanket of white made it appear clean and peaceful. For long moments, the Whitecloaks vanished. Only when they appeared in a gap between two buildings, on a street heading north, did Steler heel his mount into motion. His gauntleted hand rested on his sword hilt and his head swiveled constantly, searching the streets ahead, as they rode down the final length of the bridge. Where there was one group of Whitecloaks, there might be another. Moiraine felt suddenly very grateful for the presence of Steler and his men. A dagger would not be much use against a Whitecloak's arrow. *None* of her preparations were turning out to be very useful.

When they reached the edge of the town, Siuan again thumped her gray up beside the bannerman, still so wrapped up in her own thoughts that she rode with something approaching . . . not grace, certainly, but at least steadiness. "Bannerman Steler." Her tone combined firmness with civility, and a strong element of certainty. It was very much a voice of command. Steler turned his head to her, blinking in surprise. "You know why we are here, of course," she went on, and barely waited for his nod. "The women most likely to leave before hearing of the bounty are those in the camps most distant from the city. Visiting them yesterday would have entailed some danger, but the Amyrlin has reports that the Aiel are retreating." Light, she sounded for all the world as though the Amyrlin regularly shared reports with her! "The Amyrlin has expressed her unwillingness to let any of these women slip away without receiving the bounty, Bannerman, so I strongly suggest that we follow the Amyrlin's urging and begin with the more distant camps." Her gesture might have seemed vague to anyone other than Moiraine, but it just happened to point straight at Dragonmount. "The Amyrlin Seat will wish it."

Moiraine held her breath. Could Siuan have found the key?

"There's not an Aiel this side of the Erinin, so I hear," Steler replied in an agreeable voice. The next moment, he dashed her hopes. "But I was told the camps closest the river, so that's what it'll be. And I was told if anybody made a fuss, I was to take her right back to the Tower. You're not making a fuss, are you? I thought not."

Reining her mount in to let Moiraine catch up, Siuan fell in alongside Arrow. She was not scowling, but her stare at the bannerman's back was blue ice. The glow of *saidar* abruptly surrounded her.

"No, Siuan," Moiraine said quietly.

Siuan frowned at her. "I could just be trying to see further ahead, you know. In case there are more Whitecloaks."

Moiraine arched an eyebrow, and Siuan blushed, the light around her vanishing. She had no right to look so surprised. After six years practically in one another's belt pouches, Moiraine knew at a glance when her friend was thinking of mischief. For someone as intelligent as she was, Siuan was blind sometimes.

"I don't see how you can stand this," the taller woman muttered, half rising in her stirrups. Moiraine had to put out a hand to keep her from toppling to the ground. "If the camp is much further, I'll need a sister for Healing."

"I have an ointment," Moiraine said, patting the scrip hanging from her saddle with a touch of satisfaction. The penknife and the dagger might be useless, but at least she had thought of the ointment.

"Now if only you had a carriage in there," Siuan grumbled, but Moiraine only smiled.

Alindaer lay empty and still. The village had been burned at least three times in the Trolloc Wars, once more near the end of the War of the Second Dragon, and twice during the twenty-year siege of Tar Valon by Artur Hawkwing's armies, and it seemed the inhabitants had expected the same again. Here a chair sat in the snow-covered street, there a table, a child's doll, a cookpot, all dropped by people hurrying to get inside the city with whatever they could take with them. Then again, every window appeared to be shuttered tightly, every door closed and no doubt locked, whatever remained behind kept safe against the people's return. But the stink of burning was stronger here than on the bridge, and the only sounds were the creak of swinging inn signs and the dull clop of the horses' hooves on the paving stones beneath the snow. The place no longer seemed so pristine; it seemed . . . dead.

Moiraine felt a great relief when they left the village behind, even if they were riding south and away from Dragonmount. The countryside was supposed to be quiet, and the smell of burning faded the farther they went. Siuan plainly was not relieved. From time to time she looked over her shoulder toward the great black peak of Dragonmount—half the time, she needed a steadying hand from Moiraine to keep her in her saddle—and more than once she ground her teeth audibly. They had often discussed what Ajah they might join, and Moiraine had long since settled on the Blue for herself, but she thought Siuan might well end choosing Green.

The first camp they came to, two miles below Alindaer, was a cookfire-dotted sprawl of wagons and carts and tents in every size and state of repair mixed with rude shelters made of brush. Hammers rang on anvils at three different forges, and children ran shouting and playing in trampled, dirty snow as though unaware that there had been a battle or that their fathers might be dead. Perhaps they were. It would be a mercy. The horselines were nearly empty, and aside from the blacksmiths, few men were in evidence, but a long line of women—well above fifty!—stood in front of a canvas pavilion where an Accepted was seated at a table with four Tower Guards arrayed behind her, so Steler did not so much as slow down. Moiraine embraced the Source briefly and felt Siuan do the same. Just to better see who it was, of course. A multitude of thin Taraboner braids surrounded the distant Accepted's face. Sarene was the most beautiful woman in the Accepted's quarters, except perhaps for Ellid, though she seemed completely unconscious of it, which Ellid definitely was not, but she had remarkably little tact for a shopkeeper's daughter. Her mother must have been glad to see Sarene's sharp tongue go off to Tar Valon.

"I hope it doesn't get her in hot water this time," Siuan said softly, just as if she could read Moiraine's thoughts. But then, they both knew Sarene all too well. A friend, but a nettlesome one at times. Her saving grace was that she seemed as unaware of what she had said wrong as she was of her face.

A hundred paces later, the light around Siuan vanished, and Moiraine released the Power, too. A sister might see them, after all.

The next camp, less than a mile farther south, was even larger and more disorderly, and without anyone taking names. It was noisier, as well, with six forges working, and twice as many children rushing about shouting. The relative absence of men was the same, and the nearly bare horselines, but surprisingly, a number of closed coaches dotted the camp. Moiraine winced when she heard the Murandian accents as they rode in. Murandians were a quarrelsome lot, prickly over points of honor no one else could see, always fighting duels. But when Steler announced the purpose of their visit in a bellow that would have frightened a bull, no one wanted to quarrel in the least. In short order two weedy young men in worn cloaks carried out a table and a pair of stools for Moiraine and Siuan. They placed the table in the open, but two other youths brought three-legged braziers that they set at either end of the table. This might not be too unpleasant after all.

CHAPTER
5

The Human Heart

O nce Moiraine was seated on one of the stools with
her lapdesk open on the table in front of her, she
changed her mind about the unpleasantness. The
warmth of the braziers dissipated rapidly in the open air,
barely lessening the chill, and eddies of the thin gray smoke
drifted into her face, stinging her eyes and sometimes making her cough. Stout shoes and extra stockings or not, her
feet had grown quite cold on the ride; resting on the trampled snow, they quickly became frigid. And what appeared
to be close to a hundred women, the greater number clutching infants, formed a crowd around the table, all clamoring
at once for their names to be taken first. Most wore plain,
thick woolens, but half a dozen or so were in silks or at
least ornately embroidered dresses of fine cut that indicated
wealth or nobility or both. They shouted as loudly as anyone, though. Noblewomen, shouting along with the commoners! Murandians had little sense of proper behavior.

Helmet held on his hip, Steler bellowed till his face turned
dark for everyone to be quiet and form a line, and no one
took any notice at all. Two of the Guardsmen moved as if to
begin pushing the women back, until a sharp motion from
the bannerman halted them, and well that it did. That sort
of thing could start a riot. Moiraine stood up to try putting
things to rights, though she was uncertain how. She had
never had to face the like on any of her estates; she doubted
any of her stewards had, for that matter, and people were
more outspoken with a steward than with the lady of the estate. But Siuan was ahead of her, climbing atop her stool

with a scowl. She gripped the edges of her cloak as though to keep from shaking her fists.

The light of *saidar* enveloped her, and she wove Air and Fire. It was a simple weave using tiny amounts of the Power, but when she spoke, her voice boomed like thunder. "Be quiet!" It was simply a command, if impressively delivered, without anger, yet startled women shrank back, suddenly as hushed as stones. Even the ring of hammers on anvils ceased. The entire camp grew still, so that Moiraine could hear picketed horses stamping hooves. Steler gave Siuan a look of approbation—bannermen approved of leather lungs, in Moiraine's experience—and the women around the table a glare. A number of babies began crying shrilly, though, and when Siuan went on, it was without the weave. Still in a loud, firm voice that carried, however. "If you want to see a penny, you'll line up and keep yourselves orderly. The White Tower does not treat with mobs of unruly children. Behave as grown women, or you'll wish you had." She nodded once, for emphasis, then frowned at the mass of women to see whether they had taken her words in. They had.

As she climbed down from the stool, the women rushed to form two lines in front of the table, with only a little elbowing and jostling that Moiraine could see. The more finely dressed women were at the front, of course, with serving women carrying their babes, yet they were not above trying to push ahead of one another and exchanging scowls. Maybe they were merchants, though what trade they could find here was beyond her. Once, she had seen two well-dressed, seemingly dignified Murandian merchants get into a fistfight in the street, bloodying noses and rolling in the gutter. Despite the petty scuffling, no one spoke a word, and those with crying children seemed to be making every effort to soothe them. A cluster of girls, perhaps ten or twelve years old, gathered off to one side, huddling in their cloaks, pointing at her and Siuan and whispering excitedly. She thought she heard Aes Sedai mentioned. Another young woman, three or four years older, about the age she had been when she came to Tar Valon, stood nearby pretending that she was not watching avidly. Many girls dreamed of becoming Aes Sedai; few had the nerve to take the first step beyond dreaming. Tossing back her cloak on the right side, Moiraine uncapped her ink jar and picked up a pen. She kept her gloves on; the thin leather did not provide a great deal of protection against the chill, yet it was better than nothing.

"Your name, my Lady?" she said. The plump, smiling woman wore a high-necked green riding dress that was not of the best silk, but it *was* silk, as was her fur-lined blue cloak, embroidered in red and gold. And she wore a jeweled ring on every finger. Perhaps she was not a noble, even so, yet flattery cost nothing. "And your babe's?"

"I am the Lady Meri do Ahlan a'Conlin, a direct descendant of Katrine do Catalan a'Coralle, the first Queen of Murandy." The plump woman's smile remained, but her voice was frosty with pride. It carried those lilting Murandian accents that made you think they must be peaceable people until you learned better. With one hand, she pulled forward a stout woman in dark wool who had a heavy shawl wrapped around her head and a gurgling infant in her arms, swaddled so that only its face showed. "This is my son, Sedrin. He was born just a week ago. I refused to stay behind when my husband rode to war, of course. I'll have the coins mounted in a frame, so Sedrin will always know he was honored by the White Tower."

Moiraine forbore to mention that Sedrin would share that honor with hundreds of others, perhaps thousands, if the other camps were anything like this. Light, she had never expected so many women to have given birth! Keeping her face smooth, she studied the infant for an instant. She was not an innocent—she had observed horse-breeding and helped at foaling; if you did not know how a thing was done, how could you know whether your servants did it properly?—but she had no experience with babies. The child could have been ten days old, or a month or two for all of her. Steler and his soldiers were keeping watch a short distance from the table against any further outbreaks, but they were no help here. At least, she could not bring herself to ask. If Lady a'Conlin was lying, a full sister would have to sort it out. Moiraine glanced sideways. The woman in front of Siuan was holding a larger child, but Siuan was writing.

Dipping her pen, she saw a woman walk past with an infant feeding at her breast. Half hidden in the woman's cloak, the child looked no larger than Sedrin, yet she was ignoring the line quite pointedly. "Why is that woman not in line? Is her babe too old?"

Lady a'Conlin's smile faded, and her eyebrows rose. The temperature of her voice dropped. "I'm not accustomed to keeping track of every brat born in the camp." She pointed imperiously at the paper on the table. The ring on that finger mounted a large but visibly flawed firedrop. "Put down my name. I want to return to the warmth of my tent."

"I will write your name, and the other information we require, just as soon as you tell me about that woman," Moiraine said, trying for that voice of command that Siuan used.

The attempt did not work very well. Meri a'Conlin's brows knitted in a frown, and her lips bunched belligerently. She appeared on the point of bursting. Or striking out. Before she could do either, the round-faced serving woman spoke up hurriedly, ducking in the semblance of a curtsy every few words.

"Careme's girl is the same age as Lord Sedrin to the day, begging your pardon for speaking, my Lady, begging your pardon, Aes Sedai. But the fellow Careme wanted to marry, he run off thinking to become a Warder, and she don't like who she did marry half so well." She gave an emphatic shake of her head. "Oh, she wants nothing from the White Tower, Careme don't."

"Even so, she will receive the bounty," Moiraine said firmly. Tamra had said to get every name, after all. She wondered whether Careme's love had achieved his goal. Few men possessed the necessary skills. A Warder did not simply use weapons, he *was* a weapon, and that was only the first requirement. "What is her full name? And the child's."

"She's Careme Mowly, Aes Sedai, and her girl's Ellya." Wonder of wonders, Lady a'Conlin appeared content to let her serving woman answer. Not only that, her scowl had vanished, and she was studying Moiraine warily. Perhaps a firm tone was all that was needed. That and being thought Aes Sedai.

"From what town or village?" Moiraine asked, writing.

"And where exactly was your girl born?" she heard Siuan saying. Siuan had doffed her gloves, a nameday present from Moiraine, to protect them from ink stains. The impatient silk-clad woman in front of her might have been a beauty if not for an unfortunate nose. She was also quite tall, nearly a hand taller than Siuan. "In a haybarn a mile west of here? No, not the place you'd expect to give birth to your heir. Perhaps you shouldn't have been out riding so close to your term, not to mention the fighting that was going on. Now, do you know any woman who's had a child in the last sixteen days and isn't here? What is her name? No backtalk, my Lady. Just answer the question." The lady did, with no further complaint. But then, Siuan's manner allowed for no complaints or difficulties. She neither raised her voice nor spoke harshly; she was just obviously in charge. How did she do it?

Whatever thoughts Moiraine had of adventure in hunting for the Dragon Reborn faded in short order, along with the thrill of being outside the city walls. Asking the same questions over and over and writing down the answers, carefully setting aside the filled pages to dry and starting anew on a fresh sheet, soon became boring drudgery. The only breaks in the routine were pauses to warm her hands over the brazier at her end of the table. An indescribable pleasure under the circumstances, with her fingers aching from the cold, yet hardly anything to thrill over. The only surprise was the number of women who were not Murandian. Soldiers gone to war, it seemed, frequently acquired foreign-born wives. The anvils started up again after a time, and some fellows working on a wagon began hammering away as well, trying to force a new wheel into place. The clanging threatened to give her a headache. It was all quite miserable.

She made a special effort not to take out her discontent on the women she spoke to, though a handful did try to give her cause. Some of the noblewomen had to be dissuaded from reciting their complete lineage back to Artur Hawkwing's day and beyond, and a few of the plainly clad women wanted to argue against giving the father's name or telling where they came from, glowering suspiciously as though this might be some sort of trick to bilk them of the coins, but it took no more than a level look to quell most. Not even Murandians wanted to go too far with women they thought Aes Sedai, a notion that was spreading fast. It made the lines move a little more smoothly, if not in any way that could be called swift.

Her eyes kept drifting to the women she saw walking by who were great with child. Some paused to look at the table as though thinking of their turn to stand in line. One of them might be the mother of the Dragon Reborn, at least if she chose to journey to Dragonmount to give birth for some reason. The only two infants born that day, after Gitara's Foretelling, were girls and, like every other newborn, birthed within a mile of the camp. Some other Accepted was going to find the boychild without knowing what she had found. She herself likely would not hear of it for years. Light, but it hardly seemed fair. She *knew,* and it meant nothing.

Coming onto midday, Moiraine looked up to find a slim young woman in dark wool standing before her with a blanket-wrapped child in the crook of her arm.

"Susa Wynn, Aes Sedai," the woman said meekly. "That's me. This is my Cyril," she added, stroking the boy's head.

Moiraine might have had no experience of babies, but she could tell a child of six or seven months from a newborn. As she opened her mouth to tell the woman not to try her for a fool, Siuan laid a hand briefly on her arm. That was all—Siuan never stopped questioning the woman whose name she was writing—but it made Moiraine take another look. Susa Wynn was not slim, she was near to gaunt, with deep shadows beneath her eyes and a lost, desperate look about her. Her dress and cloak were worn and much-darned. Neatly darned, but in places there seemed to be more darning than original dress.

"The father's name?" Moiraine asked, playing for time to decide. This child was too old by far, and that was that. Except. . . .

"Jac, Aes Sedai. Jac Wynn. He. . . ." Tears welled in the woman's sunken eyes. "Jac died before the fighting even started. Slipped in the snow and cracked his head on a stone. Hardly seems right, to come all this way and die for slipping in the snow." The baby began to cough, a chesty sound, and Susa bent over him anxiously.

Moiraine was not certain whether it was the child's cough, or the tears, or a dead husband, but she entered the woman's particulars carefully. The Tower could afford a hundred gold crowns for a woman and child who might die without some sort of help. The child seemed plump enough, true, but Susa clearly was starving. And Meri a'Conlin intended to *frame* her coins. It was all she could do not to demand to know who Jac Wynn had served. Whoever it was should never have allowed matters to come to this state! Noble blood carried as many responsibilities as rights! More, as she had been taught. On top of that, where were the woman's friends? Murandians!

"The Light bless you, Aes Sedai." Susa tried to gulp back more tears and failed. She did not sob; the tears simply spilled down her cheeks. "The Light shine on you forever."

"Yes, yes," Moiraine said gently. "Do you have a Reader in this camp?" No, Murandians had another name for women who knew herbs and cures. What was it? Verin Sedai had lectured on the subject the first year she and Siuan were Accepted. "A Wisdom? A Wise Woman?" At Susa's nod, she took her purse from her belt pouch and pressed a silver penny into the woman's free hand. "Take your child to her."

That brought still more weeping and more thanks, and an attempt to kiss her hand that she barely avoided. Light, Susa was not her liege woman. It was hardly decent.

"With the bounty to come," Siuan whispered once Susa had finally gone, "the Wise Woman would have given credit." She did not move her eyes from what she was writing in a precise hand, but what Moiraine could see of her face expressed disapproval. Siuan was very careful with the little money she had.

Moiraine sighed—done was done—and then again when she realized that a flurry of whispers was rushing along the two lines of women. Word that one of the "Aes Sedai" had accepted Susa Wynn's child spread like wildfire in dry grass, and in no time she saw women hurrying to join the end of the line, at least one *leading* her child by the hand.

"My Danil, he's been real peaky lately, Aes Sedai," the roundfaced woman in front of her said with a hopeful smile. And a glint of avarice in her pale eyes. The infant cradled in her arms made happy, burbling noises. "I surely wish I could afford to see the Wise Woman." The woman's gray woolen dress looked almost new.

Moiraine's temper flared, and for once, she made no effort to force it down. "I could Heal him," she replied coolly. "Of course, he is very young. He might not survive. Very likely not." At that age, he certainly would not survive the rigors of Healing, and besides, that was one of the few weaves that Accepted were forbidden to make without a sister watching. A mistake with Healing could harm more than the weaver. The woman did not know any of that, however, and when

Moiraine stretched out a gloved hand, she jerked back, clutching the infant protectively, her eyes nearly coming out of her head with fright.

"No, Aes Sedai. Thank you, but no. I . . . I'll scrape together the coin, I will."

Temper faded—it never lasted long—and for a moment, Moiraine felt ashamed of herself. Only for a moment. The Tower could afford to be generous, yet no one could be allowed to take Aes Sedai for fools. A good part of the Tower's power came from the belief that sisters were the very opposite of fools in every way. Whispers again flashed down the lines, and the woman leading her child by the hand scurried away more quickly than she had come. At least that would not have to be dealt with. There would have been no way to avoid harsh words with someone who thought the Tower could be gulled so easily.

"Well done," Siuan murmured, her pen scratching away. "Very well done."

"Danil," Moiraine said, writing. "And your name?" Her smile was for the compliment, but Danil's mother seemed to take it as a sign of forgiveness, offering her answers in a relieved voice. Moiraine was glad to hear it. Many people feared the White Tower, occasionally with reason—the Tower could be stern when it must—but fear was a poor tool, and one that always cut the user eventually. She had learned that long before coming to the Tower.

Once the sun passed its zenith, Siuan and she went to fetch the food from their saddlebags. There was certainly no point in asking one of Steler's men to do it. They were already squatting on their heels, making a meal from dried meat and flatbread, not far from where their mounts were tethered on one of the horselines. None looked ready to stir a foot short of being attacked. But Steler bowed his head to her and Siuan as they turned from their mounts, only the slightest bob, yet approving she thought. Men were decidedly . . . odd.

With fewer than half the women's names recorded, she expected grumbling at least, but those remaining scattered to find their own food without a single complaint. A dark woman with a Tairen accent brought a battered tin teapot filled to the brim with hot, dark tea to the table, and a pair of green mugs with cracked glazing, and a lean, gray-haired woman brought two steaming wooden tankards that gave off the scent of hot spiced wine. Her leathery face looked as though a smile had never touched it.

"Susa Wynn's too proud to take more than a little food from anybody, except for her babe," she said, in a deep voice for a woman, as she set the tankards down. "What you did was kindly done, and well." With a nod, she turned and strode away across the snow, her back as straight as a Guardsman on parade. That was certainly a peculiar manner with an Aes Sedai.

"She knows who we really are," Siuan said softly, picking up the tankard in both hands to let the warmth soak in. Moiraine did the same, gloves or no. Poor Siuan's fingers must have been freezing.

"She will not tell," Moiraine said after a moment, and Siuan nodded. Not that the truth would cause any real problems, not with Steler and his men present, but it was better to avoid the embarrassment. To think that one of the commoners would know an Aes Sedai's face when none of the noblewomen had. An Aes Sedai's face or an Accepted's dress. Or both. "She went to the Tower when she was young, I think." A woman who could not be taught to channel was sent away, yet she would have seen Aes Sedai and Accepted.

Siuan gave her a sideways look, as though she had said water was wet. Sometimes it could be irritating when Siuan puzzled things out ahead of her.

They spoke little while they ate their bread and fruit and cheese. Novices were expected to keep silent during meals, and Accepted to maintain a measure of dignity, so they had grown accustomed to eating quietly. The wine they barely touched—Accepted had wine with meals, but watered, and it would never do for one of them to grow tipsy—yet Moiraine was surprised to find that she had devoured every scrap of the meal she had been certain was too much. Perhaps being out in the cold had increased her appetite.

She was folding up the cloths the food had been bundled in—and wishing there had been a few more of the dried apricots—when Siuan suddenly muttered, "Oh, no."

Moiraine looked up, and her heart sank.

Two sisters were riding into the camp, slowly picking

their way between the tents and wagons. In the current state of affairs, women dressed in silk yet moving about the countryside without an entourage had to be sisters, and these were followed by just one man, a dark fellow in a cloak that shifted colors and blended with what lay behind him so that parts of him and parts of his black gelding seemed not to be there at all. His eyes never rested long in one place; he made the Tower guards seem half-asleep lapdogs compared to a hunting leopard. A Warder's cloak was a disconcerting sight, and murmurs rose in the camp, people gaping and pointing. The blacksmiths lowered their hammers in silence once more.

It was not the appearance of just any sisters that made Moiraine's stomach feel hollow. She recognized the faces framed by the hoods of their cloaks. Meilyn Arganya, with her silver-gray hair and thrusting chin, was one of the most respected women in the Tower. It was said that no one had a bad word for Meilyn. By herself, she would not have given Moiraine a moment's pause. The other, however, was Elaida a'Roihan. Light, what was *she* doing here? Elaida had become advisor to the Queen of Andor nearly three years ago. She did return to the Tower for occasional visits, to confer with the Amyrlin on events in Andor, but Siuan and Moiraine always learned of her arrival very quickly, to their regret.

They offered curtsies as soon as the sisters came near, and Siuan burst out with, "We have permission to be here." Even Meilyn might become upset if she began to berate them only to learn she had no cause. Elaida would be furious; she absolutely hated looking foolish. "The Amyrlin Seat ordered us—"

"We know about that," Meilyn cut in mildly. "The way word is spreading, I suspect the cats in Seleisin know by now." From her tone, you could not say whether she agreed with Tamra's decision. Meilyn's smooth face never showed any hint of emotion. Her startling blue eyes held serenity as a cup held water. With a dark-gloved hand she carefully adjusted one of her divided skirts, so slashed with white that it seemed white trimmed with blue. She was one of the relatively few Whites to have a Warder; wrapped up in questions of rationality and philosophy, the greater number saw no need. Moiraine wished she would dismount. Meilyn's dappled gelding was tall, and she herself was as tall as most men. Most Cairhienin men, at least. Looking up at her in the saddle threatened to give Moiraine an ache in her neck.

"You are surprised to see me?" Elaida said, looking down from her fine-ankled bay mare. Her brocaded dress was not a muted red or a faint red, but a bright hue, as though she were screaming her Ajah to the world. Her cloak, lined with black fur, was exactly the same shade. A color fit for a Tinker's wagon, Moiraine thought. Elaida was smiling, yet that failed to lessen the severity of her face. She might have been beautiful except for that. Everything about her was severe. "I reached Tar Valon just before the Aiel, and I've been busy since, but never fear, I will call on both of you."

Moiraine had been sure her heart could sink no further, but she had been mistaken. It was very hard not to groan in despair.

Meilyn sighed. "You pay these girls too much mind, Elaida. They'll get above themselves if they start thinking they're your pets. They may already."

Moiraine exchanged shocked glances with Siuan. Pets? Goats staked out for lions, perhaps, but never *pets*.

Since gaining the shawl, Elaida had never deferred to anyone other than the Amyrlin Seat or a Sitter that Moiraine had seen, yet she bowed her head and murmured, "As you say, Meilyn. But it seems possible they might test before the end of the year. I expect them to, and I expect them to pass easily. I'll accept nothing less from either." Even that lacked her usual intensity. Normally, Elaida seemed as stiff-necked as a bull. Normally, she browbeat everyone who crossed her path.

The White sister gave a slight shrug, as though the matter was not important enough to say more. "Do you children have everything you need? Good. Some of you children came very poorly prepared, I must say. How many names do you have left to take here?"

"About fifty, Meilyn Sedai," Siuan told her. "Maybe a few more."

Meilyn glanced up at the sun, its fall toward the western horizon well begun. The dark clouds that threatened snow were moving south, leaving behind clear sky. "In that case, write quickly. You must be back in the Tower before dark, you know."

"Are all the camps like this?" Moiraine asked. "I would

think that men fighting a war would have their minds on that, not on. . . ." She trailed off, her face heating.

". . . spawning like silverpike," Siuan whispered under her breath. Moiraine only just heard, but the words deepened her blush. Why *ever* had she asked such a question in the first place?

"Cairhienin," Meilyn breathed. She sounded very nearly . . . *amused*! But she went on in a serious tone. "When a man believes he may die, he wants to leave something of himself behind. When a woman believes her man may die, she wants that part of him desperately. The result is a great many babies born during wars. It's illogical, given the hardship that comes if the man does die, or the woman, but the human heart is seldom logical."

Which explained a great deal, and left Moiraine feeling that her face might burn off. There were things one did in public and talked about, and things that were done in private and definitely *not* talked about. She struggled to regain control of herself, performing mental exercises for seeking calm. She was the river, contained by the bank; she was the bank, containing the river. She was a flower bud, opening to the sun. It did not help that Elaida was studying her and Siuan like a sculptor hefting hammer and chisel, deciding which piece of stone to remove next in order to bring out the form she wanted.

"Yes, yes, Andro," Meilyn said suddenly. "We will go in a moment." She had not even looked back at her Warder, yet he nodded as though she had responded to something he had said. Lean and no taller than his Aes Sedai, he appeared youthful. Until you noticed his eyes.

Moiraine found herself gaping, embarrassment forgotten, and not because of Andro's unblinking gaze. A sister and her bonded Warder could sense each other's emotions and physical condition, and each knew exactly where the other was, if they were close enough, and at least a direction if they were far apart, but this seemed on the order of reading minds. Some said that full sisters could do that. There were a number of things that you were not taught until you had attained the shawl, after all. Such as the weave for bonding a Warder.

Meilyn looked straight into her eyes. "No," she said

softly, "I can't read his thoughts." Moiraine's scalp prickled as though her hair were trying to stand on end. It must be true, since Meilyn had said it, yet. . . . "When you've had a Warder long enough, you will know what he is thinking, and he will know what you are. A matter of interpretation." Elaida sniffed, though quietly. Alone among the Ajahs, the Red refused to bond Warders. Most Reds seemed to dislike men altogether.

"Logically," Meilyn said, her serene gaze going to the other sister, "Reds have greater need of Warders than any except Greens, perhaps greater even than Greens. But no matter. The Ajahs choose as they will." She lifted her fringed reins. "Are you coming, Elaida? We must reach as many of the children as possible. Some are certain to lose their heads and remain too long without a reminder. Remember, children; before dark."

Moiraine expected some sort of eruption from Elaida, or at least a flash of anger in her eyes. That comment about Warders came very close to violating the codes of courtesy and privacy that governed sisters' lives, all the rules of what an Aes Sedai could say to or ask of another and what not. They were not laws, but rather customs stronger than law, and every Accepted had to memorize them. Surprisingly, Elaida merely turned her bay to follow.

Watching the two sisters leave the camp trailed by Andro, Siuan heaved a relieved sigh. "I was afraid she'd stay to supervise us."

"Yes," Moiraine said. There was no need to say which woman Siuan meant. It would have been right in Elaida's character. *Nothing* they did could escape her demands for absolute perfection. "But why did she not?"

Siuan had no answer for that, and in any event, there was no time to discuss it. With Moiraine's and her meal clearly finished, the women had taken their places in line again. And after Meilyn and Elaida's visit, they no longer seemed so certain that the two were Aes Sedai. A level look and a firm voice failed to squelch argument, now. Siuan took to shouting when necessary, which it frequently was, and running her hands through her hair in frustration. Three times Moiraine had to threaten to cease taking down any names at all before a woman carrying a child that was obviously too old would leave the line. She might have been tempted had one of them resembled Susa, but they were well fed and plainly no poorer than anyone else, just greedy.

To cap it off, with above a dozen women still in front of the table, Steler appeared, helmet on his head and leading his mount. The other soldiers were not far behind, two of them holding the reins of Arrow and Siuan's animal. "Time to go," Steler said in that gravelly voice. "I left it as long as I could, but leave it any longer, and we'll be hard-pressed to make the Tower by sunset."

"Here now," one of the women protested. "They've got to take our names!" Angry mutters rose from the rest.

"Look at the sun, man," Siuan said, sounding harassed. She looked it, as well, with hair sticking up from the constant raking of her fingers. "We have plenty of time."

Moiraine did look at the sun, sitting low in the west, and she was not so sure. It was six miles back to the Tower, the last of it through streets that would be just as crowded come nightfall as they had been that morning. Excuses would not be admitted.

Frowning, Steler opened his mouth, but abruptly the leathery-faced woman who had given them wine was right in front of him with six or seven others, all gray-haired or graying, crowding him and forcing him back. "You leave those girls be," the lean woman shouted at him. "You hear me?"

More women came running from every direction, until Steler was surrounded ten deep, and his Guardsmen as well. Half the women seemed to be screaming and shaking fists, while the rest scowled in sullen silence and gripped the hilts of their belt knives. The anvils went still once more, the blacksmiths watching the crowd of women closely and hefting their hammers. Young men, boys really, began to gather, all hot-eyed and angry. Some had their belt knives drawn. Light, they *were* going to have a riot.

"Write!" Siuan commanded. "They won't hold him long. Your name?" she demanded of the woman in front of her.

Moiraine wrote. The women waiting to give their names seemed to agree with Siuan. There were no more arguments. By this time, they knew the questions and spilled out the answers as soon as they came in front of her, some so quickly that she had to ask them to start over. When Steler and his men finally managed to push through the women encircling them without doing anything that would have brought the men and boys still in the camp running, Moiraine was blowing on the last name to dry the ink, and Siuan was hastily straightening her hair with her carved blackwood comb.

The bannerman's face was grim behind the steel bars of his faceguard, but all he said was "We'll need a bit of luck, now."

He led them out of the camp at a trot, with the horses' hooves flinging clods of snow and Siuan bouncing in her saddle so badly that he assigned men to ride on either side of her and keep her from falling. Clinging desperately to the tall pommel of her saddle, she grimaced at them, but she did not order them away. Moiraine realized that Siuan had never asked for the ointment; she was going to have more need of it than ever. After half a mile, Steler slowed to a walk, but only for another half mile, and then he picked up the trot again. Only the two soldiers kept Siuan in the saddle. Moiraine started to protest, but a glance at Siuan's determined face—and another at the sun—held her quiet. Siuan would take days to forgive her calling attention to how badly she rode. She might never forgive her if she caused them to be called to Merean's study for being late.

That was the pace Steler kept all the way back to the city, trot then walk, trot then walk, and Moiraine suspected he would have maintained it there if not for the crowded streets. A walk was the best they could manage in that throng. The sun was just a low dome of red-gold atop the walls of the Tower grounds when they rode into the yard of the West Stable. Grooms came out to take Arrow and Siuan's mount, along with a sour-faced young under-lieutenant who scowled up at Steler even as he returned the bannerman's salute, an arm laid across the chest.

"You're the last," he growled, sounding as if he wanted an excuse to lash out at anyone who was handy. "Did they cause problems?"

Helping a groaning Siuan dismount, Moiraine held her breath.

"No more than lambs," Steler replied, and she exhaled. Stepping down from his horse, the bannerman turned to his men. "I want the horses rubbed down and the tack oiled before anybody even thinks of supper. You know why I'm looking at you, Malvin."

Moiraine inquired of the young officer what they should do with the lapdesks. He glared at her before saying, "Leave them where they are. They'll be collected." And he stalked off so quickly that his cloak flared behind him.

"Why is he so angry?" she wondered aloud.

Steler glanced at the Guardsmen leading their animals into the stable, then answered in a voice too low for them to hear. "He wanted to go fight the Aiel."

"I don't care whether the fool man wanted to be a hero," Siuan said sharply. She was leaning on Moiraine, who suspected that only her arm around the other woman's waist was keeping her upright. "I want a hot wash and my bed, never mind supper."

"That sounds lovely," Moiraine breathed. Except the part about supper, anyway. She thought she could eat a whole sheep!

Siuan managed to walk on her own, but she hobbled, tight-jawed and clearly suppressing groans. She refused to let Moiraine carry her scrip, though. Siuan never gave in to pain. She never gave in to anything. When they reached their gallery in the Accepted's quarters, thoughts of hot water vanished. Katerine was waiting.

"About time," she said, huddling in her banded cloak. "I thought I'd freeze to death before you got back." A sharp-faced woman with a mass of wavy black hair that hung to her waist, she could have an acid tongue. With novices and other Accepted, she could. With Aes Sedai, she was milder than milk-water, all obsequious smiles. "Merean wants you in her study, Moiraine."

"Why does she want us?" Siuan demanded. "It isn't full sunset even now."

"Oh, Merean always tells me her reasons, Siuan. And it's just Moiraine this time, not you. Well, you've been told, and I want my supper and my bed. We have to do this whole miserable thing over again tomorrow, starting at sunrise. Who'd have thought I'd rather stay in and study than go for a ride in the countryside?"

Siuan frowned at Katerine's back as the other woman flounced away. "One day she'll cut herself with that tongue. Do you want me to come with you, Moiraine?"

Moiraine wanted nothing more. She had not done anything, not lately, yet a summons to Merean's study was never good. Many of the novices and Accepted visited that room to cry on Merean's shoulder when homesickness or the strain of learning grew too great. A summons was another matter entirely. But she shook her head and handed her cloak and scrip to Siuan. "The jar of ointment is in there. It is very good for soreness." Her friend's face lit up.

"I could still come with you. I don't need salving that badly."

"You can barely walk. Go on. Whatever Merean wants, I am sure she will not keep me long." Light, she hoped Merean had not uncovered some prank she thought safely hidden. But if so, at least Siuan would escape punishment. In her present state, she could not have borne that.

The study of the Mistress of Novices lay on the other side of the Tower, near the novices' quarters and one level below the Amyrlin's study, on a wide hallway where the floor tiles were red and green and the runner blue. Moiraine took a deep breath in front of the plain door between two bright wall hangings and patted her hair, wishing she had taken time to use her brush, then knocked twice, firmly. Merean told everyone not to tap like mice in the wainscoting.

"Come," a voice inside called.

Taking another deep breath, Moiraine went in.

Unlike the Amyrlin's study, Merean's was rather small and quite plain, the walls paneled in dark wood, the furniture sturdy and completely unadorned for the most part. Moiraine suspected that women who had been Accepted a hundred years ago would recognize everything in the room. Maybe two hundred years ago. The narrow tea-table beside the door, lightly carved on the legs in a strange pattern, might well have been older than that, and one wall held a mirror, its frame spotted with faded fragments of gilding. Against the opposite wall stood a narrow cabinet that she avoided looking at. The strap and the switch were kept in there, along with a slipper that was worse in a way.

To her surprise, Merean was on her feet rather than seated behind her writing table. She was tall—Moiraine's head only reached Merean's plump chin—with hair that was more gray than not, gathered at the nape of her neck, and a motherly look to her that almost overwhelmed the agelessness of her features. That was one reason most of the young women in training felt comfortable weeping on Merean's shoulder despite her having made them weep herself often enough. She was also kind and gentle and understanding. So long as you did not break the rules. Merean had a positive Talent for finding out what you most wanted to keep hidden.

"Sit down, child," she said gravely.

Moiraine warily seated herself on the stool in front of the writing table. It had to be bad news of some sort. But what?

"There is no way to make this easy, child. King Laman was killed yesterday, along with both of his brothers. Remember that we are all threads in the Pattern, and the Wheel weaves as the Wheel wills."

"The Light illumine their souls," Moiraine said solemnly, "and may they shelter in the Creator's hand until they are born again."

Merean's eyebrows twitched upward, doubtless in surprise that she had not burst into tears on hearing that she had lost three uncles in one day. But then, Merean did not know Laman Damodred, a distant man who burned with ambition, the only warmth in him. Moiraine's opinion was that he had remained unmarried for the simple reason that even the inducement of becoming Queen of Cairhien was not enough to convince any woman to marry him. Moressin and Aldecain had been worse, each filled with sufficient heat for ten men, which they had expressed in anger and cruelty. And in contempt for her father because he was a scholar, because he had taken another scholar for his second wife rather than marrying to bring lands or connections to House Damodred. She would pray for their souls, yet she felt more sadness for Jac Wynn than for all three of her uncles combined.

"Shock," Merean murmured. "You're in shock, but it will pass. When it does, come to me, child. Until then, there's no need for you to go out tomorrow. I'll inform the Amyrlin." The Mistress of Novices had the final say when it came to novices and Accepted. Merean must have been put out to learn that Tamra had sent them out of the city without consulting her.

"Thank you for the kindness," Moiraine said quickly, "but please, no. Having something to do will help, and being with friends. If I remain behind tomorrow, I will be alone."

Merean seemed doubtful, but after more soothing words— words to soothe the hurt she seemed sure Moiraine must be hiding—she let Moiraine return to her room, where she found both of her oil lamps lit and a fire crackling on her hearth. Siuan's work, no doubt. She thought of dropping into Siuan's room, but the other woman was certainly fast asleep by now.

Supper would be available in the dining halls for at least another hour, but she put away any thought of food and instead spent that time kneeling in prayer for her uncles' souls. A penance. She did not mean to be one of those sisters who took on penances at every turn—maintaining a balance in their lives, they called it; she thought it ostentatious foolishness—yet she should feel something for the deaths of her own blood kin, however horrible they had been. It was wrong not to. Only when she knew that the dining halls would be full of serving women mopping the floors did she rise and undress to wash herself. After using a trickle of Fire to heat the water. Cold water would have been another penance, but there were limits.

Extinguishing her lamps, she wove a ward to keep her dreams from affecting anyone else's—that could happen with those who could channel; others nearby could find themselves sharing your dreams—and crawled beneath her blankets. She truly was tired, and sleep came quickly. Unfortunately, nightmares came, too. Not of her uncles, or even of Jac Wynn, but of an infant lying in the snow on Dragonmount. Lightning flashed in the pitch-black sky, and his wails were the thunder. Dreams of a faceless young man. There was lightning in those dreams, too, but he called this lightning from the sky, and cities burned. Nations burned. The Dragon was Reborn. She woke weeping.

The fire had burned down to a few glowing coals. Rather than adding more wood, she used the fire-shovel to scoop ashes over the coals, and rather than climbing back into bed, she wrapped a blanket around herself and went out into the night. She was not sure she could go back to sleep, but one thing she was certain of. She did not want to sleep alone.

She was certain that Siuan must be asleep, but when she slipped into her friend's room, quickly closing the door behind her, Siuan said softly, "Moiraine?" A few flames still flickered on Siuan's small hearth, giving enough light to see her pull one side of her blankets back.

Moiraine wasted no time climbing in. "Did you have nightmares, too?"

"Yes," Siuan breathed. "What can they do, Moiraine? Even if they find him, what can they do?"

"They can bring him to the Tower," Moiraine replied, putting more confidence into her voice than she felt. "He can be protected here." She hoped he could. More than the Reds might want him dead or gentled, whatever the Prophecies said. "And educated." The Dragon Reborn would have to be educated. He would need to know as much of politics as any queen, as much of war as any general. As much of history as any scholar. Verin Sedai said that most mistakes made by rulers came from not knowing history; they acted in ignorance of the mistakes others had made before them. "He can be guided." That would be the most important of all, to make sure that he made the right decisions.

"The Tower can't teach him to channel, Moiraine."

That was true. What men did was . . . different. As different as men and women, Verin said. A bird could not teach a fish to fly. He would have to survive learning on his own. The Prophecies did not say that he would, or that he would avoid going mad before the Last Battle, only that he had to be at Tarmon Gai'don for any hope of victory, yet she had to believe. She had to!

"Do you think Tamra is having bad dreams tonight, Siuan?"

Siuan snorted. "Aes Sedai don't have bad dreams."

They were not yet Aes Sedai, however. Neither of them could close her eyes through the rest of the night. Moiraine did not know what Siuan saw, lying there staring up at the ceiling—she could not make herself ask—but she saw a babe crying in the snow on Dragonmount, and a faceless man calling down lightning. Being awake was no protection against these nightmares.

CHAPTER
6

Surprises

A scratching at Siuan's door near morning proved to be a timid novice named Setsuko, a stocky girl shorter than Moiraine, who told them that the Amyrlin had ordered all Accepted to be at the West Stable before Third Rise, ready to carry on with their task. By the light of the lamp she carried, Setsuko's pale eyes were bleak with envy. The Arafellin girl already knew that her stay in the Tower would end in a few months.

Setsuko had talked openly of running away until a visit to Merean's study taught her discretion if not wisdom. Bitter as the knowledge must be, she could never reach the shawl, but she must be kept until the sisters were certain she could channel without harming herself or others. Despite that, she still might have flight in mind. Novices did run from time to time, and even the rare Accepted who flinched at what lay ahead of her, but they were always caught eventually, and their return to the Tower was painfully unpleasant to say the least. It was much better for everyone if that could be avoided.

Another time, weary as she was, Moiraine might have offered comforting words. Or a caution. This morning, however, the gong for First Rise had already sounded, and it was no more than half an hour to Second. They could snatch a bite to eat and reach the stable before Third, but only just. Yawning, Moiraine gave Siuan a last hug and hurried out into the darkness, wrapped in her blanket, before Setsuko reached the next door and began scratching, trying to wake Sheriam. The child would have to do better. Sheriam slept like the dead.

Half a dozen novices carrying lamps were tapping at other doors, ghostly images in the night. At hers, a very tall girl with golden hair spilling down her back offered a sulky curtsy when Moiraine dismissed her. Lisandre would be allowed to test for Accepted, but only if her sulkiness could be cured. Likely it would be. When the Tower saw a fault in one of its students, that fault usually was cured, one way or another.

She washed and dressed hastily, barely taking time to scrub her teeth with salt and soda and brush her hair into some semblance of order, yet when she reached the gallery with her scrip hanging beneath the edge of her cloak, the darkness was definitely gray. Siuan was already outside, cloaked and ready, talking to a visibly chafing, flame-haired Sheriam, and other Accepted were already scurrying to breakfast.

"Sheriam says the Aiel really are retreating, Moiraine," Siuan said excitedly, hitching her scrip on her shoulder. "She says they're all leagues east of the river."

Sheriam nodded and started to follow the others, but Moiraine caught the edge of her cloak.

"Are you certain?" Moiraine nearly winced. Had she been less tired, she would have used greater care choosing her words; you learned nothing if you put someone's back up to start.

Luckily, the slim Accepted had none of the temper that her hair and her tilted green eyes might have indicated. She merely sighed and looked longingly toward the door leading from the gallery. "I had it first from a Guardsman who had it from a Shienaran soldier, a courier, but later, I was told the same by Serafelle, by Ryma, *and* by Jennet. One sister may be mistaken, but when three tell you something, you may be sure they have the right of it." She was an enjoyable companion to pass an evening with, yet she did have a way of making casual statements sound like lectures. "Why are you two grinning like fools?" she demanded suddenly.

"I didn't know I was grinning," Siuan replied, schooling her features. She still looked eager, rising up on her toes as though to run.

"Is not a chance to ride in the countryside worth grinning over?" Moiraine asked. Now, perhaps they could convince their escort to take them to the camps closest to Dragon-

mount. She was unsure exactly when she had adopted
Siuan's view, yet it was her own, now. They would find him
first. Somehow, they would. Grin? She could have laughed
aloud and danced.

"Sometimes, you two are passing strange," Sheriam said.
"I'm saddle-sore near to hobbling, myself. Well, you can
stand here and talk if you wish. I want my breakfast." But
as she turned to go, she stopped dead and exhaled in shock.

Merean had come onto the gallery in the fading darkness, her vine-woven shawl draped over her arms so the
blue fringe almost brushed the floor. She attracted a good
many stares from the Accepted. Sisters seldom wore their
shawls inside the Tower except for official occasions. An
appearance here by the Mistress of Novices, wearing hers,
meant someone was in very deep trouble. Or else being
summoned for testing. A few of the women lingered on the
gallery hopefully, while a handful sped off as fast as they
could short of running, no doubt propelled by guilty con-
sciences. They should have known better. All they achieved
was to have Merean note them with a glance, and she
would dig until she discovered what they felt guilt about. In
Cairhien, a gooseherd would have known as much. She paid
them no heed now, however, as she glided calmly along the
gallery, the Accepted she passed rising from their curtsies
with regret painting their faces.

Sheriam was one of those who lingered, and it was in
front of her, Siuan and Moiraine that Merean stopped. Moiraine's heart fluttered, and she struggled to breathe evenly as
she curtsied. She struggled just to breathe in the first place.
Maybe Siuan had been right. Well, she *was* right, in point of
fact. When Merean said an Accepted might test soon, it always came within the month. But she was not ready! Siuan's
face shone with eagerness, of course, her eyes bright. Sheriam's lips were parted in hopeful anticipation. Light, every
last Accepted must think herself more ready than Moiraine
Damodred did.

"You'll be late if you don't hurry, child," the Blue sister
told Sheriam sharply. And surprisingly. Merean was *never*
sharp, even when there was punishment in the offing. When
she lectured on your misdeeds while applying switch or
strap or the hated slipper, her voice was merely firm.

As the fire-haired woman darted away, the Mistress of

Novices focused her attention on Siuan and Moiraine. Moiraine thought her heart would pound its way through her ribs. Not yet. Light, please, not yet.

"I've spoken with the Amyrlin, Moiraine, and she agrees with me that you must be in shock. The other Accepted will have to make do without you today." Merean's mouth tightened for an instant before serenity returned to her face. Her voice remained a needle, though. "I'd have kept you all in, but people will cooperate better with initiates of the Tower than with clerks, even White Tower clerks, and the sisters would be up in arms if they were asked to do the task. The Mother was right about that much."

Light! She must have argued with Tamra to be upset enough to say all of that to Accepted. No wonder she was being sharp. Relief welled up in Moiraine that she was not to be whisked off and tested for the shawl immediately, yet it could not compete with disappointment. They could reach the camps around Dragonmount today. Well, one of the camps, at least. They could!

"Please, Merean, I—"

The sister raised one finger. That was her warning not to argue, and however kind and gentle she was in the general course of things, she never gave a second. Moiraine closed her mouth promptly.

"You shouldn't be left to brood," Merean went on. Smooth face or no, the way she shifted her shawl to her shoulders spoke of irritation. "Some of the girls' writing is like chicken scratches." Yes, she was definitely upset. When she had any criticism, however slight, it was delivered to the target of it and no one else. "The Mother agreed that you can copy out the lists that are near unreadable. You have a clear hand. A bit over-flowery, but clear."

Moiraine tried desperately to think of something to say that the sister would not take for argument, but nothing came. How was she to escape?

"That's a very good idea, Moiraine," Siuan said, and Moiraine gaped at her friend in amazement. Her friend! But Siuan went merrily ahead with betrayal. "She didn't sleep a wink last night, Merean. No more than an hour at most, anyway. I don't think she's safe to go riding. She'll fall off inside a mile." *Siuan* said that!

"I'm glad you concur with my decision, Siuan," Me-

rean said dryly. Moiraine would have blushed to have that
tone directed at her, yet Siuan was made of sterner material, meeting the sister's raised eyebrow with an open-eyed
smile of innocence. "She shouldn't be left alone, either, so
you can help her. You have a good clear hand yourself." The
smile froze on Siuan's face, but the sister affected not to notice. "Come along, then. Come along. I've more to do today
than usher the pair of you around."

Gliding ahead of them like a plump swan on a stream, a
fast-swimming swan, she led the way to a small windowless room a little down from the Amyrlin's apartments and
across the corridor. A richly carved writing table, with two
straight-backed armchairs behind it, held a tray of pens,
large glass ink jars, sand jars for blotting, stacks of good
white paper, and a great disorderly stack of pages covered
in writing. Hanging her cloak on a peg and setting her scrip
on the floor by the table, Moiraine stared at that ragged
pile as glumly as Siuan did. At least there was a fireplace,
and a fire going on the narrow hearth. The room was warm
compared to the corridors. Much warmer than a ride in the
snow. There was that.

"Once you've finished breakfast," Merean said, "come
back here and set to work. Leave the copies in the anteroom
of the Amyrlin's study."

"Light, Siuan," Moiraine said with feeling as soon as
the sister was gone, "what made you think this was a good
idea?"

"You—" Siuan grimaced ruefully. "We will get a look at
more names this way. Maybe all the names, if Tamra keeps
us in the job. We could be the first to know who he is. I
doubt there could be two boys born on Dragonmount. I just
thought it would be 'you,' not 'us.'" She breathed a gloomy
sigh, then suddenly frowned at Moiraine. "Why would you
be brooding? Why are you supposed to be in shock?"

Last night, revealing her woes had seemed out of place,
a trifle compared to what they knew the world faced, but
Moiraine had no hesitation in telling her now. Before she
finished, Siuan enveloped her in a strong, comforting hug.
They had wept on each other's shoulders much more often
than either had availed herself of Merean's. She had never
been as close to anyone as she was to Siuan. Or loved anyone as much.

"You know I have six uncles who are fine men," Siuan said softly, "and one who died proving how fine a man he was. What you don't know is, I have two others my father wouldn't let cross his doorstep, one his own brother. My father wouldn't even say their names. They're street robbers, shoulderthumpers and drunkards, and when they've guzzled enough ale, or brandy if they've stolen enough to afford it, they start fights with anyone who looks at them the wrong way. Usually, it's both of them together setting on the same poor fellow with fists and boots and anything that comes to hand. One day, they'll hang for killing somebody, if they haven't already. When they do, I won't shed a tear. Some people just aren't worth a tear."

Moiraine hugged her back. "You always know the right thing to say. But I will still pray for my uncles."

"I'll pray for those two scoundrels when they die, too. I just won't fret myself over them, alive or dead. Come. Let's go to breakfast. It's going to be a long day, and we won't even have a nice ride for exercise." She had to be joking, yet there was not so much as a twinkle of mirth in her blue eyes. Then again, she truly did hate doing clerical work. *No* one enjoyed that.

The dining hall most often used by Accepted lay on the lowest level of the Tower, a large room with stark white walls and a white-tiled floor, full of long, polished tables, and plain benches that could hold two women, or three at a pinch. The other Accepted ate quickly, sometimes gulping their food with unseemly haste. Sheriam spilled porridge on her dress and hurried from the room proclaiming that she had time to change. She very nearly ran. Everyone was hurrying. Even Katerine all but trotted off, still eating a crusty roll and brushing crumbs from her dress. It seemed a chance to leave the city was not so miserable, at that. Siuan dawdled over her porridge, laced with stewed apples, and Moiraine kept her company with another cup of strong black tea containing just a drop of honey. After all, the chance that the boychild's name was among those awaiting them had to be vanishingly small.

Soon they were alone at the tables, and one of the cooks came out to frown at them, fists planted on her hips. A plump woman in a long, spotless white apron, Laras was short of her middle years and more than pretty, yet she could frown a hole through a stone. No Accepted was ever fool enough to come over high-handed with Laras, at least not more than once. Even Siuan gave way beneath that unwavering gaze, hastily spooning the last bits of apple from her bowl. Laras began calling for the scullions to bring their mops before Siuan and Moiraine reached the door.

Moiraine expected the work to be drudgery, and it was, though not so bad as she had feared. Not quite so bad. They began by digging their own lists out of the mound, and added those already in a readable hand, which reduced the stack by half. But only by half. If you came to the Tower unable to write, you were taught a decent hand as a novice, but those who came writing badly often took years to reach legibility, if they ever did. Some full sisters used the clerks for anything they wanted someone else to understand.

Most of the lists appeared to be shorter than hers and Siuan's, yet even counting Meilyn's explanation, it seemed that an astonishing number of women had given birth. And this was only from the camps nearest the river! Noticing Siuan scanning each page before setting it to one side, she began doing the same. Without any great hope, yet vanishingly small was not the same as impossible. Except that the more she read, the further her spirits fell.

Many of the entries were shockingly vague. Born within sight of Tar Valon's walls? The city's walls were visible for leagues, visible from the slopes of Dragonmount. This particular child was a girl, with a Tairen father and a Cairhienin mother, yet the note boded ill for locating the boychild. There were far too many like that. Or, born in sight of the White Tower. Light, the Tower could be seen from nearly as far as Dragonmount! Well, from a good many miles, at least. Other entries were sad. Salia Pomfrey had given birth to a boy and had left to return to her village in Andor after her husband died on the second day of fighting. There was a note beneath the name, in Myrelle's flowing script. *Women in the camp tried to dissuade her, but she was said to be half mad or more from grief. Light help her.* Sad to weeping. And in a colder vein, as troubling as the inexact entries. No name was recorded for her village, and Andor was the largest nation between the Spine of the World and the Aryth Ocean. How could she be found? Salia's child had been born on the wrong side of the Erinin and too early by six days, but if the Dragon Reborn's mother was like her, how could he be found? The pages were dotted with names like that, though usually they seemed to be women others had heard of, so the information might be written in full elsewhere. Or it might not. The task had seemed so simple when Tamra set it.

The Light help us, Moiraine thought. *The Light help the world.*

They wrote steadily, sometimes putting their heads together to decipher a hand that really did resemble chicken scratches, took an hour at midday to go down to the dining hall for bread and lentil soup, then returned to their pens. Elaida appeared, in a high-necked dress even redder than that she had worn the day before, to stride around the table and silently stare over first Siuan's shoulder and then Moiraine's as though to study their writing. Her red-fringed shawl was richly embroidered with flowered vines. Flowered and, more fittingly, barbed with long thorns. Finding nothing to criticize, she left as abruptly as she had come, and Moiraine echoed Siuan's sigh of relief. Other than that, they were left alone. When Moiraine dusted her last page with fine sand and poured it into the wooden box sitting on the floor between the chairs, the hour for supper had come. A number of boychildren had been born yesterday—the birth had to come after Gitara's Foretelling—but not one had seemed remotely possible for the child they sought.

After a night of troubled, restless sleep, she needed no urging from Siuan to return to that small room rather than joining the other Accepted hurrying to the stables. Though some were not hurrying so quickly, today. It seemed that even a trip outside the city could pall when all you had to do was sit on a bench and write names all day. Moiraine was looking forward to writing names. No one had told them not to, after all. And they had been wakened by the sounds of the other women getting ready, not by a novice bringing orders to ride out with the rest. As Siuan often said, it was easier to ask forgiveness than permission. Though the Tower was rather short on forgiveness for Accepted.

Yesterday's gleanings were waiting on the table, an untidy stack as tall as the first had been. While they were sorting out the readable lists, two clerks walked in and stopped in surprise, a stout woman with the Flame of Tar Valon worked on one dark sleeve, her gray hair in a neat roll on the nape of her neck, and a strapping young fellow who looked more suited to armor than to his plain gray woolen coat. He had beautiful brown eyes. And a lovely smile.

"I dislike being set a task only to learn someone else is already performing it," the woman said acerbically. Noticing the younger clerk's smile, she shot him a cold stare. Her voice turned to ice. "You know better than that if you want to keep your place, Martan. Come with me." Smile sliding away in worry and red-faced with embarrassment, Martan followed her from the room.

Moiraine looked apprehensively at Siuan, but Siuan never stopped sorting. "Keep working," she said. "If we look to be busy enough. . . ." Her voice trailed off. It was a small hope, if clerks had been assigned the work, but it was all they had.

By a matter of minutes they managed to be copying names by the time Tamra herself walked into the room. Wearing plain blue silk today, the Amyrlin was Aes Sedai calm made flesh. No one would have thought that her friend had died right in front of her only the day before yesterday, or that she was waiting on a name that would save the world. Tamra was followed closely by the gray-haired clerk, who wore satisfaction on her face like too much rouge, and young Martan stood behind her, smiling over her shoulder at Moiraine and Siuan. He really would lose his place if he did that too often.

Moiraine bobbed to her feet and offered her courtesies so fast that she forgot the pen in her hand. She felt it twist, though, and winced at the ink stain it left, a black smear spreading to the size of a coin on the white wool. Siuan was just as quick, but much more steady. She remembered to lay her pen on the tray before spreading her skirts. *Calm,* Moiraine thought. *I must be calm.* Running through the mental exercises did little good.

The Amyrlin studied them closely, and when Tamra scrutinized someone, the most thick-skinned and insensitive felt measured to the inch and weighed to the ounce. Moiraine only just managed not to shift in unease. Surely that gaze would see everything they planned. If that could be graced with the name of plan.

"I had intended you to have a freeday, to read or study as you chose," Tamra said slowly, still considering them. "Or perhaps to practice for your testing," she added with a smile that did nothing to lessen her scrutiny. A long pause, and then she nodded slightly to herself. "You are still troubled by your uncles' deaths, child?"

"I had nightmares again last night, Mother." True, but once more they had been of a baby crying in the snow, and a faceless young man breaking the world anew even while he saved it. The steadiness of her own voice amazed her. She had never thought she would dare give an Aes Sedai answer to the Amyrlin Seat.

Tamra nodded again. "Very well, if you think you need to be occupied, you may continue. When the boredom of copying all day overcomes you, leave a note with your finished work, and I will see to replacing you." Half turning, she paused. "Ink is very difficult to remove, especially from white cloth. I won't tell you not to channel to do it; you know that already." Another smile, and she gathered up the gray-haired clerk, herding her from the room. "No need to look so indignant, Mistress Wellin," she said soothingly. Only fools upset clerks; their mistakes, accidental or on purpose, could cause too much damage. "I'm sure you have much more important tasks than. . . ." Her voice faded to a receding murmur in the corridor.

Moiraine lifted her skirt to look at the stain. It had spread to the size of a large coin. Ordinarily, removing it would require hours of careful soaking in bleach that stung your hands and offered no guarantee of success. "She just told me to use the Power to clean my dress," she said wonderingly.

Siuan's eyebrows attempted to climb atop her head. "Don't talk nonsense. I heard her as well as you, and she said nothing of the sort."

"You have to listen to what people mean as well as what they say, Siuan." Interpreting what others really meant was integral to the Game of Houses, and put together, Tamra's smile, the cast of her eye, and the phrasing she had used were as good as written permission.

Embracing the Power, she wove Air, Water and Earth exactly so, laying the weave atop the stain. Just because Accepted were forbidden to channel to do chores did not mean they were not taught how; there was no such prohibition for sisters, who frequently traveled without a maid. The black smear suddenly glistened wetly and began to shrink, rising onto the surface of the wool as it did. Smaller and smaller it became, until it was only a small ebon bead of dried ink that fell into her cupped palm.

"I might keep this as a memento," she said, setting the black bead on the edge of the table. A reminder that Siuan had been correct. There were times when the rules could be broken.

"And if a sister had walked in?" Siuan asked wryly. "Would you have tried to tell *her* it was all part of the Game of Houses?"

Moiraine's face grew hot, and she released the Source. "I would have told her. . . . I would have. . . . Must we talk of this now? There must be as many names as yesterday, and I would like to finish before supper is done."

Siuan laughed uproariously. You might have thought the redness of Moiraine's face was a fool's paint.

They had been writing above an hour when Moiraine came to an entry that gave her pause. Born in sight of Dragonmount, it said, which was as ridiculous as saying in sight of the Tower. But Willa Mandair had given birth to a son, west of the river, and on the day of Gitara's Foretelling. She copied the entry slowly. Raising her pen at the end, she did not dip it in the ink jar or look for the next name in Ellid's spiky hand. Her gaze rose to the ebon bead. She was one of the Accepted, not a sister. But she would be tested soon. Bili Mandair could have been born on the riverbank and his mother still have been in sight of Dragonmount. But nothing Ellid had written indicated how far the camp she had gone to was from the mountain. Or how close. The earlier entries just said "born in Lord Ellisar's encampment outside Tar Valon."

The white page in front of her was only half filled with her writing, but she drew another blank sheet across the table and copied the particulars for Bili Mandair. A humble name, if he was the one. But it was more likely the Dragon Reborn would be the son of a simple soldier than of a lord.

Suddenly she noticed Siuan writing in a little leather-bound book, small enough to fit in her belt pouch, while keeping one eye on the doorway. "You have to be prepared," Siuan said.

Nodding, Moiraine slid the page bearing a single entry across the table to Siuan, who carefully copied the information into her little book. Tomorrow, Moiraine would bring her own book.

The day produced quite a few names of children "born in sight of Dragonmount" or even "born near Dragonmount," a number of them on the east side of the Erinin. Moiraine knew she should have expected it. The mountain was the most easily identifiable landmark for leagues, after all. But this was only the second day's list, and they added nine more boys to Siuan's book. Light, how many names would they gather before it was done?

There were other surprises. Shortly after midmorning, Jarna Malari swept into the room, elegant in dark gray silk, with slashes of white at her temples that added to her commanding presence, sapphires in her long black hair, and more around her neck. The silken fringe on her shawl was so long that it nearly touched the floor with the shawl resting on her shoulders. Jarna was a Sitter for the Gray. Sitters rarely seemed to notice Accepted, but she motioned to Moiraine. "Walk with me a brief while, child."

In the corridor, Jarna strolled slowly in silence for a time, and Moiraine was content to have it so. Light, what could a Sitter want with her? A task to be done, or a message to be carried, would have been mentioned right away. In any case, Accepted did not try to hurry sisters. As well attempt hurrying the Amyrlin as a Sitter. The drafts that made the stand-lamps flicker did not bother Jarna, of course, but Moiraine began to wish she had her cloak.

"I hear you are troubled by your uncles' deaths," the Sitter said at last. "That is understandable."

Moiraine made a sound that she hoped Jarna took for agreement. Aes Sedai answers were all very well, but she wanted to avoid outright lying. If she could. She tried not to strain for every inch, but the top of her head only came to the other woman's shoulder. What *did* the woman want?

"I fear that affairs of state never wait on grief, Moiraine. Tell me, child, who in House Damodred do you think will ascend to the Sun Throne now that Laman and his brothers are dead?"

Tripping over her own feet, Moiraine staggered and would have fallen had Jarna not steadied her with a hand. A *Sitter* was asking her opinion on politics? Of her native land, to be sure, but Sitters knew more of most countries' politics than their own rulers did. Jarna's liquid brown eyes gazed at her serenely, patiently. Waiting.

"I have given the matter no thought, Aes Sedai," Moiraine said truthfully. "I think perhaps the Sun Throne will pass to another House, but I cannot say which."

"Perhaps," Jarna murmured, half lidding her eyes for the space of the word. "House Damodred has acquired an ill reputation that Laman only made worse."

Moiraine frowned before she could stop herself, and hurriedly smoothed away the lines hoping that Jarna had not noticed. It was true. Her father had been alone among his generation in lacking a dark character, men and women alike. The preceding generations had been nearly as bad, when not worse. The deeds done by House Damodred had blackened the name. But she did not like hearing anyone say it.

"Your half-brother Taringail is denied by his marriage to the Queen of Andor," Jarna went on. "A ridiculous law, but he cannot change it unless he is king, and he cannot become king until it is changed. What of your elder sisters? Are they not well thought of? The . . . taint . . . seems largely to have skipped your generation."

"Well thought of, but not for the throne," Moiraine replied. "Anvaere cares for nothing except horses and hawking." And no one would trust her temper, far worse than Moiraine's had ever been, on the Sun Throne. But that was something she would say only to Siuan. "And if Innloine gained the throne, everyone knows affairs of state would come a poor second, at best, to playing with her children." Likely because in playing with her children, she had forgotten all about the affairs of state. Innloine was a warm and loving mother, but the truth was, she was not terribly bright, although very stubborn. A dangerous combination in a ruler. "No one will support either for the throne, Aes Sedai, even within House Damodred."

Jarna peered down into Moiraine's eyes for a long moment, reminding her uncomfortably of Meilyn saying she could not read thoughts. There was nothing for it but to meet that gaze with patience and apparent openness. As well as a fervent hope that Meilyn had not found a way around the Three Oaths.

"I see," Jarna said finally. "You may return to your work, child."

"What did she want?" Siuan asked when Moiraine returned to the room.

"I am not sure," she said slowly, taking up her pen. That was the first lie she had ever told Siuan. She was all too afraid that she knew exactly what Jarna wanted.

By the time they laid the completed copies on the rose-carved writing table that had been Gitara's, in the spacious anteroom to the Amyrlin's study, six more Sitters had come to take Moiraine aside. One from each Ajah, all with very much the same questions. Tsutama Rath, beautiful and hard-eyed enough to make Moiraine flinch, put it to her directly.

"Have you never thought," Tsutama said casually, toying with the red fringe of her shawl, "of being Queen of Cairhien yourself?"

Thus she gained another nightmare to join the babe in the snow and the faceless man. She sat on the Sun Throne wearing the shawl of an Aes Sedai, and in the streets outside, the mobs were destroying the city. No Aes Sedai had been a queen in over a thousand years, and even before that, the few who admitted it openly had fared badly. But if that was the goal of the Hall of the Tower, how could she forestall it? Only by fleeing the Tower as soon as she did gain the shawl and staying away until matters resolved themselves in Cairhien. She spent most of that sleepless night praying to be tested soon. Even tomorrow would not be too soon. Light, she was not ready, but she had to escape. Somehow.

CHAPTER

7

The Itch

The following day brought still more names that met the criteria, and in larger number, all with vague reference to Dragonmount for the place of birth. Moiraine realized she and Siuan would never see a name with "born on the slopes of Dragonmount" attached. The Prophecies of the Dragon were known to many people, though often known wrongly, especially among the common folk, but the mountain's connection remained in even the most nonsensical versions. No woman would want to admit that she had birthed a son who would channel the Power one day, with all that entailed, the child of her body doomed to madness and terror. How much less would she admit to bearing a child who might become the Dragon Reborn? She could not deny Dragonmount entirely, or her acquaintances might call her on it, yet "near the mountain" or "in sight of it" was safe enough. The child they sought would surely be hidden behind such a half truth.

Someone would need to visit each of those women with closer questions, prudently phrased and carefully asked. She rehearsed those questions in her mind, the delicate probing to elicit information while giving away nothing. Rouse the mother's suspicions, and she would lie again. And likely run as soon as the questioner's back was turned. It would be playing *Daes Dae'mar* with the world at stake. Far from a task she would relish, yet how to resist imagining?

The morning also brought a visit from Tamra, who abruptly walked in just as Moiraine was slipping her little book, bearing a fresh name, back into her belt pouch. She tried to disguise the movement, make it part of her curtsy, a touch of clumsiness brought on by surprise. She thought it well done, yet she held her breath as the Amyrlin studied her. Had the other woman seen the book? Suddenly, the notion of asking forgiveness rather than permission seemed very frail. Discovery would gain them neither. In all likelihood, discovery would bring rustication, working on an isolated farm from sunrise to sunset, cut off from friends and studies, forbidden to channel. For novices and Accepted, that was the penultimate penalty, one last chance to learn correct behavior, before being sent away forever. Far worse than blistered hands, though, it would certainly separate them forever from the hunt for the child.

"I'd have thought yesterday would have sated your appetites for boredom," Tamra said finally, and Moiraine breathed again. "Especially yours, Siuan."

Siuan seldom blushed, but her face colored at that. Everyone knew her dislike of clerical work. Copying lines was the punishment she dreaded most.

Moiraine put in, "The lists help me govern my thoughts, Mother." Once you began giving misleading answers, they came more and more easily, even to the Amyrlin Seat.

In truth, those thoughts still flashed into her head when least expected, lists or no lists. Thoughts of a babe in the snow and a faceless man. Equally dire, of the Sun Throne. She wanted to beg Tamra to halt that scheme, yet she knew begging would be useless. The Tower was no less implacable in its weaving than the Wheel of Time itself. In both cases, the threads were human lives, and the pattern they made more important than any individual thread.

"Very well, child. So long as your studies don't suffer." Tamra held out a folded paper that Moiraine had not noticed, sealed with a circle of green wax. "Take this to Kerene Nagashi. She should be in her rooms. Give it to no one else." As if she would do that!

Some Accepted complained, very quietly and very privately, over having to climb the wide corridors that spiraled upward through the Tower, but even with a climb halfway to the top, Moiraine enjoyed any errand that took her to the Ajah quarters. A great deal could be learned through seeing people where they lived. Even Aes Sedai let their guard down in those circumstances. They did a little, at any rate; enough for one who knew how to listen and observe.

The Ajah quarters were identical in number of rooms and how they were laid out, but the details differed widely. The impression of a full-sized sword was worked into each of the huge white floorstones of the Green Ajah quarters, swords in two dozen different styles, single-edged and double, curved and straight. Every door along the hallways was carved with a sword, point-up, gilded for the rooms of Sitters and silvered or lacquered for many others. The tapestries on the walls, between tall gilded stand-lamps on bases worked in the form of stacked halberds, were of martial scenes, charging horsemen and battles and famous last stands, alternating with ancient battle standards from lands long dead, many torn and stained and all preserved through the centuries by weaves of the One Power. No Aes Sedai had ridden to war since the Trolloc Wars, but when the Last Battle came, the Battle Ajah would ride in the forefront. Until then, they fought for justice where it often could be obtained only through their Warders' swords, but that was just what they did while they waited on Tarmon Gai'don.

Another difference here was the number of men. Not just any men, of course. Warders. Tall or short, wide or slim, even quite stout in one case, they moved like lions or leopards. None wore the distinctive cloak indoors, but the cloak was a mere decoration for a discerning eye. You could see Warders in any Ajah's quarters, excepting the Red, but most kept rooms in the Guards' barracks or even in the city. Greens' Warders often lived in the same apartments as the sister!

A green-eyed Warder who made up for his lack of height through width glanced at her as he strode by quickly, as if on an errand. Three others, standing together, fell silent at her approach, their quiet conversation taken up again after she passed. One wore silver bells in his dark Arafellin braids, one had a thick Taraboner mustache, and the third was very dark, perhaps a Tairen or a southern Altaran, yet aside from the grace of their movements, there was another thing they shared with each other, and with the heavyset man, and with every man to be seen here. Once, while hawking with cousins, she had looked into the eyes of a caped eagle, with its ruff of black feathers around its head. Meeting a Warder's gaze was akin to that. Not fierce, but full of self-knowledge, absolutely aware of their own capabilities, their capacity for violence.

And yet, it was a violence in restraint, disciplined by their own wills and their bonds to their Aes Sedai. Here, they were simply going about their daily lives. A lean man, his head shaven except for a Shienaran topknot, was resting against a wall with one booted foot up, tuning a fiddle and ignoring the good-natured gibing of another Warder, who said that it sounded like a wet cat caught in a net. Two others, in shirtsleeves, were practicing with wooden swords in a broad side corridor, the bundled lathes clattering with each swift blow.

Rina Hafden, who somehow made a square face lovely and a stocky build both elegant and graceful, was urging them on with a wide smile, calling, "Well struck, Waylin! Oh, very well struck, Elyas!" For size, they might have been twins, though one was dark and clean-shaven, the other fair, with a short beard. Grinning, they moved faster and faster. Their sweat-sodden shirts clung to broad shoulders and backs, yet the pair seemed fresh and untired.

Through an open door, Moiraine saw a round-faced Warder playing a stately melody on a flute while gray-haired Jala Bandevin, an imposing woman despite standing near a hand shorter than Moiraine, attempted to teach a new Warder the steps of a court dance. He had to be new, a blushing, pale-haired boy of no more than twenty, yet no man gained the bond unless he already possessed all the requisite skills. All save dancing, at least.

Kerene's door, bearing a sword lacquered in red, gold and black, also stood open, with the sounds of merry music coming out. Moiraine had no idea what the lacquering meant, or the colors, and she suspected she never would unless she chose the Green. That would not be, yet she disliked not knowing. Once she identified something she did not know, the ignorance became an itch on her shoulder blade, just beyond reach. Not for the first time, she filed the swords in the back of her mind, beside many other things seen in Ajah quarters. The itch receded, yet she knew it would return when next she saw these doors.

The few tapestries in Kerene's sitting room were scenes of war or hunting, but most of the wall space was given over to bookshelves carved in the styles of half a dozen countries. Along with a few books, they held a large lion's skull and an even bigger from a bear, glazed bowls, vases in odd shapes, daggers adorned with gems and gold and daggers with plain wooden hilts, one with just the nub of a broken blade. A blacksmith's hammer with the head split in two lay next to a cracked wooden bowl that held a single fat firedrop, fine enough to grace a crown. A gilded barrel clock with the hands frozen at just before noon, or midnight, stood beside a steel-backed gauntlet stained black with what Moiraine was sure was blood. They and all the rest were mementos of well over a hundred years wearing the shawl.

Of memories before the shawl, there were few. Just a row of painted miniatures on the wave-carved mantel over the fireplace, showing a plainly dressed, dignified man, a plump, smiling woman, and five children, three of them girls. They were Kerene's family, long since passed into the grave along with her nieces and nephews, and their children, and their children's children and more. That was the pain borne by Aes Sedai. Families died, and everything you knew vanished. Except the Tower. The White Tower always remained.

Two of Kerene's Warders were in the sitting room with her. Massive Karile, whose hair and beard gave him the aspect of a golden-maned lion, was reading a book in front of the fireplace with his boots resting on the ornate brass fender, a feather of blue smoke rising from the bowl of his long-stemmed pipe. Stepin, looking more a clerk than a Warder, with his narrow shoulders and sad brown eyes, sat on a stool playing a lively jig on a twelve string bittern, fingers flashing as skillfully as any hired musician's. Neither man stopped what he was doing for the arrival of an Accepted.

Kerene herself stood working at an embroidery frame mounted on a stand. It always seemed incongruous to see a Green doing needlework. Especially when, as now, the subject was a field of wildflowers. How did that accord with the violence and death decorating her walls? A tall, slim woman, Kerene looked exactly what she was, her ageless face strong and beautiful, her nearly black eyes pools of serenity. Even here, she wore a riding dress, the divided skirts slashed with emerald green, and her dark hair, lightly touched with white, was cut shorter than either Karile's or Stepin's, above her shoulders, and gathered in a thick braid.

No doubt it was easier to care for while traveling, cut like that. Kerene seldom remained in the Tower long before setting out again. She placed her needle on the embroidery frame, took the letter, and broke the green sealing wax with a thumb. Tamra always sealed her messages to sisters with wax in the Ajah color of the recipient. Of all Ajahs and none.

Whatever Tamra had written was quickly read, and no change came to Kerene's face, but before the Green finished, Stepin leaned his bittern against a side table and began buttoning up his coat. Karile placed his book on a shelf, tapped the dottle from his pipe onto the hearth and stuffed the pipe into a capacious coat pocket. That was all, but they were plainly waiting and ready. Despite his sad eyes, Stepin did not look a clerk any longer. They were both leopards awaiting the command to hunt.

"Will there be a reply, Aes Sedai?" Moiraine asked.

"I'll carry it myself, child," Kerene replied, starting for the door with a brisk stride that made her silk skirts rasp softly. "Tamra wants me *urgently*," she told the two Warders, who were heeling her like hunting hounds, "but she doesn't say why."

Moiraine allowed herself a brief smile. As with servants, sisters often forgot Accepted had ears. Sometimes, the best way to learn was to keep silent and listen.

As she was making her way back down along the drafty, spiraling corridor, thinking about what she had learned and trying to ignore the cold, Siuan came running up behind her. There were no sisters to be seen, but still. . . .

"Another message," Siuan explained. "To Aisha Raveneos. She kept muttering something about urgent, making it a question. I'll wager it was the same as you carried to Kerene. What do you suppose Tamra wants with a Gray and a Green together?"

The Gray handled matters of mediation and justice, where it came from laws rather than swords, and Aisha was reputed to adhere to the strictest letter of the law no matter her own feelings, whether pity or contempt. A trait she shared with Kerene. And both women had worn the shawl for a very long time, though that could be unimportant. Moiraine might not be so handy with puzzles as Siuan, but this truly was like the Game of Houses.

She looked around carefully, including a glance over her shoulder. A maid was trimming the wicks on a stand-lamp farther along the hallway, and two liveried men, one atop a tall ladder, were doing something concerning one of the wall hangings. There still was not a sister in sight, but she lowered her voice anyway. "Tamra wants . . . searchers . . . to look for the boychild. Oh, this changes everything. I was wrong, Siuan. And you were right."

"Right and wrong about what? What makes you think she's recruiting these searchers?" How *could* the woman be so deft with puzzles and not see the pattern here?

"What matter could be more urgent to Tamra right now than the boychild, Siuan?" she said patiently. "Or more secret, so she dares not put the reason on paper? That secrecy means that she believes the Reds cannot be trusted. That is what you were right about. More than that, how many other sisters will at first want to deny that this child really is the one prophesied? Particularly if he evades discovery until he is a grown man and already channeling. No, she means to use sisters she is sure of to search for him. Where I was wrong was in thinking he would be brought to the Tower. That would only expose him to the Reds, and others who might be untrustworthy. Once found, Tamra will send him into hiding. His education will be at the hands of her searchers, the women she trusts most."

Siuan clapped a hand atop her head. "I think my skull will explode," she muttered. "You built all of that from two messages, and you don't even know what they said."

"I know one thing they said and one they did not. It is simply a matter of seeing the patterns and fitting the pieces together, Siuan. Really, you should be able to do it easily."

"Oh? Ellid gave me a blacksmith's puzzle last week. Said she was bored with it, but I think she couldn't solve it. Want to try your hand?"

"Thank you, no," Moiraine said politely. And, after a quick look for lurking sisters, stuck her tongue out at the other woman.

The next day, Tamra sent three more messages. The first went to Meilyn Arganya, the second to Valera Gorovni, a plump little Brown who always wore a smile and seemed to be bustling even while standing still, and the third to Ludice Daneen, a bony Yellow whose long, grim face was framed by brightly beaded Taraboner braids that hung to her waist. None let slip a hint of the messages' content, yet all three had worn the shawl well over a hundred years, and all three shared that reputation for strict adherence to the law. Moiraine saw it as confirmation, and even Siuan began to believe.

Five seemed too few to undertake the search for the boychild—day by day the names entered into their small notebooks filled more and more pages—yet Tamra sent no further messages. At least, not by them. Aeldra Najaf was raised Keeper of the Chronicles to replace Gitara, and she might have carried them, or more likely sent them by a novice. For a time, Moiraine and Siuan tried keeping an unobtrusive watch on the Amyrlin's study and her apartments, taking turns to peek around the edge of the doorway, but Tamra had a steady flow of visitors. Not constant, but steady. Sitters could be dismissed from consideration, since Sitters rarely left the confines of the city while they held a chair in the Hall of the Tower, yet any of the others could have been searchers. Or not. It was extremely frustrating for Moiraine. That itch on the shoulder blade, just where her fingers could not reach.

Soon enough they gave up attempts to spy. For one thing, there seemed no point. For another, with only one copying, recording the names went much too slowly. And Aeldra, returning to the Amyrlin's study, caught Moiraine lurking in the doorway.

White hair was the sole similarity between Aeldra and Gitara, and Aeldra's was straight and cut as short as Kerene's. The new Keeper was lean, her coppery skin turned to leather from long exposure to sun and wind, yet assuredly no one had ever called her a beauty, with her narrow jaw and sharp nose. For jewelry, she wore the Great Serpent ring alone; her dress was of blue wool, finely woven but simply cut, and the deep blue stole on her shoulders was no more than two fingers wide. A very different woman from Gitara.

"What are you looking at, child?" she asked gently.

"Just the sisters going in and out of the Amyrlin's study, Aes Sedai," Moiraine replied. Every word true.

Aeldra smiled. "Dreaming of the shawl? Perhaps your time would be better spent in study, and practice."

"We find time for both, Aes Sedai, and this work oc-

cupies my mind otherwise." Also true. The search for the
boychild occupied every scrap of her mind not given to
thoughts she would rather not have.

A faint frown creasing her forehead, Aeldra laid a hand
on Moiraine's cheek, almost as if checking for fever. "Do
those other dreams still trouble you? Some of the Browns
know a great deal about herbs. I'm sure one will give you
something to help you sleep, if you need it."

"Verin Sedai already has." The concoction had had a foul
taste, but it did help her sleep. A pity it did not help her
forget the nightmares that came when she did. "The dreams
are not so bad, now." Sometimes, there was no way to use
evasion.

"Good, then." Aeldra's smile returned, but she shook a
mildly reproving finger under Moiraine's nose. "Neverthe-
less, daydreaming in doorways is not proper for one of the
Accepted, child. If I see it again, I will have to take notice.
You understand me?"

"Yes, Aes Sedai." There would be no more spying.
Moiraine began to think she would scream from that cursed
itch.

CHAPTER
8

Shreds of Serenity

There was no evading their private lessons with the sisters, either. Not that Moiraine wanted to, or Siuan, either, but long hours sitting and writing left them surprisingly tired, and also left only the evenings free, after supper. The Accepted who still rode out every day at sunrise did the same, though many grumbled at it—when there were no Aes Sedai around to overhear. At least, they took lessons when lessons were offered. Some sisters refused, saying they would teach Accepted again when they no longer had to give novice classes that should have been taught by Accepted. All too many Aes Sedai disliked the situation. Gossip said that petitions had been presented to the Amyrlin requesting a return to normal routines, but if so, Tamra rejected them. The sisters' faces remained masks of serenity, yet frequently the eyes of even the mildest flashed with a fire that made novices squeak and Accepted step very gingerly. In the depths of winter's cold, the Tower seemed feverish.

Siuan never spoke of her own experiences, but Moiraine quickly realized that she herself attracted particularly heated looks from nearly every Aes Sedai she encountered, and she understood why. Unlike the rest, she and Siuan could have given novice classes and taken their own lessons at a more reasonable hour. A few sisters who taught others at night pronounced themselves busy when either of them tried to schedule a lesson. In some ways, Aes Sedai could be as petty as anyone else, though that was something no Accepted dared say aloud. Moiraine hoped these small enmities would fade soon. Paltry irritations sometimes had a way of festering into lifelong antagonisms. What could she do, though? Apologize humbly to those who seemed most angry, begging their indulgence, and hope. She would not give up the lists.

Not all sisters were so reluctant. Kerene met with her to discuss the relatively few facts known to historians of Artur Hawkwing's empire, Meilyn tested her on the ancient writer Willim of Maneches and his influence on the Saldaean philosopher Shivena Kayenzi, and Aisha questioned her closely on the differences in the structure of law in Shienar and Amadicia. That was the sort of lesson she took, now. What they could teach her of the Power, what she could learn of it—not always the same—had been imparted months past. Had she dared, she would have asked why they were still in the Tower. Why were they not out hunting down the names on the list? Why?

And yet, she knew the answer. What had to be the answer. Nothing else fit. But they felt no urgency. Taking the boy from his mother straightaway would be cruel. Maybe they thought they had years to find him, but if that was the case, they had not even seen the list yet, with so many entries lacking as much as a home village. Maybe they were waiting for its completion. She hoped there *were* other searchers, because Siuan reported Valera and Ludice were still in the Tower.

No urgency! Moiraine burned with it. Rumor said the fighting continued, many leagues southeast, but only in skirmishes, though some were said to be fierce. Apparently no one among the commanders of the Coalition army wanted to press too hard on dangerous foes who were, after all, in retreat. That last was certain, at least, reported by Aes Sedai. Rumor said many of the Murandians and Altarans had already packed up and headed south for home, that the Amadicians and Ghealdanin planned on following soon. Rumor added that word had come of troubles along the Blight, and the Borderlanders would soon ride north. Aes Sedai, it seemed, paid no heed to rumors. She tried bringing the tales up with them, but. . . .

"Rumor is irrational and has no place here, child," Meilyn told her firmly, her gaze serene above the teacup balanced on her fingertips. "Now. When Shivena said that reality is illusion, where did she gain insight from Willim and what was her own?"

"If you want to talk of rumors, make them rumors of Hawkwing," Kerene said, voice sharp. She always toyed with one of her knives while teaching, using it for a pointer. Tonight, it was a poor man's belt knife, so old that the wooden handle was cracked and warped. "The Light knows, half what we have of him is rumor."

Aisha sighed and pointed a stout finger, her soft brown eyes suddenly quite hard. A plain-faced woman who could have passed for a farmer's wife, she wore a wealth of jewelry, earrings with large firedrops, long necklaces of both emeralds and rubies, but only the golden Great Serpent for a finger ring. "If you cannot keep your mind on the matter at hand, perhaps a visit to Merean is in order. Yes, I thought you'd say that."

No, making them see the urgency was just impossible! All she could do was wait. And practice not grinding her teeth. Light, let her test soon. With the shawl on her shoulders, she would be out of the Tower and searching for the boy like an arrow leaving the bow. Soon, but not before she had all of the names. Oh, it was *such* a quandary!

The Accepted's quarters seethed with rumors more than usual, though not about who had had a spat with whom or which Green was said to be behaving scandalously with a Warder. These tales were gotten from Guardsmen, from soldiers, from men and women in the camps, about the fighting, about men who had died heroically, and those who had been heroes and still lived. Those were particularly talked over; such a one might have the qualities of a Warder, a subject much discussed by Accepted, save the few who already knew they wanted the Red. There were tales of camps breaking, though no one knew whether they were moving east after the army or returning home, and tales of small groups remaining behind to make sure that women's names were entered for the Tower's bounty. At least that reduced the chances that the right woman would slip away unknown, but if she was already entered and already gone, would she be among those who would be easily found? Moiraine could have *screamed* from frustration.

Ellid Abareim had a story from an Aes Sedai, though she insisted it was no rumor.

"I heard Adelorna tell Shemaen," Ellid said with a smile. Ellid always smiled when she saw herself in a mirror, and when she smiled, she always seemed to be looking into one. A gusting evening breeze in the well rippled the waves of golden hair framing her perfect face. Her eyes were like large sapphires, her skin like rich cream. The only fault in her appearance that Moiraine could see was an over-abundance of bosom. And she was very tall, nearly as tall as most men. Men smiled at Ellid, when they did not leer. Novices mooned after her, and too many fools among the Accepted envied her. "Adelorna said Gitara had a Foretelling that Tarmon Gai'don will come during the lifetimes of sisters now breathing. I can't wait. I intend to choose Green, you know." Every Accepted knew that. "I mean to have six Warders when I ride to the Last Battle." Every Accepted knew that, too. Ellid was always telling you what she intended to do. She almost always did it, too. That hardly seemed fair.

"So," Moiraine said softly when Ellid had joined the others streaming off to supper. "Gitara did have other Foretellings. At least one, and if one, then perhaps more."

Siuan frowned. "We already know the Last Battle is coming." She fell silent while Katerine and Sarene passed, talking wearily of whether they were too tired to eat, then went on once they were beyond earshot. "What does it matter if Gitara had a dozen Foretellings, or a hundred?"

"Siuan, did you never wonder how Tamra could be *certain* this is the time, that the boy will be born *now*? I would say it is very likely that at least one of those other Foretellings spoke of him. Something that, put with what we heard her say, told Tamra that now is the time." It was Moiraine's turn to frown, in thought. "Do you know how the Foretelling was with Gitara?" It took different women in different ways, including how they gave voice to a Foretelling. "The way she spoke, he could have been being born at that instant. Maybe the shock of that was what killed her."

"The Wheel weaves as the Wheel wills," Siuan said glumly, then gave herself a shake. "Light! Let's go eat. You still need practice."

They had resumed the practicing, too, at least at night, and Myrelle continued to help, when she was not so tired that she went straight to her bed after supper. Or sometimes before. Enough of the Accepted did one or the other that the galleries were still and silent long before the lamps were extinguished. The practice went poorly for Moiraine, especially in the beginning. The very first night, Elaida entered her room while she was suffering Siuan and Myrelle's torments on her flowered rug. The fire had been built as high as the small hearth would accept, but the best that could be said was that the blaze took the edge off the chill. At least it was not freezing.

"I'm glad to see you're not taking the excuse of your work to avoid practice," the Red sister said. Her tone said she was surprised to see it, and contempt wrapped the word "work." Once again her dress was pure red, and she wore her fringed shawl as though on appointed duties. Moving to a corner facing Moiraine, she folded her arms beneath her breasts. "Continue. I wish to observe." There was nothing for it but to obey.

Perhaps spurred by Elaida's presence, Siuan and Myrelle did their very best. Which meant their very worst for startling slaps and pinches, sudden bangs beside Moiraine's ear and switch-like blows across her legs, always just when she needed her concentration most. She tried not to look at Elaida, but the sister stood where she could not avoid seeing her. Elaida's judgmental gaze made her nervous, yet maybe it inspired her, as well. Or drove her. Focusing herself, concentrating with all she had, she managed to complete sixty-one weaves before the sixty-second collapsed in a tangle of Earth, Air, Water and Spirit that left her skin clammy until she let it dissipate. Not a wonderful performance, but neither was it so terrible. She had come close to completing all one hundred on numerous occasions, but she had actually done it only twice, once by the skin of her teeth.

"Pitiful," Elaida said, cold as ice. "You'll never pass like that. And I *want* you to pass, child. You *will* pass, or I'll make you take off your skin and dance in your bones before you're sent away. You two are pitiful friends, if that's how you help her. We knew how to practice when I was Accepted." Directing Siuan and Myrelle to the corner where she had been standing, she took their place at the table. "This will show you how it is done properly. Again, child."

Wetting her lips, Moiraine turned her back. Myrelle gave her an encouraging smile, and Siuan nodded confidently, but she could see their worry. What would Elaida do? She began. As soon as she embraced the Power, flashes of light began streaking across her line of vision, leaving black and silver flecks dancing in her eyes. Bangs and piercing whistles made her ears ring. Blows as from hard-swung straps or switches struck her one after another. It was all continuous, with no letup until she completed a weave, and then only a short pause until she began to weave again.

And all the while, Elaida harangued her in a cold, matter-of-fact tone. "Faster, child. You must weave faster. The weave must almost leap into being complete. Faster. Faster."

Clutching at serenity with her fingernails, Moiraine reached only the twelfth weave before her concentration broke completely. The weave not only collapsed, she lost *saidar* entirely. Blinking, she tried to clear the dancing flecks from her sight. And more successfully, to blink back tears. Pain covered her from shoulders to ankles, bruises aching, welts throbbing, stinging from sweat. A constant chime was sounding in her ears.

"Thank you, Aes Sedai," Siuan said quickly. "We see what we must do, now." Myrelle's hands were clutching her skirts in fists; her face was ashen, her eyes wide with horror.

"Again," Elaida said. It took everything Moiraine had in her to make herself turn her back once more.

The only difference was that she finished just nine weaves this time.

"Again," Elaida said.

On the third try, she completed six weaves, and only three on the fourth. Sweat rolled down her face. After a while, the flashing lights and ear-piercing whistles hardly seemed more than annoyances. Only the incessant beating mattered. Only the endless beating, and the endless pain. On the fifth attempt, she fell to her knees weeping beneath the first shower of blows. The pummeling ceased instantly, but huddling in on herself, she sobbed as though she would never stop. Oh, Light, she had never hurt like this before. Never.

She was not even aware of Siuan kneeling beside her until the other woman said gently, "Can you stand, Moiraine?" Raising her head from the rug, she stared up at Siuan's face, full of concern. With an effort she had not thought in her, she managed to master her weeping, barely, then nodded and began to push herself up laboriously. Bruised muscles did not want to lift her. Every movement scrubbed her shift against the sweat-stung welts, clothing her in burning agony.

"She will live," Elaida said dryly. "A little pain tonight will drive the lesson home. You must be fast! I will come back in the morning to Heal her. And you, too, Siuan. Help her to the bed and begin."

Siuan's face paled, but when an Aes Sedai commanded. . . .

Moiraine did not want to watch, yet Siuan had been forced to, so she held her eyes open by force of will. It made her want to begin weeping all over again. Often when they practiced, Siuan managed to complete every last weave despite anything Moiraine could do. She never failed less than two-thirds of the way through. Tonight, under Elaida's strict tutelage, she managed twenty the first time. The second, it was seventeen, and fourteen on the third. Her face was drained of color and slick with sweat. Her breath came raggedly. But she had not shed a tear. And when a weave failed, she started from the beginning again without so much as a moment's pause. On the fourth try, she finished twelve. And twelve on the fifth, the sixth. Doggedly, she began to weave once more.

"That's enough for tonight," Elaida said. Not one drop of pity touched her voice. Slowly, painfully, Siuan turned, the light of *saidar* vanishing. Her face was absolutely devoid of expression. Elaida went on calmly, adjusting the shawl on her shoulders. "Even if you managed to finish, as you are, you would still fail. There isn't a shred of serenity in you." She fixed first Siuan and then Moiraine with a stern eye. "Remember, you must be serene *whatever* is done to you. And you *must* be fast. If you are slow, you will fail as surely as if you fall to panic or fear. Tomorrow night, we will see if you can do better."

Siuan waited until the door closed behind the Aes Sedai, then threw back her head. "Oh, Light!" she wailed, falling to her knees with a thud, and the tears she had held back came in torrents.

Moiraine bounded from the bed. Well, she tried to bound. It was actually more of a pained hobble, and Myrelle reached Siuan first. The three of them knelt there, holding one another and weeping, Myrelle as hard as she or Siuan.

Finally, Myrelle pushed back, sniffing and wiping tears from her cheeks with her fingers. "Wait here," she said, as if they were in condition to go anywhere, and darted from the room. Soon she returned with a red-glazed jar the size of her two fists, and also Sheriam and Ellid to help get Siuan and Moiraine undressed and apply the ointment in the jar.

"This is wrong!" Ellid said fiercely once the pair of them were naked and she was opening the jar, all the gasping over their welts and bruises finished. Sheriam and Myrelle nodded quick agreement. "The law forbids using the Power to discipline an initiate!"

"Oh?" Siuan growled. "And how often have you had your ear flicked with the Power by a sister, or gotten a stripe across your bottom?" A gasp broke from her mouth. "There's no need to rub that clear to the bone, is there?"

"I'm sorry," Ellid said in contrite tones. "I'll try to be easier." Vanity was a powerful fault, but that was her only real fault. Her only one. It was very hard to like Ellid. "You two should report this. We could all go to Merean."

"No," Moiraine breathed hoarsely. Going on, the salve stung worse than the welts. It was better after. A little better. "I think Elaida really is trying to help us. She said she *wants* us to pass."

Siuan stared at her as though she had sprouted feathers. "I don't recall hearing her say that. Myself, *I* think she's trying to make us fail!"

"Besides," Moiraine added, "who ever heard—? Oh! Oh!" Sheriam muttered an apology, but the ointment still stung. "Who ever heard of an Accepted complaining without paying for it?"

That brought three nods. Grudgingly given, yet they nodded. Novices who complained received a gentle if firm explanation of why matters were how they were. Accepted were expected to know better. They were required to learn endurance every bit as much as history or the One Power.

"Maybe she'll decide to leave you alone," Sheriam said, but she did not sound as if she believed it would happen.

When they finally departed, Myrelle left the jar of ointment behind. Only Verin's vile-tasting concoction let them sleep, huddled beneath the blankets in Moiraine's narrow bed, and it was the grim reminder of that jar sitting on the mantel that warred with sleep as much as their welts and bruises.

Elaida was as good as her word, appearing before daybreak to use Healing on them. And it *was* used, not offered. She merely cupped their heads between her hands and wove without asking. When the intricate weave of Spirit, Air and Water touched her, Moiraine gasped and convulsed. For a moment it felt as though she were totally immersed in icy water, but when the weave vanished, her yellowing bruises were gone. Unfortunately, Elaida supplied a new crop that night, and another on the following. Moiraine lasted through seven attempts and then ten before pain and tears overwhelmed her. Siuan made ten on the second night and twelve on the third. And Siuan never wept until Elaida was gone. Not one tear.

Sheriam, Myrelle and Ellid must have kept watch, for each night, after Elaida left, they appeared to offer commiseration while undressing Siuan and her and spreading the salve on their injuries. Ellid even tried telling jokes, but no one felt like laughing. Moiraine began to wonder whether the jar held enough ointment to last. Had she misheard? Could Siuan be right, that Elaida wanted them to fail? A cold terror settled in her belly, a leaden lump of ice. She was afraid that the next time, she would beg Elaida to stop. But Elaida would not; she was certain of that, and it made her want to cry.

On the morning after Elaida's third visit, though, it was Merean who woke them in Siuan's bed and offered Healing.

"She will not trouble you in this manner again," the motherly Aes Sedai told them once their bruises were gone.

"How did you find out?" Moraine asked, hurriedly pulling her shift over her head. With them sleeping like the dead under the influence of Verin's mixture, the fire had burned down to ashes in the night, and the air in the room was cold, if not quite so cold as it had been only days earlier, but the floor was little warmer. She snatched up her stockings from where they had been left draped over a chairback.

"I have my ways, as you should know," Merean replied mysteriously. Moraine suspected Myrelle or Sheriam or Ellid, if not all three, but Merean *was* Aes Sedai. Never a straight answer when mystery would do, and perhaps do better. "In any case, she very nearly earned herself an imposed penance, and I informed her that I'd ask the Amyrlin for Mortification of the Flesh. And I reminded her that what I must deal to sisters is harsher than what I give novices or Accepted. She was convinced."

"Why shouldn't she get a penance for what she did to

us?" Siuan asked, reaching behind herself to do up the buttons on her dress.

The Mistress of Novices raised an eyebrow at her tone, which came very close to demanding. But perhaps she believed they deserved a little leeway after Elaida. "Had she used *saidar* to punish or coerce you, I'd have seen her strapped to the triangle for birching, yet what she did broke no law." Merean's eyes twinkled suddenly, and her lips curved in a small smile. "Perhaps I shouldn't tell you, but I will. Her penance would have been for helping you cheat in the test for the shawl. All that saved her was the question of whether it actually was cheating. I trust you will accept her gift in the spirit it was given. After all, she paid a price in humiliation for giving it when I confronted her."

"Believe me, Aes Sedai, I will," Siuan said flatly. What she meant was plain. Merean sighed and shook her head, but said nothing more.

The icy lump that had melted from Moiraine's middle when she learned there would be no further lessons from Elaida returned twice as large. She had almost helped them cheat? Could she have given them a foretaste of the actual test for the shawl? Light, if the test meant being beaten the whole way . . . ! Oh, Light, how could she possibly pass? But whatever comprised the test, every woman who wore the shawl had undergone it and succeeded. She would, as well. Somehow, she would! She pushed Myrelle and Siuan to be harder on her, but though they sometimes made her weep, they refused to do what Elaida had done. Even so, again and again she failed to complete all one hundred weaves. That lump of ice grew a little larger every day.

They did not see Elaida again for two days, and then it was on their way to dinner at midday. The Red sister stopped beside a tall stand-lamp at the sight of them, speaking not a word as they curtsied. Still silent, she turned to watch as they passed her. Her face was a severe mask of serenity, but her eyes burned. Her gaze should have scorched the wool of their dresses.

Moiraine's heart sank. Clearly, Elaida thought they had gone to the Mistress of Novices themselves. And she had "paid a price in humiliation," according to Merean. Moiraine could think of several ways that the threat of a penance could be used to make Elaida give way, and every one of them would have wrung the sister with humiliation. The only question was, how hard had Merean wrung? Very hard, likely; she *did* speak of the novices and Accepted as being hers. Oh, this was no small enmity that might fester over time. What was in Elaida's eyes was full-blown animosity. They had acquired an enemy for life.

When she told Siuan as much, and her reasoning, the taller woman grunted sourly. "Well, I never wanted to be her friend, did I? I tell you, once I gain the shawl, if she ever tries to harm me again, I'll make her pay."

"Oh, Siuan," Moiraine laughed, "Aes Sedai do *not* go about harming one another." But her friend would not be assuaged.

One week to the day after Gitara made her Foretelling, the weather warmed suddenly. The sun rose in a cloudless sky on what seemed like a cool spring day, and before sunset most of the snow had melted. All of it was gone around Dragonmount, except on the very peak. The ground around the mountain had its own warmth, and snow always melted there first. The limit had been set. It was a boy born within those ten days that they sought. Two days later, the number who met the criteria began to dwindle sharply, and near a week on, five days had passed without another name being added to their small books. They could only hope that no more were found, though.

Nine days after the thaw, in the dim light before dawn. Merean appeared on the gallery as Siuan and Moiraine were leaving for breakfast. She was wearing her shawl. "Moiraine Damodred," she said formally, "you are summoned to be tested for the shawl of an Aes Sedai. The Light keep you whole and see you safe."

CHAPTER
9

It Begins

Merean barely allowed time for a quick hug from Siuan before leading Moiraine away, and with every step, the lump of ice in Moiraine's middle grew. She was not ready! In all of her practices, she had managed to complete all of the weaves only twice, and never under anything approaching the pressure Elaida had put on her. She was going to fail and be put out of the Tower. She was going to fail. Those words throbbed in her head, a drumbeat marking the walk to the headsman's axe. She was going to fail.

As she followed Merean down a narrow staircase that spiraled deep into the bedrock beneath the Tower, a thought occurred to her. If she failed, she would still be able to channel, at least so long as she remained circumspect. The Tower frowned on ostentation in the women who were sent away, and when the Tower frowned on something, only fools failed to take heed. The sisters said those sent away all but gave up touching *saidar* for fear of overstepping the Tower's strictures inadvertently, but giving up that rapture was beyond her comprehension. She knew she never would, whatever happened. Another thought, seemingly unconnected. If she failed, she would still be Moiraine Damodred, scion of a powerful if disreputable House. Her estates would no doubt need years to recover from the ravages of the Aiel, but surely could still supply an adequate income.

A third thought, and it all came together, so obvious that clearly she had been thinking of it all along on some deeper level. She still had her book with its hundreds of names in her belt pouch. Even if she failed, she could take up the search for the boy. That carried dangers, of course. The Tower more than merely disliked outsiders meddling in its affairs, and she would be an outsider, then. Rulers had learned bitter regret for interfering where the Tower planned. How much worse for a young exile, however powerful her House? No matter. What would be, would be.

"The Wheel weaves as the Wheel wills," she murmured, earning a sharp look from Merean. The ritual was far from complex, but it must be adhered to. That she had forgotten that once below ground she must be silent until addressed said little for her chances in the actual test.

It was very odd. She wanted to be Aes Sedai more than she wanted life, yet the knowledge that she could take up the search, whatever happened here, the knowledge that she would, quieted that drumbeat in her head. It even made the frozen lump dwindle. A little. One way or another, in a few days she would begin her own search. Light let it be as Aes Sedai.

The lofty passages Merean led her along, carved through the rock of the island, as wide as any in the Tower, were lit by lamps in iron brackets high on the pale walls, though many crossing corridors lay shrouded in darkness, or with only widely spaced lamps making small lonely pools of light. The smooth stone floor was free of any speck of dust. The way had been prepared for them. The air was cool and dry, and, beyond the faint scuff of their slippers, silent. Except for storerooms on the highest levels, these basements were seldom used, and everything was plain and unadorned. Dark wooden doors lined the corridors, all shut, and, as they went deeper, securely locked. Many things were kept down here safe from prying eyes. What was done down here was never for outside eyes, either.

On the very lowest level, Merean stopped before paired doors larger than any they had passed, as tall and wide as fortress gates, but polished to glistening and lacking iron straps. The Aes Sedai channeled, and flows of Air swung the doors open silently on well-oiled hinges. Taking a deep breath, Moiraine followed her into a large, round, domed chamber ringed by stand-lamps. Their light, reflected from the polished white stone walls, dazzled after the comparative dimness of the passages.

Blinking, her eyes went immediately to the object centered beneath the dome, a great oval ring, narrow at top and bottom, its rounded rim little thicker than her arm. Well above a span in height and perhaps a pace across at its widest, it glittered in the lamplight, now silver, now gold or green or blue or swirls of all, never the same for more than a moment, and—a seeming impossibility—it stood unsupported. That was a *ter'angreal*, a device made to use the One Power in the long-ago Age of Legends. Within it, she would be tested. She would not fail. She would not!

"Attend," Merean said formally. The other Aes Sedai already in the chamber, one from each Ajah, came to stand in a ring around them, fringed shawls draped on their shoulders. One was Elaida, and Moiraine's heart fluttered uneasily. "You come in ignorance, Moiraine Damodred. How would you depart?"

Light, why had Elaida been allowed to be part of this? She wanted desperately to ask, but the words were prescribed. She was surprised to hear her voice come out steady. "In knowledge of myself."

"For what reason have you been summoned here?" Merean intoned.

"To be tried." Calm was all-important, but though her voice sounded it, within was another matter. She could not shake Elaida from her thoughts.

"For what reason should you be tried?"

"So that I may learn whether I am worthy." All of the sisters would try to make her fail—that *was* the test, after all—but Elaida might try the hardest. Oh, Light, what could she do?

"For what would you be found worthy?"

"To wear the shawl." And with that, she began to disrobe. According to ancient custom, she must test clad in the Light, symbolizing that she trusted to the Light's protection alone.

As she undid her belt, she suddenly remembered the small book in her pouch. If that were discovered . . . ! But to falter now was to fail. She laid belt and pouch on the floor beside her feet and reached behind her back to work at her buttons.

"Therefore I will instruct you," Merean went on. "You will see this sign upon the ground." She channeled, and her finger drew a six-pointed star in the air, two overlapping triangles written for an instant in fire.

Moiraine felt one of the sisters behind her embrace *saidar,* and a weave touched the back of her head. "Remember what must be remembered," the sister murmured. It was Anaiya, the Blue. But this was not part of what she had been taught. What did it mean? She made her fingers march steadily along the buttons down her back. It had begun, and she must proceed in utter calm.

"When you see that sign, you will go to it immediately, at a steady pace, neither hurrying nor hanging back, and only then may you embrace the Power. The weaving required must begin immediately, and you may not leave that sign until it is completed."

"Remember what must be remembered," Anaiya murmured.

"When the weave is complete," Merean said, "you will see that sign again, marking the way you must go, again at a steady pace, without hesitation."

"Remember what must be remembered."

"One hundred times you will weave, in the order you have been given and in perfect composure."

"Remember what must be remembered," Anaiya murmured for a final time, and Moiraine felt the weaving settle into her, much as Healing did.

All of the sisters save Merean moved away and formed a circle around the *ter'angreal.* Kneeling on the stone floor, each embraced *saidar.* Surrounded by the light of the Power, they channeled, and the color-shifting of the oval ring increased in speed, until it flashed like a kaleidoscope attached to a mill wheel. All of the Five Powers they wove, in a complexity nearly as great as anything required in the test, every sister concentrating on her task. No, not true. Not completely. Elaida glanced away, and her gaze was stern and heated when it touched Moiraine. A red-hot awl fit to bore into her skull.

She wanted to wet her lips, yet "perfect composure" meant exactly that. Protection of the Light or no, removing her clothes in front of so many was not easy, but most of the sisters were concentrating on the *ter'angreal.* Only Merean was watching her, now. Watching for hesitation, for a break in her outward serenity. It was begun, and a break now brought failure. Yet it was just outward calm, a mask of smooth features that carried no deeper than her skin.

Continuing to undress, she carefully folded each garment and placed it in a neat pile atop her belt and pouch. That should do. All of the sisters save Merean would be occupied until her test was done—at least, she thought they would—and she doubted the Mistress of Novices would rummage through her clothing. In any case, there was nothing else to do, now. Slipping off her Great Serpent ring, last of all, and laying the circlet of gold atop the rest brought a pang. Since winning that, she had worn it even when bathing. Her heart was racing, thudding so hard she was certain Merean must be able to hear. Oh, Light, Elaida. She would have to be very wary. The woman knew how to break her. She must watch and be ready.

After that, she could only stand and wait. Her skin quickly pebbled with gooseflesh in the cool air, and she wanted to shift her bare feet on the stone floor, which was more than cool. Perfect composure. She stood still, back straight, hands at her sides, and breathed evenly. Perfect composure. Light, help her. She refused to fail just because of Elaida. She refused! But that lump of ice in her belly spread its chill along her bones. She let none of it show. A perfect mask of composure.

The air in the opening of the ring suddenly turned to a sheet of white. It seemed somehow whiter than the wool of her skirts, whiter than snow or the finest paper, yet rather than reflect the stand-lamps, it seemed to absorb some of their light, making the chamber grow dim. And then, the tall oval ring began to revolve slowly on its base, without the slightest sound of stone grating against whatever it was made of.

No one spoke. They did not need to. She knew what must be done. Unwavering, at least on the outside, she walked toward the turning ring at a steady pace, neither hurrying nor hanging back. She *would* pass, whatever Elaida did. She would! She stepped into the whiteness and through, and. . . .

. . . Wondered where in the Light she was and how she had come there. She was standing in a plain stone corridor lined with stand-lamps, and the only door, at the far end, stood open on sunlight. In fact, the only way out. Behind her was a smooth wall. Very strange. She was certain she had never seen this place before. And why was she there . . . *unclothed*? Only the certainty that she must display absolute calm kept her from covering herself with her hands.

Anyone might walk in through that far door at any moment, after all. Suddenly she noticed a dress lying on a narrow table halfway down the hall. She was positive neither table nor dress had been there a moment earlier, but things did not suddenly appear from thin air. She thought she was certain of that.

Fighting not to hurry, she walked to the table and found a full set of garments. The slippers were embroidered black velvet, the white shift and stockings of the finest silk, the dress of only slightly heavier material, in a dark, shimmering green, well cut and meticulously sewn. Bars of red, green and white, each two inches tall, made a narrow line of color down the front of the dress from the high neck to below knee-level. How could a dress with her own House colors be here? She could not recall the last time she had worn a dress in that style, which was very odd, for surely it had passed out of fashion no more than a year or two ago. Her memory seemed full of holes. Chasms. Still, once she was clothed again, looking over her shoulder to do up the tiny mother-of-pearl buttons by her reflection in the stand-mirror. . . . Where had that come from? No, best not to worry over what seemed beyond explanation. The garments fit as though her own seamstress had measured her. Once she was dressed, she began to feel every inch the Lady Moiraine Damodred. Only having her hair arranged in elaborate coils on the sides of her head could have made it more so. When had she begun wearing her hair loose? No matter. Inside Cairhien, only a handful of people could order Moiraine Damodred. Most obeyed her commands. She had no doubt she could maintain whatever serenity was necessary. Not now.

The door at the end of the hallway opened onto a large, circular courtyard surrounded by tall brick arches supporting a columned walk. Gilded spires and domes suggested a palace, yet there was no one in sight. All lay silent and still beneath a clear spring sky. Spring, or a cool summer day, perhaps. She could not even remember what time of year it was! But she remembered *who* she was, the Lady Moiraine, who had been raised in the Sun Palace, and that was sufficient. She paused only long enough to locate the six-pointed star, made of polished brass set into the paving stones in the center of the courtyard, and, gathering her skirts, stepped outside. She moved as one born in a palace, head high, un-hurrying.

At her second step, the dress vanished, leaving her in her shift. That was impossible! By force of will, she continued her regal walk. Serene. Confident. Two more steps, and her shift melted away. By the time silk stockings and lace garters went, halfway to the shiny brass star, they seemed a grievous loss. That made no sense, but at least they had been *some* covering. A steady pace. Serene and confident.

Three men strolled out from one of the brick arches, bulky, unshaven fellows in rough-woven coats, the sort who wasted their days drinking in taverns or the common rooms of inns. Certainly not men who would be allowed to wander inside a palace. Color touched her checks even before they noticed her and began leering. Ogling *her*! Anger flashed in her, and she suppressed it. Serenity. A steady movement, neither hurrying nor hanging back. It had to be so. She did not know why, only that it must be.

One of the men raked his fingers through his greasy hair as though to straighten it, making a greater mess in the process. Another straightened his ragged coat. They began sauntering toward her, oily smirks twisting their faces. She had no fear of them, just the burning consciousness that these ... these ... *ruffians* ... were seeing her without a stitch—without a single stitch!—yet she dared not channel until she reached the star. Utter calm and a steady pace. Deep-buried anger twitched and strained, but she held it down.

Her foot touched the brass star, and she wanted to gasp with relief. Instead, she turned to face the three louts and, embracing *saidar,* channeled Air in the required weave. A solid wall of Air, three paces high, flashed into being around them, and she tied it off. That was allowed. It rang with the sound of steel when one of them struck it.

There was a six-pointed star gleaming in the brickwork at the top of the very arch the men had come out of. She was certain it had not been there earlier, yet it certainly was now. Walking at a steady pace became difficult passing the wall of Air, and she was glad she still held the Power. By the curses and shouts she could hear from inside it, the men were attempting to climb out by scrambling atop one another's shoulders. Again, she was not afraid of them. Just of them seeing her naked again. Color stained her cheeks once more. It was very hard not to pick up her step. But she concentrated on that, on keeping her face smooth and unruffled however red.

Stepping through the arch, she turned, ready in case they. . . .

Light, where was she? And why was she . . . *unclothed*? Why was she holding *saidar*? She released it uneasily as well as reluctantly. She knew she had completed the first weave of one hundred she must make, out there in that empty courtyard. She knew that much and no more. Except that she must go on.

Luckily, a set of garments lay on the floor just inside the arch. They were rough wool and thick, the stockings scratchy, yet they fit as though made for her. Even the heavy leather shoes. Ugly things, but she put them on.

It was very strange, given that what had seemed a palace courtyard lay behind her, but the doorless corridor she walked along was rough-dressed stone, lit by lamps set in iron brackets high on the walls. More suited to a fortress than a palace. It was not entirely doorless, of course; it could not be. She had to go on, and that meant she had to go *somewhere*. Even odder than the corridor was what the lone doorway at the far end revealed.

A tiny village lay before her, a dozen small thatch-roofed houses and ramshackle barns, apparently abandoned in a dire drought. Warped doors creaked on their hinges as the wind blew dust along the single dirt street beneath a pitiless noonday sun. The heat struck her like a hammer, drenching her in sweat before she had gone ten paces. She was suddenly glad for the stout shoes; the ground was rocky, and might well have burned her in slippers. One stone well stood in the middle of what might once have been called the village green, a patch of dry dirt with scattered tufts of desiccated grass. On the cracked green tiles that made a rim around the well, where once men and women had stood to draw water, someone had painted a six-pointed star in red paint now faded pale and chipped.

As soon as she stepped onto that star, she began to channel. Air and Fire, then Earth. As far as she could see lay parched fields and twisted, bare-branched trees. Nothing moved in that landscape. How had she come here? However it had happened, she wanted to be away from this dead place. Suddenly, she was ensnared in blackclaw bushes, the dark inch-long thorns driving through her woolens, pricking her cheeks, her scalp. She did not bother with thinking it was impossible. She just wanted out. Every piercing burned, and she could feel blood trickling from some. Calm. She must display complete calm. Unable to move her head, she tried to feel for a way to pull at least a few of the tangled brown branches away, and very nearly gasped as sharp points dug into her flesh. Fresh blood dribbled down her arms. Calm. She could channel other weaves than what was required, but how to get rid of these cursed thorns? Fire was useless; the bushes looked dry as tinder, and burning them would envelop her in flames, too. She continued weaving while she thought, of course. Spirit, then Air. Spirit followed by Earth and Air together. Air, then Spirit and Water.

Something moved on one of the branches, a small dark shape on eight legs. A memory drifted up from somewhere, and her breath caught in spite of herself. Keeping her face smooth strained her abilities to the utmost. The death's-head spider came from the Aiel Waste. How did she know that? Its name came from more than the gray marking on its back that resembled a human skull. One bite could sicken a strong man for days. Two could kill him.

Still weaving the useless snarl of the Five Powers—why *would* she want to weave such a thing? but she must—still weaving, she swiftly divided the flows and touched the spider with a tiny but very intricate weave of Fire. The thing flashed to ash so quickly it did not so much as scorch the branch. It would not take much to set the bushes alight. Before she could feel relief, however, she spotted another spider crawling toward her, and killed it with that small weave, and then another, and another. Light, how many were there? Her eyes, the only part of her that could move, searched hurriedly, and almost everywhere they lit, she found another death's-head, crawling toward her. Every one she saw, she killed, but so many where her eyes could find them begged the question. How many were below her sight? Or behind her? Calm!

Burning spiders as rapidly as she could locate them, she began to weave faster at that great useless lump. In several places, thin tendrils of smoke rose from blackened spots on the branches. Holding her face in a smooth, frozen mask, she wove faster and faster. Dozens more spiders died, and more tendrils of smoke rose, some thicker. Once the first flame showed, it would spread like the wind. Faster. Faster.

The last threads fell into place in the worthless weave, and as soon as she stopped weaving, the blackclaw bushes vanished. They were simply gone! The thorn-pricks were not, but they hardly concerned her right then. She very much wanted to scramble out of her clothes and shake them out thoroughly. Using flows of Air. The spiders on the bushes had disappeared with the bushes, but what about any that might have crawled onto her dress? Or inside it? Instead, she searched for another six-pointed star, and found it carved above the door of one of the thatch-roofed houses. Once inside, she could search her clothing. Calmly. She stepped through into pitch blackness.

And found herself wondering where she was and how she had gotten there. Why was she dressed in a farmer's woolens, and why was she bleeding as though she had rolled in a thornbush? She knew that she had completed two of the one hundred weaves she must make, and nothing more. Not even where the first had been made. Nothing except that the way she must go lay through this house. She did look back at the bleak landscape behind her.

All she could see ahead was a faint patch of light across the room. Strange; she was sure the windows had been unshuttered. Perhaps that glow indicated some way out, a crack beside a door, perhaps. She could have made a light, but she must not embrace the Power again yet. Darkness held no fears for her, but she walked carefully to avoid bumping into anything. Nothing impeded her, though. For nearly a quarter of an hour she walked, with the patch of light slowly growing larger, before realizing that what she saw was a doorway. A quarter of an hour, in a house she could have walked around twice in a quarter of that. A very peculiar place, this. A dream, she would have thought, had she not known it was not.

It took almost as long again to reach the doorway, which opened onto a scene as strange as that long walk. A solid wall of massive stones, five paces high and thirty on a side, surrounded a stone-paved square, but she saw nothing beyond it, not one building, not a tree. Nor were there any gates or doors; the one she had come out of was gone when she glanced back. A very casual glance, with her face holding its mask of calm as though it were carved. The air was moist and spring-like, the sky bright and clear save for a few drifting white clouds, yet that failed to dent the ominous feel of the place.

The six-pointed star, a span across, was carved into the center of the square, and she walked toward it as close to quickly as she dared. Just before she reached it, a massive form in spiked mail pulled itself up on the wall and dropped down inside. It was as tall as an Ogier, but no amount of squinting could make it seem human, though the body was human in form. A wolf's jaws and twitching ears made a horror of a face otherwise that of a man. She had seen drawings of Trollocs, but never before one in the flesh. Shadowspawn born of the war that ended the Age of Legends, servants of the Dark One, Trollocs inhabited the Shadow-corrupted Blight along the Borderlands. Could she be in the Blight? Her blood chilled at the thought. Behind her, she heard the thud of boots landing heavily, and of hooves. Not all Trollocs had human feet. The wolf-muzzled creature drew a huge, scythe-curved sword that had been hanging on its back and began to run at her. Light, the thing was fast! She heard more running feet, running hooves. More Trollocs dropped over the wall ahead of her, faces marred with eagles' beaks and boars' tusked snouts.

One more step, and she was on the star. Straightaway, she embraced *saidar* and began to weave. The required weave first, but as soon as the first strands of Air, Earth and Spirit were laid down, she divided her flows, making a second weave, and a third, of Fire. There were a number of ways to produce balls of fire, and she chose the simplest. Throwing with both hands, she hurled them at the nearest Trollocs and spun, still weaving Fire. She had to pause in the more important weave, but so long as she was quick enough. . . . Light, there were a dozen Trollocs in the square with her, and more climbing over the walls! With both hands she threw, as fast as she could weave, aiming for those closest, and where her fireballs struck, they exploded, decapitating a creature with a ram's snout and horns, blowing a goat-horned Trolloc in two, ripping off legs. She felt no pity. Trollocs took human prisoners only for food.

Completing her spin, she was just in time to catch the major weave on the point of collapse. Just in time to hurl balls of fire that removed an eagle-beaked head, only paces away, and half the torso of a wolf-muzzled Trolloc that staggered across the edge of the star before toppling in a lifeless sprawl. It was not going to work. There were too many Trollocs, with more crossing the walls all the while, and she could not neglect the important weave even spinning as quickly as she could. There had to be a way. She *would* not fail! Somehow, the thought of being killed and eaten by Trollocs never entered into it. She would not fail; that was the whole.

Abruptly, the way came to her, and she smiled and began to hum the quickest court dance that she knew. Perhaps the way; a chance, in any case. The rapid steps took her around the rim of the star without ever requiring her to lose sight of the weave she had to complete above all else. After all, however quickly her feet moved, what could be more serene than a court dance, with her face properly smooth, as though she were dancing in the Sun Palace? She wove the Five Powers as fast as she could, faster than she had ever woven before, she was certain. In some way, the dancing helped, and the intricate weave began to take shape like the finest Mardina lace. Dancing, she wove, hurling fire with both hands, killing Shadowspawn with both hands. Sometimes they came so close that their blood spattered her face, sometimes so close that she had to dance out of their way as they fell, dance away from their down-curving swords, but she ignored the blood and danced.

The final weave fell into place, and she let the whole thing evaporate, but there were still Trollocs in the square. A quick step took her to the center of the star, where she danced in a tiny circle, back-to-back with an imaginary partner. Working three separate weaves at once had left her exhausted, but she summoned the strength to manage three again. Dancing, she hurled fire and called lightning from the sky, harrowing the square with explosions.

At last, nothing moved except for her, dancing. She circled three more times before she realized it and stopped.

Stopped humming. There was an archway in the wall now, a shadowed opening with the star carved above it. Her heart turned to ice. An archway that led out to where the Trollocs had come from. Into the Blight. Only madmen entered the Blight willingly. Gathering her rough skirts, she made herself cross that charnel square toward the gate. It was the way she had to go.

CHAPTER
10

It Finishes

Ninety-nine weaves. She found the six-pointed star laid out in round river stones amid the towering dunes of a desert where the heat made her light-headed and sucked the moisture from her skin before sweat had time to form. She found it drawn in the snow on a mountainside where gale winds beat at her and lightning struck all around, and in a great city of impossible towers where people babbled at her incomprehensibly. She found it in a night-shrouded forest, in a blackwater swamp, in a marsh of tall grass that cut like knives, on farms and plains, in hovels and palaces. Sometimes she found it while she was clothed, but her clothing frequently vanished, and just as often, she had none to begin. Sometimes she was suddenly bound with ropes or manacles, bent into contorted positions that twisted her joints, or hanging suspended by her wrists or ankles. She faced poisonous serpents and toothed water lizards three spans long, rampaging wild boars and hunting lions, hungry leopards and stampeding herds of wild cattle. She was stung by hornets and groundwasps, bitten by swarms of ants and horseflies and insects she did not recognize. Mobs carrying torches tried to drag her away for burning, Whitecloaks to hang her, robbers to stab her, footpads to strangle her. And every time, she forgot, and wondered how she had gotten a slash across her cheek, what had to be a sword-cut along her ribs, three gouges down her back that must have come from claws, other wounds and injuries and bruises that left her bleeding, limping. And she was weary. Oh, so weary, down to the bone. More than channeling even ninety-nine weaves could explain. Perhaps her wounds did. Ninety-nine weaves.

Clutching her plain woolen skirts, she hobbled to the six-pointed star, marked out in red tiles beside a burbling marble fountain in a small garden surrounded by a colonnade of thin, fluted columns. She could barely stand, and maintaining a smooth face took her to the limits of her ability. Pain throbbed in every part of her. No, agony was a better description than pain. But this was the last. Once it was done, this would be done as well, whatever this was, and she would be free to seek Healing. If she could find an Aes Sedai. Otherwise, a Reader would do.

This was another of the useless weaves, producing only a shower of shining colorful flecks if woven correctly. Incorrectly woven, it would redden her skin, painfully, as from a bad sunburn. She began very carefully.

Her father walked out of the colonnade right in front of her, in a long coat of a style at least a year out of fashion, with bars of the House Damodred colors marching from his high collar down to below his knees. He was very tall, for a Cairhienin man, just an inch short of six feet, with hair more gray than not worn in a club at the nape of his neck. He had always stood straight as a blade, except when bending to let her leap into his arms as a child, but now his shoulders were slumped. She could not understand why the sight of him made her suddenly teary.

"Moiraine," he said, worry adding lines to his gentle face, "you must come with me immediately. It is your mother, child. She is dying. There is just time, if you come now."

It was too much. She wanted to weep. She wanted to rush off with him. She did neither. The weave seemed to complete itself in a sudden blur, and gaily glittering flecks fell around them. The display seemed especially bitter. She opened her mouth to ask where her mother was, and saw the second star behind him, worked in red tile above the colonnade just where he had first appeared. A steady pace, without hesitation.

"I love you, Father," she said calmly. Light, how could she stay calm? But she must. "Please tell Mother that I love her with all my heart."

Brushing past him, she limped toward the second star.

She thought he called after her, that he ran after and plucked at her sleeve, but her mind was a haze from the effort of keeping a smooth face and a steady tread. A stumble, really, but she neither hung back nor hurried. She stepped between the fluted columns, beneath the star, and. . . .

. . . found herself staggering into a round white chamber, the reflected light of stand-lamps dazzling her eyes. Memory crashed back into her, nearly buckling her knees. Unable to think as that torrent flooded in on her, she managed three more steps before stumbling to a halt. She remembered everything, the making of every weave, where every injury had been received. All of her missteps, her frantic efforts to hold on to some outward semblance of serenity.

"It is done," Merean intoned, clapping her hands together with a loud crack. "Let no one ever speak of what has passed here. It is for us to share in silence with she who experienced it. It is done." Again she clapped her hands loudly, the blue fringe of her shawl swinging. "Moiraine Damodred, you will spend tonight in prayer and contemplation of the burdens you will take up on the morrow, when you don the shawl of an Aes Sedai. It is done." For a third time she clapped her hands together.

Gathering her skirts, the Mistress of Novices started for the doors, but the rest of the sisters came quickly to Moiraine. All except Elaida, she realized. Shawl wrapped around her as though she felt the coolness, Elaida was leaving with Merean.

"Will you accept Healing, child?" Anaiya asked. A hand taller than Moiraine, her plain features nearly overwhelmed agelessness and made her look more a farmer than an Aes Sedai despite her finely cut blue woolens with their intricate embroidery on the sleeves. "I don't know why I ask. You're not in as bad a state as some I've seen, but bad enough."

"I . . . passed?" she said in amazement.

"If blushes counted as breaking calm, no one would ever reach the shawl," Anaiya replied, adjusting her own with a laugh.

Light, they had seen everything! Of course, they would have to, but she remembered a stunningly handsome man who had snatched her up and begun kissing her quite thoroughly just as she started the forty-third weave, and her face reddened. They had *seen* that!

"You really should Heal the child before she falls over, Anaiya," Verin said. Short and dreamy-eyed, she was quite plump in her fine russet wool and brown-fringed shawl. Moiraine liked Verin, yet she felt a chill at the sight of her clothing in the Brown sister's hands.

"I suppose I should at that," Anaiya said, and clasping Moiraine's head between her hands, she channeled.

These injuries were far worse than the welts and bruises Elaida had given, and this time Moiraine felt as though she were caked in ice rather than dunked in cold water. When it passed, though, all of the cuts and gouges and gashes were gone. The weariness remained, seeming even heavier than before. And she was starving. How long had she been down here? Her carefully learned sense of time seemed utterly scrambled.

One touch at her pouch told her the book was still there, but she could do no more in front of the sisters. Besides, she very much wanted to be clothed once more. But there was a question she wanted answered. Her tests had not been simply a matter of chance, completely a product of the *ter'angreal*. The continual assaults on her modesty left no doubts. "The last test was very cruel," she said, pausing with her dress ready to lift over her head. Pausing to watch their faces.

"It is not to be spoken of, however cruel," Anaiya said firmly. "Not ever, to anyone."

But Yuan, a slim Yellow, half glanced toward the door, displeasure in her gray eyes. So. Merean had been no part of the test. Elaida *had* tried to make her fail, and harder than anyone else, or the Arafellin sister would not have disapproved. So.

The other three sisters went their own way, but Anaiya and Verin escorted her back above ground, using a different route than she had come down by. When they left her, she went to the room where she and Siuan had spent so many days copying names, and found two clerks doing the work, harassed-looking women who were none too pleased to be interrupted with questions about an Accepted of whom they knew nothing. Could it be? Oh, Light, could it?

She hurried to the Accepted's quarters—and was three times called down for it by sisters; she was still only Accepted, until tomorrow—she all but ran, and found Siuan's room and her own both empty. Some of the name-taking excursions were ending earlier, now, and it was well past midday, so she searched through the other rooms until she found Sheriam and Myrelle sitting before the fire in Myrelle's room, where the small rug had a ragged red fringe and the washbasin and pitcher were blue.

"Merean came for Siuan a little while ago," Myrelle said excitedly. "For her test."

"Did you . . . ? Did you pass?" Sheriam asked.

"Yes," she replied, and felt a touch of sadness at the sudden withdrawal in their faces. They even stood, hands going to skirts, almost making to curtsy. A gulf had opened between them. She was still Accepted, until tomorrow, but friendship was at an end, until they also gained the shawl. They did not ask her to leave, yet neither did they ask her to stay, and they seemed relieved when she said she wanted to go to her room to wait alone for Siuan's return.

Once in her room, she examined the book in her belt pouch, but nothing indicated that it had been touched, no pages creased by someone reading carelessly. Which did not mean no one *had* read. But then, no one would have known what they were looking at unless they knew what Moiraine and Siuan did. And Tamra's searchers. She offered a silent prayer of thanks that none of them had been among the sisters testing her. So far as she knew.

A serving woman, or perhaps a novice, had laid a fire on the hearth and placed a tray on her small table, and removing the crisp white cloth that covered it revealed a larger meal than she thought she had ever eaten in her life, piled slices of roasted beef, turnips with a cream sauce, broad beans with crumbly white goat cheese, cabbage with pine nuts. There was a round loaf of crusty brown bread, and a huge pot of tea. The tray must only just have been left, because everything was still warm. The Tower had a way of timing things to a nicety.

Much too much food, yet she ate every shred, even the bread. The whole loaf. Her whole body yearned for sleep, but that would never do. If Siuan failed, and survived failing—Light, let her live, at least—she would be brought back only long enough to gather her possessions and say her goodbyes. Moiraine refused to take the risk. So she curled up on her bed, but with a small leather-bound book. *Hearts of Flame* might be unsuitable for a novice, but it was one of *her* favorites. And Siuan's. Now, she stared at the first page for minutes before realizing she had not read a word. She got up to pace awhile before taking up the book again, yawning, but she still could not manage to hold a sentence. Siuan *would* come back. She would *not* be put out of the Tower. But there were so many ways to misstep, so many ways to fail. No! Siuan would pass. She had to. It would be unfair for Moiraine to reach the shawl and not Siuan. She knew her friend would be a better Aes Sedai than she could ever manage.

Throughout the afternoon she heard the sounds of other Accepted returning, some laughing, others complaining, all loudly. The noise always turned to stillness very quickly, though, as word spread that she had been tested and had passed, that she was in her room. Tomorrow she would be raised Aes Sedai, yet they behaved as though she already was, moving in a hush so as not to disturb her. The hour for supper came and passed. She actually thought she could eat a little something in spite of her huge, and late, dinner, but she did not go to the dining hall. For one thing, she doubted she could bear the stares of the others or, worse, their downcast gazes. For another, Siuan might return while she was gone.

She was on her bed, yawning and making yet another attempt at reading, when Siuan walked in, her expression unreadable.

"Did you . . . ?" Moiraine began, and could not finish.

"It was as easy as falling off a boat," Siuan answered. "Into a school of silverpike. I almost swallowed my heart when I remembered this . . ." she slapped her belt pouch, where she also carried her book of names, "but after that, it went well." Her whole face suddenly turned bright red. She managed a smile through it. "We'll be raised together, Moiraine."

Moiraine leaped to her feet, and laughing, they danced hand in hand for joy. She ached to ask what had happened in Siuan's test. That furious blush—from Siuan!—begged intriguing questions, but. . . . To be shared in silence, and only then with the women who had shared it with you. How long since they two had failed to share everything? Even here, the shawl brought separations.

"You must be starved," Moiraine said, stopping the dance.

She was so tired, she had begun to stagger, and Siuan was not much steadier. "And there must be a tray waiting in your room." She indicated the one on her table. It might have been brought up to her on this special occasion, but she was expected to carry the dirty dishes down herself. And feel lucky if she did not have to wash them, for waiting so long.

"I could eat an oar, but there's better than food in my room." Siuan grinned suddenly. "I got six mice from one of the grooms this morning."

"We are practically sisters," Moiraine protested. "We cannot put mice in someone's bed. Anyway, beyond improper, it would not be fair. Nearly everyone has been out for most of the day, and they must be as tired as you are."

"Practically sisters isn't the same as being, Moiraine. Think. It's our last chance. It really won't be proper once we have the shawl." Siuan's grin faded to grimness. "And Elaida hasn't been out of the Tower that I know. Mice are a small repayment for those beatings, Moiraine. We owe her. We owe her!"

Moiraine drew breath. Without Elaida, she might never have practiced trying to weave faster, and without that, she might well have failed. But she suspected her father had not been Elaida's only special addition to her test. Too often, her weaknesses had been laid bare by someone who knew them particularly well. The woman had tried to *make* her fail.

"Only after you have eaten," she said.

CHAPTER
11

Just Before Dawn

By the light of a single lamp and the low fire on her narrow hearth, Moiraine dressed herself carefully, making an effort to stifle her yawns. It needed effort. A night of contemplation meant a night of no sleep; her eyes were grainy, her limbs leaden. Well, sleep would have been beyond her in any case, simply because of what lay ahead this morning. Oh, why had she not argued Siuan out of that mad prank? It was a question she had asked herself often during the night, and as foolish this time as the first. She rarely won arguments with Siuan.

If only Siuan were with her now. Contemplating the burdens and duties of an Aes Sedai turned inevitably to the task Moiraine meant to take up, and the scale of that search had loomed larger and larger as the night went on, until it reared before her like unscalable Dragonmount itself. Company would have helped. But the ritual was explicit. Each must be alone when they came for her. Missteps now brought no penalties beyond embarrassment, and likely a reputation as flighty dunces that they might never shake off—of course, they might already have achieved the reputation—yet it had seemed best to be beyond reproach as far as they could.

Once dressed, she laid out her few belongings on the bed, but except for a change of shift and stockings, she left the remaining garments in the wardrobe. They would be washed and put away against a novice gaining the ring who could wear them. None among those currently in white would be able to wear those dresses, without huge alterations, anyway, but no matter; the White Tower was patient. The little book was snug in her belt pouch, the safest place she could think of. She had just put her small rosewood box on the bed, containing the few pieces of jewelry she had brought with her to the Tower, when a knock came at the door, three firm raps. She jumped at the noise, and her heart fluttered. Suddenly, she was almost as nervous as before the test. It was very hard not to run to answer. Instead, she checked her hair carefully in the mirror on the washstand, used her hairbrush to tame a few strands that really did not need taming, laid the brush on the bed and only then went to the door.

Seven sisters awaited her in the night, one from each Ajah, all wearing their vine-covered shawls over silks or fine woolens, their faces ageless masks. So the ritual required. Elaida was the Red, but Moiraine managed to meet the woman's stern gaze levelly, her features smooth. Well, as smooth as she could make them. Another hour, or just a little more, and they would be equals, at least to some degree. Never again would Elaida be able to make her quail.

Without a word, she stepped outside, closing the door behind her for the last time, and wordlessly they formed a ring around her, escorting her along the dark gallery to Siuan's door. Silence was required. Jeaine, a slim, copper-skinned Domani, knocked three times, the green fringe of her shawl swaying. Siuan opened the door so quickly she must have been waiting on her toes for the third knock. The ring of sisters parted to let her in, and her eyebrow twitched at the sight of Elaida, but at least she did not grimace, the Light be thanked. Moiraine clenched her jaw to suppress a yawn. She *would* finish without breaking the proprieties.

With the soft brush of their slippers on floor tiles they passed along corridors of the Tower where nothing moved save themselves and the flames flickering atop the standlamps. Moiraine was surprised not to see any servants. Much of their work was done in the hours before the sisters rose or after they retired for the night. In silence they climbed down into the levels beneath the Tower, along well-lighted passages and past dark. The doors to the chamber where she and Siuan had been tested stood open wide, but there in the corridor, they all stopped, the ring of Aes Sedai breaking apart to form a line behind the two of them as they turned to face the gaping doorway.

"Who comes here?" Tamra's voice demanded from within.

"Moiraine Damodred," Moiraine answered clearly, and if her face remained smooth, her heart fluttered. With joy, this time. Siuan spoke her own name at the same instant, defiance touching her tone, if only lightly. She insisted that Elaida would still find some way to rob them of the shawl, if she could.

Their teachers had never brought up the matter of precedence—perhaps they had never expected the two of them to march this far in complete lockstep—but Moiraine heard someone's breath catch behind her, and when Tamra spoke again, it was after a pause so slight that she might have imagined it.

"For what reason do you come?"

"To swear the Three Oaths and thereby claim the shawl of an Aes Sedai," they answered together. Breach of the proprieties or not, they intended to do everything together this morning insofar as possible.

"By what right do you claim this burden?"

"By right of having made the passage, submitting myself to the will of the White Tower."

"Then enter, if you dare, and bind yourself to the White Tower."

Hand in hand, they entered. Together. A smooth face and a steady tread, neither hurrying nor lagging back. The will of the Tower awaited them in the flesh.

Tamra, in pale brocaded blue with the Amyrlin's striped stole around her neck, stood framed by the oval *ter'angreal,* its colors slowly shifting through silver and gold, blue and green, with Aeldra at her side in a darker shade of blue, holding a black velvet cushion in both hands. Along the circular wall stood the shawl-draped Sitters in the Hall of the Tower, grouped by Ajah, and in front of each three Sitters, two more sisters of that Ajah, shawled and each with another shawl folded over one arm. Expressionless eyes watched Siuan and Moiraine cross the floor.

The *ter'angreal* presented the first problem to their plan. The tall oval was too narrow for both to pass through at once, not without squeezing together, and that hardly conformed to the required dignity. This was one argument Moiraine had won. Siuan gave her a look—it seemed impossible those blue eyes could turn sharp without altering her smooth expression, yet they did—and, gathering her skirts, stepped through with Moiraine following behind. Side by side they knelt in front of the Amyrlin Seat.

From the velvet cushion Aeldra held, Tamra took the Oath Rod, a smooth ivory-white cylinder a foot long and only slightly thicker than Moiraine's wrist. A *ter'angreal*, the Oath Rod would bind them to the Three Oaths, and thus to the Tower.

For an instant, Tamra hesitated, as though uncertain which of them to bind first, but only for an instant. Moiraine promptly raised her hands in front of her, palms upward, and Tamra placed the Rod there. This was the price Siuan had exacted, a favor to be granted, for Moiraine's yielding precedence through the oval. Needless to say, she had not revealed her "favor" until Moiraine accepted. She would become Aes Sedai first by minutes. It was so unfair!

But there was no time for thinking of how she should have known Siuan was up to something when she gave in so easily. The glow of *saidar* surrounded Tamra, and she touched the Oath Rod with a thin flow of Spirit.

Moiraine closed her hands around the Rod. It felt like glass, only somehow smoother. "Under the Light and by my hope of salvation and rebirth, I vow that I will speak no word that is not true." The Oath settled on her, and suddenly the air seemed to press harder against her skin. *Red is white,* she thought. *Up is down.* She could still think a lie, but her tongue would not work to utter it now. "Under the Light and by my hope of salvation and rebirth, I vow that I will make no weapon for one man to kill another." The pressure grew abruptly; it felt as though she had been sewn into an invisible garment, much too tight, that molded her from the crown of her head to the soles of her feet. To her chagrin, sweat popped out on her forehead, yet she managed to keep her face calm. "Under the Light and by my hope of salvation and rebirth, I vow that I will never use the One Power as a weapon except against Darkfriends or Shadowspawn, or in the last extreme of defending my life or that of my Warder or another sister." That garment shrank to still greater snugness, and she breathed heavily through her nose, clamping her jaws to keep it from becoming a gasp. Invisible and utterly flexible, yet oh, so tight! This feeling that her flesh was being compressed would fade, but not entirely for a whole year. Light! She wondered how Elaida had enjoyed taking that last oath, with its mention of Warders. The Three Oaths remained unchanged whatever Ajah you intended to join. Thinking of that helped, a little.

"It is half done," the Amyrlin intoned, "and the White Tower is graven on your bones." But she did not complete the ceremony. Instead, she took the Rod and placed it in Siuan's hands. Moiraine fought down a smile. She could have kissed Tamra.

There was no sweating or gasping from Siuan. She rendered the Oaths in a clear, strong voice, never so much as blinking as each settled onto her. No physical hardship could faze Siuan, who had never wept until after Elaida was gone, had never shed a tear until they left Merean's study. Siuan had the heart of a lion.

"It is half done, and the White Tower is graven on your bones," Tamra said, replacing the Oath Rod on Aeldra's cushion. "Rise now, Aes Sedai, and choose your Ajah, and all will be done that may be done under the Light."

However much equanimity Siuan had shown swearing the Oaths, she moved no less stiffly than Moiraine as they rose and curtsied formally to Tamra, bending to kiss her Great Serpent ring.

Together, they walked toward the Blue sisters. Slowly, with as much grace as they could muster, and not holding hands; that would never have done, not now. Like any Accepted, they had often discussed which Ajah they might enter, arguing merits and faults as though they knew more than the surface, yet for the last year or more, those discussions had been merely to prove a choice already made. The Blue sought to right wrongs, which was not always the same as seeking justice, like Greens and Grays. "Seekers after Causes," Verin had called Blues, and the capitals were there to be heard in her voice. Moiraine could not imagine belonging elsewhere. Siuan was smiling, which she should not have done. But then, so was she herself, she realized, and she could not make it go away.

Once their direction became clear, the sisters from other Ajahs began making their courtesies to the Amyrlin and departing, first the Yellows, then the Greens, gliding from the chamber with their Sitters leading the way in regal procession. The Browns left, and then the Whites. What set the order, Moiraine did not know, but once the Reds were gone, the last, Tamra glided from the chamber after them. What passed here now was for the Blue alone. Aeldra remained to watch.

The three remaining Sitters gathered around as copper-skinned Leane, willowy and as tall as most men, bent to lay the blue-fringed shawl around Moiraine's shoulders and Rafela, slim, dark and pretty, performed the same office for Siuan. Neither had the ageless face yet, but they wore dignity like cloaks. The Sitters were dignity incarnate.

Stout Eadyth, with white hair spilling to her waist, kissed Siuan lightly on both cheeks and then Moiraine, each time murmuring, "Welcome home, sister. We have waited long for you." Anlee, grave-faced and graying in green-slashed blue and almost as many rings and necklaces as Gitara had worn, repeated the kisses and the words, and then Lelaine, whose solemn expression broke into a smile as she spoke. Lelaine became a great beauty when she smiled.

"Welcome home, sister," Leane said, bending once more to kiss Moiraine. "We have waited long for you."

Aeldra also kissed their cheeks and spoke words, then surprisingly added, "You each owe me a pie, made with your own hands. It's customary among us for the sixth sister who gives you the welcome kiss."

Moiraine blinked and exchanged glances with Siuan. Was the ceremony done so abruptly? A *pie*? She doubted Aeldra would be able to eat hers. She had never cooked anything in her life.

Eadyth clicked her tongue and adjusted her shawl along her arms. "Really, Aeldra," she said firmly. "Just because these two have chosen to step beyond the bounds in so many ways is no reason for you to forget *your* dignity. Now." Long blue silk fringe swung as she raised her hands. "I charge you, Leane Sharif, escort Moiraine Damodred that the White Tower may see that a Blue sister has come home. I charge you, Rafela Cindal, escort Siuan Sanche that the White Tower may see that a Blue sister has come home."

Gathering Aeldra, Eadyth led the other Sitters from the chamber, but it seemed the rest of them were not entirely done.

"Custom is a precious thing that should not be allowed to wither," Rafela said, eyeing Siuan and her each in turn.

"Will you proceed to the Blue Ajah quarters clad in the Light, as ancient custom required?" Siuan clutched at her shawl as though she never meant to remove it, and Rafela added hastily, "And in your shawl, of course. To show that you need no protection beyond the Light and the shawl of an Aes Sedai."

Moiraine realized she was clutching her own shawl in identical fashion, and made her hands relax, stroking the silk softly with her fingers. The Three Oaths had made her Aes Sedai, yet she had not felt Aes Sedai until the shawl was put onto her shoulders. But if she was required to go out in public wearing nothing else . . . ! Oh, Light, now her face was turning hot! She had *never* seen an Aes Sedai blush.

"Oh, do give over, Rafela," Leane said with a quick, reassuring smile shared between Moiraine and Siuan. She had been Accepted with them for a time, and by the warmth of that smile it seemed their friendship might be taking up where it had left off. "A thousand years ago, women came to be raised clad in the Light and left the same way— everyone here would have been—but the only part of that custom left is keeping the hallways clear until you reach the Ajah's quarters," she explained briskly. Leane did everything briskly. "I doubt anyone but a few Browns even remembers the custom. Rafela is half mad with trying to bring back dead customs. Don't deny it, Rafela. Remember the apple blossoms? Even the Greens don't remember what battle that was supposed to commemorate."

Strangely, though Rafela had reached the shawl a year before Leane, she only sighed. "Customs should not be forgotten," she said, but without any force.

Leane shook her head. "Come along. I know you must want your breakfast, but that has to wait on a few things, including this walk. Which will not include all of the public corridors," she added, cocking an eyebrow at Rafela. "Nor will we stop at each Ajah's quarters calling for them to come out and see a sister of the Blue." Shaking her head, she herded them through the doors, channeling briefly to swing them shut. "I've never been so embarrassed in my life. You should have been the one blushing, Rafela. Verin told her she had such a sweet voice, she should take up singing. One Red came out to tell us to stop caterwauling and go away. And the Greens! Some Greens have a . . . rough . . .

sense of humor." Whether or not Rafela had blushed then, color tinged her cheeks faintly now.

How rough had those Greens' sense of humor been, Moiraine wondered. At least Rafela's blushes made her stop worrying about her own. Of course the sisters would present a different face to each other than they did to those who did not wear the shawl. Which she did, now. It made her feel inches taller, even if Leane did tower head and shoulders above her. The other woman had shortened her stride, yet Moiraine still had to trot to keep up as they climbed back up through the basements to Tower corridors empty of life save for them. The hallways were seldom crowded, but the absence of people made them seem cavernous. Imagining the Tower completely empty became all too easy. It would be, one day, if matters continued as they were.

"Is the ceremony done with this walk?" she asked. "The Blue Ajah part, I mean. May we ask questions?" She supposed she should have asked that first, but she wanted the sound of voices to chase away ill thoughts.

"Not completely done," Leane replied, "but you can ask whatever you like. Some questions, though, can't be answered till you've met the First Selector, the head of our Ajah."

"You must never reveal that title," Rafela put in quickly.

Moiraine nodded, though she already knew that. Accepted were taught that every Ajah had secrets, as Rafela had to be aware. More than one sister had told Moiraine that she would have almost as much to learn once she gained the shawl as before. She intended to step very carefully until she learned more.

"I have a question," Siuan said with a frown. "Are there many customs like this pie? I can cook, but my eldest sister did all the baking."

"Oh, yes," Rafela said happily, and she regaled them with arcane customs while they walked along the Tower's first level, some as silly as wearing blue stockings when leaving Tar Valon, some as sensible as refraining from marriage. Aes Sedai did marry now and then, but Moiraine could not see how that could end other than poorly. The torrent of information continued as they climbed one of the spiraling hallways, only stopping when they reached the plain, polished doors that led into the Blue quarters.

"You can hear the others later," Rafela said, shifting her shawl down to her arms. "Be sure to learn them all quickly. Some are enforced as strictly as Tower law. I think they all should be, but at least some are."

"Give over, Rafela," Leane said, and she and the dark sister each took a brass door handle and pushed one of the doors open.

They had not channeled. Perhaps that was another custom. Riding would be uncomfortable for a few days, and she intended using the time until she could leave the city to memorize those customs, at least those that were enforced. She was not about to have the beginning of her search delayed by something as ridiculous as not wearing all blue on the first day of the month. Light, surely they did not enforce that one. Safer to be sure, though.

She and Siuan stepped through the doorway, and stopped in surprise. The Blue was the second smallest Ajah, after the White, but every Blue sister currently in Tar Valon was lining the main corridor, all save Aeldra formally wrapped in their shawls.

CHAPTER
12

Entering Home

A naiya was the first to step forward and kiss their cheeks, saying, "Welcome home, sister. We have waited long for you. Aeldra told me how she stole my pies," she added, giving her shawl a twitch of irritation that was obvious pretense, betrayed by a laugh. "It wasn't fair of her to take advantage of her position that way."

"Or mine, perhaps, if I'd been a trifle quicker," Kairen said after giving the formal greeting. A beautiful woman, and not overly tall, her smile belied the coolness of her steady blue eyes. "May we at least hope you two bake poorly? Aeldra likes pranks almost as much as you two, and it would be nice to see her repaid properly."

Moiraine laughed and hugged Siuan. She could not help it. She truly had come home. *They* had come home.

The Blue quarters held none of the flamboyance of the Green's and Yellow's, though they were not so plain as the Brown's or the White's. The brightly colored winter wall hangings along the main corridor were scenes of spring gardens and fields of wildflowers, brooks running over stones and birds in flight. The stand-lamps against the pale walls were gilded, but quite simple in decoration. Only the floor tiles, in every shade of blue from a pale morning sky to the deep violet of twilight and laid in a wavy pattern, gave any hint of grandeur. Moving slowly along those waves, she and Siuan received the welcome kiss thirty-nine more times before reaching Eadyth and the other two Sitters.

"Rooms have been prepared for you," the round-faced sister told them, "along with proper clothing and some breakfast, but change and eat quickly. There are things I must tell you, things you must know before it is really safe for you to set foot outside our quarters. Or even to walk within it, in truth, though most are tolerant of a new sister. Cabriana, will you show them the way?"

A pale-eyed sister, light golden hair hanging almost to her waist, spread her blue-slashed skirts in a slight curtsy. Not all sisters taught classes by far, and Moiraine did not recognize her. There was a fierce directness in her gaze suitable for a Green, yet her tone was quite meek as she said, "As you say, Eadyth." And to Siuan and Moiraine, almost as meekly, "Will you come with me, please?" It was very odd, that blend of fierceness and . . . well, docility seemed the closest description.

"Is she the First Selector?" Moiraine asked cautiously as soon as they were out of Eadyth's earshot. And of anyone else's, she hoped. The sisters who had gathered were dispersing by ones and twos, removing their shawls.

"Oh, yes," Anaiya said, joining them with Kairen. Cabriana had her mouth open to answer, but she closed it without a trace of protest at being overridden. "It's unusual for the First Selector also to be a Sitter," Anaiya went on, "but unlike some, we Blues like to make full use of ability."

Folding her shawl and laying it across one arm, Kairen nodded. "Eadyth is perhaps the most capable Blue in the last hundred years, but if she were a Brown or a White, they'd let her potter off wherever she wanted."

"Oh, yes," Cabriana said, making a tssking sound. "Some of the Brown Sitters have been disgraceful. For Sitters, at least. But Browns always let their minds wander. In any case, you may rest assured that whatever talents you have, a use will be found for them."

Disliking the sound of that, Moiraine exchanged a guarded glance with Siuan. Well, neither of them had any special abilities. But what danger was Eadyth going to warn them about? A danger even here. She wanted to ask the three sisters escorting them down the hallway, but she was certain the information had to come from Eadyth, and in private; otherwise she would simply have told them then and there. Light! Their new home might have as many undercurrents as the Sun Palace. A definite time for caution. A time to listen and observe and say little.

The apartments chosen for Siuan and her were side by

side a little off the main corridor, each containing a spacious bedchamber, a large sitting room, a dressing room, and a study, with fireplaces of carved marble whose crackling fires had taken the chill from the air. The polished wall panels were bare, but patterned carpets, some fringed, from half a dozen countries lay on the blue-tiled floors. The furniture was disparate, too, here a table inlaid with mother-of-pearl in a fashion used in Cairhien a hundred years ago, there a chair with vine-carved legs from the Light alone knew where, and the lamps and mirrors in as many styles as there were lamps and mirrors, but nothing was chipped or cracked and every piece of wood or metal had been polished till it shone softly. The belongings they had left laid out in the Accepted's quarters had been brought up, and Moiraine's own brush and comb on the washstand, her blackwood lapdesk on the writing table in the study, her jewelry box on a side table in the bedchamber, already put her mark on her rooms.

"We thought you'd like to be close together," Anaiya said when they finished up in Moiraine's sitting room. Kairen and Cabriana stood flanking her on the scroll-worked carpet, and looking to her as often as at Siuan or Moiraine, as well. They talked among themselves with the ease of long friendship, yet Kairen and Cabriana clearly took their lead from Anaiya. It was quite subtle, but obvious to eyes trained in the Sun Palace. Not that it meant anything—in any group there was always one who took the lead—but Moiraine filed it away.

"You can choose other rooms, if you wish," Kairen added. "We have all too many empty, though I fear some are as dusty as the worst of the basements." She was leaving Tar Valon soon, had spoken casually of some business she had in Tear. Could she be one of Tamra's searchers? There was no way to know. Aes Sedai were always leaving the Tower, and others returning.

"If you want to change rooms, I can arrange for the cleaning," Cabriana said, gathering her skirts as if to see to it immediately. She sounded almost anxious! Why was she behaving so strangely? Plainly she was the low woman among the three, yet she acted the same way toward Siuan and her, too.

"Thank you, no." Fingering the lace edging a chair's

cushion, she tried to say the rooms were very nice—the three sisters had seen to preparing everything, though the carpets and furnishings were a gift from the Ajah—but her tongue refused to form the lie, so she settled for, "These are more than adequate." Every last cushion in the rooms had lace ruffles, and so did the coverlets on the beds *and* the pillowcases. Some of the *ruffles* seemed to have ruffles! The rooms would be much more than adequate once she got rid of all those frills. Siuan had actually smiled at the lace on her bed, as though she would enjoy sleeping in a sea of froth. Moiraine shuddered at the thought.

She offered tea or hot spiced wine before realizing she had no idea how to procure either, but Anaiya said that they must be eager to change and have breakfast, with the other two nodding agreement, and they gathered their skirts together.

"Food can wait," Siuan said as soon as the door closed behind the three sisters. "Eadyth first. Have you winkled out any hint of what she has to tell us? It sounds like your Game of Houses, to me."

"Eadyth first, breakfast later," Moiraine agreed, though the smell of warm porridge and stewed apricots from the cloth-covered tray on a side table made her mouth water. "But I have no clue, Siuan. None." Yet it *was* reminiscent of *Daes Dae'mar.*

Four dresses of fine blue wool, plain but well cut, were hanging in the dressing room, two of them with skirts divided for riding, and she changed into one with a full skirt and left the banded Accepted's dress folded in the wicker laundry basket. The small notebook she transferred from the white belt pouch that would be taken away to the plain blue pouch she found in the capacious wardrobe. Even here, perhaps especially here, there seemed no safer place than on her own person. Unsurprisingly, the new dress fit perfectly. It was said the Tower knew more of its initiates than their seamstresses and hairdressers combined. Not that she had had either in some time, of course, a lack she intended to remedy. The seamstress, at least. She had grown accustomed to wearing her hair loose, but she would need more than four dresses before she left Tar Valon, and in better than wool. Silk was hardly cheap, but it did wear wonderfully.

From her carved jewelry box, she took her favorite piece,

a *kesiera*. She had regretted not being able to wear that
here, but even after six years her hands remembered how
to weave the thin gold chain into her hair so the small sap-
phire hung in the middle of her forehead. Studying herself
in a wall mirror with a scroll-worked wooden frame, she
smiled. She might lack the ageless face yet, but now she
looked the Lady Moiraine Damodred, and Lady Moiraine
Damodred had navigated the Sun Palace where hidden currents could pull you under even at fifteen or sixteen. Now
she was ready to navigate the currents here. Settling her
blue-fringed shawl on her shoulders, she went in search of
Siuan, and met her in the hall, wrapped in her own shawl
and coming the other way.

The first sister they saw, Natasia, a slim Saldaean with
dark tilted eyes and high cheekbones who was a lenient
teacher, gave them directions to Eadyth's rooms with a twist
of distaste on her full lips. Moiraine wondered whether Natasia had some dislike for Eadyth, which it surely would be
odd for her to display openly, but Eadyth herself imitated
the expression with near exactness as she showed them to
tall, cushioned chairs before her sitting room's broad fireplace, where flames danced. And then she stood warming
her hands as though reluctant to speak. There was no offer
of tea or wine, or any sort of welcome. Siuan fidgeted impatiently on the edge of her chair, but Moiraine schooled
herself to stillness. With difficulty, but she did it. The tightness of the Three Oaths was particularly harsh, sitting. Be
quiet, listen, and observe.

Eadyth's sitting room was larger than theirs, with a cornice carved in rolling waves, and two tapestries, of flowers
and brightly colored birds, on the walls, though her stand-
lamps were as plain. The massive furnishings were of dark
wood inlaid with ivory and turquoise, except for one delicate little table that appeared to be carved ivory or bone.
However long Eadyth had occupied these rooms, she had
added few personal touches here, just a tall vase of glistening yellow Sea Folk porcelain, a wide bowl of hammered
silver, and a pair of crystal figures, a man and a woman
each reaching a hand toward the other, on the mantel above
the fireplace. All of which told her nothing except that the
white-haired sister had good taste and restraint. Be silent,
listen, and observe.

Squirming on her seat cushion, Siuan appeared about to stand when Eadyth finally turned to face them. Folding her arms beneath her breasts, she took a deep breath. "For six years you have been taught that the second greatest rudeness is to speak directly of someone's strength in the One Power." Her mouth twisted again briefly. "In truth, I find it difficult to do so now, necessary though it is. For six years, you have been strongly discouraged from thinking of your own strength in the Power or anyone else's. Now, you must learn to compare your strength to that of every sister you meet. In time, it will become second nature, and you will do it without thought, but you must be very careful until you reach that point. If another sister stands higher than you in the Power, whatever her Ajah, you must defer to her. The higher she stands above you, the greater your deference. Failure in that is the third greatest rudeness, and third only by a hair. The most common reason for new sisters to be given penance is a misstep of that sort, and since the penance is set by the offended sister, it is seldom light. A month or two of Labor or Deprivation is the least you can expect. Mortification of the Spirit and Mortification of the Flesh are not unheard of."

Moiraine nodded slowly. Of course. That explained Elaida's deference to Meilyn, and Rafela yielding to Leane. And Cabriana; Cabriana was not very strong at all. That thought came very hard. When the White Tower wanted to strongly discourage something, it was well and truly discouraged. Light, the Tower rooted something out of you, then made you use that very thing to determine precedence. What a tangle. At least she and Siuan were near identical in strength, and likely would be as they gained their full potential. They had moved in lockstep so far. It would have seemed unnatural if Siuan had been forced to defer to her.

"Do we have to obey them?" Siuan asked, finally giving in and standing, and Eadyth sighed heavily.

"I thought I was quite clear, Siuan. The higher she stands above you, the greater your deference. I truly dislike talking about this, so please don't make me repeat myself. It works the other way around as well, of course, but remember that it doesn't apply if your Ajah or the Tower has set someone above you. If you're attached to an embassy, for example, you obey the Tower's emissary as you would me, if she was barely allowed to test for Accepted. Now. Do you have that clear in your heads? Good. Because I myself feel an urgent need to clean my teeth." And she hustled them from her rooms as if she really did intend to rush for the salt and soda.

"I was scared half out my wits," Siuan said once they were back in the corridor, "but that wasn't so bad. I thought we'd have to start at the bottom, but we're not so far from the top already. In another five years, we'll be close." Whether or not they thought about it, everyone knew when they would reach their full strength; the length of time could vary considerably from woman to woman, but it was always a smooth climb in a straight line.

"I was frightened, too," Moiraine said with a sigh, "but it is not so simple as you make it sound. At what point does deference become obedience? Even if she did not call it so, that is what she meant. We must observe the other sisters closely, and until we know for certain, we must err on the side of prudence. A month from now, I mean to be leagues from Tar Valon, not sweating on a farm across the river."

Siuan snorted. "So we step carefully. What else have we been doing for six years? But it still could be worse. What say I bring my tray to your rooms and we breakfast together."

Before they reached their rooms, however, another Aes Sedai intercepted them, a tall, square-faced woman in sky-blue silk with her steel-gray hair in a multitude of blue-beaded braids that hung to her waist. Moiraine had been certain that every Blue in the Tower had been at the welcome, but she did not recall seeing this sister ever before. She made herself aware of the woman's ability, her strength, and realized that it was nearly as great as her own and Siuan's would be eventually. Surely more than simple deference was required here. Should she curtsy? She settled for waiting politely with her hands folded at her waist.

"I am Cetalia Delarme," the sister said in a strong Taraboner accent, eyeing her up and down. "By your description, the pretty little porcelain doll, you are Moiraine."

Moiraine stiffened. A . . . pretty . . . little . . . porcelain . . . *doll*? It was all she could do to keep her face smooth, to keep her hands from clutching her shawl in fists. The thought of that farm helped.

But Cetalia's attention had already left her. "Which makes you Siuan, no? I am told you are a great solver of puzzles. What do you make of this little puzzle?" she said, thrusting a thin stack of pages at Siuan.

Siuan frowned as she read, and so did Moiraine, reading past her friend's shoulder. Siuan riffled through the pages too quickly for her to catch everything, but it seemed to be nothing but the names of playing cards, in no particular order she could see. The Ruler of Cups was followed by the Lord of Winds, the Ruler of Flames by the Lady of Rods, but then it was the Five of Coins followed by the Four of Cups. A puzzle? It was nonsense.

"I'm not certain," Siuan said finally, handing the pages back. Which settled it. If the thing were a puzzle, she would have seen the solution.

"Oh?" That word held a world of disappointment, but after a moment, Cetalia went on, the beads in her braids rattling softly as she tilted her head thoughtfully. "You don't say you do not know, so you have the glimmer of something. Of what are you uncertain?"

"There's a game I've read about," Siuan said slowly, "a game wealthy women play with cards, called Arrays. You have to put the cards in descending order in one of a set of patterns, but only certain suits can be played on others. I think someone wrote down each card as it was played. In a winning game."

Cetalia arched one eyebrow. "You have only read of the game?"

"Fishermen's daughters can't afford playing cards," Siuan replied dryly, and Cetalia's eyes took on a dangerous look. For a moment, Moiraine thought a penance hovered.

But all the Taraboner sister said was "I'll wager Moiraine has played the Arrays, yet I suspect she would have called it just the nonsensical list of playing cards or some such. Most would. But you, who have only read of the game, deduced the correct answer. Come with me. I have some more puzzles I wish to test you on."

"I haven't had my breakfast yet," Siuan protested.

"You can eat later. Come." Obviously, *Cetalia* thought more than mere deference was due.

Watching a reluctant Siuan follow Cetalia up the corridor, Moiraine let herself glare at the woman's back. Surely that behavior at least skirted rudeness. Apparently there were gradations. Well, nuance was everything in the Sun Palace, too. They would only have to bear it a short time, though. Inside the week, they would be gone, and she for one did not intend to return until she was at her full strength. Except to let Tamra know where the boychild was, of course. Actually being the ones to find him would be wonderful.

Her own breakfast porridge still held enough warmth to be edible, and she settled gingerly onto a plump-cushioned chair at the table, but before she could take a second bite, Anaiya walked in. Anaiya was nearly as strong in the Power as Cetalia, so she set down her silver spoon and stood.

"I'd tell you to sit down and eat," the motherly woman said, "but Tamra sent a novice to fetch you. I told the child I'd carry her message because I wanted to offer you Healing. It can help with the tightness of the Oaths in some cases."

Moiraine reddened. Of course everyone knew by now. Light! "Thank you," she said, both for the Healing—the tightness did not loosen by a hair, but it was *much* more comfortable, after—and for the clue. If she did not have to stand for Anaiya, she surely did not have to obey her. Unless Anaiya was simply being courteous, of course. She very nearly sighed. More observation was in order before she reached any conclusions.

Leaving the Blue quarters with her shawl wrapped firmly around her shoulders—she did not mean to go without that just yet; for one thing, it helped with the chill—she wondered what Tamra wanted with her. Only one possibility came to mind. Now that she and Siuan were full sisters, Tamra might mean to put them among her searchers. After all, they already knew. Nothing else made sense. Her steps quickened eagerly.

"But I don't want a job," Siuan protested, her belly rumbling with hunger yet again. She felt wrung out after hours in Cetalia's rooms, so full of books and stacked boxes of papers that they seemed to belong to a Brown. And the woman seemed never to have heard of a chair cushion. Her chairs were hard as stone!

"Don't be ridiculous," the gray-haired sister said dismissively, crossing her legs. She tossed the last pages she had given Siuan carelessly onto a writing table already littered six deep with others. "You didn't do too badly for a beginner. I have need of you, and that is that. I expect you here at Second Rise tomorrow morning. Now go get something to eat. You are Aes Sedai, now; you cannot go around sounding like the leaky drain pipe."

There was no point in protesting again. The bloody woman had already made it clear that two protests in succession came dangerously close to rudeness in her book. Bloody, *bloody* woman! She let nothing of anger touch her face, a lesson learned long before Tar Valon. On the fishing docks, displaying anger or fear either one could lead to trouble. Sometimes it could lead to a knife in your back.

"As you say, Cetalia," she muttered, earning yet another raised eyebrow, and just managed not to stalk out of the woman's apartments. Outside, she did stalk, and the Dark One take anyone who did not like it!

Burn her, why had she been fool enough to let the woman goad her? Moiraine had counseled caution, and instead, she had tried to wipe the doubt from bloody Cetalia's bloody voice by thinking like Moiraine. Unskilled hands on the tiller put the boat aground when they did not capsize it. Her unskilled steering meant she would not be leaving the Tower any time soon. Not for years, until she was strong enough to tell Cetalia what she could do with her job. At least the woman had not gotten her claws on Moiraine. With her mind, she would have been a wonder as Cetalia's assistant.

Hungry or not, she went in search of Moiraine rather than dinner, to let her know she would be searching by herself. The sight of Moiraine always made her smile. Cetalia had been wrong in one particular. She was not a pretty little porcelain doll; she was a beautiful little porcelain doll. On the outside, anyway. Inside, where it counted, was another matter. The first time Siuan saw her, she had been sure the Cairhienin girl would crack like a spindle-shell in a matter of days. But Moiraine had turned out to be as tough as she herself if not tougher. No matter how often she was knocked down, she climbed back to her feet straightaway. Moiraine did not know the meaning of "give up." Which was why it was a surprise to find her slumped in a chair in her sitting room, her shawl slung over the chairback, with a sulky expression on her face. A green-glazed teapot on a tray gave off the smell of hot tea, but the white cups looked unused.

"What happened to you?" Siuan asked. "You haven't earned a penance already, have you?"

"Worse," Moiraine replied disconsolately. Her voice usually minded Siuan of silver bells, but Moiraine hated hearing that. "Tamra has put me in charge of distributing the bounty."

"Blood and bloody ashes!" Siuan tested the words on her tongue. There would be no switchings now for speaking like herself. She had heard Aes Sedai who could have made any dockman blush. She did seem to sense a faint taste of soap, though. "Does she suspect? Is she trying to make sure you can't interfere?" Maybe that was why Cetalia had latched hold of her. No, she had done well on the bloody woman's tests, the more fool her.

"I think not, Siuan. I was taught to manage an estate, though I only did it for a few months before coming to the Tower. She said that gave me all the skills I needed." Her mouth twisted wryly. "I was 'lying around loose,' as she put it, and I suspect she decided to give an onerous task to a Blue as a way of being fair. What about you? What sort of puzzles did Cetalia want you to look at?"

"A lot of old reports," Siuan grumbled, easing down onto a cushioned chair. If only her skin did not feel three sizes too small! Without asking, she poured herself a cup of tea. They never asked about things like that. "She wanted me to puzzle out what happened forty or fifty years ago in Tarabon and Saldaea and Altara." As soon as the words were out of her she wanted to clap a hand over her mouth, but it was too late for that.

Moiraine sat up straight, suddenly very interested. "Cetalia heads the Blue Ajah eyes-and-ears." It was not a question. Trust her to see straight to the heart right away.

"Don't even whisper that. The bloody woman will boil me down like an oil fish if she learns I let it slip. She'll probably have it anyway, but I don't want to give her cause before she finds it." She certainly would, if today had been any guide. "Look now, handing out the bounty can't last more than a few months. After, you're free to go. Let me know where you're going, and if I learn anything, I'll try to get word to you." The Blue had an extensive network of eyes-and-ears, as useful for passing messages out as for sending reports in.

"I do not know that I can afford a few months," Moiraine said in a small voice, dropping her eyes, very unlike herself. "I. . . . I have been keeping a secret from you, Siuan." But they never kept secrets from each other! "I am very afraid the Hall means to put me on the Sun Throne."

Siuan blinked. Moiraine, a queen? "You'd make a wonderful queen. And don't bring up those Aes Sedai queens who came to bad ends. That was a very long time ago. There's hardly a ruler anywhere who doesn't have an Aes Sedai advisor. Who's ever said a word against them except the Whitecloaks?"

"It is a long step from advisor to queen, Siuan." Moiraine sat up, carefully arranging her skirts, and her voice took on that infuriatingly patient tone she used explaining things. "Obviously, the Hall thinks I could take the throne without bringing mobs into the streets, but I do not want to take the chance they are wrong. Cairhien has endured enough these last two years without that. And even if they are right, no one has ruled Cairhien for long without being willing to stoop to kidnapping, assassination and worse. My great-grandmother, Carewin, ruled more than fifty years, and the Tower calls her a very successful ruler because Cairhien prospered and had few wars under her, but her name is still used to frighten children. Better to be forgotten than remembered like Carewin Damodred, but even with the Tower behind me, I will have to try matching her if the Hall succeeds." Suddenly, her shoulders slumped, and her face broke close to tears. "What can I do, Siuan? I am caught like a fox in a trap, and I cannot even chew off my own foot to escape."

Setting her teacup on the tray, Siuan knelt beside Moiraine's chair and put her hands on the other woman's shoulders. "We'll find a way out," she said, putting far more confidence into her voice than she felt. "We'll find a way." She was a little surprised the First Oath allowed her to say those words. She could imagine no way out for either of them.

"If you say so, Siuan." Moiraine did not sound as if she believed, either. "There is one thing I can remedy. May I offer you Healing?"

Siuan could have kissed her. In fact, she did.

There was still considerable snow close to the mountains that rose up ahead of Lan, and the trampled tracks of a large body of men lay clear beneath the afternoon sun, leading straight across the hills toward the cloud-capped heights that reared higher and higher the deeper you looked. He raised his looking glass, but he could discern no movement ahead. The Aiel must already be into the mountains. Cat Dancer stamped a hoof impatiently.

"Are those the Spine of the World?" Rakim called in that rasping voice. "Impressive, but somehow I thought they'd be taller."

"That's Kinslayer's Dagger," a well-traveled Arafellin laughed. "Call them the foothills to the Spine and you won't be far wrong."

"Why are we just standing here?" Caniedrin demanded, low-voiced enough not to be called down for it but loud enough for Lan to hear. Caniedrin liked to press the edges where he could.

Bukama relieved him of the necessity to answer. "Only fools try fighting Aiel in mountains," he said loudly. Twisting toward Lan in his saddle, he lowered his own voice to a near whisper, and the creases of his permanent scowl deepened. "The Light send Pedron Niall doesn't choose now to paint his face." Niall, Lord Captain Commander of the Children of the Light, had the command today.

"He won't," Lan said simply. Only a handful knew war as well as Niall. Which meant that this particular war might very well end this day. He wondered whether it would be called a victory. Sliding the looking glass back into its saddle-case, he found himself looking north. Feeling the pull, an iron filing feeling the lodestone. It was almost pain, after so long. Some wars could not be won, yet they still must be fought.

Studying his face, Bukama shook his head. "And only a fool jumps from one war straight into another." He did not bother to speak softly, and several Domani in Lan's sight gave him odd looks, clearly wondering what Bukama was talking about. No Borderlander needed to wonder. They knew who he was.

"A month or two will rest me, Bukama." That was how long it would take to ride home. A month, with luck.

"A year, Lan. Just one year. Oh, all right. Eight months." Bukama made that sound a great concession. Perhaps he felt tired? He had always seemed made of iron, but he was no longer young.

"Four months," Lan conceded. He had borne waiting two years; he could bear another four months. And if Bukama still felt weary then. . . . That was a chasm he would have to cross when he came to it.

As it happened, Niall had not chosen to become a fool, which was very well indeed, given that above half the army had already departed in the belief the victory had been won days ago if not when the Aiel first began their retreat. And they were calling it a great victory. At least, those who had not fought were, the hangers-on and bystanders, and the historians already writing as if they knew everything. Lan was willing to let them. His mind was already two hundred leagues to the north.

Saying their goodbyes, he and Bukama turned their faces southward toward softer lands, avoiding Tar Valon altogether. It was a great and wondrous city by all accounts, but too full of Aes Sedai for any comfort. Bukama talked animatedly of what they might see, in Andor and perhaps Tear. They had been in both lands, but contending with Aiel, they had not seen even the fabled Stone of Tear or any of the great cities. Lan did not speak at all unless Bukama addressed him. He felt the pull of home sharply. All he wanted was a return to the Blight. And no encounters with Aes Sedai.

CHAPTER
13

Business in the City

They could have had food brought to their rooms,
but after Moiraine Healed Siuan, they went down
to the first sitting of dinner. Neither was willing to
miss her first meal as Aes Sedai in the sisters' main dining
hall, where Accepted came only by rare invitation and novices only to serve at table. It was a spacious high-ceilinged
room, colorful winter tapestries decorating the white walls,
broad cornice gleaming under a weight of gold leaf. The
square tables, their slender legs elegantly carved, were only
large enough for four, and most spaced far apart for privacy of conversation, though today some were placed together to accommodate larger groups. The only women in
the room wearing their shawls, they attracted looks from
other sisters, not to mention a few amused smiles. Moiraine
felt her cheeks heating, but it would take more than smiles
to make her give up wearing the shawl every time she left
her rooms. More than outright laughter. She had worked too
hard to earn it. Siuan marched across the bright floor tiles,
patterns of all the Ajah colors, with a queenly grace, casually adjusting her shawl along her arms as though to draw
attention to it. Siuan was seldom shy.

There were no benches here, but low-backed chairs
carved to match the table legs, and where, in their own
dining hall, Accepted ate whatever the kitchen prepared, a
young serving woman with the Flame of Tar Valon on her
breast curtsied before reciting what the kitchens here had to
offer in the singsong voice of one who made the same reci-
tation often. Where Accepted ate on heavy glazed pottery
and had to serve and clear away their own plates, the same

serving woman brought their food on a ropework silver tray, in dishes of thin white Taraboner porcelain impressed with the Flame of Tar Valon all around the rim. Tarabon's work could not compare with what came from the islands of the Atha'an Miere, but it was hardly inexpensive.

Siuan complained that her fish was too heavily seasoned, yet she left nothing except the bones, and looked around as though thinking of asking for another. Moiraine had a rich soup of vegetables and beef, but she found she had little appetite, and in the end ate only a small piece of dark bread and drank a single cup of tea. She had to escape, but there was no escape. Just walking away from a task assigned by the Amyrlin Seat was unthinkable. Maybe the Hall would decide the plan was untenable. No one had approached her concerning the matter since Tsutama had asked whether she had thought of being Queen of Cairhien. They might decide so. It seemed a thin hope, but thin hopes were all she could find.

As soon as they returned to the Blue quarters, Eadyth summoned them to her rooms again and without ceremony handed each a letter-of-rights in the amount of one thousand crowns gold. "You will receive the same from the Tower each year on this day," she said, "or if you are not here, it will be deposited as you specify." The distaste of her earlier lecture had departed entirely. She wore a serene smile, serene and pleased at having gained two new Blues. "Spend wisely. You can obtain more if need be, but ask too often, and you will have to answer questions in the Hall. Believe me, being questioned in the Hall is never pleasant. Never."

Siuan's eyes grew very round reading the amount, and impossible as it seemed, wider still at mention of getting more. Few merchants cleared more gold in a year, and many minor nobles made do with far less, but the Tower could not afford to have sisters seen in poverty. The Sun Palace had taught Moiraine that power often grew from others deciding that you already had power, and an appearance of wealth could give that.

She had her own banker, but Siuan deposited her letter-of-rights with the Tower, in spite of an offered introduction. Siuan's father had not earned a thousand crowns over his entire life, and she was not about to put that sum at any risk whatsoever. Nothing Moiraine said could convince her.

Safety alone concerned her, and it seemed a banking house old enough to have loaned gold to Artur Hawkwing could not be challenged in that regard by the first bank founded after the Breaking.

Wearing her blue-fringed shawl displayed proudly on her shoulders, Moiraine hired a sedan chair in the great square in front of the Tower, where the milling midafternoon crowd of strollers and hawkers, tumblers and jugglers, musicians and barrowmen selling meat pies and roasted nuts, all kept their distance from the huge structure. Few people went nearer than a hundred paces unless they had business with the Tower, or wanted to present a petition. The two bearers, husky fellows in dark brown coats with their long hair neatly tied back, carried her smoothly through the streets, the lead man crying, "Make way for an Aes Sedai! Make way for an Aes Sedai!"

The shouting seemed to impress no one, and perhaps was not believed. Even with the heavy curtains tied back, the fringe on her shawl would remain hidden unless she propped her arms inelegantly on the windowsills. No one moved aside any faster than they did for wagon drivers' shouts and often more slowly, since the wagon drivers carried long whips and were not reluctant to use them. Even so, soon enough they reached what appeared to be a small palace, on a broad boulevard with tall leafless trees marching down the center strip, and unfastened the poles so she could open the door. The building was in a southern style, with a high white dome, and narrow spires at the four corners, and broad marble stairs climbing to a wide, white-columned portico, yet there was a restraint about it. The stone carvings, friezes of vines and leaves, were well done, yet simple and not overly plentiful. No one would leave money with a banking house that was poor, but neither would anyone with a bank that spent too lavishly on itself.

A doorman with two bands of red on his dark coatsleeves bowed her through the tall front doors and handed her over to a plain-coated footman, a pretty young man, if too tall, who gravely guided her to the study of Mistress Dormaile, a slim, graying little woman a full hand shorter than Moiraine. Her father had banked with Ilain Dormaile's elder brother, who still handled her own accounts in Cairhien, making her choice easy in Tar Valon.

A slight smile broke Mistress Dormaile's usual solemn expression when she saw the shawl, and she spread her dark, red-banded skirts in a precise curtsy, neither too brief nor too deep. But then, she had given the same courtesy even when Moiraine had come in an Accepted's dress. After all, she knew how much Moiraine had left with the bank on her first arrival in the city, and how much more her estates had sent over the years. Still, the smile was genuine.

"May I offer congratulations, Moiraine Sedai?" she said warmly, escorting Moiraine to a cushioned chair with a high, carved back. "Will you have spiced wine, or tea? Perhaps some honeyed cakes, or poppy seed?"

"The wine, thank you," Moiraine replied with a smile. "That will suffice." Moiraine Sedai. This was the first time anyone had called her that, and she rather liked the sound.

Once the other woman had issued orders to the footman, she took a chair facing Moiraine without asking. You did not require your banker to stand too far on ceremony. "I assume you have come to deposit your stipend." Of course a banker would know of that. "If you seek further information, I fear I put everything I knew into the letter I sent to you, and I have learned nothing more."

For an instant, Moiraine's smile froze in place. With an effort, she unfroze it, made her voice casual. "Suppose you tell it to me again. I may winnow out something hearing it fresh."

Mistress Dormaile inclined her head slightly. "As you say. Nine days ago a man came to me, a Cairhienin, wearing the uniform of a captain in the Tower Guard and giving the name Ries Gorthanes. He spoke with cultured accents, an educated man, perhaps even nobility, and he was tall, a good three hands or more taller than me, and broad-shouldered, with a soldier's bearing. He was clean-shaven, of course, and his face was well-proportioned, and good-looking despite a scar about an inch long, here." With one finger, she drew a line from the corner of her left eye back toward her ear.

Neither name nor description jogged anything in Moiraine's memory, not that she would have spoken if they had. She made a small gesture for the banker to go on.

"He presented an order purportedly signed and sealed by the Amyrlin Seat directing me to lay open your finances to him. Unfortunately for him, I know Tamra Ospenya's signature well, and the White Tower knows I would never reveal the affairs of my patrons in any respect. I had several footmen overpower him and lock him in an empty strong-room, and then I sent for real Tower Guards. I regret failing to take the opportunity to thrash his mistress or master's name out of him, but as you know, White Tower law takes a dim view of that."

The footman returned with an ornate silver pitcher and two silver goblets on a tray, and the banker fell silent until he had gone. "He escaped before the Guards arrived," she went on, pouring dark wine that gave off the sweet scent of spices. "A matter of bribery." A grimace of distaste twisted her mouth for a moment as she offered Moiraine a goblet with a small bow. "I had the young man involved strapped so I wager he still feels it when he sits down. I then hired him out as a bilgeboy on a rivership running ice peppers to Tear where he will be put ashore penniless, unless he persuades the captain to keep him on. I made sure of that by convincing her to give me his wages in advance. He is a pretty youth. He might persuade her. I think she had it in mind when she handed over the coins."

Directing a level look at the other woman across her goblet, Moiraine raised a quizzical eyebrow. She was quite proud of her outer coolness, as great as anything she had displayed while being tested.

"The false Guard captain broke Tower law, Moiraine Sedai," Mistress Dormaile blandly answered the unspoken question, "and I was required to hand him over to the justice of the Tower, but internal matters I prefer to keep internal. I tell you only because you were involved. You understand?"

Moiraine nodded. Of course. No bank could afford to have it known one of its employees took bribes. She sus-pected the young man had gotten off so lightly because he was someone's son or nephew, else he might well have floated downriver on his own. Bankers were hard folk.

Mistress Dormaile did not ask what Moiraine knew or thought of the matter. Such was no business of hers. Her face did not even show curiosity. This discretion was one reason Moiraine had never kept more than a little coin with the Tower. As a novice, without access to the city, it had been unnecessary, but her own sense of privacy made her continue the practice as Accepted. Tower law required equal representation of every Ajah in the Tower's bank, and now that she wore the shawl, she did not want her affairs known to other Blues, much less other Ajahs, especially after what she had just been told.

The only reason the Tower would have held back Mistress Dormaile's letter was that the Hall hoped to lull her into thinking they had decided against putting her on the Sun Throne. But they had made their first moves, or rather, since they would have been as careful as thieves trying to cut a well-guarded lady's purse, many more than the first. Enough for someone to puzzle out their intention. Nothing else explained a Cairhienin trying to find out how she was dispersing money, and to whom. Oh, Light, they were going to do it before she knew what was happening, unless she found a way out.

She let nothing show on her face, of course, merely sipping her wine, letting the warm sweetness slide down her throat, all outward serenity. "You have done very well by me, Mistress Dormaile, to the pain of your house. Please transfer a suitable recompense from my accounts to your own." Very properly, the banker demurred twice, bowing her head, before accepting with a show of reluctance that Moiraine barely noticed. Light, she had to find a way out!

She began laying plans. Not to run away, but to be ready. She signed over her letter-of-rights and, before leaving, gave instructions at which Mistress Dormaile displayed no hint of surprise. Perhaps that was because she also was Cairhienin and so accustomed to *Daes Dae'mar,* or maybe bankers were all stoic. Perhaps she had other Aes Sedai as patrons. If so, Moiraine would learn of it only if the sisters told her. The grave was less discreet than Ilain Dormaile.

Back in the Tower, she asked around until she settled on the name of a seamstress. No fewer than five Blues named Tamore Alkohima as the best in Tar Valon, and even those who spoke other names allowed that Tamore was very good, so the following afternoon, she and Siuan took sedan chairs to Mistress Alkohima's shop, with Siuan grumbling about the fare. Really. It was only a silver penny. It had taken considerable effort to induce Siuan to go with her. How *could* the woman think four dresses sufficient? She was going to have to learn not to be parsimonious.

Mistress Alkohima's establishment, its walls lined with

tall shelves bearing stacked bolts of silk and fine wool in every hue imaginable, was one of a number of large shops that occupied the ground floor of a building that seemed to be all curves. It suited Tamore very well. Fair-skinned for a Domani, she would have made Gitara seem almost boyish in comparison. When she came to greet them—their fringed shawls assured a personal greeting—rather than simply walking, she seemed to flow gracefully between the smaller shelves full of laces and ribbons, and the dressmaker's forms clothed in half-finished garments. Her half-dozen assistants all curtsied deeply, young pretty women garbed in finely sewn examples of their native lands' styles, each different, but there were no curtsies from the seamstress. She knew her place in this world. Her pale green dress, elegant and simple at the same time, spoke well of her talents, though it did cling in an alarming manner, molding her in a way that left no doubts of exactly what lay beneath the silk.

Tamore's languorous smile widened at hearing their order, and well it should have. Few of her patrons would come for an entire wardrobe in one visit. At least, it widened for Moiraine. Under prodding, Siuan had agreed on six dresses, to make up one for each day of the week with what she already had, but she wanted them in wool. Moiraine ordered twenty, half with skirts divided for riding, all in the best silk. She could have done with fewer, but the Hall might check. An order for twenty would make them think her settled in Tar Valon.

She and Siuan quickly found themselves in a back room, where Tamore watched as four of her assistants undressed them to the skin and measured them, turning them this way and that for the seamstress to see what she had to work with. Under almost any other circumstances, that would have embarrassed Moiraine near to death. But this was for a seamstress, and that made all the difference. Then it was time for the fabric to come out, for choices. Tamore knew what the fringe on their shawls meant, and shades of blue predominated.

"I want decent dresses, mind," Siuan said. "High necks, and nothing too snug." That with a pointed look at Tamore's garment. Moiraine nearly groaned. Light send Siuan did not mean to go on this way!

"I think perhaps this is too light for me," Moiraine murmured as a tall yellow-haired girl, in green with a square-cut neckline that displayed too much cleavage, draped sky-blue silk over her. "I was thinking of Cairhienin styles, without House colors or embroidery," she suggested. She could never wear Damodred colors inside the Tower.

"A Cairhienin cut, of course," Tamore said, thumbing her full lower lip thoughtfully. "That will suit you very well. But that hue is lovely against your pale skin. Half of your dresses must be of light color, and half embroidered. You require elegance, not plainness."

"Perhaps only a quarter in each?" A Cairhienin cut suited her very well? Was the woman implying she could not succeed in wearing a Domani dress? Not that she would. Tamore's garment was indecent! But there was the principle of the thing.

The seamstress shook her head. "At least a third in light colors," she said firmly. "At least. And half embroidered." Frowning slightly, she rubbed her thumb across her under-lip again.

"A third and half," Moiraine agreed before the woman could go higher, as she seemed to be considering. With a good seamstress, it was always a matter of negotiation. She could live with a little embroidery.

"Do you have anything cheaper, Mistress Alkohima?" Siuan demanded, frowning down at the fine blue wool draped on her. Light, she had been asking prices! No wonder the girls with her looked scandalized.

"Will you excuse me just a brief moment, Tamore?" Moiraine said, and when the seamstress nodded, she handed the length of silk to the Andoran girl and hurriedly took Siuan aside.

"Listen to me, Siuan, and do not argue," she whispered in a rush. "We must not keep Tamore waiting long. Do *not* ask after prices; she will tell us the cost after we make our selections. Nothing you buy here will be cheap, but the dresses Tamore sews for you will make you look Aes Sedai as much as the shawl does. And it *is* Tamore, not Mistress Alkohima. You must observe the proprieties, or she will believe you are mocking her. But try thinking of her as a sister who stands just a little above you. A touch of deference is necessary. Just a touch, but she will tell you what to wear as much as she asks."

Siuan scowled over her shoulder at the Domani woman. Light, she *scowled*! "And will the bloody shoemaker tell us what kind of slippers to buy and charge us enough to buy fifty new sets of nets?"

"No," Moiraine said impatiently. Tamore was only arching one eyebrow, yet her face might as well have been like a thunderhead. The meaning of that eyebrow was clear as the finest crystal. They had already made the seamstress wait too long, and there would be a price for it. And that scowl! She hurried on, whispering as fast as she could. "The shoemaker will make what we want, and we will bargain the price with him, but not too hard if we want his best work. The same with the glovemaker, the stockingmaker, the shiftmaker, and all the rest. Just be glad neither of us needs a hairdresser. The best hairdressers are true tyrants, nearly as bad as perfumers." Siuan barked a laugh, as if she were joking, but she would learn if she ever sat for a hairdresser, not knowing how her hair was to be arranged until the hairdresser was finished and allowed her to look in a mirror. At least, that was how it was in Cairhien.

Once the choices of colors had been agreed upon, and the forms of embroidery—negotiation was necessary even there, as well as on which dresses were to be embroidered—they still had to stay for the first dress to be cut and pinned on them, a task Tamore deftly performed herself with a pincushion fastened to her wrist. Moiraine quickly learned what the price would be for making the woman wait. The fabric she pinned for Moiraine was a blue even paler than the sky blue, almost a blue-tinged white, and the way she pinned Siuan's dark blue wool, it was going to be nearly as snug at bosom and hips as her own garment. It could have been worse. The seamstress could have "accidentally" stuck them a dozen times *and* demanded a pinning for every dress. But Moiraine was sure her first dresses would all be the lightest shades.

The prices Tamore mentioned, once the pinned garments had been slipped off them and onto dressmaker's forms, made Siuan's eyes pop, though at least she remained silent. She *would* learn. In a city like Tar Valon, one gold crown for a woolen dress and ten for a silk were reasonable from a seamstress of Tamore's quality. Still, Moiraine murmured that she would give a generous gratuity for speedy completion. Otherwise, they might not see anything for months.

Before leaving, she told Tamore that she had decided on five more riding dresses, in the strictest Cairhienin style, which was to say dark, though she did not put it that way, each with six slashes across the breast in red, green and white, far fewer than she had a right to. The Domani woman's expression did not alter at this evidence that she was a rather minor member of a noble House. Sewing for Aes Sedai would count with sewing for the High Seat of a House, or perhaps even a ruler.

"I would like them made last, if you please," Moiraine told her. "And do not send them. Someone will pick them up."

"I can promise you they will be last, Aes Sedai."

Oh, yes; her first dresses were going to be pale. But the second part of her plan was accomplished. For the moment, she was as ready as she could be.

CHAPTER
14

Changes

The sisters who had said there was almost as much to learn after gaining the shawl as before were proven right in short order. Moiraine and Siuan had learned the complexities of White Tower customs as Accepted, especially which ones had been in existence so long they had the force of law, and the penalties for violating them. Now Rafela and others spent hours instructing them in the long list of Blue Ajah customs, accreted over three thousand years. Siuan actually retained most of what Rafela had told them during their first walk to the Blue quarters, and Moiraine had to work hard to catch up. It would have been a shame to gain a penance for something so trivial as wearing red inside the Tower. Red gems were allowed, firedrops or rubies or garnets, but the color was forbidden in clothing, a matter of some long-standing animosity between the Blue and the Red, so old no one was actually certain what had begun it or when. Blue and Red opposed each other as a matter of course, at times bringing the Hall to a near standstill.

The very idea of enmity between Ajahs startled her, yet there were other oppositions. While the Green and the Blue had seen few breaks in their accord for several centuries, the situation was far different regarding other Ajahs. At the moment, there was a slight strain with the White, for reasons known only to the White, and something more tense with the Yellow, with sisters of each accusing sisters of the other of interfering with their actions in Altara some hundred years past. Strong custom forbade interference with another sister, a custom that provided the sole release from the customary deference. Outside the Tower, at least. And then there were the permutations. For example, the Brown supported the White against the Blue, but supported the Blue against the Yellow. For the time being, anyway. These things could last for centuries, or shift in the blink of an eye. It also was necessary to learn what antagonisms and rivalries existed between other Ajahs, too, where they were known. Each was a snare lying in wait for an unwary step or a careless word. Light, the tangle of it all made *Daes Dae'mar* child's play!

Siuan heard her recitations every night, just as they had as novice and Accepted, and she heard Siuan's, though there hardly seemed a point. Siuan never made any mistakes.

They found themselves studying the Power again, with Lelaine and Natasia and Anaiya and others taking turns, learning the Warder bond and other weaves not trusted to Accepted, including a few known only to the Blue. Moiraine found that very interesting. If the Blue included weaves among their Ajah secrets, surely the other Ajahs did as well, and if the Ajahs, perhaps individual sisters. After all, she had had one, her first learned, before coming to Tar Valon, and had carefully concealed it from the sisters. They had been aware the spark was already ignited in her, but she told them only about lighting candles and making a ball of light to find her way in the dark. No one lived in the Sun Palace without learning to keep secrets. Did Siuan have any secret weaves? It was not the sort of question you could ask your closest friend.

Although they knew enough now of *saidar* to learn quickly, there simply was too much for a day or a week. At least, Moiraine could not do it. The method of ignoring heat or cold turned out to be a trick of mental concentration simple enough once you knew how, or so Natasia pronounced.

"The mind must be as still as an unruffled pond throughout," she said pedantically, just as she lectured in the classroom. They were in her rooms, where almost every flat surface was covered with figurines and small carvings and painted miniatures. These lessons always took place in the teacher's rooms. "Focusing on a point behind your navel, in the center of your body, you begin to breathe at an unvarying pace, but not as normally. Each inhalation must take exactly the same length of time, and each exhalation, and between, for that same space, you do not breathe. In time, that will come quite naturally. Breathing so, focused so, soon your mind becomes detached from the outer world, no longer acknowledging heat or cold. You might walk naked in a blizzard or across a desert without shivering or sweating." Taking a sip of tea, Natasia laughed, her dark tilted eyes twinkling. "Frostbite and sunburn would still present difficulties, after a time. Only the mind is truly distanced, the body much less so."

Simple perhaps, yet for above a week Moiraine's focus might slip at any time, sitting at supper or walking down a corridor, and she would let out a gasp as the cold suddenly rushed in and bit down three times as hard as before she began the meditation. In public, all that huffing attracted stares from other sisters. She very much feared she was gaining a reputation as a dreamer. And as a constant blusher. It was hardly to be borne. Needless to say, Siuan picked up the trick straightaway and never shivered again that Moiraine saw.

The Feast of Lights came to mark the turning of the year, and for two days every window in Tar Valon shone brightly from twilight till dawn. In the Tower, servants entered chambers that had been unused for centuries, to light lamps and make sure they burned the whole two days. It was a joyous celebration, with processions of citizens carrying lamps through the night-cloaked streets and merry gatherings that frequently lasted until sunrise in even the poorest homes, but it filled Moiraine with sadness. Chambers unused for centuries. The White Tower was dwindling, and she could not see what was to be done about it. But then, if women who had worn the shawl two hundred years or more could find no solution, why should she be able to?

Many sisters received ornately inscribed invitations to balls during the feast, and quite a number accepted. Aes Sedai could like dancing as well as any other woman. Moiraine got invitations, too, from Cairhienin nobles of two dozen Houses and almost as many merchants wealthy enough to rub shoulders with the nobility. Only the Hall's plans for her could have placed so many powerful Cairhienin in the city at one time. She tossed the stiff white cards into the fireplace unanswered. A dangerous move in *Daes Dae'mar,* with no way to tell how it might be interpreted, but she was not playing the Game of Houses. She was hiding.

Surprisingly, their first dresses were delivered early on the first day of the feast. Either Tamore was eager for her gratuity, or more likely, she thought they would want the garments for feastday festivities. She came with two of her assistants to see whether any adjustments were necessary, but none were. Tamore was excellent at what she did. Moiraine had been right, though. The darkest of her six was in a hue little deeper than sky blue, and only two were embroidered, which meant nearly everything else would be. She would have to keep on wearing the woolens the Ajah had given her a while longer. At least all of her riding dresses would be dark. Even Tamore could not ask for a riding dress in too light a hue. Siuan's dresses, only one divided for riding, displayed all the elegance Tamore was capable of, making them suitable for a palace despite being wool, but they emphasized her bosom and hips quite strongly. Siuan affected not to notice, or perhaps did not. She really cared very little about clothing.

Some things were not easy for Siuan, either. She returned from Cetalia's apartments with a face that grew stiffer by the day. Every day she became more prickly and irritable, but she refused to reveal what the problem was, and even snapped at Moiraine when she persisted in asking. That was worrying; she could count on the fingers of one hand, with fingers left over, the times Siuan had gotten angry with her in six years. The day Tamore delivered the dresses, however, Siuan joined her for tea in her rooms before going down to supper, but instead of taking a cup, she flung herself down in a leaf-carved armchair and folded her arms angrily beneath her breasts. Her face was anything but stiff, and her eyes were blue fire.

"That bloody fangfish of a woman will be the bloody death of me yet," she growled. That half a week had undone every scrap of the sisters' hard work with her language. "Fish guts! She expects me to jump like a spawning redtail! I never jumped so fast when I was a—!" She gave a strangled grunt and her eyes popped as the First Oath clamped down. Coughing, her face turning pale, she pounded a fist on her chest. Moiraine hastily poured a cup of tea, but it was minutes before Siuan could drink. Her mind must have been racing for her to come that close.

"Well, not when I was Accepted, anyway," she muttered once she could speak again. "From the moment I arrive it's 'Find this, Siuan' and 'Do that, Siuan' and 'Aren't you finished yet, Siuan?' Cetalia snaps her fingers and bloody well expects me to jump."

"That is how things are," Moiraine said judiciously. The situation could have been much worse, but Siuan's mind apparently had changed on that point, and she did not want to start an argument. "It will not last forever, and only a handful of sisters stand so high above us."

"That's easy for you to say," Siuan grumbled. "You don't have bloody Cetalia snapping her fingers at you."

That was true, yet it hardly meant her task was easy. The new lessons left her little free time, but she had hoped distributing the bounty would allow her to search among the camps that still remained. Instead, for two or three hours each morning she sat in a windowless room, on the eighth level of the Tower, just large enough for a plain writing table and two straight-backed chairs. Mirrored stand-lamps of unadorned brass stood in the four corners, giving a good and very necessary light. Lacking them, the chamber would have been twilight dark at noon. Normally, a senior clerk sat there, but whoever that was, she or he had left no imprint on the room at all. Only inkwell, pen tray, sand jar and a small white bowl of alcohol for cleaning the pens sat on the table, and the pale stone walls were bare.

The considerably larger outer room was crowded by rows of high, narrow writing desks and tall stools, but as soon as she arrived, the clerks formed a line that stretched from her writing table and nearly circled their own room, bringing her lists of women who had received the bounty and reports on arrangements to send the money to women who had already left. The number of those reports was distressing. Few camps remained, and the last were melting away like frost in sunlight. None of the clerks used her second chair, only stood respectfully while she read each page and signed her approval at the bottom, then curtsied or bowed and made way for the next without a word. Very quickly she began to think it really might be possible to die of boredom.

She tried to make them arrange the distribution faster—

the Tower's vast resources could have seen to it in a week, surely; the Tower held hundreds more clerks—but clerks worked at their own pace. They even seemed to slow down after her suggestion of speed. She considered begging Tamra to release her from the task, but why put herself to useless effort? What better way to keep her shackled in Tar Valon until the Hall's schemes came to fruition? Boredom *and* frustration. Still, she had her plan. That helped, a bit. Slowly, a conviction settled in her. If worse came to worst, she *would* run, whatever penance that earned her. Any penance lay in the future, and must end eventually. The Sun Throne would be a sentence for life.

The day after the Feast of Lights, Ellid was summoned to her testing, though Moiraine only heard of it after. The beautiful Accepted who wanted to become a Green failed to come out of the *ter'angreal*. There was no announcement; the White Tower never flaunted its failures, and a woman dying in her test was counted a great failure on the Tower's part. Ellid simply disappeared, and her belongings were taken away. There was a day of mourning, however, and Moiraine wore white ribbons in her hair and tied a long, lace-edged white silk kerchief around each arm so they dangled to her wrists. She had never liked Ellid, but the woman deserved her grief.

Not every sister who was strong enough to make them jump showed any desire to do so. Elaida avoided them, or at least they did not see her again before hearing she had left to return to Andor. Even so, learning she was gone was a relief. She stood as high as they would one day, and could have made their lives a misery almost as badly as she had when they were novice and Accepted. Perhaps worse. The petty errands novice and Accepted took as expected would have been near a penance for them as Aes Sedai. Perhaps more than near.

Lelaine, who stood as high as Elaida and was a Sitter to boot, had them to tea several times, to ease the strain of the first weeks as she put it. Siuan got on very well with her, though she made Moiraine a little nervous with that penetrating gaze. It always seemed that Lelaine knew more of you than she revealed, that you had no secrets with her. But then, Siuan appeared unable to understand Moiraine's liking for Anaiya. It was not the Healing. Anaiya was warm and open, and made you feel that all would come out well in the end. Almost any conversation with Anaiya turned out comforting. Moiraine thought that in time she might become as close a friend as Leane, if not so close as Siuan.

That friendship with Leane took up right where it had left off, for her and Siuan both, and brought with it Adine Canford, a plump, blue-eyed woman with short-cut black hair who displayed not a hint of arrogance despite being Andoran. Of course, she was not very strong in the Power. It really was becoming second nature to consider that. They renewed acquaintance with sisters of other Ajahs who had been Accepted with them and found that in some cases friendship revived within a few words and in others had shrunk to mere amity, while a few had grown too accustomed to the gap between Aes Sedai and Accepted to close it again now they wore the shawl, too. It was enough. Friends lightened many burdens, even those they did not know of.

Friends or no friends, though, the days passed with glacial slowness. Meilyn finally departed the Tower, and then Kerene, followed in turn by Aisha, Ludice and Valera, but Moiraine's relief that the search was under way at last was tempered by frustration at being kept out of it. Siuan began to grow interested in her job, to the point where her complaints started to seem more for the form of the thing. She headed off to Cetalia's rooms earlier than need be, and often remained until the second or third sitting of supper. Moiraine had no such buffer. Her nightmares continued, of the babe in the snow and the faceless man and the Sun Throne, although not as frequently, save the last. Ever as bad, though. She banished most of the lace and ruffles from her rooms, which required only a visit to a cushionmaker and a small wait for their alteration by twos and threes. Not all, because of Anaiya's obvious if silent disappointment at seeing them go, so her bed remained an ocean of froth that made Siuan giggle with delight. But she spent more time in her other rooms, so the bed it had to be. After numerous efforts, she managed to bake a pie without burning it black, but Aeldra took one bite and turned pale green. Siuan produced a fish pie that the gray-haired sister declared quite tasty, only within the hour she was running for the privy and required Healing. No one accused them of doing anything deliberate, which they had not, but Anaiya and Kairen thought it an excellent repayment for greediness.

Only a week after Ellid, on High Chasaline, Sheriam was tested and passed. Technically, Siuan was the newest Blue by a hair, but Cetalia refused to lose her services for even a few hours, so it was Moiraine who laid the shawl on the fire-haired Saldaean's shoulders when she chose the Blue the following day, and escorted her beaming back to the Blue quarters for the welcome. Where Siuan managed to nip in for the sixth kiss. Sheriam was a very good cook, and loved to bake.

It was the Day of Reflection in Cairhien, yet Moiraine could not manage to dwell on her sins and faults. She and Siuan had regained a friend they had feared might be lost for a year. Siuan even suggested bringing Sheriam into their search, and talking her out of it required hours. It was not that Moiraine feared Sheriam would expose them to Tamra, but Sheriam had been one of the biggest gossips in the Accepted's quarters. She never told what she promised to keep hidden, yet she would be unable to resist giving hints of such a juicy secret, hints that she had a secret, as Siuan should have known very well. Let others know you possessed a secret, and some would work to learn it; that was a fact of nature. Sometimes Siuan did not known the meaning of caution. Sometimes? No; never.

Sisters began to talk of a resurgence in the Tower, with so many passing for the shawl in so short a time, and perhaps another one or two who might very soon. By custom, none spoke of Ellid, but Moiraine thought of her. One woman dead and three raised to the shawl in the space of two weeks, but the only novice to test for Accepted in that time had failed and been sent away, and not one name was added to the novice book, while above twenty novices too weak ever to reach the shawl were put out. Those chambers would remain unused for centuries more at this rate. Until they were all unused. Siuan tried to soothe her, but how could she be happy when the White Tower was destined to become a monument to the dead?

Three days later, Moiraine wished she had spent the Day of Reflection properly. She was not superstitious, but failure to do so always brought ill luck to someone you cared for, so it was said. She was at the second sitting of breakfast, slowly eating her porridge and fretting over the boredom of torture by clerk to come, when Ryma Galfrey glided into the dining hall. Slim and elegant in yellow-slashed green, much of a height with Moiraine, she was not one of those Moiraine needed to defer to, but she had a regal bearing accentuated by the rubies in her hair like a crown, and a haughty cast typical of Yellows to her face. Startlingly, she wove Air and Fire to make her voice clearly audible in every corner of the dining hall.

"Last night, Tamra Ospenya, the Watcher of the Seals, the Flame of Tar Valon, the Amyrlin Seat, died in her sleep. May the Light shine on her soul." Her voice was perfectly self-possessed, as though she had announced it would rain that day, and she waited only long enough to run a cool eye over the room to make sure her words had been absorbed before leaving.

A buzz of talk started up immediately at the other tables, but Moiraine sat stunned. Aes Sedai died before their time as often as anyone else, and sisters did not grow feeble with the years—death came in apparent full good health—yet this was so unexpected that she felt hit on the head by a hammer. The Light illumine Tamra's soul, she prayed silently. The Light illumine her soul. Surely it would. What would happen to the search for the boychild now? Nothing, of course. Tamra's chosen searchers knew their task; they would inform the new Amyrlin of their task. Perhaps the new Amyrlin would release her from her own labor, if she got to the woman before the Hall informed her of their scheme.

Self-disgust immediately stabbed her heart, and she pushed the bowl of porridge away, all appetite gone. A woman she admired with all her soul had died, and she thought of *advantage* in it! *Daes Dae'mar* truly was ingrained in her bones, and maybe all the darkness of the Damodreds.

She very nearly asked Merean for a penance, but the Mistress of Novices might give her something that would hold her in Tar Valon longer. Considering that just added to her guilt. So she set her own penance. Only one dress she owned came close to the white of grieving, the blue so pale it seemed more white tinged with blue, and she put that on for Tamra's funeral rites. Tamore had embroidered the garment front and back and sleeves with a fine, intricate blue mesh that looked innocent enough until she actually donned the dress. Then it seemed as blatant as what the seamstress herself had worn. No, not seemed; it was. She very nearly wept after examining herself in the stand-mirror.

Siuan blinked at the sight of her in the corridor outside their rooms. "Are you sure you want to wear that?" She sounded half-strangled. Long white ribbons were tied in her hair, and longer tied around her arms. The passing sisters all wore variations of the same. Aes Sedai never put on full mourning, except for Whites, who did not consider it so.

"Sometimes a penance is required," Moiraine replied, deliberately moving her shawl down into the crooks of her elbows, and Siuan asked no more. There were questions one asked, and questions one did not. That was strong custom. And friendship.

Wearing their shawls, every sister residing in the Tower gathered at a secluded clearing in a woody part of the Tower grounds, where Tamra's body lay on a bier, sewn into a simple blue shroud. The morning air was more than brisk—Moiraine was aware of that despite feeling no urge to shiver—and even the surrounding oaks were still leafless beneath a gray sky, their thick twisted limbs suitable framing for a funeral. Moiraine's garment earned more than a few raised eyebrows, but the sisters' disapproval was part of her penance. Mortification of the Spirit was always the hardest to endure. Strangely, the Whites all wore glossy *black* ribbons, yet it must have been an Ajah custom, for it garnered no frowns or stares from the other sisters. They must have seen it before. Any who wished were allowed to speak a prayer or a few words in memory, and most did. Only the Sitters spoke among the Reds, and then in very few words, but perhaps that was custom as well.

Moiraine made herself go forward and stand before the bier, shawl loosely draped, exposing herself, knowing she would be the focus of every eye. The hardest to bear. "May the Light illumine Tamra's soul, brightly as she deserved, and may she shelter in the Creator's hand until her rebirth. The Light send her a radiant rebirth. I cannot think of any woman I admired more than Tamra. I admire her and honor her still. I always will." Tears welled in her eyes, and not from the humiliation that stabbed her like long thorns. She had never really known Tamra—novices and Accepted never really knew sisters, much less the Amyrlin Seat—but, oh, Light, she would miss her.

According to Tamra's wishes, her body was consumed by flows of Fire, and her ashes scattered across the grounds of the White Tower by the sisters of the Ajah she had been raised from, the Ajah to which she had returned in death. Moiraine was not alone in weeping. Aes Sedai serenity could not armor against all things.

The rest of the day she wore that shaming dress, and that night burned it. She would never have been able to look at it again without remembering.

Until a new Amyrlin was raised, the Hall of the Tower reigned over the Tower, but there were increasingly strict measures in the law to insure they did not dally too long, and by the evening after Tamra's funeral, Sierin Vayu had been raised from the Gray. An Amyrlin was supposed to grant indulgences and relief from penances on the day she assumed the stole and the staff. None came from Sierin, and in the space of half a week, every last male clerk in the Tower had been dismissed without a character, supposedly for flirting with novices or Accepted, or for "inappropriate looks and glances," which could have meant anything. Even men so old their grandchildren had children went, and some who had no liking for women at all. No one commented on it, however. No one dared, not where it might come to Sierin's ears.

Three sisters were exiled from Tar Valon for a year, and twice Moiraine was forced to join the others in the Traitor's Court to watch an Aes Sedai stripped and stretched tight on the triangle, then birched till she howled. A ward that formed a shimmering gray dome over the stone-paved Court held in the shrieks till they seemed to crowd in on Moiraine, stifling thought, stifling breath. For the first time in a week she lost focus and shivered in the cold. And not only from the cold. She feared those screams would ring in her ears for a very long time, waking or sleeping. Sierin watched, and listened, with utter calm.

A new Amyrlin chose her own Keeper, of course, and could choose a new Mistress of Novices if she wished. Sierin had done both. Oddly, Amira, the stocky woman whose long beaded braids flailed as she worked the birch with a will, was a Red, and so was the new Keeper, Duhara. Neither law nor custom demanded that either Keeper or Mistress of Novices be of the Amyrlin's former Ajah, yet it was expected. But then, whispers told of considerable surprise when Sierin had chosen the Gray over the Red. Moiraine did not think any of Tamra's searchers would tell Sierin of the hunt for the boychild.

On the day after the second birching, she presented herself in the anteroom to the Amyrlin's study, where Duhara sat rigidly upright behind her writing table with a red stole a hand wide draped around her neck. Her dark dress was so slashed with scarlet it might as well have been all scarlet. A Domani, Duhara was slim and beautiful despite being near a hand and a half taller than she, but the woman's full lips had a meanness about them, and her eyes searched for fault. Moiraine reminded herself that, without the Keeper's stole, Duhara would have had to jump when she snapped her fingers, should she have chosen to. As she opened her mouth, the door to the Amyrlin's study banged open, and Sierin strode out with a paper in her hand.

"Duhara, I need you to—now, what do *you* want?" That last was barked at Moiraine, who curtsied promptly, and as deeply as she had as a novice, kissing the Great Serpent ring on the Amyrlin's right hand before rising. That ring was Sierin's only display of jewelry. Her seven-striped stole was half the width of Duhara's stole, and her dark gray silks were simply cut. Quite plump, her round face appeared to have been constructed for jolliness, but she wore implacable grimness as though it had been carved there. Moiraine could almost look her straight in the eyes. Hard eyes.

Her mouth felt dry, and she fought not to shiver in a cold that suddenly seemed worse than the heart of winter, but quick calming exercises failed to produce the composure necessary. She had learned a great deal about Sierin from the whispers about the new Amyrlin. One fact struck deep, right that moment, like a sharp knife. To Sierin, her own view of the law *was* the law, and without a shred of mercy to be found in it. Or in her.

"Mother, I ask to be relieved of my duties regarding the bounty." Her voice was steady, thank the Light. "The clerks are carrying out the task as quickly as they can, but making them stand in line each day for a sister to approve what they have done only robs them of hours they could be working."

Sierin pursed her mouth as though she had bitten a sour persimmon. "I'd stop that fool bounty entirely if it wouldn't put the Tower in bad odor. A ridiculous waste of coin. Very well; the clerks may send their papers to another for signature. A Brown, perhaps. They like that sort of thing." Moiraine's heart soared before the Amyrlin added, "You will remain in Tar Valon, of course. As you know, we will have need of you, soon."

"As you say, Mother," Moiraine replied, heart sinking into her stomach, down to her ankles after that brief flight. Offering another deep curtsy, she kissed the Amyrlin's ring once again. With a woman like Sierin, best to take no chances.

Siuan was waiting in her rooms when she returned. Her friend leaned forward expectantly and looked a question.

"I am free of the bounty, but I am ordered to remain in Tar Valon. 'As you know, we will have need of you, soon.'" She thought that a fine mimicry of Sierin's voice, if a bit streaked with bitterness.

"Fish guts!" Siuan muttered, leaning back. "What will you do now?"

"I am going for a ride. You know where I will be, in what order."

Siuan's breath caught. "The Light protect you," she said after a moment.

There was no point in waiting, so Moiraine changed into a riding dress, with Siuan's help to make the changing faster. The dress was a suitably dark blue, with a few leafy silver vines climbing the sleeves to encircle the high neck. All of her darkest garments were embroidered, but she had begun to think a little needlework might not be so bad. Leaving her shawl folded in the tall wardrobe, she took out a cloak lined with black fox, and tucked her hairbrush and comb into one of the small pockets the cloakmaker had sewn inside and her sewing kit into the other. Gathering her riding gloves, she gave Siuan a hug and hurried out. Long goodbyes would have turned to tears, and she could not risk that.

Sisters in the corridor glanced at her as she passed, but most seemed intent on their own affairs, though Kairen and Sheriam both said it seemed a cool day for a ride. Only Eadyth said more, stopping her with a half-raised hand, eyeing her in a way that seemed all too like Lelaine.

"Ruined farms and villages will hardly make for a re-freshing outing, I fear," the white-haired Sitter murmured.

"Sierin has ordered me to remain in Tar Valon," Moi-raine replied, her face a perfect Aes Sedai mask, "and I think she might see crossing one of the bridges for a few hours as disobedience."

Eadyth's mouth tightened for an instant, so briefly it might have been Moiraine's imagination. Clearly she had read Sierin's revelation of the plans in that response, and she was displeased. "The Amyrlin can be fearsome toward anyone who goes against her wishes in the smallest way, Moiraine."

Moiraine almost smiled. Light, the woman had given her a chance to say it straight out. Well, nearly straight. A suit-able Aes Sedai answer. "As well I do not intend to cross a bridge, then. I have no wish to be birched."

In the West Stable, she had Arrow saddled, without sad-dlebags. There was no need for them for a ride in the city, and no matter what she had told Eadyth, the Sitter might send someone to check. Moiraine would have. With luck, no one would suspect anything before nightfall.

Her first stop was Mistress Dormaile's, where the banker had a number of letters-of-rights ready in various amounts and four fat leather purses containing two hundred crowns in gold and silver between them. The coin would sustain Moiraine for some time. The letters-of-rights were for after the coin was gone, and for emergencies. Once she used one, she would need to move fast. The Tower's eyes-and-ears would be looking for her, and no matter how discreet bankers were, the Tower generally learned what it wanted to learn. Mis-tress Dormaile asked no questions, of course, but on learn-ing that Moiraine was alone, she offered four of her footmen as escort, and Moiraine accepted. She had no fear of foot-pads, who were few in Tar Valon and easily handled in any event, but if anyone did think of robbery, better they were frightened off by a bodyguard than chased away with the Power. That would attract attention. Wealthy women often rode with bodyguards, even in Tar Valon.

The men who walked in a box around Arrow as she de-parted the banker's might have been called footmen, but though they wore plain gray coats, they were muscular men who looked accustomed to the swords hanging from their

belts. Doubtless they were the "footmen" who had over-
come Master Gorthanes, or whatever his true name was,
they or men like them. Banks always had guards, though
never called that.

At Tamore's shop, she sent two of the men with coin
to purchase a travel trunk and hire a pair of porters, then
changed into one of the riding dresses that marked her as
a minor Cairhienin noble. Three of the five were embroidered, but lightly, and she did not complain. Too late to have
it picked out in any case. Tamore asked no more questions
than Mistress Dormaile had; one deferred to one's seamstress, but in the end, she *was* a seamstress. And, too, seamstresses had their own sense of discretion, or they did not
remain in business long. Before leaving, Moiraine tucked
her Great Serpent ring into her belt pouch. Her hand felt
oddly naked without it, her finger itched for the small circle
of gold, but too many in Tar Valon knew what it meant. For
now, she truly must hide.

With her small entourage, she progressed northward,
making stops that filled the chest on the porters' shoulder-
poles with the needful things she could not have brought
out of the Tower unnoticed, until at last they reached Northharbor, where the city walls curved out into the river and
made a ring near a mile across, broken only by the harbor
mouth. Wooden-roofed docks lined the inside of that huge
ring, and moored riverships in every size. A few words with
the dockmistress, a heavyset, graying woman with a harassed expression, gained her directions to the *Bluewing,*
a two-masted vessel. *Bluewing* was not the largest vessel at
the docks, but it was scheduled to sail within the hour.

Soon enough, Arrow had been hoisted aboard by a long
wooden boom, with straps beneath her belly, and secured
on deck, the porters had been paid off, the footmen sent
away with a silver mark each in thanks, and her trunk
made snug in a small quarterdeck cabin. Still, she would
be spending more time than she would like in that cabin,
so she remained on deck scratching Arrow's nose while the
rivership was untied and pushed off, and the long sweeps
pushed out to maneuver *Bluewing* across the harbor like
some immense waterbug.

That was why she saw the dockmistress pointing to

Bluewing and talking to a man who held his dark cloak around him tightly while he stared at the vessel. Immediately, she embraced *saidar,* and everything became clearer in her sight, sharper. The effect was not so good as a fine looking glass, yet she could make out the man's face, peering avidly from his hood. Mistress Dormaile's description had been exact. He was not pretty, but good-looking despite the scar at the corner of his left eye. And he was very tall for a Cairhienin, close to two paces. But how had he found her here, and why had he been searching? She could not think of a pleasant answer to either question, least of all the second. For someone who wanted to stop the Hall's scheme, someone who wanted another House than Damodred on the Sun Throne, the easiest way would be the death of the Hall's candidate. Fixing the fellow's face in memory, she let the Power drain away. Another reason to take great care, it appeared. He knew the vessel she traveled by, and likely every stop intended between here and the Borderlands. That had seemed the best place to begin, far from Cairhien and easily reached by the river.

"Is *Bluewing* a fast ship, Captain Carney?" she asked.

The captain, a wide, sun-dark man with narrow mustaches waxed to spikes, stopped shouting orders and put on a semblance of a respectful smile. He had been quite pleased to take a noblewoman's gold for herself and a horse. "The fastest on the river to be sure, my Lady," he said, and returned to shouting at his crew. He already had half the gold, and only needed to show respect enough to ensure he got the rest.

Any captain might have said the same of his vessel, but when the wind caught the triangular sails, *Bluewing* leaped like its namesake, all but flying out of the harbor mouth.

At that moment, Moiraine passed into disobedience to the Amyrlin Seat. Oh, Sierin surely would have seen it from the instant she left the Tower, but intention was not action. Whatever penance the woman set likely would combine Labor, Deprivation, Mortification of the Flesh *and* Mortification of the Spirit. On top of which, she almost certainly had an assassin trailing her. Her knees should have been shaking in fear of Sierin, if not Master Gorthanes, but as Tar Valon and the Tower began shrinking behind her, all she felt was a great burst of freedom and excitement. They could not put her on the Sun Throne, now. By the time the Hall found her, another would be secure in it. And she was off to find the boychild. She was off on an adventure as grand as any ever undertaken by an Aes Sedai.

CHAPTER

15

Into Canluum

The air of Kandor held the sharpness of new spring when Lan returned to the lands where he had always known he would die. Long past the arrival of spring in more southerly lands, here trees bore the first red of new growth, and a few scattered wildflowers dotted winter-brown grass where shadows did not cling to patches of snow, yet the pale sun offered little warmth after the south, gray clouds hinted at more than rain, and a cold, gusting breeze cut through his coat. Perhaps the south had softened him more than he knew. A pity, if so. He was almost home. Almost.

A hundred generations had beaten the wide road nearly as hard as the stone of the surrounding hills, and little dust rose, though a steady stream of ox-carts was leaving the morning farmers' markets in Canluum, and merchant trains of tall wagons, surrounded by mounted guards in steel caps and bits of armor, flowed toward the city's high gray walls. Here and there the chains of the Kandori merchants' guild spanned a chest or an Arafellin wore bells in her hair, a ruby decorated this man's ear, a pearl brooch that woman's breast, but for the most part the traders' clothes were as subdued as their manner. A merchant who flaunted too much profit discovered it hard to find bargains.

By contrast, farmers showed off their success when they came to town. Bright embroidery decorated the striding country men's baggy breeches, the women's wide trousers, their cloaks fluttering in the wind. Some wore colored ribbons in their hair, or a narrow fur collar. They might have been dressed for the coming Bel Tine dances and feasting.

Yet country folk eyed strangers as warily as any guard, eyed them and hefted spears or axes and hurried along. The times carried an edge in Kandor, maybe all along the Borderlands. Bandits had sprung up like weeds this past year, and more troubles than usual out of the Blight. Rumor even spoke of a man who channeled the One Power, but then, rumor often did.

Leading Cat Dancer toward Canluum, Lan paid as little attention to the stares he and his companion attracted as he did to Bukama's scowls and carping. For all his talk of taking a rest, the longer they had remained in the south, the grumpier Bukama had grown. This time his mutters were for a stone-bruised hoof that had him afoot.

They did attract attention, two very tall men walking their mounts and a packhorse with a pair of tattered wicker hampers, their plain clothes worn and travel-stained. Their harness and weapons were well tended, though. A young man and an old, hair hanging to their shoulders and held back by a braided leather cord around the temples. The *hadori* drew eyes. Especially here in the Borderlands, where people had some idea what it meant.

"Fools," Bukama grumbled. "Do they think we're bandits? Do they think we mean to rob the lot of them, at midday on the high road?" He glared and shifted the sword at his hip in a way that brought considering stares from a number of merchants' guards. A stout farmer prodded his ox wide of them.

Lan kept silent. A certain reputation clung to Malkieri who still wore the *hadori,* though not for banditry, but reminding Bukama would only send him into an even blacker humor for days. His mutters shifted to the chances of a decent bed that night, of a decent meal before. Bukama expected little, and trusted to less.

Neither food nor lodging entered Lan's thoughts, despite the distance they had traveled. His head kept swinging north. He remained aware of everyone around him, especially those who glanced his way more than once, aware of the jingle of harness and the creak of saddles, the clop of hooves, the snap of wagon canvas loose on its hoops. Any sound out of place would shout at him. He remained aware, but the Blight lay north. Still miles away across the hills, yet he could feel it, feel the twisted corruption.

Just his imagination, but no less real for that. It had pulled at him in the south, in Cairhien and Andor, even in Tear, almost five hundred leagues distant. Two years away from the Borderlands, his personal war abandoned for another, and every day the tug grew stronger. He should never have let Bukama talk him into waiting, letting the south soften him. The Aiel had helped maintain his edge.

The Blight meant death to most men. Death and the Shadow, in a rotting land tainted by the Dark One's breath, where anything at all could kill, an insect bite, the prick of the wrong thorn, a touch of the wrong leaf. Abode of Trollocs and Myrddraal and worse. Two tosses of a coin had decided where to begin anew. Four nations bordered the Blight, but his war covered the length of it, from the Aryth Ocean to the Spine of the World. One place to meet death was as good as another. He was almost home. Almost back to the Blight. He had been away too long.

A drymoat surrounded Canluum's wall, fifty paces wide and ten deep, spanned by five broad stone bridges with towers at either end as tall as those that lined the wall itself. Raids out of the Blight by Trollocs and Myrddraal often struck much deeper into Kandor than Canluum, but none had ever made it inside the city's wall. The Red Stag waved above every tower. A proud man, was Lord Varan, the High Seat of House Marcasiev; Queen Ethenielle did not fly so many of her own banners even in Chachin itself.

The guards at the outer towers, in helmets with Varan's antlered crest and the Red Stag on their chests, peered into the backs of wagons before allowing them to trundle onto the bridge, or occasionally motioned someone to push a hood further back. No more than a gesture was necessary; the law in every Borderland forbade hiding your face inside village or town, and no one wanted to be mistaken for one of the Eyeless trying to sneak into the city. Hard gazes followed Lan and Bukama onto the bridge. Their faces were clearly visible. And their *hadori*. No recognition lit any of those watching eyes, though. Two years was a long time in the Borderlands. A great many men could die in two years.

Lan noticed that Bukama had gone silent, always a bad sign. "Be easy, Bukama."

"I never start trouble," the older man snapped, but he did stop fingering his sword hilt.

The guards on the wall above the open iron-plated gates and those on the bridge wore only back- and breastplates for armor, yet they were no less watchful, especially of a pair of Malkieri with their hair tied back. Bukama's mouth grew tighter at every step.

"Al'Lan Mandragoran! The Light preserve us, we heard you were dead fighting the Aiel at the Shining Walls!" The exclamation came from a young guard, taller than the rest, almost as tall as Lan. Young, perhaps a year or two less than he, yet the gap seemed ten years. A lifetime. The guard bowed deeply, left hand on his knee. *"Tai'shar Malkier!"* True blood of Malkier. "I stand ready, Majesty."

"I am not a king," Lan said quietly. Malkier was dead. Only the war still lived. In him, at least.

Bukama was not quiet. "You stand ready for *what,* boy?" The heel of his bare hand struck the guard's breastplate right over the Red Stag, driving the man upright and back a step. "You cut your hair short and leave it unbound!" Bukama spat the words. "You're sworn to a Kandori lord! By what right do you claim to be Malkieri?"

The young man's face reddened as he floundered for answers. Other guards started toward the pair, then halted when Lan let his reins fall. Only that, but they knew his name, now. They eyed his bay stallion, standing still and alert behind him, almost as cautiously as they did him. A warhorse was a formidable weapon, and they could not know Cat Dancer was only half-trained yet.

Space opened up as people already through the gates hurried a little distance before turning to watch, while those still on the bridge pressed back. Shouts rose in both directions from people wanting to know what was holding traffic. Bukama ignored it all, intent on the red-faced guard. He had not dropped the reins of the packhorse or his yellow roan gelding. There was that for a hope to walk on without blades being bared.

An officer appeared from the stone guardhouse inside the gates, crested helmet under his arm, but one hand in a steel-backed gauntlet resting on his sword hilt. A bluff, graying man with white scars on his face, Alin Seroku had soldiered forty years along the Blight, yet his eyes widened slightly at the sight of Lan. Plainly he had heard the tales of Lan's death, too.

"The Light shine upon you, Lord Mandragoran. The son of el'Leanna and al'Akir, blessed be their memories, is always welcome." Seroku's eyes flickered toward Bukama, not in welcome. He planted his feet in the middle of the gateway. Five horsemen could have passed easily on either side, but he meant himself for a bar, and he was. None of the guards shifted a boot, yet every one had hand on sword hilt. All but the young man meeting Bukama's glares with his own. "Lord Marcasiev has commanded us to keep the peace strictly," Seroku went on, half in apology. But no more than half. "The city is on edge. All these tales of a man channeling are bad enough, but there have been murders in the street this last month and more, in broad daylight, and strange accidents. People whisper about Shadowspawn loose inside the walls."

Lan gave a slight nod. With the Blight so close, people always muttered of Shadowspawn when they had no other explanation, whether for a sudden death or unexpected crop failure. He did not take up Cat Dancer's reins, though. "We intend to rest here a few days before riding north." Rest, and try to regain his edge.

For a moment he thought Seroku was surprised. Did the man expect pledges to keep the peace, or apologies for Bukama's behavior? Either would shame Bukama, now. A pity if the war ended here. Lan did not want to die killing Kandori.

His old friend turned from the young guard, who stood quivering, fists clenched at his sides. "All fault here is mine," Bukama announced to the air in a flat voice. "I had no call for what I did. By my mother's name, I will keep Lord Marcasiev's peace. By my mother's name, I will not draw sword inside Canluum's walls." Seroku's jaw dropped, and Lan hid his own shock with difficulty.

Hesitating only a moment, the scar-faced officer stepped aside, bowing and touching sword hilt, then heart. "There is always welcome for Lan Mandragoran Dai Shan," he said formally. "And for Bukama Marenellin, the hero of Salmarna. May you both know peace, one day."

"There is peace in the mother's last embrace," Lan responded with equal formality, touching hilt and heart.

"May she welcome us home, one day," Seroku finished. No one really wished for the grave, but that was the only place to find peace in the Borderlands.

Face like iron, Bukama strode ahead pulling Sun Lance and the packhorse after him, not waiting for Lan. This was not well.

Canluum was a city of stone and brick, its paved streets twisting around tall hills. The Aiel invasion had never reached the Borderlands, but the ripples of war always diminished trade a long way from any battles, and now that fighting and winter were both finished, the city had filled with people from every land. Despite the Blight practically on the city's doorstep, gemstones mined in the surrounding hills made Canluum wealthy. And, strangely enough, some of the finest clockmakers anywhere. The cries of hawkers and shopkeepers shouting their wares rose above the hum of the crowd even away from the terraced market squares. Colorfully dressed musicians, or jugglers, or tumblers performed at every intersection. A handful of lacquered carriages swayed through the mass of people and wagons and carts and barrows, and horses with gold- or silver-mounted saddles and bridles picked their way through the throng, their riders' garb embroidered as ornately as the animals' tack and trimmed with fox or marten or ermine. Hardly a foot of street was left bare anywhere.

Lan even saw several Aes Sedai, women with serene, ageless faces. Enough people recognized them on sight that they created eddies in the crowd, swirls to clear a way. Respect or caution, awe or fear, there were sufficient reasons for a king to step aside for a sister. Once you might have gone a year without seeing an Aes Sedai even in the Borderlands, but the sisters seemed to be everywhere since their old Amyrlin Seat died. Maybe it was those tales of a man channeling; they would not let him run free long, if he existed.

He kept his eyes away from them, walked on quickly to avoid notice. The *hadori* could be enough to attract the interest of a sister seeking a Warder. Supposedly, they asked before bonding a man, but he knew several who had taken that bond, and every time it had come as a surprise. Who would give up his freedom to trot at an Aes Sedai's heels unless there was more to it than asking?

Shockingly, lace veils covered many women's faces. Thin lace, sheer enough to reveal that they had eyes, and no one had ever heard of a female Myrddraal, but Lan had never

expected law to yield to mere fashion. Next they would take
down the oil lamps lining the streets and let the nights grow
black. Even more shocking than the veils, Bukama looked
right at some of those women and did not open his mouth.
Then a jut-nosed man named Nazar Kurenin rode in front
of Bukama's eyes, and he did not blink. The young guard
surely had been born after the Blight swallowed Malkier,
but Kurenin, his hair cut short and wearing a forked beard,
was twice Lan's age. The years had not erased the marks of
his *hadori* completely. There were many like Kurenin, and
the sight of him should have set Bukama spluttering. Lan
eyed his friend worriedly.

They had been moving steadily toward the center of the
city, climbing toward the highest hill, Stag's Stand. Lord
Marcasiev's fortress-like palace covered the peak, with
those of lesser lords and ladies on the terraces below. Any
threshold up there offered warm welcome for al'Lan Mandragoran. Perhaps warmer than he wanted now. Balls and
hunts, with nobles invited from as much as fifty miles away,
including from across the border with Arafel. People avid
to hear of his "adventures." Young men wanting to join his
forays into the Blight, and old men to compare their experiences there with his. Women eager to share the bed of a
man fool stories claimed the Blight could not kill. Kandor
and Arafel were as bad as any southland at times; some of
those women would be married.

And there would be men like Kurenin, working to sub-
merge memories of lost Malkier, and women who no longer
adorned their foreheads with the *ki'sain* in pledge that they
would swear their sons to oppose the Shadow while they
breathed. He could ignore the false smiles while they named
him al'Lan Dai Shan, diademed battle lord and uncrowned
king of a nation betrayed while he was in his cradle. In his
present mood, Bukama might do murder. Or worse, given
his oaths at the gate. He would keep those to the death. But
Bukama's hands and feet were dangerous enough to maim a
man for life.

"Varan Marcasiev will hold us a week or more with ceremony," Lan said, turning down a narrower street that led
away from the Stand. "With what we've heard of bandits
and the like, he will be just as happy if I don't appear to
make my bows." True enough. He had met the High Seat

of House Marcasiev only once, years past, but he remembered a grave-faced man given entirely to his duties. Lord Marcasiev would arrange those balls and hunts, and regret every one.

Bukama followed without complaint about missing a palace bed or the feasts the cooks would prepare. It was worrying. Along with regaining his own edge, he needed to find a way to sharpen Bukama's, or they might as well open their veins now.

CHAPTER
16

The Deeps

No palaces rose in the hollows toward the north wall, only shops and taverns, inns and stables and wagon yards. Bustle surrounded the factors' long warehouses, but no carriages came to the Deeps, and most streets were barely wide enough for carts. They were just as jammed with people as the wide ways, though, and every bit as noisy. Here, the street performers' finery was tarnished, yet they made up for it by being louder, and buyers and sellers alike bellowed as if trying to be heard in the next street. Likely some of the crowd were cutpurses, slipfingers and other thieves, finished with a morning's business higher up or headed there for the afternoon. It would have been a wonder otherwise, with so many merchants in town. The second time unseen fingers brushed his coat in the crowd, Lan tucked his purse under his shirt. Any banker would advance him more against the Shienaran estate he had been granted on reaching manhood, but loss of the gold on hand meant accepting the hospitality of Stag's Stand.

At the first three inns they tried, slate-roofed cubes of gray stone with bright signs out front, the innkeepers had not a cubbyhole to offer. Lesser traders and merchants' guards filled them to the attics. Bukama began to mutter about making a bed in a hayloft, yet he never mentioned the feather mattresses and linens waiting on the Stand. Leaving their horses with ostlers at a fourth inn, The Blue Rose, Lan entered determined to find some place for them if it took the rest of the day.

Inside, a graying woman, tall and handsome, presided over a crowded common room where talk and laughter almost drowned out the slender girl singing to the music of her zither. Pipe smoke wreathed the ceiling beams, and the smell of roasting lamb floated from the kitchens. As soon as the innkeeper saw Lan and Bukama, she gave her blue-striped apron a twitch and strode toward them, dark eyes sharp.

Before Lan could open his mouth, she seized Bukama's ears, pulled his head down, and kissed him. Kandori women were seldom retiring, but even so it was a remarkably thorough kiss in front of so many eyes. Pointing fingers and snickering grins flashed among the tables.

"It's good to see you again, too, Racelle," Bukama murmured with a small smile when she finally released him. "I didn't know you had an inn here. Do you think—?" He lowered his gaze rather than meeting her eyes rudely, and that proved a mistake. Racelle's fist caught his jaw so hard that his hair flailed as he staggered.

"Six years without a word," she snapped. "Six years!" Grabbing his ears again, she gave him another kiss, longer this time. Took it rather than gave. A sharp twist of his ears met every attempt to do anything besides standing bent over and letting her do as she wished. At least she would not put a knife in his heart if she was kissing him. Perhaps not.

"I think Mistress Arovni might find Bukama a room somewhere," a man's familiar voice said dryly behind Lan. "And you, too, I suppose."

Turning, Lan clasped forearms with the only man in the room beside Bukama of a height with him, Ryne Venamar, his oldest friend except for Bukama. The innkeeper still had Bukama occupied as Ryne led Lan to a small round table in the corner. Five years older, Ryne was Malkieri, too, but his hair fell in two long bell-laced braids, and more silver bells lined the turned-down tops of his boots and ran up the sleeves of his yellow coat. Bukama did not exactly dislike Ryne—not exactly—yet in his present mood only Nazar Kurenin could have had a worse effect.

While the pair of them were settling themselves on benches, a serving maid in a striped apron brought hot spiced wine. Apparently Ryne had ordered as soon as he saw Lan. Dark-eyed and full-lipped, she stared Lan up and down openly as she set his mug in front of him, then whispered her name, Lira, in his ear, and an invitation, if he was staying the night. All he wanted that night was sleep, so he lowered his gaze, murmuring that she honored him too much. Lira did not let him finish. With a raucous laugh, she bent to bite his ear, hard.

"By tomorrow," she announced in a throaty voice, and loudly, "I'll have honored you till your knees won't hold you up." Raucous laughter flared at the tables around them.

Ryne forestalled any possibility of righting matters, tossing her a fat coin and giving her a slap on the bottom to send her off. Lira offered him a dimpled smile as she slipped the silver into the neck of her dress, but she left sending smoky glances over her shoulder at Lan that made him sigh. If he tried to say no now, she might well pull a knife over the insult.

"So your luck still holds with women, too." Ryne's laugh had an edge. Perhaps he fancied her himself. "The Light knows, they can't find you handsome; you get uglier every year. Maybe I ought to try some of that coy modesty, let women lead me by the nose."

Lan opened his mouth, then took a drink instead of speaking. He should not have to explain, but it was too late for explanation with Ryne in any case. His father had taken him to Arafel the year Lan turned ten. The man wore a single blade on his hip instead of two on his back, yet he was Arafellin to his toenails. He actually started conversations with women who had not spoken to him first. Lan, raised by Bukama and his friends in Shienar, had been surrounded by a small community who held to Malkieri ways. If Lira did share his bed tonight, as seemed certain, she would discover there was nothing shy or retiring about him once they were abed, yet the woman chose when to enter that bed and when to leave.

A number of people around the room were watching their table, sidelong glances over mugs and goblets. A plump copper-skinned woman wearing a much thicker dress than Domani women usually did made no effort to hide her stares as she spoke excitedly to a fellow with curled mustaches and a large pearl in his ear. Probably wondering whether there would be trouble over Lira. Wondering whether a man wearing the *hadori* really would kill at the drop of a pin.

"I didn't expect to find you in Canluum," Lan said, setting the wine mug down. "Guarding a merchant train?" Bukama and the innkeeper were nowhere to be seen.

Ryne shrugged. "Out of Shol Arbela. The luckiest trader in Arafel, they say. Said. Much good it did him. We arrived yesterday, and last night footpads slit his throat two streets over. No return money for me this trip." He flashed a rueful grin and took a deep pull at his wine, perhaps to the memory of the merchant or perhaps to the lost half of his wages. "Burn me if I thought to see you here, either."

"You shouldn't listen to rumors, Ryne. I've not taken a wound worth mentioning since I rode south." Lan decided to twit Bukama if they did get a room, about whether it was already paid for and how. Indignation might take him out of his darkness.

"The Aiel," Ryne snorted. "I never thought *they* could put paid to you." He had never faced Aiel, of course. "I expected you to be wherever Edeyn Arrel is. Chachin, now, I hear."

That name snapped Lan's head back to the man across the table. "Why should I be near the Lady Arrel?" he demanded softly. Softly, but emphasizing her proper title.

"Easy, man," Ryne said. "I didn't mean. . . ." Wisely, he abandoned that line. "Burn me, do you mean to say you haven't heard? She's raised the Golden Crane. In your name, of course. Since the year turned, she's been from Fal Moran to Maradon, and coming back now." Ryne shook his head, the bells in his braids chiming faintly. "There must be two or three hundred men right here in Canluum ready to follow her. You, I mean. Some you'd not believe. Old Kurenin wept when he heard her speak. All ready to carve Malkier out of the Blight again."

"What dies in the Blight is gone," Lan said wearily. He felt more than cold inside. Suddenly Seroku's surprise that he intended to ride north took on new meaning, and the young guard's assertion that he stood ready. Even the looks here in the common room seemed different. And Edeyn was part of it. Always she liked standing in the heart of the storm. "I must see to my horse," he told Ryne, scraping his bench back.

Ryne said something about making a round of the taverns that night, but Lan hardly heard. He hurried through the kitchens, hot from iron stoves and stone ovens and open hearths, into the cool of the stableyard, the mingled smells of horse and hay and wood-smoke. A graylark warbled on

the edge of the stable roof. Graylarks came even before rob-
ins in the spring. Graylarks had been singing in Fal Moran
when Edeyn first whispered in his ear.

The horses had already been stabled, bridles and saddles
and packsaddle atop saddle blankets on the stall doors, but
the wicker hampers were gone. Plainly Mistress Arovni
had sent word to the ostlers that he and Bukama were being
given accommodation.

There was only a single groom in the dim stable, a lean,
hard-faced woman mucking out. Silently she watched him
check Cat Dancer and the other horses as she worked,
watched him begin to pace the length of the straw-covered
floor. He tried to think, but Edeyn's name kept spinning
though his head. Edeyn's face, surrounded by silky black
hair that hung below her waist, a beautiful face with large
dark eyes that could drink a man's soul even when filled
with command.

After a bit the groom mumbled something in his direction, touching her lips and forehead, and hurriedly shoved
her half-filled barrow out of the stable, glancing over her
shoulder at him. She paused to shut the doors, and did that
hurriedly, too, sealing him in shadow broken only by a little
light from open haydoors in the loft. Dust motes danced in
the pale golden shafts.

Lan grimaced. Was she that afraid of a man wearing
the *hadori*? Did she think his pacing a threat? Abruptly he
became aware of his hands running over the long hilt of
his sword, aware of the tightness in his own face. Pacing?
No, he had been in the walking stance called Leopard in
High Grass, used when there were enemies on all sides. He
needed calm.

Seating himself cross-legged on a bale of straw, he assumed the *ko'di* and floated in calm emptiness, one with the
bale beneath him, the stable, the scabbarded sword folded
behind him. He could "feel" the horses, cropping at their
mangers, and flies buzzing in the corners. They were all
part of him. Especially the sword. This time, though, it was
only the emotionless void that he sought.

From his belt pouch he took a heavy gold signet ring
worked with a flying crane and turned it over and over in
his fingers. The ring of Malkieri kings, worn by men who
had held back the Shadow nine hundred years and more.

Countless times it had been remade as time wore it down, always the old ring melted to become part of the new. Some particle might still exist in it of the ring worn by the rulers of Rhamdashar, that had lived before Malkier, and Aramaelle that had been before Rhamdashar. That piece of metal represented over three thousand years fighting the Blight. It had been his almost as long as he had lived, but he had never worn it. Even looking at the ring was a labor, usually. One he disciplined himself to every day. Without the emptiness, he did not think he could have done so today. In *ko'di,* thought floated free, and emotion lay beyond the horizon.

In his cradle he had been given four gifts. The ring in his hands and the locket that hung around his neck, the sword on his hip and an oath sworn in his name. The locket, containing the painted images of the mother and father he could not remember seeing in life, was the most precious, the oath the heaviest. "To stand against the Shadow so long as iron is hard and stone abides. To defend the Malkieri while one drop of blood remains. To avenge what cannot be defended." And then he had been anointed with oil and named Dai Shan, consecrated as the next King of Malkier and sent away from a land that knew it would die.

Nothing remained to be defended now, only a nation to avenge, and he had been trained to that from his first step. With his mother's gift at his throat and his father's sword in his hand, with the ring branded on his heart, he had fought from his sixteenth nameday to avenge Malkier. But never had he led men into the Blight. Bukama had ridden with him, and others, but he would not lead men there. That war was his alone. The dead could not be returned to life, a land any more than a man. Only, now, Edeyn Arrel wanted to try.

Her name echoed in the emptiness within him. A hundred emotions loomed like stark mountains, but he fed them into the flame until all was still. Until his heart beat time with the slow stamping of the stalled horses, and the flies' wings beat rapid counterpoint to his breath. She was his *carneira,* his first lover. A thousand years of tradition shouted that, despite the stillness that enveloped him.

He had been fifteen, Edeyn more than twice that, when she gathered the hair that had still hung to his waist in her hands and whispered her intentions. Women had still called him beautiful then, enjoying his blushes, and for half a year she had enjoyed parading him on her arm and tucking him into her bed. Until Bukama and the other men gave him the *hadori*. The gift of his sword on his tenth nameday had made him a man by custom along the Border, though years early for it, yet among Malkieri that band of braided leather had been more important. Once that was tied around his head, he alone decided where he went, and when, and why. And the dark song of the Blight had become a howl that drowned every other sound. The oath that had murmured so long in his heart became a dance his feet had to follow.

Almost ten years past now that Edeyn had watched him ride away from Fal Moran, and been gone when he returned, yet he still could recall her face more clearly than that of any woman who had shared his bed since. He was no longer a boy, to think that she loved him just because she had chosen to become his first lover, yet there was an old saying among Malkieri men. *Your* carneira *wears part of your soul as a ribbon in her hair forever.* Custom strong as law made it so.

One of the stable doors creaked open to admit Bukama, coatless, shirt tucked raggedly into his breeches. He looked naked without his sword. As if hesitant, he carefully opened both doors wide before coming all the way in. "What are you going to do?" he said finally. "Racelle told me about . . . about the Golden Crane."

Lan tucked the ring away, letting emptiness drain from him. Edeyn's face suddenly seemed everywhere, just beyond the edge of sight. "Ryne says even Nazar Kurenin is ready to follow," he said lightly. "Wouldn't that be a sight to see?" An army could die trying to defeat the Blight. Armies had died trying. But the memories of Malkier already were dying. A nation was memory as much as land. "That boy at the gates might let his hair grow and ask his father for the *hadori*." People were forgetting, trying to forget. When the last man who bound his hair was gone, the last woman who painted her forehead, would Malkier truly be gone, too? "Why, Ryne might even get rid of those braids." Any trace of mirth dropped from his voice as he added, "But is it worth the cost? Some seem to think so." Bukama snorted, yet there had been a pause. He might be one of those who did.

Striding to the stall that held Sun Lance, the older man

began to fiddle with his roan's saddle on the stall door as though suddenly forgetting why he had moved. "There's always a cost for anything," he said, not looking up. "But there are costs, and costs. The Lady Edeyn. . . ." He glanced at Lan, then turned to face him. "She was always one to demand every right and require the smallest obligation be met. Custom ties strings to you, and whatever you choose, she will use them like a set of reins unless you find a way to avoid it."

Carefully Lan tucked his thumbs behind his sword belt. Bukama had carried him out of Malkier tied to his back. The last of the five who survived that journey. Bukama had the right of a free tongue even when it touched Lan's *carneira*. "How do you suggest I avoid my obligations without shame?" he asked more harshly than he had intended. Taking a deep breath, he went on in a milder tone. "Come; the common room smells much better than this. Ryne suggested a round of the taverns tonight. Unless Mistress Arovni has claims on you. Oh, yes. How much will our rooms cost? Good rooms? Not too dear, I hope."

Bukama joined him on the way to the doors, his face going red. "Not too dear," he said hastily. "You have a pallet in the attic, and I . . . ah . . . I'm in Racelle's rooms. I'd like to make a round, but I think Racelle. . . . I don't think she means to let me. . . . I. . . . Young whelp!" he growled. "There's a lass named Lira in there who's letting it be known you won't be using that pallet tonight, *or* getting much sleep, so don't think you can—!" He cut off as they walked into the sunlight, bright after the dimness inside. The graylark still sang of spring.

Six men were striding across the otherwise empty yard. Six ordinary men with swords at their belts, like any men on any street in the city. Yet Lan knew before their hands moved, before their eyes focused on him and their steps quickened. He had faced too many men who wanted to kill him not to know. And at his side stood Bukama, bound by oaths that would not let him draw even had he been wearing his blade. Bare hands were poor weapons against swords, especially at these odds. If they both tried to get back inside the stable, the men would be on them before they could haul the doors shut. Time slowed, flowed like cool honey.

"Inside and bar the doors!" Lan snapped as his hand went to his hilt. "Obey me, armsman!"

Never in his life had he given Bukama a command in that fashion, and the man hesitated a heartbeat, then bowed formally. "My life is yours, Dai Shan," he said in a thick voice. "I obey."

As Lan moved forward to meet his attackers, he heard the bar drop inside with a muffled thud. Relief was distant. He floated in *ko'di,* one with the sword that came smoothly out of its scabbard. One with the men rushing at him, boots thudding on the hard-packed ground as they bared steel.

A lean heron of a fellow darted ahead of the others, and Lan danced the forms. Time like cool honey. The graylark sang, and the lean man shrieked as Cutting the Clouds removed his right hand at the wrist, and Lan flowed to one side so the rest could not all come at him together, flowed from form to form. Soft Rain at Sunset laid open a fat man's face, took his left eye, and a ginger-haired young splinter drew a gash across Lan's ribs with Black Pebbles on Snow. Only in stories did one man face six without injury. The Rose Unfolds sliced down a bald man's left arm, and ginger-hair nicked the corner of Lan's eye. Only in stories did one man face six and survive. He had known that from the start. Duty was a mountain, death a feather, and his duty was to Bukama, who had carried an infant on his back. For this moment he lived, though, so he fought, kicking ginger-hair in the head, dancing his way toward death, danced and took wounds, bled and danced the razor's edge of life. Time like cool honey, flowing from form to form, and there could only be one ending. Thought was distant. Death was a feather. Dandelion in the Wind slashed open the now one-eyed fat man's throat—he had barely paused when his face was ruined—a fork-bearded fellow with shoulders like a blacksmith gasped in surprise as Kissing the Adder put Lan's steel through his heart.

And suddenly Lan realized that he alone stood, with six men sprawled across the width of the stableyard. The ginger-haired youth thrashed his heels on the ground one last time, and then only Lan of the seven still breathed. He shook blood from his blade, bent to wipe the last drops off on the blacksmith's too-fine coat, sheathed his sword as formally as if he were in the training yard under Bukama's eye.

Abruptly people flooded out of the inn, cooks and stablemen, maids and patrons shouting to know what all the noise was about, staring at the dead men in astonishment. Ryne was the very first, sword already in hand, his face blank as he came to stand by Lan. "Six," he muttered, studying the bodies. "You really do have the Dark One's own flaming luck."

Dark-eyed Lira reached Lan only moments before Bukama, the pair of them gently parting slashes in his clothes to examine his injuries. She shivered delicately as each was revealed, but she discussed whether an Aes Sedai should be sent for to give Healing and how much stitching was needed in as calm a tone as Bukama, and disparagingly dismissed his hand on the needle in favor of her own. Mistress Arovni stalked about, holding her skirts up out of patches of bloody mud, glaring at the corpses littering her stableyard, complaining in a loud voice that gangs of footpads would never be wandering in daylight if the Watch was doing its job. The Domani woman who had stared at Lan inside agreed just as loudly, and for her pains received a sharp command from the innkeeper to fetch the Watch, along with a shove to start her on her way. It was a measure of Mistress Arovni's shock that she treated one of her patrons so, a measure of everyone's shock that the Domani woman went running without complaint. The innkeeper began organizing men to drag the bodies out of sight.

Ryne looked from Bukama to the stable as though he did not understand—perhaps he did not, at that—but what he said was "Not footpads, I think." He pointed to the fellow who looked like a blacksmith. "That one listened to Edeyn Arrel when she was here, and he liked what he heard. One of the others did, too, I think." Bells chimed as he shook his head. "It's peculiar. The first she said of raising the Golden Crane was after we heard you were dead outside the Shining Walls. Your name brings men, but with you dead, she could be el'Edeyn."

He spread his hands at the looks Lan and Bukama shot him. "I make no accusations," he said hastily. "I'd never accuse the Lady Edeyn of any such thing. I'm sure she is full of all a woman's tender mercy." Mistress Arovni gave a grunt hard as a fist, and Lira murmured half under her breath that the pretty Arafellin knew little about women.

Lan shook his head. Not in denial. Edeyn might decide to have him killed if it suited her purposes, she might have left orders here and there in case the rumors about him proved false, but if she had, that was still no reason to speak her name in connection with this, especially in front of strangers.

Bukama's hands stilled, holding open a slash down Lan's sleeve. "Where do we go from here?" he asked quietly.

"Chachin," Lan after a moment. There was always a choice, but sometimes every choice was grim. "You'll have to leave Sun Lance. I mean to depart at first light tomorrow." His gold would stretch to a new mount for the man.

"Six!" Ryne growled, sheathing his sword with considerable force. "I think I'll ride with you. I'd as soon not go back to Shol Arbela until I'm sure Ceiline Noreman doesn't lay her husband's death at my boots. And it will be good to see the Golden Crane flying again."

Lan nodded. To put his hand on the banner and abandon what he had promised himself all those years ago, or to stop her, if he could. Either way, he had to face Edeyn. The Blight would have been much easier.

CHAPTER

17

An Arrival

C hasing after prophecy, Moiraine had decided by the end of the first month, involved very little adventure and a great deal of boredom. Now, three months out of Tar Valon, her grand search consisted mainly of frustration. The Three Oaths still made her skin feel too tight, and now saddlesoreness added to the mix. The wind rattled the closed shutters against their latches, and she shifted on the hard wooden chair, hiding impatience behind a sip of honeyless tea. In Kandor, comforts were kept to a minimum in a house of mourning. She would not have been overly surprised to see frost on the leaf-carved furniture or the steel-cased clock above the cold hearth.

"It was all so strange, my Lady," Jurine Najima sighed, and for the tenth time hugged her daughters to her fiercely, as though she would never release them. They seemed to find comfort in the crushing grip. Perhaps thirteen or fourteen, standing on either side of Jurine's chair, Colar and Eselle had her long black hair and large blue eyes still full of loss. Their mother's eyes seemed big, too, in a face shrunken by tragedy, and her plain gray dress appeared made for a larger woman. "Josef was always careful with lanterns in the stable," she went on, "and he never allowed any kind of open flame. The boys must have carried little Jerid out to see their father at his work, and. . . ." Another hollow sigh. "They were all trapped. How could the whole stable be ablaze so fast? It makes no sense."

"Little is ever senseless, Mistress Najima," Moiraine said soothingly, setting her cup on the small table at her elbow. She felt sympathy, but the woman had begun repeating herself. "We cannot always see the reason, yet we can take some comfort in knowing there is one. The Wheel of Time weaves us into the Pattern as it wills, but the Pattern is the work of the Light."

Hearing herself, she suppressed a wince. Those words required dignity and weight her youth failed to supply. For a moment, she wished for the agelessness, but the last thing she could afford was to have the name Aes Sedai attached to her visit. No sister had come calling on Jurine yet, but one would sooner or later.

"As you say, my Lady Alys," the other woman murmured politely, though an unguarded shift of pale eyes spoke her thoughts. This outlander was a foolish child, noble or not.

The small blue stone of the *kesiera* dangling onto Moiraine's forehead and one of Tamore's riding dresses, in dark green, upheld her supposed rank. People allowed questions from a noble they never would from a commoner, and accepted odd behavior as natural. Supposedly, she was making sympathy calls in mourning for her own king. Not that many people seemed to be mourning Laman in Cairhien itself. The latest news she had from there, a month old, spoke of four Houses laying claim to the throne and fierce skirmishes, some approaching battles. Light, how many would die before that was settled? There would have been deaths had she gone along with the Hall—the succession to the Sun Throne was always contested, whether through open warfare or assassination and kidnapping—but at least she had been gone long enough to put paid to that. And *she* would pay for doing so, atop whatever Sierin imposed for disobedience.

Perhaps she let something of her anger show, and Mistress Najima took it to mean her own thoughts had been too clear, because she started up again, speaking anxiously. No one wanted to anger a noble, even an outland noble. "It's just that Josef was always so lucky, my Lady Alys. Everyone spoke of it. They said if Josef Najima fell down a hole, there'd be opals at the bottom. When he answered the Lady Kareil's call to go fight the Aiel, I worried, but he never took a scratch. When camp fever struck, it never touched us or the children. Josef gained the Lady's favor without trying. Then it seemed the Light truly did shine on us. Jerid was born safe and whole, and the war ended, all in a matter of days, and when we came home to Canluum, the Lady gave us the livery stable for Josef's service, and . . . and. . . ." She swallowed tears she would not shed. Colar began to weep, and her mother pulled her closer, whispering comfort.

Moiraine rose. More repetition. There was nothing here for her. Jurine stood, too, not a tall woman, yet almost a hand taller than she. Either of the girls could look her in the eyes. Forcing herself to take time, she murmured more condolences and tried to press a washleather purse on the woman as the girls brought her fur-lined cloak and gloves. A small purse. In the beginning, instinct had made her generous, even with the bounty to come if not already received, but before long, she would need to find a bank.

The woman's stiff-necked refusal to take the purse irritated her. No, she understood pride, and besides, Lady Kareil had provided. The presence of a clock spoke of a prosperous household. The real irritant was her own desire to be gone. Jurine Najima had lost her husband and three sons in one fiery morning, but her Jerid had been born in the wrong place by almost twenty miles. Moiraine disliked feeling relief in connection with the death of an infant. Yet she did. The dead boy was not the one she sought.

Outside under a gray sky, she gathered her cloak tightly. Anyone who went about the streets of Canluum with an open cloak would draw stares. Any outlander, at least, unless clearly Aes Sedai. Besides, not allowing the cold to touch you did not make you entirely unaware of it. How these people could call this "new spring" without a hint of mockery was beyond her. Mentally she drew a line through the name of Jurine Najima. Other names in the notebook residing in her belt pouch already had real lines inked through them. The mothers of five boys born in the wrong place or on the wrong day. The mothers of three girls. Her initial optimism that she would be the one to find the boychild had faded to a faint hope. The book contained hundreds of names. Surely one of Tamra's searchers would locate him first. Still, she intended to go on. Years might pass before it was safe for her to return to Tar Valon. A great many years.

Despite the near freezing wind that gusted over the rooftops, the winding streets were packed with milling people and carts and wagons, and hawkers with their trays or barrows. Wagon drivers shouted and cracked their long

whips to gain some headway, the women coming nearer
to striking flesh than the men, and so managed to move
in straight lines, but for her, it was a matter of picking her
way, dodging around wagons and high-wheeled carts. She
was certainly not the only outlander afoot in the streets. A
Taraboner with heavy mustaches pushed past her muttering
a hasty apology, and an olive-skinned Altaran woman who
scowled at her, then a smiling Illianer with a beard that left
his upper lip bare, a very pretty fellow and not too tall. A
dark-faced Tairen in a striped cloak, even prettier, eyed her
up and down and pursed his lips in betrayal of lascivious
thoughts. He even moved as though to speak to her, but she
let the wind catch one side of her cloak, flinging it open
long enough to reveal the slashes on her breast. That sent
him scurrying. He might have been willing to approach a
merchant with his beautiful face and lewd suggestions, but
a noble was another matter.

Not everyone was forced to crawl. Twice she saw Aes
Sedai strolling through the crowds, and those who recognized the ageless face leaped out of their paths and hastily
warned others to move aside, so they walked in pools of
open space that flowed along the street with them. Neither
was a woman she had met, but she kept her head down and
stayed to the other side of the street, far enough that they
could not sense her ability. Perhaps she should put on a veil.
A stout woman brushed by, features blurred behind lace.
Sierin Vayu herself could have passed unrecognized at ten
feet in one of those. She shivered at the thought, ridiculous
at it was.

The inn where she had a small room was called The
Gates of Heaven, four sprawling stories of green-roofed
stone, Canluum's best and largest. Nearby shops, jewelers
and goldsmiths, silversmiths and seamstresses, catered to
the lord and ladies on the Stand, looming behind the inn.
She would not have stopped in it had she known who else
was staying there before paying for her room. There was
not another room to be found in the city, but a hayloft would
have been preferable. Taking a deep breath, she hurried inside. Neither the sudden warmth from fires on four large
hearths nor the good smells from the kitchens eased her
tight shoulders.

The common room was large, and every table beneath

the bright red ceiling beams was taken. The customers were plainly dressed merchants for the most part, bargaining in low voices over wine, and a sprinkling of well-to-do crafts-folk with rich embroidery covering colorful coats or dresses. She hardly noticed them. No fewer than five sisters were staying at The Gates of Heaven—none known to her from the Tower, the Light be thanked—and all sat in the common room when she walked in. Master Helvin, the innkeeper, would always make room for an Aes Sedai even when he had to force other patrons to double up.

The sisters kept to themselves, barely acknowledging one another, and people who might not have recognized an Aes Sedai on sight knew them now, knew enough not to intrude. Every other table was jammed, yet where any man sat with an Aes Sedai, it was her Warder, a hard-eyed man with a dangerous look about him however ordinary he might seem otherwise. One of the sisters sitting alone was a Red, a fact known only through an overheard comment. Only Felaana Bevaine, a slim yellow-haired Brown in plain dark wool-ens, wore her shawl. She had been the first to corner Moi-raine when she arrived. They had felt her ability as soon as she came close, of course.

Tucking her gloves behind her belt and folding her cloak over her arm, she started toward the stone stairs at the back of the room. Not too quickly, but not dawdling, either. Look-ing straight ahead. The sisters' eyes following her seemed the touch of fingers. Not quite grasping. None spoke to her. They thought her a wilder, a woman who had learned to channel on her own. That lucky deception had come about by accident, a misperception on Felaana's part, but it was bolstered by the presence of a true wilder at the inn. No one knew what Mistress Asher was, except the sisters. Many Aes Sedai disliked wilders, considering them a loss to the Tower, yet few went out of their way to make their lives dif-ficult. A merchant in dark gray wool who wore only a red-enameled circle pin for jewelry, Mistress Asher dropped her eyes whenever a sister glanced at her, but they had no interest in her. Her gray hair ensured that.

Then, just as Moiraine reached the staircase, a woman did speak behind her. "Well, now. This is a surprise."

Turning quickly, Moiraine kept her face smooth with an effort as she made a brief curtsy suitable from a minor

noblewoman to an Aes Sedai. To two Aes Sedai. Short of
Sierin herself, she could hardly have encountered two worse
than this pair in sober silks.

The white wings in Larelle Tarsi's long hair emphasized
her serene, copper-skinned elegance. She had taught Moiraine in several classes, as both novice and Accepted, and
she had a way of asking the last question you wanted to
hear. Worse, the other was Merean. Seeing them together
was a surprise; she had not thought they particularly liked
one another.

Larelle was as strong as Merean, requiring deference,
but they were outside the Tower, now. They had no right
to interfere with whatever she might be doing here. Yet if
either said the wrong thing here, word that Moiraine Damodred was wandering about in disguise would spread with
the sisters in the room, and it would reach the wrong ears
as surely as peaches were poison. That was the way of the
world. A summons back to Tar Valon would find her soon
after. Disobeying the Amyrlin Seat once was bad enough.
Twice, and very likely sisters would be sent to bring her
back. She opened her mouth hoping to forestall the chance,
but someone else spoke first.

"No need trying that one," Felaana said, twisting around
on her bench at a nearby table where she was sitting alone.
She had been writing intently in a small leather-bound
book, and there was an ink stain on the tip of her nose, of
all places. "Says she has no interest in going to the Tower.
Stubborn as stone about it. Secretive, too. You would think
we'd have heard about a wilder popping up even in a lesser
Cairhienin House, but this child likes to keep to herself."

Larelle and Merean looked at Moiraine, Larelle arching a thin eyebrow, Merean apparently trying to suppress
a smile.

"It is quite true, Aes Sedai," Moiraine said carefully, relieved that someone else had laid a foundation. "I have no
desire to enroll as a novice, and I will not."

Felaana fixed her with considering eyes, but she still
spoke to the others. "Says she's twenty-two, but that rule
has been bent a time or two. A woman says she's eighteen,
and that's how she's enrolled. Unless it's too obvious a lie,
anyway, and this girl could easily pass for—"

"Our rules were not made to be broken," Larelle said

sharply, and Merean added in a wry voice, "I don't believe this young woman will lie about her age. She doesn't want to be a novice, Felaana. Let her go her way." Moiraine almost let out a relieved sigh.

Enough weaker than they to accept being cut off, Felaana still began to rise, plainly meaning to continue the argument. Halfway to her feet she glanced up the stairs behind Moiraine, her eyes widened, and abruptly she sat down again, focusing on her writing as if nothing in the world existed beyond her book. Merean and Larelle gathered their shawls, gray fringe and blue swaying. They looked eager to be elsewhere. They looked as though their feet had been nailed to the floor.

"So this girl does not want to be a novice," said a woman's voice from the stairs. A voice Moiraine had heard only once, two years ago, and would never forget. A number of women were stronger than she, but only one could be as much stronger as this one. Unwillingly, she looked over her shoulder.

Nearly black eyes studied her from beneath a bun of iron-gray hair decorated with golden ornaments, stars and birds, crescent moons and fish. Cadsuane, too, wore her shawl, fringed in green. "In my opinion, girl," she said dryly, "you could profit from ten years in white."

Everyone had believed Cadsuane Melaidhrin dead somewhere in retirement until she reappeared at the start of the Aiel War, and a good many sisters probably wished her truly in her grave. Cadsuane was a legend, a most uncomfortable thing to have alive and staring at you. Half the tales about her came close to impossibility, while the rest were beyond it, even among those that had proof. A long-ago King of Tarabon winkled out of his palace when it was learned he could channel, carried to Tar Valon to be gentled while an army that did not believe chased after to attempt rescue. A King of Arad Doman and a Queen of Saldaea *both* kidnapped, spirited away in secrecy, and when Cadsuane finally released them, a war that had seemed certain simply faded away. It was said she bent Tower law where it suited her, flouted custom, went her own way and often dragged others with her.

"I thank the Aes Sedai for her concern," Moiraine began, then trailed off under that stare. Not a hard stare. Simply implacable. Supposedly even Amyrlins had stepped warily around Cadsuane over the years. It was whispered that she had actually *assaulted* an Amyrlin, once. Impossible, of course; she would have been executed! Moiraine swallowed and tried to start over, only to find she wanted to swallow again.

Descending the stair, Cadsuane told Merean and Larelle, "Bring the girl." Without a second glance, she glided across the common room. Merchants and craftsfolk looked at her, some openly, some from the corner of an eye, and Warders, too, but every sister kept her gaze on her table.

Merean's face tightened, and Larelle sighed extravagantly, yet they prodded Moiraine after the bobbing golden ornaments. She had no choice but to go. At least Cadsuane could not be one of the women Tamra had called in; she had not returned to Tar Valon since that visit at the beginning of the war.

The Green sister led them to one of the inn's private sitting rooms, where a fire blazed on the black stone hearth and silver lamps hung along the red wall panels. A tall pitcher stood near the fire to keep warm, and a lacquered tray on a small carved table held silver cups. Merean and Larelle took two of the brightly cushioned chairs, but when Moiraine put her cloak on a chair and started to sit, Cadsuane pointed to a spot in front of the other sisters. "Stand there, child," she said.

Fighting down a searing flare of temper, Moiraine made an effort not to clutch her skirt in fists. Even a woman as strong as Cadsuane had no right to order her here. Yet under that remorseless gaze, she stood as directed. Quivering with outrage, she struggled not to utter words she would regret, but she did it. There was something of Siuan about this woman, only magnified. Siuan had been born to lead. Cadsuane had been born to command.

She circled the three of them slowly, once, twice. Merean and Larelle exchanged wondering frowns, and Larelle opened her mouth, but after one look at Cadsuane closed it again. They assumed smooth-faced serenity; any watcher would have thought they knew exactly what was going on. Sometimes Cadsuane glanced at them, but the greater part of her attention stayed on Moiraine.

"Most new sisters," the legendary Green said abruptly, "hardly remove their shawls to sleep or bathe, but here you are without shawl or ring, in one of the most dangerous spots you could choose, short of the Blight itself. Why?"

Moiraine blinked. A direct question. The woman really did ignore custom when it suited her. She made her voice light. "New sisters also seek a Warder." Why was the woman singling her out in this manner? "I have not bonded mine, yet. I am told Bordermen make fine Warders." The Green sent her a stabbing look that made her wish she had been just a little less light.

Stopping behind Larelle, Cadsuane laid a hand on her shoulder. "What do you know of this child?"

Every girl in Larelle's classes had thought her the perfect sister and been intimidated by that cool consideration. They all had been afraid of her, and wanted to be her. "Moiraine was studious and a quick learner," she said thoughtfully. "She and Siuan Sanche were two of the quickest the Tower has ever seen. But you must know that. Let me see. She was rather too free with her opinions, and her temper, until we settled her down. As much as we did settle her. She and the Sanche girl had a continuing fondness for pranks. But they both passed for Accepted on the first try. She needs seasoning, of course, yet she may make something of herself."

Cadsuane moved behind Merean, asking the same question, adding, "A fondness for . . . pranks, Larelle said. A troublesome child?"

Merean shook her head with a smile. "Not troublesome, really. High-spirited. None of the tricks Moiraine played were mean, but they were plentiful. Novice and Accepted, she was sent to my study more often than any three other girls. Except for her pillow-friend Siuan. Of course, pillow-friends frequently get into tangles together, but with those two, one was never sent to me without the other. The last time the very night after passing for the shawl." Her smile faded into a frown very much like the one she had worn that night. Not angry, but rather disbelieving of the mischief young women could get up to. And a touch amused by it. "Instead of spending the night in contemplation, they tried to sneak mice into a sister's bed—Elaida a'Roihan—and were caught. I doubt any other women have been raised Aes Sedai while still too tender to sit from their last visit to the Mistress of Novices."

Moiraine kept her face smooth, kept her hands from knotting into fists, but she could do nothing about burning cheeks. That ruefully amused frown, as if she were still Accepted. She needed seasoning, did she? Well, perhaps she did, some, but still. And spreading out all these intimacies!

"I think you know all of me that you need to know," she told Cadsuane stiffly. How close she and Siuan had been was no one's business but theirs. And their punishments, *details* of their punishments. "If you are quite satisfied, I must pack my things. I am departing for Chachin."

She swallowed a groan before it could form. She still let her tongue go too free when her temper was up. If Merean or Larelle was part of the search, they must have at least part of the list in her little book. Including Jurine Najima here, the Lady Ines Demain in Chachin, and Avene Sahera, who lived in "a village on the high road between Chachin and Canluum." To strengthen suspicion, all she need do now was say she intended to spend time in Arafel and Shienar next.

Cadsuane smiled, not at all pleasantly. "You'll leave when I say, child. Be silent till you're spoken to. That pitcher should hold spiced wine. Pour for us."

Moiraine quivered. Child! She was no longer a novice. The woman could not order her coming and going. Or her tongue. But she did not protest. She walked to the hearth—stalked, really—and picked up the long-necked silver pitcher.

"You seem very interested in this young woman, Cadsuane," Merean said, turning slightly to watch Moiraine pour. "Is there something about her we should know?"

Larelle's smile held a touch of mockery. Only a touch, with Cadsuane. "Has someone Foretold she'll be Amyrlin one day? I can't say that I see it in her, but then, I don't have the Foretelling."

"I might live another thirty years," Cadsuane said, putting out a hand for the cup Moiraine offered, "or only three. Who can say?"

Moiraine's eyes went wide, and she slopped hot wine over her own wrist. Merean gasped, and Larelle looked as though she had been struck in the forehead with a stone.

"A little more care with the other cups," the Green said, unperturbed by all the gaping. "Child?" Moiraine returned to the hearth still staring, and Cadsuane went on. "Meilyn is considerably older. When she and I are gone, that leaves Kerene the strongest." Larelle flinched. Did the woman mean to violate *every* custom all in one go? "Am I disturbing you?"

Cadsuane's solicitous tone could not have been more false, and she did not wait for an answer. "Holding our silence about age doesn't keep people from knowing we live longer than they. Phaaw! From Kerene, it's a sharp drop to the next five. Five once this child and the Sanche girl reach their potential. And one of those is as old as I am and in retirement to boot."

"Is there some point to this?" Merean asked, sounding a little sick. Larelle pressed her hands against her middle, her face gray. They barely glanced at the wine Moiraine offered before gesturing it away, and she kept the cup, though she did not think she could swallow a mouthful.

Cadsuane scowled, a fearsome sight. "No one has come to the Tower in a thousand years who could match me. No one to match Meilyn or Kerene in almost six hundred. A thousand years ago, there would have been fifty sisters or more who stood higher than this child. In another hundred years, though, she'll stand in the first rank. Oh, someone stronger may be found in that time, but there won't be fifty, and there may be none. We dwindle."

Moiraine's ears pricked. Did Cadsuane have some solution to the problem? But how could any solution involve her?

"I don't understand," Larelle said sharply. She seemed to have gathered herself, and to be angry for her previous weakness. "We are all aware of the issue, but what does Moiraine have to do with it? Do you think she can somehow attract more girls to the Tower, girls with . . . with stronger potential?" She had to force that last out, grimacing in disgust, and her snort said what she thought of the notion.

"I would regret her being wasted before she knows up from down. The Tower can't afford to lose her out of her own ignorance. Look at her. A pretty little doll of a Cairhien noble." Cadsuane put a finger under Moiraine's chin, tilting it up. "Before you find a Warder like that, child, a brigand who wants to see what's in your purse will put an arrow through your heart. A footpad who'd faint at the sight of a sister in her sleep will crack your head, and you'll wake at the back of an alley minus your gold and maybe more. I suspect you'll want to take as much care choosing your first man as you do your first Warder."

Moiraine jerked back, spluttered with indignation. First

her and Siuan, now this. There were things one talked about, and things one did not!

Cadsuane ignored her outrage. Calmly sipping her wine, she turned back to the others. "Until she does find a Warder to guard her back, it might be best to protect her from her own enthusiasm. You two are going to Chachin, I believe. She'll travel with you, then. I expect you not to let her out of your sight."

Moiraine found her tongue, but her protests did as much good as her indignation had. Merean and Larelle objected, too, just as vociferously. Aes Sedai did not need "looking after," no matter how new. They had interests of their own to look after. They did not make clear what those were or whether they were shared between them—few sisters would have—but plainly neither wanted company. Cadsuane paid no attention to anything she did not want to hear, assumed they would do as she wished, pressed wherever they offered an opening. Soon the pair were twisting on their chairs and reduced to saying that they had encountered each other only the day before and were not sure they would be traveling on together. In any event, both meant to spend two or three days in Canluum, while Moiraine wanted to leave today.

"The child will stay until you leave," Cadsuane said briskly. "Good; that's done, then. I'm sure you two want to see to whatever brought you to Canluum. I won't keep you."

Larelle shifted her shawl irritably at the abrupt dismissal, then stalked out muttering that Moiraine would regret it if she got underfoot or slowed her reaching Chachin. Merean took it better, saying she would look after Moiraine like a daughter, though her smile hardly looked pleased.

When they were gone, Moiraine stared at Cadsuane incredulously. She had never seen anything like it. Except an avalanche, once. The thing to do now was keep silent until she had a chance to leave without Cadsuane or the others seeing. Much the wisest thing. "I agreed to nothing," she said coolly. Very coolly. "What if I have affairs in Chachin that will not wait? What if I do not choose to wait here two or three days?" Perhaps she did need to learn to school her tongue a little more.

Cadsuane had been looking thoughtfully at the door that had closed behind Merean and Larelle, but she turned a

piercing gaze on Moiraine. "You've worn the shawl only
four months or so, and you have affairs that cannot wait?
Phaaw! You still haven't learned the first real lesson, that
the shawl means you are ready to truly begin learning. The
second lesson is caution. I know better than most how hard
that is to find when you're young and have *saidar* at your
fingertips and the world at your feet. As you think." Moiraine tried to fit a word in, but she might as well have stood
in front of that avalanche. "You will take great risks in your
life, if you live long enough. You already take more than
you know. Heed carefully what I say. And do as I say. I will
check your bed tonight, and if you are not in it, I will find
you and make you weep as you did for those mice. You can
dry your tears afterward on that shawl you believe makes
you invincible. It does not."

Staring as the door closed behind Cadsuane, Moiraine
suddenly realized she still held the cup of wine and gulped it
dry. The woman was . . . formidable. Custom forbade physical violence against another sister, but Cadsuane had not
sidestepped a hair in her threat. She had said it right out,
so by the Three Oaths she meant it exactly. Incredible. Was
it happenstance that she had mentioned Meilyn Arganya
and Kerene Nagashi? They were two of Tamra's searchers.
Could Cadsuane be another? Either way, she had very neatly
cut Moiraine out of the hunt for the next week or more. If
she actually went with Merean and Larelle, at least. But why
only a week? If the woman was part of the search. . . . If
Cadsuane knew about her and Siuan. . . . If. . . . Standing
there fiddling with an empty winecup was getting her nowhere. She snatched up her cloak.

CHAPTER
18

A Narrow Passage

A number of people looked around at Moiraine when she came out into the common room, some with sympathy in their eyes. Doubtless they were imagining what it must be like to be the focus of attention for three Aes Sedai, and they could not imagine any good in it. There was no commiseration on any sister's face. Most took hardly any notice of her at all. Felaana wore a pleased smile, though, probably thinking the Lady Alys' name as good as written in the novice book. At least she did not know the truth, not with that smile. There was some hope of staying hidden from Sierin a while longer. Cadsuane was nowhere in sight, nor the other two.

Picking her way through the tables, Moiraine felt as though she had been spun like a top. There were too many questions, and not an answer to be found. She wished Siuan were there, with her ability to solve puzzles. And nothing shook Siuan. She could have used Siuan's presence for the steadying alone.

A young woman looked in at the door from the street, then jerked out of sight. Moiraine missed a step. Wish for something hard enough, and you could think you saw it. The woman peeked in again, the hood of her cloak fallen atop the bundle on her back, and it really was Siuan, sturdy and handsome in one of Tamore's plain blue riding dresses. This time she saw Moiraine, but instead of rushing to greet her, Siuan nodded up the street and vanished again.

Heart climbing into her throat, Moiraine swept her cloak around her and went out. Down the street, Siuan was slipping through the traffic, glancing back at every third step. A wagon driver hauled her reins hard to avoid running Siuan down, and cracked her whip over Siuan's head, but Siuan seemed unaware of the horses snorting in their traces or the whip or the wagon driver's angry shouts. Moiraine followed quickly, worry growing. Another three or four years would pass before Siuan gained enough strength to tell Cetalia she was leaving the job as Cetalia's assistant. There would be snow at Sunday before the woman let her go short of that. And the only other possibility for her being in Canluum. . . . Moiraine groaned, and a big-eared fellow selling pins from a tray gave her a concerned look. She glared so hard that he started back.

Perhaps Siuan had let something slip, or maybe her book of names had been found, or. . . . No; how it happened did not matter. Sierin must have found out, about everything. It would be just like the woman to send Siuan to bring her back, so their worry could feed on each other during the long ride. Maybe she was building phantasms, but she could not imagine another explanation.

A hundred paces from the inn, Siuan looked back once more, paused till she was sure that Moiraine saw her, then darted into an alley. Moiraine quickened her stride and followed.

Her friend was pacing beneath the still-unlit oil lamps that lined this narrow, dusty passage. The dark blue dress showed signs of hard travel, creases and stains, dust. Nothing frightened Siuan, yet fear glittered in those sharp blue eyes now. Moiraine opened her mouth to confirm her own fears about Sierin, but the taller woman spoke first.

"Light, I thought I'd *never* bloody find you. Tell me you've found him, Moiraine. Tell me the Najima boy's the one, and we can hand him to the Tower with a hundred sisters watching, and it's done."

A hundred sisters? "No, Siuan, he is not." This did not sound like Sierin. "What is the matter? Why did you come yourself instead of sending a message?"

Siuan began to weep. Siuan, who had a lion's heart. Tears spilled down her cheeks. Throwing her arms around Moiraine, she squeezed hard enough to make Moiraine's ribs ache. She was trembling. "I couldn't trust this to a pigeon," she mumbled, "or to any of the eyes-and-ears. I wouldn't have dared. They're all dead. Aisha and Kerene, Valera and Ludice and Meilyn. They say Aisha and her Warder were killed by bandits in Murandy. Kerene supposedly fell off a ship in the Alguenya during a storm and drowned. And Meilyn . . . Meilyn. . . ." Sobs racked her so she could not go on.

Moiraine hugged her back, making soothing sounds. And staring past Siuan's shoulder in consternation. "Accidents do happen," she said slowly. "Bandits. Storms. Aes Sedai can die as easily as anyone else."

She was having a hard time making herself believe. *All* of them? Her father used to say that once was happenstance, twice might be coincidence, but thrice or more indicated the actions of your enemies. He said he had read it somewhere. But *what* enemies? A thought occurred, and she forced it down. Some things did not bear thinking.

Siuan pushed herself away from Moiraine's embrace. "You don't understand. Meilyn!" Grimacing, she scrubbed at her eyes. "Fish guts! I'm not making this clear. Get hold of yourself, you bloody fool!" That last was growled to herself. Guiding Moiraine to an upended cask with no bung, she sat Moiraine down and shrugged off the bundle from her own back. If that was all she was traveling with, likely she did not have so much as a spare dress. "You won't want to be standing when you hear what I have to say. For that matter, I bloody well don't want to be standing myself."

Dragging a crate with broken slats from further up the alley, she settled on it, fussing with her skirts, peering toward the street, muttering about people looking in as they passed. Her reluctance did nothing to soothe Moiraine's fluttering stomach. It seemed to do little for Siuan's, either. When she started again, she kept pausing to swallow, like a woman who wanted to sick up.

"Meilyn returned to the Tower almost a month ago. I don't know why. She didn't say where she had been, or where she was going, but she only meant to stay a few nights. I. . . . I'd heard about Kerene the morning Meilyn came back, and the others before that. So I decided to speak to her. Don't look at me that way! I know how to be cautious!"

Cautious? Siuan? Moiraine could have laughed. Only she knew if she did, it might well tip over into tears of her own. This was madness. It had to be madness. She shoved that horrible thought away again. There had to be another explanation. There *had* to be.

"Anyway, I sneaked into her rooms and hid under the bed. So the servants wouldn't see me when they turned down her sheets." Siuan grunted sourly. "I fell asleep under there. Sunrise woke me, and her bed hadn't been slept in. So I sneaked out again—not easy that time of morning, but I'm sure nobody saw me—and went down to the second sitting of breakfast. And while I was spooning my porridge, Chesmal Emry came in to. . . . She. . . . She announced that Meilyn had been found in her bed, that she'd died during the night." She finished in a rush and sagged, staring at Moiraine.

Moiraine was very glad to be sitting. Her knees would not have supported a feather. It *was* madness. Murder had been done. "The Red Ajah?" she suggested finally. A Red might kill a sister she thought intended to protect a man who could channel. It was possible. But she could not have said it aloud, because she did not believe it

Siuan snorted. "Meilyn didn't have a mark on her. Yellows delved her, of course. They'd have detected poison, or smothering. They found nothing and called it a natural death. But I know it wasn't. It couldn't be, not the way they found her. No marks. That means the Power, Moiraine. Could even a Red do that?" Her voice was fierce, but she pulled the bundle up, clutching it on her lap. She seemed to be hiding behind it. Still, there was less fear on her face than anger, now.

"Think, Moiraine. Tamra supposedly died in her sleep, too. Only we know Meilyn didn't, no matter where she was found. First Tamra, then the others started dying. The only thing that makes sense is that someone noticed her calling sisters in and wanted to know why badly enough that they bloody risked putting the Amyrlin Seat herself to the question. They had to have something to hide to do that, something they'd hazard anything to keep hidden. They killed her to hide it, to hide what they'd done, and then they set out to kill the rest. Which means they don't want the boy found, not alive. They don't want the Dragon Reborn at the Last Battle. Any other way to look at it is tossing the slop bucket into the wind and hoping for the best."

Unconsciously, Moiraine peered toward the mouth of the alley. A few people walking by glanced in, but none more than once. No one paused at seeing them seated there.

Some things were easier to speak of when you were not too specific. "The Amyrlin" had been put to the question; "she" had been killed. Not Tamra, not a name that brought up the familiar face. "Someone" had murdered her. "They" did not want the Dragon Reborn found. Putting someone to the question with the Power violated none of the Three Oaths, but murder using *saidar* certainly did, even for. . . . For those Moiraine did not want to name any more than Siuan did.

Forcing her face to smoothness, forcing her voice to calm, she forced the words out. "The Black Ajah." Siuan flinched, then nodded, glowering.

Almost any sister grew angry at the suggestion that a secret Ajah existed, hidden inside the others, an Ajah dedicated to the Dark One. Most sisters refused to listen to any mention of it. The White Tower had stood for the Light for over three thousand years. But some sisters did not deny the Black straight out. Some believed. Very few would admit it even to another sister, though. Moiraine did not want to admit it to herself.

Siuan plucked fretfully at the ties on her bundle, but she went on in a brisk voice. "I don't think they have our names—Tamra never really thought us part of it; she told us to be quiet, put us aside, and forgot us—else I'd have had an 'accident,' too. Just before I left, I slipped a note with my suspicions under Sierin's door. Not about the boy; about the. . . . About the Black. Only, I didn't know how much to trust her even there. The Amyrlin Seat! But if it's real, then anybody could belong. Anybody! I wrote with my left hand, but I was shaking so hard, no one could recognize my writing if I'd used my right. Burn my liver! Even if we knew who to trust, we have bilgewater for proof."

"Enough for me." Light, the Black Ajah! "If they know everything, all the women Tamra chose, there may be none left except us. We will have to move fast if we have a hope of finding the boy." It all seemed hopeless—who could say how many Black sisters there might be? twenty? fifty? and a terrible thought: more?—but Moiraine tried for a vigorous tone, too. It was gratifying that Siuan only nodded. She would not give up for all her talk of shaking, and she never considered that Moiraine might. *Most* gratifying. Especially when she still doubted her knees. "Perhaps they know us, and perhaps not. Perhaps they think they can leave two new sisters for last. In any case, we cannot trust anyone but ourselves." The blood drained from her face, and she suddenly felt light-headed. "Oh, Light! I just had an encounter at the inn, Siuan."

She tried to recall every word, every nuance, from the moment Merean first spoke. Siuan listened with a distant look, filing and sorting. "Cadsuane could be Black Ajah," she agreed when Moiraine finished. She barely hesitated over the words. "Maybe she's just trying to get you out of the way until she can dispose of you without rousing suspicion. Or she could be one of Tamra's chosen. Just because we think she hasn't been in Tar Valon for two years doesn't make it so." Sisters did slip in and out of the Tower quietly sometimes, but Moiraine thought that anywhere Cadsuane arrived shook as though struck by an earthquake. "The trouble is, any of them could be either." Leaning across her bundle, she touched Moiraine's knee. "Can you bring your horse from the stable without being seen? I have a good mount, but I don't know if she can carry both of us. We should be hours from here before they know we're gone."

Moiraine smiled in spite of herself. She very much doubted the good mount. Any horse trader could pass off a broken-down cart horse as a charger to Siuan, whose eye for horseflesh was no better than her seat in the saddle. The ride north must have been agony for her. And full of fear. "No one knows you are here at all, Siuan," she said. "Best if it stays so. You have your book? Good. If I remain until morning, I will have a day's start on them instead of hours. You go on to Chachin now. Take some of my coin." By the state of Siuan's dress, she had spent the last part of that trip sleeping under bushes. She would not have dared draw much from the Tower's bank before leaving. "Start searching for the Lady Ines, and I will catch you up there, looking for Avene Sahera on the way."

It was not that easy, of course. Siuan had a stubborn streak as wide as the Erinin.

"I have enough for my needs," she grumbled, but Moiraine insisted on handing her half the coins in her purse, and when Moiraine reminded her of their pledge during their first months in the Tower, that what one owned belonged to the other as well, she muttered, "We swore we'd find beautiful young princes to bond, too, and marry them besides. Girls say all sorts of silly things. You watch after yourself, now. You leave me alone in this, and I'll wring your neck."

Embracing to say goodbye, Moiraine found it hard to let go. An hour ago, her worries had been how long she could escape Sierin's justice and the birch. Now, that seemed like worrying over stubbing her toe. The Black Ajah. She wanted to empty her stomach. If only she had Siuan's courage. Watching Siuan slip down the alley adjusting that bundle on her back again, Moiraine wished she were Green. She would have liked at least three or four Warders to guard her back right then.

Walking back up the street, she could not help looking at everyone she passed, man or woman. If the Black Ajah—her stomach twisted every time she thought that name—if they were involved, then ordinary Darkfriends were, too. No one denied that some misguided people believed the Dark One would give them immortality, people who would kill and do every sort of evil to gain that hoped-for reward. And if any sister could be Black Ajah, anyone she met could be a Darkfriend. She hoped Siuan remembered that.

As she approached The Gates of Heaven, a sister appeared in the inn's doorway. Part of a sister, at least; all she could see was an arm with a fringed shawl over it, and that just for an instant. A very tall man who had just come out, his hair in two belled braids, turned back to speak for a moment, but a hand gestured peremptorily, and he strode past Moiraine wearing a scowl. She would not have thought twice of it if not for thinking about the Black Ajah and Darkfriends. The Light knew, Aes Sedai did speak to men, and some did more than speak. She had been thinking of Darkfriends, though. And Black sisters. If only she could have made out the color of that fringe. She hurried the last thirty-odd paces frowning.

Merean and Larelle were seated together by themselves near the door, both still wearing their shawls. Few sisters did that except for ceremony, or for show. Both women were watching Cadsuane go into that private sitting room followed by a pair of lean, gray-haired men who looked hard as last year's oak. She still wore her shawl, too, with the white Flame of Tar Valon bright on her back amid the woven vines. It could have been any of them. Cadsuane might be looking for another Warder; Greens always seemed to be looking. Merean or Larelle might be, too; neither had one, unless bonded since she left Tar Valon. The fellow's scowl might have been for hearing he did not measure up. There were a hundred possible explanations, and she put the man out of her head. The sure dangers were real enough without inventing more.

Before she was three steps into the common room, Master Helvin bustled up in a green-striped apron, a bald-headed man nearly as wide as he was tall, and handed her a new irritation. "Ah, Lady Alys; just who I was looking for. With three more Aes Sedai stopping here, I fear I need to shuffle the beds again. Certainly you won't mind sharing yours, under the circumstances. Mistress Palan is a most pleasant woman."

Under the circumstances? Under any normal circumstances, he would never have dared suggest doubling to a noblewoman, no matter how many merchants he had to push into one bed. But what he meant was, since she would soon be off to the White Tower. In fact, he more than suggested. He had already moved the woman in! And when she protested. . . .

"If you're displeased, I suggest you speak to one of the Aes Sedai," he said in a firm voice. A firm voice! To her! "Now, if you'll excuse me, I have many things to take care of. We're very busy right now." And off he bustled without another word. Or even a bow!

She could have screamed. She very nearly channeled, to give him a clout on the ear.

Haesel Palan was a rug merchant from Murandy with the lilt of Lugard in her voice. Moiraine heard more of it than she wanted from the moment she stepped into the small room that had been hers alone. Her clothes had been moved from the wardrobe to pegs on the wall, her comb and brush displaced from the washstand for Mistress Palan's. The plump, graying woman in fine brown woolens surely would have been diffident with "Lady Alys," but not with a wilder who everybody said was off in the morning to become a novice in the White Tower. She lectured Moiraine on the duties of a novice, all of her information wrong. Some of what she suggested would have killed most of the novices in a week if not on the first day, and the rest was just impossible. Learn to fly? The woman was mad! She followed Moiraine down to supper and gathered other traders of her acquaintance at the table, every woman of them eager to share what she knew of the White Tower. Which was nothing at all. They shared it in great detail, though. If Moiraine truly had been a potential novice, they would have frightened her out of going anywhere near the Tower! She thought to escape by retiring early, but Mistress Palan appeared almost as soon as she had her dress off and talked until she dropped off to sleep.

It was not an easy night. The bed was narrow, the woman's elbows sharp and her feet icy despite thick blankets trapping the warmth of the small, tiled stove built in beneath the bed. Ignoring cold air was one thing; icy feet were quite something else. The rainstorm that had threatened all day broke, wind and thunder rattling the shutters for hours. Moiraine doubted she could have slept in any event. Darkfriends and the Black Ajah danced in her head. She saw Tamra being dragged from her sleep, dragged away to somewhere secret and tortured by women wielding the Power. Sometimes the women wore Merean's face, and Larelle's, and Cadsuane's, and every sister's she had ever seen. Sometimes Tamra's face became her own.

When the door creaked slowly open in the dark hours of morning, Moiraine embraced the Source in a flash. *Saidar* filled her to the point where the sweetness and joy came close to pain. Not as much of the Power as she would be able to handle in another year, much less five, yet a hair more would burn the ability out of her now, or kill her. One was as bad as the other, but she wanted to draw more, and not just because the Power always made you want more.

Cadsuane put her head in. Moiraine had forgotten her promise, her threat. The Green sister saw the glow, of course, could feel how much she held. "Fool girl" was all the woman said before leaving.

Moiraine counted to one hundred slowly, then swung her feet out from under the covers. Now was as good a time as any. Mistress Palan heaved onto her side and began to snore. It sounded like canvas ripping. Even so, Moiraine took care to be quiet. Channeling Fire, she lit one of the lamps and dressed hurriedly. A riding dress, this time, in dark blue silk and embroidered on the neck and sleeves in a golden pattern like Maldine lace. Reluctantly she decided to abandon her saddlebags along with everything else she had to leave behind. Anyone who saw her moving about might not think too much of it even this time of the morning, but not if she had saddlebags over her shoulder. All she took was what she could fit into the pockets sewn inside her cloak, her brush and comb and sewing kit, some spare stockings and a clean shift. There was no room for more. It was enough, with the letters-of-rights and the remaining gold in her belt pouch. Mistress Palan was still snoring as she closed the door behind her.

CHAPTER
19

Pond Water

T he common room was empty at that hour, though the clatter of pots and the murmur of voices through the kitchen door told of preparations for breakfast. She hurried out through a side door, into the inn's stable-yard. Unseen, she was sure. So far, so good. The sky was just beginning to turn gray, and the air retained every ounce of the night's chill, but at least the rain had stopped. There was a weave to keep rain off, but it did tend to attract notice. Gathering her skirts and cloak to keep them out of the puddles on the paving stones, she quickened her step. The faster gone, the less chance of being seen.

Not that she could avoid every eye. The hinges creaked softly as she opened one of the stable doors to slip inside, and the coatless groom on night duty jumped to his feet from the stool where he had no doubt been dozing with his back against a thick roof post. A skinny, hook-nosed fellow with the tilted eyes of Saldaea, he raked his fingers through his hair in a useless effort to straighten it and made a jerky bow.

"How may I help my Lady?" he asked in a raspy voice.

"Saddle my mare, Kazin," she said, putting a silver penny in his ready hand. It was very good luck that this same man had been on duty when she arrived, too. Master Helvin had written a description of Arrow in the stable book, sitting on a slanted ledge by the doors, but she very much doubted Kazin could read. The silver had him knuckling his forehead and scurrying for Arrow's stall. Likely, he more often received coppers.

She regretted leaving her packhorse behind, but not even

a fool noble—she had heard Kazin mutter "who but a fool noble would ride out at this hour?"—would take a pack animal for a morning jaunt. At best, he would hurry inside to find out whether she was paid in full with the innkeeper. She was, and for another night besides, but there was always the chance Cadsuane had promised the servants rewards to watch her movements. In the Green sister's place, she would have. This way, no one would suspect anything until she failed to return that night.

Climbing into Arrow's high-cantled saddle, she gave the groom a cool smile, because of his comment, and rode slowly out into damp, nearly empty streets. Just out for a ride, however early. It looked to be a good day. The sky looked rained out, for one thing, with barely a cloud blocking the stars, and there was little wind.

The lamps high on the walls of every building were still lit all along the streets and alleys, leaving no more than the palest shadow anywhere, yet the only people to be seen were the Night Watch's helmeted patrols with their halberds and crossbows, and the Lamplighters, just as heavily armed as they made their rounds to make sure no lamp went out. A wonder that people could live so close to the Blight that a Myrddraal could step out of any dark shadow. Night Watchmen and Lamplighters alike eyed her with surprise as she rode by. No one went out in the night. Not in the Borderlands.

Which was why she was surprised to see she was not the first to reach the western gates. Slowing Arrow, she stayed well back from the three very large men waiting with a packhorse behind their mounts. None wore helmet or armor, but each wore a sword at his hip and carried a heavy horsebow, with a bristling quiver tied in front of his saddle. Few men went unarmed in these lands. Their attention was all on the barred gates, with now and again a word shared with the gate guards. They seemed impatient for the gates to open, and barely glanced in her direction. The lamps near the gates showed their faces clearly. A grizzled old man and a hard-faced young one, in dark, knee-long coats, with braided leather cords tied around their heads. Malkieri? She thought that was what that cord meant. The third was an Arafellin with belled braids, in a dark yellow coat sewn with more bells. The same fellow she had seen leaving The Gates of Heaven.

By the time a bright sliver of sunrise on the horizon allowed the gates to be swung wide, several merchants' trains had lined up to depart. The three men were first through, but Moiraine let a dozen tall, canvas-covered wagons behind six-horse teams rumble ahead of her, with their outriding guards in helmets and breastplates, before she followed across the bridge and onto the road through the hills. She kept the three in sight, though. They were heading in the same direction so far, after all.

They moved quickly, good riders who barely shifted a rein, but speed suited her. The more distance she put between herself and Cadsuane, the better. She stayed only close enough to maintain sight of the men. No need to attract their attention until she wished. At that pace, the merchants' wagons and their guards fell behind long before she saw the first village near midday, a small cluster of tile-roofed two-story stone houses around a tiny inn on a forested hill slope beside the road. Even after several months it still seemed odd to see villagers wearing swords, and at least one halberd racked outside every door. Crossbows and quivers, too. It made stark contrast to the children rolling hoops and tossing beanbags in the street.

The three men never slowed or turned an eye toward the village, but Moiraine paused long enough to purchase part of a loaf of crusty pale bread and a narrow wedge of hard yellow cheese and ask whether anyone knew a woman named Avene Sahera. The answer was no, and she galloped on until the three appeared on the hard-packed road ahead, their horses still in that ground-eating pace. Maybe they knew nothing more than the name of the sister the Arafellin had spoken to, but anything at all she learned about Cadsuane or the other two would be to the good.

She formulated several plans for approaching them, and discarded each. Three men on a deserted forest road could well decide a young woman alone was a heaven-sent opportunity, especially if they were what she feared. Handling them presented no difficulty, if it came to it, but she wanted to avoid that. Should they turn out to be Darkfriends, or simply brigands, she would have to hold them prisoner long enough to hand them over to some authority. No telling how long that would take, and besides, there would be no hiding that she was Aes Sedai then. News of a woman capturing three outlaws, hardly an event of every day, would spread like wildfire in dry timber. She might as well weave a great column of Fire above her head to help anyone who wanted to find her.

Forest gave way to scattered farms, and farms faded to more forest, towering fir and pine and leatherleaf, massive oaks with only tiny red leaf-buds on their thick branches. A red-crested eagle soared overhead, not twenty paces up, and became a shape against the descending sun. The road ahead was empty except for the three men and their pack animal, and bare of life behind as well. Decent people would be at their suppers. Not that there was so much as a farmhouse in evidence here. As her shadow stretched out behind her, she decided to forget the men and begin looking for a place to sleep. With luck she might see more farms soon, and if a little silver did not bring a bed, a hayloft would have to do. Without luck, her saddle would suffice for a pillow, if a hard one. A meal would be nice, though. That bread and cheese seemed a very long time back.

Ahead, the three men suddenly stopped in the middle of the road, conferring for a moment. She drew rein where she was. Even if they noticed, proper caution for a woman alone called on her not to ride up on them. Then one of the fellows took the packhorse and turned aside into the forest. The others dug in their heels and rode on at a quicker pace, as though suddenly remembering somewhere they needed to be.

Moiraine frowned. The Arafellin was one of the pair rushing off, but since they were traveling together, maybe he had mentioned meeting an Aes Sedai to his companion left behind. The younger Malkieri, she thought. People did talk about encounters of that sort. Relatively few people had actually met a sister and known who or what she was. And one man would certainly be less trouble than three, if she was careful.

Riding to where rider and packhorse had vanished, she dismounted and began searching for sign. Most ladies left tracking to their huntsmen, but she had taken an interest in the years when climbing trees and getting dirty had seemed equal fun. It appeared this man was no woodsman, though. Broken twigs and kicked winter-fall leaves left a trail a child could have followed. A hundred paces or so into the forest, she spotted a wide pond in a hollow through the trees. And the younger of the Malkieri.

He had already unsaddled and hobbled his bay—a fine-looking animal; much too fine for his worn coat, perhaps the sign of a bandit—and was setting the packsaddle on the ground. He looked even larger, this close, with very wide shoulders and a narrow waist. Far from a pretty man, too. Not handsome, with that hard, angular face. A suitable face for a brigand. Unbuckling his sword belt, he sat down cross-legged facing the pond, laid sword and belt beside him, and put his hands on his knees. He seemed to be staring off across the water, still glittering through the late afternoon shadows, toward the water reeds that rimmed the far bank. He did not move a muscle.

Moiraine considered. Plainly he had been left to make camp. The others would return, but not quickly, since he was slacking his task. A question or two would not take long. "Which of you met an Aes Sedai recently?" might be enough. And if he was unnerved a little—say at finding her suddenly standing right behind him—he might answer before he thought. *Saidar* must be left till last. She would have to use it almost certainly, but let the fact that she could channel come as an added surprise.

Tying Arrow's reins to a low branch on a leatherleaf, she gathered her cloak and skirts and moved forward as silently as possible. A small hummock lay behind him, and she stepped up onto that. Added height could help. He was a very tall man. And it might also help if he found her with her belt knife in one hand and his sword in the other. Channeling, she whisked the scabbarded blade from his side. Every little bit of shock she could manage for him—

He moved faster than thought. No one so large could move so fast, yet her grasp closed on the scabbard, and he uncoiled, whirling, one hand clutching the scabbard between hers, the other seizing the front of her dress. Before she could think to channel, she was flying through the air. She had just time to see the pond coming up at her, just time to shout something, she did not know what, and then she struck the surface flat, driving all the wind out of her, struck with a great splash and sank. The water was *freezing*! *Saidar* fled in her shock.

Floundering to her feet, she stood up to her waist in the

icy water, coughing, wet hair clinging to her face, sodden cloak dragging at her shoulders. Furiously she twisted around to confront her attacker, furiously embraced the Source once more, prepared to knock him down and drub him till he squealed!

He stood shaking his head and frowning in puzzlement at the spot where she had stood, a long stride from where he had been sitting. She might as well have been a fish! When he *deigned* to notice her, he put down the scabbarded sword and came to the edge of the pond, bending to stretch out a hand.

"Unwise to try separating a man from his sword," he said, and after a glance at the colored slashes on her dress added, "my Lady." Hardly an apology. His startlingly blue eyes did not quite meet hers. If he was hiding mirth . . . !

Muttering under her breath, she splashed awkwardly to where she could take his outstretched hand in both of hers. And heaved with all of her might. Ignoring icy water tickling down your ribs was not easy, and if she was wet, so would he be, and without any need to use the One. . . .

He straightened, raised his arm, and she came out of the water dangling from his hand. In consternation she stared at him until her feet touched the ground and he backed away.

"I'll start a fire and hang up blankets so you can dry yourself," he murmured, still not meeting her gaze. What *was* he hiding? Or perhaps he was shy. She had never heard of a shy Darkfriend, though she supposed there could be some.

He was as good as his word, and by the time the other men reappeared, she was standing beside a small fire surrounded by blankets dug from his packsaddles and hung from the branches of an oak. She had no need of the fire for drying, of course. The proper weave of Water had taken every drop from her hair and clothes while she stayed in them. As well he did not see that, though. Or her, until her hair was combed straight and brushed. And she did appreciate the flame's warmth. Anyway, she had to stay inside the blankets long enough for the man to think she had used the fire as he intended. She very definitely held on to *saidar*. So far, she had proof of nothing.

"Did she follow you, Lan?" a man's voice said as he dismounted to the jingle of bells. The Arafellin.

"Why are those blankets up?" a sour voice demanded gruffly.

Moiraine stared at nothing, missing what reply her assailant made to the questions. They had known? Men watched for bandits in these times, but they had noticed a lone woman and decided she was following them? It made no sense. But why lure her into the woods instead of just confronting her? Three men had no reason to fear one woman. Unless they knew she was Aes Sedai. They would step very cautiously, then. But she was certain the fellow had no idea how she had gotten hold of his sword.

"A Cairhienin, Lan? I suppose you've seen a Cairhienin in her skin, but I never have." That certainly caught her ear, and with the Power filling her, so did another sound. Steel whispering on leather. A sword leaving its sheath. Preparing several weaves that would stop the lot of them in their tracks, she made a crack in the blankets to peek out.

To her surprise, the man who had dunked her—Lan?—stood with his back to her blankets. He was the one with bared steel in hand. The Arafellin, facing him, looked surprised.

"You remember the sight of the Thousand Lakes, Ryne," Lan said coldly. "Does a woman need protection from your eyes?"

For a moment, she thought Ryne was going to draw despite the blade already in Lan's hand, but the older man—Bukama, she heard him called—a much-battered, graying fellow though as tall as the others, calmed matters, took the other two a little distance away with talk of some game called "sevens." A strange game it seemed to be, and more than dangerous in the failing daylight. Lan and Ryne sat cross-legged facing one another, their swords sheathed, then without warning drew, each blade flashing toward the other man's throat, stopping just short of flesh. The older man pointed to Ryne; they sheathed swords, and then did it again. For as long as she watched, that was how it went. Perhaps Ryne had not been so overconfident as he seemed.

Waiting inside the blankets, she tried to recall what she had been taught of Malkier. It had not been a great deal, except as history. Ryne remembered the Thousand Lakes, so he must be Malkieri, too. There had been something about distressed women. Now that she was with them, she might as well stay until she learned what she could.

When she came out from behind the blankets, she was ready. "I claim the right of a woman alone," she told them formally. "I travel to Chachin, and I ask the shelter of your swords." She also pressed a fat silver coin into each man's hand. She was not really sure about this ridiculous "woman alone" business, but silver caught most men's attention. "And two more each, paid in Chachin."

The reactions were not what she expected. Ryne glared at the coin as he turned it over in his fingers. Lan looked at his without expression and tucked it into his coat pocket with a grunt. She had given them some of her last Tar Valon marks, she realized, but Tar Valon coins could be found anywhere, along with those of every other land.

Bukama bowed with his left hand on his knee. "Honor to serve, my Lady," he said. "To Chachin, my life above yours." His eyes were also blue, and they, too, would not quite meet hers. She hoped he did not turn out to be a Darkfriend.

Learning anything proved to be difficult. Impossible. First the men were busy setting up camp, tending the horses, making a larger fire. They did not seem eager to face a new spring night without that. Bukama and Lan barely said a word over a dinner of flatbread and dried meat that she tried not to wolf down. Ryne talked and was quite charming, really, with a dimple in his cheek when he smiled, and a sparkle in his blue eyes, but he gave no opening for her to mention The Gates of Heaven or Aes Sedai. When she finally inquired why he was going to Chachin, his face turned sad.

"Every man has to die somewhere," he said softly, and went off to make up his blankets. A very odd answer. Worthy of an Aes Sedai.

Lan took the first watch as the moon rose above the trees, sitting cross-legged not far from Ryne, and when Bukama doused the fire and rolled himself up in his blankets near Lan, she wove a ward of Spirit around each man. Flows of Spirit she could hold on to sleeping, and if any of them moved in the night, the ward would wake her without alerting them. It meant waking every time they changed guard, which they did frequently, but there was nothing for it. Her own blankets lay well away from the men, and as she settled her head on her saddle for the third time, Bukama murmured something she could not catch. She heard Lan's reply plainly enough.

"I'd sooner trust an Aes Sedai, Bukama. Go to sleep."

All the anger she had tamped down flared up. The man threw her into an icy pond, he did not apologize, he . . . ! She channeled, Air and Water weaving with a touch of Earth. A thick cylinder of water rose from the surface of the pond, stretching up and up in the moonlight, arching over. Crashing down on the fool who was so free with his tongue!

Splattered, Bukama and Ryne bounded to their feet with oaths, but she continued the torrent for a count of ten before letting it end. Freed water splashed down across the campsite. She expected to see a sodden, half-frozen man beaten to the ground and ready to learn proper respect. He *was* dripping wet, a few small fish flopping around his feet. He was standing on his feet. With his sword out.

"Shadowspawn?" Ryne said in a disbelieving tone, and atop him, Lan said, "Maybe! I've never heard the like, though. Guard the woman, Ryne! Bukama, take west and circle south; I'll take east and circle north!"

"Not Shadowspawn!" Moiraine snapped, stopping them in their tracks. They stared at her. She wished she could see their expressions better in the moonshadows, but those cloud-shifting shadows aided her, too, cloaking her in mystery. With an effort she gave her voice every bit of cool Aes Sedai serenity she could muster. "It is unwise to show anything except respect to an Aes Sedai, Master Lan."

"Aes Sedai?" Ryne whispered. Despite the dim light, the awe on his face was clear. Or maybe it was fear.

No one else made a sound, except for Bukama's grumbles as he shifted his bed away from the mud. Ryne spent a long time moving his blankets in silence, giving her small bows whenever she glanced his way. Lan made no attempt to dry off. He started to choose a new spot for his watch, then stopped and sat back where he had been, in the mud and water. She might have thought it a gesture of humility, only he glanced at her, very nearly meeting her eyes this time. If that was humility, kings were the most humble men on earth.

She wove her wards around them again, of course. If anything, revealing herself only made it more necessary. She did not go to sleep for quite a while, though. She had a great deal to think about. For one thing, none of the men had asked *why* she was following them. The man had been on his *feet*! When she drifted off, she was thinking of Ryne, strangely. A pity if he was afraid of her, now. A great pity if he turned out to be a Darkfriend. He was charming, and quite pretty, really. She did not mind a man wanting to see her unclothed, only his telling others about it.

CHAPTER
20

Breakfast in Manala

Y ou may call me Lady Alys," the strange little woman
told them when she climbed drowsily from her
blankets at sunrise, stifling yawns with a fist. Apparently she was unused to sleeping on the ground. Lan was
certain she had been awake every time he took a turn at
guard. People breathed differently awake and asleep. Well,
women who wore silks seldom encountered hardships or
discomfort.

He doubted the name as much as he did the Great Serpent
ring she produced, especially after she tucked it back into her
belt pouch and said no one must know she was Aes Sedai, not
even other sisters. True, Aes Sedai often pretended to be ordinary women, and carried it off with those who did not know a
sister's face, and true, once he had encountered an Aes Sedai
who had not yet attained the ageless look, but one and all they
practiced serenity to a fault. Oh, they got angry, but it was a
cold anger. He had seen "Alys'" face in the moonlight when
the water stopped, though he had not realized what he was
seeing till later. Childish glee at playing a prank, and childish
disappointment that it had not worked as she wished. Aes
Sedai were many things, and convoluted enough with it to
make other women seem simple, but they were never childish.

When they had first seen her behind them, outpacing the
merchant trains and the shield of their guards, Bukama offered a reason for a woman alone to follow three men. If
six swordsmen could not kill a man in daylight, perhaps
one woman could in darkness. Bukama had not mentioned
Edeyn, of course. In truth, it plainly could not be that, or he
would be dead now, yet Edeyn might set a woman to watch

him, thinking he would be less on his guard. Only a fool believed women less dangerous than men, but women often seemed to think men fools when it came to women.

In the night, despite his earlier misgivings, Bukama had expressed displeasure at Lan's refusal to make proper pledge to her, though his own pledge sufficed to tie them to this "Lady Alys" to Chachin. Besides, she had given them money. The woman did not know insult when she offered it. This morning, he grumbled while saddling his black gelding, a horse he claimed was not a patch on Sun Lance. That was going some even for Bukama. The black was a fine animal, with excellent conformation and a good turn of speed, if untrained as a warhorse yet. "Aes Sedai or not, a decent man follows certain forms," he muttered as he tightened his front saddle girth. "It's a matter of common decency."

"Give over, Bukama," Lan told him quietly. Bukama did not, of course.

"It's disrespectful to her, Lan, and shameful on your part. An honorable man protects whoever needs protecting, but children above all, and women above men. Pledge her protection for your own honor."

Lan sighed. Likely, Bukama would keep this up the whole way to Chachin. He should understand. If the woman really was Aes Sedai, Lan wanted no more strings binding him to her. Bukama had already tied one, but his own pledge might lead to worse. If she was Aes Sedai, she might be hunting a Warder. If.

Ryne only waited for the woman to finish brushing out her hair, which she did seated on her saddle on the ground, before offering her a flourishing bow that set his bells chiming. "A beautiful morning, my Lady," he murmured, "though no sunrise could compare in beauty with the deep, dark pools of your eyes." And then he twitched, his own eyes going wide as he searched to see whether she was offended. "Ah. . . . May I saddle your mare, my Lady?" As diffident as a scullion in the withdrawing room.

"Why, thank you," she said, smiling. A very warm smile. "A gracious offer, Ryne."

She went with him to saddle her bay, or rather to flirt, as it seemed. She stood very close while he worked, looking up at him with those big eyes he so admired, and whatever she said, Lan heard answering murmurs about her "skin of silky snow." Which brought a delighted laugh from her.

Lan shook his head. He understood what drew Ryne. The woman's face was beautiful, and however childishly she behaved, the slim body inside that blue silk belonged to no child. But Ryne was right; he had seen a Cairhienin in her skin, more than one. And they had all tried to mesh him in a scheme, or two, or three. Over one particularly memorable ten days in the south of Cairhien, he had almost been killed six times and nearly married twice. An Aes Sedai, if she really was one, *and* a Cairhienin? There could be no worse combination.

Strangely, she made no complaint about riding on without a bite of breakfast, but when they reached Manala, a considerable village less than an hour along the road, she commanded a halt. And it was a command.

"Hot food now will make the day's ride easier," she said firmly, sitting very straight in her saddle and staring a challenge at them. That was certainly like an Aes Sedai, but then, it was like most women. "I wish to reach Chachin as swiftly as possible, and I will not have you falling over from hunger in a foolish attempt to show me how tough you are." Only Ryne met her gaze directly, with an uneasy smile. The man needed to decide whether he was besotted or afraid.

"It was our plan to stop briefly for food, my Lady," Bukama said, lowering his eyes respectfully. He did not add that they would have eaten there last night, and slept in beds, if not for her. Had she followed them to Manala, it would have meant nothing. Following Lan into the forest meant she had some interest in them or their plans.

A sprawling collection of stone houses roofed in red or green tiles, Manala was not far short of being called a town, with above twenty streets crisscrossing a pair of low hills. Three inns fronted a large green in the hollow between the hills, alongside the road. There the men of two large merchant trains headed east were reluctantly hitching their horses under the watchful eye of the mounted merchants. A train of some thirty or so wagons was already lumbering away to the west, with some of the outriding guards looking over their shoulders instead of keeping watch as they should. The Bel Tine festivities were under way in Manala.

They had not come to the games of skill and strength and speed yet, but newly married men and women were formally dancing the Spring Pole in the center of the green, feet flashing but bodies rigidly upright as they entwined the two-span-tall pole in long brightly dyed linen ribbons, while older and unmarried adults were dancing in more lively fashion to the music of fiddles and flutes and drums in half a dozen sizes. Everyone wore their feastday best, the women's pale blouses and wide trousers and the men's bright coats encrusted with elaborate embroidery. They crowded the wide, open space, yet they were not the whole population of Manala. A steady trickle flowed up the hills, men and women bound on some errand, and a steady trickle flowed back down, often carrying dishes of food to the long tables set out on the far side. It was a merry sight. Laughing children, their faces smeared with honey often as not, ran and played through it all, some of the older ones occasionally feeding the small Bel Tine fires at the corners of the green. Lan was not sure how many really believed that leaping those low flames would burn away any bad luck accumulated since the previous Bel Tine, but he did believe in luck. Both kinds. In the Blight, you lived or died by luck as often as by skill or lack of it.

In stark counterpoint to the merriment on the green, beside the road stood six stakes holding the large heads of Trollocs, wolf-snouted, ram-horned, eagle-beaked below all too human eyes. They looked no more than two or three days old, although the weather was still cool enough to retard decay, too cool for flies. These were the reasons each of those dancing men wore a sword, and the women carried long knives at their belts. He smelled no charred wood, though, so it had been a small raid, and unsuccessful.

"Lady Alys" stopped her mare beside the stakes and stared at them. Not in amazement or fear or disgust. Her face was a perfect mask of calm. For an instant, he could almost believe she truly was Aes Sedai.

"I should have hated to face these creatures armed only with a sword," she murmured. "I cannot imagine the courage needed to do that."

"You have faced Trollocs?" Lan asked in surprise. Ryne and Bukama exchanged startled looks.

"Yes." She grimaced faintly, as if the word had slipped out before thought.

"Where, if I may ask?" he said. Few southerners had ever seen a Trolloc. Some called them tales to frighten children.

Alys eyed him coolly. Very coolly. "Shadowspawn can be found in places you never dream of, Master Lan. Choose us an inn, Ryne," she added with a smile. The woman actually believed she was in charge. From the way Ryne jumped to obey, so did he.

The Plowman's Blade was two stories of red-roofed stone with arrowslits rather than windows on the ground floor and a two-handed sword of the sort farmers carried on their plows hanging point-down above a door of heavy planks. This near the Blight, inns served as strong-points against a Trolloc attack, and so did many houses. The innkeeper, a stout graying woman, her billowing blouse worked with red and yellow flowers and her wide trousers covered in red and blue, came from the green when she saw them tying their horses to the hitching rings set in the front of the inn. Mistress Tomichi looked uneasy about two Malkieri stopping at her inn, but she brightened when Alys began issuing commands for her breakfast.

"As you say, my Lady," the round-faced innkeeper murmured, giving Alys a deep curtsy. The Cairhienin had given no name, but her manner and dress did suggest a Lady. "And will you want rooms for yourself and your retainers?"

"Thank you, no," Alys replied. "I intend to ride on soon."

Ryne showed no offense at being called a retainer, accepting the word as easily as Alys did, but Bukama's perpetual scowl darkened. He said nothing, of course, not here, and perhaps would not ever, given his pledge. Lan decided he would have a few quiet words with Alys when he had the chance. There was a limit to how many insults a man could swallow in silence.

He and the other men ordered dark bread and strong tea, and bowls of porridge with slivers of ham in it. Alys did not invite them to share her table in the large common room, so they took benches at another. There were plenty to choose from, given that they were alone except for Mistress Tomichi, who served them with her own hands, explaining that she did not want to pull anyone from the festivities. Indeed, once she had taken payment, she returned to them herself.

Taking advantage of their privacy, Lan and the others discussed the diminutive woman who had attached herself to them. Or rather, they argued about her, in low voices so as not to be overheard. Utterly convinced that Alys was Aes Sedai, Ryne recommended asking no questions. Questions could be dangerous with Aes Sedai, and you might not like the answers. Bukama maintained that they needed to know what she wanted with them, especially if she were Aes Sedai. Tangling in some unknown Aes Sedai scheme could be hazardous. A man could acquire enemies without knowing it, or be sacrificed without warning to further her plans. Lan forbore mentioning that it was Bukama who had placed their feet in that snare. He himself just could not believe she was a sister. He thought her a wilder placed to watch him—by Edeyn, though he did not mention her name, of course. Edeyn likely had eyes-and-ears the breadth of the Borderlands. It did seem an unlikely coincidence that she would happen to have a wilder waiting for him in Canluum, but there had been those six men, and he could not think of anyone else who might have sent them.

"I still say," Bukama began, then bit off an oath. "Where did she go?"

Alys' bowl sat empty on the table where she had been sitting, but there was no sign of the woman herself. Lan's eyebrows rose in admiration in spite of himself. He had not heard a sound of her leaving.

Scraping his bench back noisily, Ryne rushed to one of the arrowslits and peered out. "Her horse is still there. Maybe she's just visiting the privy." Lan winced inwardly at the crudity. There were matters one spoke of and matters one did not. Ryne fingered one of his braids, then gave it a hard tug that made its bells jingle. "I say we leave her her silver and go before she comes back."

"Go if you wish," Lan said, rising. "Bukama pledged to her, and I'll honor his pledge."

"Better if you honor your own," Bukama grumbled.

Ryne grimaced and gave his braid another hard pull. "If you stay, I stay."

Perhaps the woman had just gone out for a glimpse of the

festivities. Telling Bukama to remain in case she returned, Lan took Ryne out to see. She was nowhere among the dancers or the onlookers, though. In her silks, she would have stood out among all that embroidered linen and wool. Some of the women asked them to dance, and Ryne smiled at the prettier ones—the man would stop to smile at a pretty face if a dozen Trollocs were charging him!—but Lan sent him off to look among the houses on the southern hill, while he climbed the one behind The Plowman's Blade. He did not want Alys meeting someone behind his back, perhaps arranging some surprise for later in the day. Just because the woman had not tried to kill him did not mean Edeyn wanted him alive.

He found her in a nearly empty street halfway up the hill, receiving the curtsy of a lean young woman whose blouse and wide trousers were embroidered in red and gold patterns as intricate as those on Alys' riding dress. Kandori were as bad as southerners when it came to embroidery. Stepping softly, he closed to listening distance of Alys' back and stopped.

"There's some Saheras live three streets that way, my Lady," the lean woman said with a gesture. "And I think there's some live on South Hill. But I don't know if any are named Avene."

"You have been a great help, Mistress Marishna," Alys said warmly. "Thank you." Accepting another curtsy, she stood watching the other woman walk on uphill. Once Mistress Marishna was beyond earshot, she spoke again, and her voice was anything but warm. "Shall I show you how eavesdropping is punished in the White Tower, Master Lan?"

He very nearly blinked. First she managed to leave the common without him hearing, and now she heard him when he was trying to be quiet. Remarkable. Perhaps she was Aes Sedai. Which meant she might be looking at Ryne for a Warder.

"I think not," he told the back of her head. "We have business in Chachin that cannot wait. Perhaps your search will go more quickly if we help you find this Avene Sahera."

She turned very quickly and peered up at him, straining for height. He thought she might be up on her toes. No, she was no Aes Sedai, despite the icy look of command on her face. He had seen shorter Aes Sedai dominate rooms full

of men who had no idea who they were, and without any
straining.

"Better for you to forget hearing that name," she said
coldly. "It is unwise to meddle in the affairs of Aes Sedai.
You may leave me, now. But I expect to find you ready to
go on when I am done. If, that is, Malkieri keep their word
as I have been told they do." With that insult, she stalked
off in the direction the lean woman had pointed. Light, the
woman had a tongue like a knife!

When he returned to The Plowman's Blade and told Bukama what he had learned, the older man brightened. Well,
his scowl lessened a little. For him, that was as good as a
grin from anyone else. "Maybe all she wants from us is protection until she finds this woman."

"That doesn't explain why she followed us for a whole
day," Lan said, dropping onto the bench in front of his
breakfast bowl. He might as well finish the porridge. "And
don't suggest she was afraid to approach us. I think that
woman frightens as easily as you do." Bukama had no answer for that.

CHAPTER
21

Some Tricks of the Power

Lan knew the ride to Chachin would be one he would rather forget, and the journey met his expectations. They rode hard, passing merchants' trains of wagons, never stopping long in a village and sleeping under the stars most nights, since no one had the coin for inns, not for four people with horses. Barns and haylofts had to do, when there was a barn or hayloft to be found come nightfall. Many of the hills along the road bore neither village nor farm, only towering oak and leatherleaf, pine and fir, with smaller beech and sourgum scattered through. In the Borderlands, there were no such things as isolated farms; sooner or later, a farm set off by itself became a graveyard.

Alys continued her search for the Sahera woman in every village they passed, though she fell silent whenever Lan or one of the others approached, and eyed them frostily until they went away. The woman had a ready way with a frosty eye. For him, anyway. Ryne twitched and peered wide-eyed at her, fetched and trotted and offered up compliments like a courtier on a leash, still bouncing between enraptured and fearful, and she accepted his subservience and his praise alike as her due while laughing at his witticisms.

Not that she focused only on him. She seldom let an hour go by without probing questions directed at each of them in turn, till it seemed she wanted to know the entire story of their lives. The woman was like a swarm of blackflies; no matter how many you swatted, there were always more to bite. Even Ryne knew enough to deflect that sort of interrogation. A man's past belonged to himself and the people who had lived it with him; it was not a matter for gossip with an inquisitive woman. Despite her questions, Bukama continued his carping. Day and night, it seemed every second comment out of his mouth regarded the pledge. Lan began to think the only way to silence the man would be to take oath *not* to give her the pledge.

Twice thick black clouds rolled down out of the Blight to unleash driving downpours of freezing rain mixed with hail large enough to crack a man's head. The worst storms in spring came from the Blight. When the first of those clouds darkened the sky to the north, he began looking for a place where the trees' branches might be thick enough to afford some shelter, maybe with the aid of blankets stretched overhead, but when Alys realized what he was doing, she said coolly, "There is no need to stop, Master Lan. You are under my protection."

Doubtful of that, he was still looking when the storm struck. Lightning flashed in blue-white streaks across a sky that seemed suddenly night and thunder crashed like monstrous kettledrums overhead, but the driving rain sheeted down an invisible dome that moved with their horses, and the hailstones bounced off it in an eerie silence, as though they had struck nothing at all. She performed the same service for the second storm, and both times, she seemed surprised at their offered thanks. Her face hardly altered in its smoothness, a very good imitation of an Aes Sedai's serene expression, but something flickered about her eyes. A strange woman.

They saw bandits, as rumored, usually a pack of ten or twelve roughly dressed men who counted the odds against three with arrows nocked and melted back into the trees before Lan and the rest reached them. He or Bukama always went after them, just far enough to make sure they really had gone, while the other two guarded Alys. It would have been foolish to ride into an ambush they knew might be waiting.

Noon on the fourth day found them riding through the forested hills along a road that stretched empty as far as the eye could see in either direction. The sky was clear, with just a few scattered white clouds drifting high up, and the only sounds were their horses' hooves and squirrels chittering on branches. Suddenly horsemen burst from the trees on both sides of the road some thirty paces ahead, twenty or so scruffy fellows who formed a line blocking the way, and the pounding of hooves told of more behind.

Dropping his reins on the pommel of his saddle, Lan snatched two more arrows and held them between his fingers as he drew the one already nocked. He doubted he would have time for even a second shot, but there was always a chance. Three of the men in front of him wore much-battered breastplates stained with rust over their dirty coats, and one had a rust-spotted helmet with a barred faceguard. None carried a bow, not that that made any great difference.

"Twenty-three behind at thirty paces," Bukama called. "No bows. On your word."

No difference at all, against a band large enough to attack most merchant trains. He did not loose, however. So long as the men only sat their horses, a chance remained. A small one. Life and death often turned on small chances.

"Let's not be too hasty," the helmeted man called, removing it to reveal a grizzled head of greasy hair and a narrow, dirty face that had last been touched by a razor a week gone. His wide smile showed two missing teeth. "You might be able to kill two or three of us before we cut you down, but there's no need for that. Let us have your coin and the pretty lady's jewelry, and you can go on your way. Pretty ladies in silk and fur always have lots of jewels, eh?" He leered past Lan at Alys. Maybe he thought it a friendly smile.

There was no temptation in the offer. These fellows wanted no casualties among themselves if they could manage it so, but surrender meant that he and Bukama and Ryne would have their throats slit. They probably intended to keep Alys alive until they decided she was a danger. If she had some trick of the Power up her sleeve, he wished she would—

"You dare impede the way of an Aes Sedai?" she thundered, and it *was* thunder, setting some of the brigands' horses snorting and plunging. Cat Dancer, knowing what dropped reins meant, remained still beneath him, awaiting the pressures of knee and heel. "Surrender or face my wrath!" And red fire exploded with a roar above the bandits' heads, sending more of their mounts into panicked bucking that tumbled two of the poorer riders to the road.

"I told you she was Aes Sedai, Coy," whined a fat, balding

fellow in a breastplate that was too small for him. "Didn't I say that, Coy? A Green with her three Warders, I said."

The lean man backhanded him across the face without taking his eyes from Lan. Or more likely, from Alys, behind him.

"No talk of surrender, now. There's still fifty of us and four of you. Rather than face the noose, we'll take our chances on how many you can kill before we take you."

"Well and good," Lan said. "But if I can see one of you at the count of ten, it begins." With the last word, he started counting in a loud voice.

The bandits did not let him reach two before they were galloping back toward the trees; by four, the dismounted pair stopped trying to gain the saddles on their wild-eyed animals and took off afoot as fast as they could go. There was no need to follow. The pounding and crackle of horses being galloped through brush rather than around it was fast fading into the distance. In the circumstances, it was the best end that could be hoped for. Except that Alys did not see it so.

"You had no right to let them go," she said indignantly, anger flashing in her eyes as she did her best to skewer each of them with her gaze. She reined her mare around to make certain they each received a dose. "Had they attacked, I could have used the One Power against them. How many people have they robbed and murdered, how many women ravished, how many children orphaned? We should have fought them and taken the survivors to the nearest magistrate."

Lan, Bukama and Ryne took turns trying to convince her how unlikely it was that any of the four of them would have been among the survivors—the bandits would have fought hard to avoid the gallows, and sheer numbers did count— but she actually seemed to believe she could have defeated close on fifty men by herself. A very strange woman.

Had it been only storms and bandits, that would have been more than he expected on any journey. Ryne's foolishness and Bukama's complaints could have been taken as a matter of course, too. But Alys was blind about a great deal, and that made all the difference.

That first night he had sat in the wet to let her know he would accept what she had done. If they were to travel together, better to end it with honors even, as she must see it. Except that she did not. The second night she remained awake till dawn and made sure he did as well, with sharp flicks of an invisible switch whenever he nodded off. The third night, sand somehow got inside his clothes and boots, a thick coating of it. He had shaken out what he could and, without water to wash, rode covered in grit the next day. The night after the bandits. . . . He could not understand how she managed to make ants crawl into his smallclothes, or make them all bite at once. It had been her doing for sure. She was standing over him when his eyes shot open, and she appeared surprised that he did not cry out.

Clearly, she wanted some response, some reaction, but he could not see what. If she felt that she had not been repaid for her wetting, then she was a very hard woman, but a woman could set the price for her insult or injury, and there were no other women here to call an end when she went beyond what they considered just. All he could do was endure until they reached Chachin. The following night she discovered a patch of blisterleaf near their campsite, and to his shame, he almost lost his temper.

He did not mention the incidents to Bukama or Ryne, of course, though he was certain they knew, but he began to pray for Chachin to loom up ahead at the next rise. Perhaps Edeyn had set the woman to watch him, but it was beginning to seem she meant to kill him after all. Slowly.

Moiraine could not understand the stubbornness of this Lan Mandragoran, though Siuan said that "stubborn" was a redundancy when it came to men. All she wanted was a display of remorse for dunking her. Well, that and an apology. An abject apology. And a proper regard for an Aes Sedai. But he never displayed the slightest scrap of penitence. He was frozen arrogance to the core! His disbelief of her right to the shawl was so plain he might as well have spoken aloud. A part of her admired his fortitude, but only a part. She *would* bring him properly to heel. Not to tame him utterly—a completely tame man was no use to himself or anyone else—but to make certain he recognized his mistakes right down to his bones.

She allowed him his days to reflect, while she planned

what she would do to him that night. The ants had been a great disappointment. That was one of the Blue Ajah secrets, a way to repel insects or make them gather and bite or sting, though not intended for the use she had put it to. But she was quite proud of the blisterleaf, which at least made him jump a bit, proving that he really was made of human flesh. She had begun to doubt that.

Oddly, neither of the other men ever offered him a word of commiseration that she heard, though they had to know what she was doing. If he voiced no complaints to her, which was peculiar enough in itself, surely he did to his friends; that was one thing friends were for. But the three were strangely reticent in other ways, too. Even in Cairhien people would talk about themselves, a little, and she had been taught that Borderlanders shunned the Game of Houses, yet they revealed almost nothing about themselves even after she primed their tongues with incidents from her own youth in Cairhien and from the Tower. Ryne at least laughed when the story was funny—once he realized he was supposed to laugh, he did—but Lan and Bukama actually looked embarrassed. She thought that was the emotion they displayed; they could have taught Aes Sedai to control their faces. They admitted having met sisters before her, but when she probed ever so delicately to learn where and when. . . .

"There are Aes Sedai so many places that they are difficult to recall," Lan replied one evening as they rode ahead of their own long shadows. "We had best stop at those farmhouses ahead and see whether we can hire the use of a hayloft for the night. We won't see another house till well after full dark."

That was typical. Those three could have taught Aes Sedai about oblique answers and deflecting questions, too.

Worst of all, she still had no idea whether any of them were Darkfriends. Of course, she had no *real* reason to think that any of the sisters in Canluum had been Black Ajah, and if they were not, Ryne's visit to The Gates of Heaven likely had had some purely innocent purpose, yet wariness made her continue her questions. She still laid a ward around each of them every night. She could not afford to trust *anyone* except Siuan until she was sure of them. Other Aes Sedai and any men who might be involved with them least of all.

Two days from Chachin, in a village called Ravinda, she finally located Avene Sahera, the very first woman she spoke to in the place. Ravinda was a thriving village, though much smaller than Manala, with a wide field of hard-packed dirt that served as a market for folk from neighboring villages to barter produce and handcrafts and buy from peddlers. Two peddlers' wagons, their tall canvas covers festooned with pots and pans, stood surrounded by crowds when she and her reticent companions arrived that morning, each peddler glaring at his competitor despite the people clamoring for his own goods. Ravinda also had an inn under construction, the second floor already building, the result of Mistress Sahera receiving the bounty. She intended to call it the White Tower.

"You think the sisters might object?" she said, frowning at the sign already carved and painted and hung above the front door, when Moiraine suggested a change in the name. By the scale, the Tower on the sign would have had to be over a thousand feet high! Avene was a plump, graying woman, with a silver-mounted, foot-long dagger hanging at her worked leather belt and yellow embroidery covering the sleeves of her bright red blouse. Apparently, the bounty had put a touch of feastday into every day for her. Finally, she shook her head. "I can't see why they would, my Lady. The Aes Sedai who took names in our camp was very soft-spoken and pleasant." The woman would learn, the first time a sister who cared to reveal herself happened by.

Moiraine wished she remembered which Accepted had taken Avene Sahera's name and had a chance to give the child a piece of her mind. Avene's son Migel—her tenth child!—had been born thirty miles from Dragonmount and a *week* before Gitara spoke her Foretelling. That sort of carelessness in writing down what you heard was intolerable! How many more names in her book would turn out to have borne children outside the specified ten days?

Riding away from Ravinda, the men's obvious delight that she had been quick turned her smoldering irritation from the unknown Accepted to them. Oh, they did not show it openly, but she heard Ryne say it—"At least she was fast with it this time"—not quite prudent enough about being overheard, and Bukama muttered a sour agreement as they fell in behind her. Lan was riding ahead, plainly shunning her company. In truth, she could understand that, but his broad back, stiffly erect, seemed a rebuke. She began to think on what she might arrange for him that night. With perhaps a touch for the other two as well.

For a time, nothing came to mind that could top what she had already done. Then a wasp buzzed past her face, and she watched it fly into the trees alongside the road. Wasps. Of course, she did not want to kill him. "Master Lan, are you allergic to wasp stings?"

He twisted in his saddle, half reining his stallion around, and suddenly grunted, his eyes growing wide. For an instant, she did not understand. Then she saw the arrowhead sticking out from the front of his right shoulder.

Without thought, she embraced the Source, and *saidar* filled her. It was as though she were back in the testing again. Her weaves flashed into being, first of all a clear shield of Air to block any more arrows away from Lan, then one for herself. She could not have said why she wove them in that order. With the Power in her and her sight sharpened, she scanned the trees where the arrow had come from, and caught motion just inside the edge of the forest. Flows of Air lashed out to seize the man just as he loosed again, the shaft going up at an angle as his bow was snapped tight against his body. Just heartbeats, that all took, beginning to end, as fast as anything she had woven in testing. Just enough time for two arrows fired by Ryne and Bukama to strike home.

With a dismayed groan, she released the bonds of Air, and the man toppled backward. He had attempted murder, but she had not intended holding him up as a target for execution. He *would* have been executed, once they had carried him to a magistrate, yet she disliked having been part of carrying out the sentence, especially before it was given. To her mind, it came very near using *saidar* as a weapon, or making a weapon for men to use in killing. Very near.

Still holding *saidar,* she turned to Lan to offer Healing, but in spite of the arrow sticking from him front and back, he gave her no chance to speak, wheeling his mount and galloping to the edge of the trees, where he dismounted and strode to the fallen man followed by Bukama and Ryne. With the Power in her, she could hear their voices clearly.

"Caniedrin?" Lan said, sounding shocked.

"You know this fellow?" Ryne asked.

"Why?" Bukama growled, and there came the thud of a boot meeting ribs.

A weak voice answered in gasps. "Gold. Why else? You still have . . . the Dark One's luck . . . turning just then . . . or that shaft . . . would have found . . . your heart. He should have . . . told me . . . she's Aes Sedai . . . instead of just saying . . . to kill her first."

As soon as she heard those words, Moiraine dug her heels into Arrow's flanks to gallop the short distance, and flung herself from the saddle already preparing the weave for Healing. "Get those arrows out of him," she called as she ran toward them, holding up her cloak and skirts to keep from tripping. "If the arrows remain, Healing will not keep him alive."

"Why Heal him?" Lan asked, sitting himself down on a storm-fallen tree. Its great spread of dirt-covered roots rose in a fan high above his head. "Are you so eager to see a hanging?"

"He's dead already," Ryne said. "Can you Heal that?" He sounded interested in seeing whether she could.

Moiraine's shoulders slumped. Caniedrin's eyes, open and staring up the branches overhead, were already glazed and empty. Strangely, despite the blood around his mouth he looked a beardless youth in his rumpled coat. Man enough to do murder, though. Man enough to die with a pair of arrows transfixing his chest. Dead, he could never tell her if it was this Gorthanes who had hired him, or where the man might be found. A nearly full quiver was fastened to his belt, and two arrows stuck upright in the ground nearby. Apparently, he had been confident he could kill four people with four shots. Even knowing Lan and Bukama, he had thought so. Knowing them, he had disobeyed his instructions and tried to kill Lan first. The most dangerous of them, as he must have thought.

As she studied the man, it came to her that he might tell her a little, even dead. With her belt knife, she sliced away the pouch hanging behind his quiver and emptied the contents beside him amid the small weeds pushing through the mulch. A wooden comb, a half-eaten piece of cheese covered with lint, a small folding knife, a ball of string that she unwound to make sure nothing was hidden inside, a filthy crumpled handkerchief that she unwadded with the tip of her knife blade. It had been too much to hope for a letter written by Master Gorthanes giving instructions on how to find him. Cutting the cords of the leather purse tied to Caniedrin's belt, she upended that over the litter. A handful of silver and copper spilled out. And ten gold crowns. So. The price of her death in Kandor was the same as the price of a silk dress in Tar Valon. Fat coins, with the Rising Sun of Cairhien on one side and her uncle's profile on the other. A fitting footnote in the history of House Damodred.

"Have you taken to robbing the dead?" Lan asked in that irritatingly cool voice. Just asking, not accusing, but still . . . !

She straightened angrily just as Ryne snapped off the feathered end of the arrow jutting from Lan's back. Bukama was knotting a narrow strip of rawhide behind the arrowhead. Once he had it tight, he gripped the cord in his fist and gave one quick yank, pulling the arrow the rest of the way through. Lan blinked. The man had an *arrow* pulled out of his body, and he *blinked*! Why that should irritate her, she did not know, but it surely did.

Ryne hurried back to the road while Bukama helped Lan off with his coat and shirt, revealing a puckered hole in his front. Likely the one behind was no better. The blood that had been soaking into coat and shirt began to pour freely down his chest and ribs. Neither man asked for Healing, and she was of half a mind not to offer it. More scars decorated Lan than she expected on a man so young, and a number of partly healed wounds crossed by neat dark stitches. Seemingly, he angered men as easily as he did women. Ryne returned carrying bandaging cloths and mouthing bread for a poultice. None of them were going to ask for Healing until the man bled to death!

"Will you accept Healing?" she asked coldly, reaching toward Lan's head. He shied back from her touch. He shied back!

"Day after tomorrow in Chachin, you may need your right arm," Bukama muttered, scrubbing a hand under his nose and not meeting anyone's eyes. A very peculiar thing to say, but she knew there was no point in asking what it meant.

After a moment, Lan nodded and leaned forward. That was all. He did not ask or even accept her offer. He just leaned forward.

She clapped her hands on his head in something near to a pair of slaps and channeled. The convulsion when the Healing weave hit him, arms flinging wide, ripped him out of her grasp. Very satisfying. Even if he did only breathe hard rather than gasp. His old scars remained, the half-healed wounds were now thin pink lines—the stitches that had been on the outside, now loose, slid down his arms and chest; he might have difficulty picking out the rest—but smooth skin marked where the arrowholes had been. He could meet the wasps in perfect health. She could always Heal him again afterward, if need be. Only if need be, however.

They left the coins lying beside Caniedrin's body, though the men plainly could have used them. They wanted nothing from the dead man. Bukama found his mount tied a short distance away in the trees, a white-stockinged brown gelding with a look of speed about him and a prancing step. Lan removed the animal's bridle and tied it to the saddle, then slapped the horse's rump and sent him racing toward Ravinda.

"So he can eat until somebody finds him," he explained when he saw her frowning after the gelding.

In all truth, she had been regretting not searching the saddlebags tied behind the gelding's saddle. But Lan had shown a surprising touch of kindness. She had not expected any such to be found in him. For that, he would escape the wasps. There had to be something memorable, in any case. She had only two more nights to crack him, after all. Once they reached Chachin, she would be too busy to attend to Lan Mandragoran. For a time she would be.

CHAPTER
22

Keeping Custom

I f Canluum was a city of hills, Chachin was a city of
mountains. The three highest rose almost a mile even
with their peaks sheared off short, and all glittered in
the noonday sun with colorful glazed tile roofs and tile-
covered palaces. Atop the tallest, the Aesdaishar Palace
shone brighter than any other in red and green, the prancing Red Horse flying above its largest dome. Three towered
ringwalls surrounded the city, as did a deep drymoat a hundred paces wide spanned by two dozen bridges, each with a
fortress hulking at its mouth. The traffic was too great here,
and the Blight too far away, for the helmeted and breast-
plated guards with the Red Horse on their chests to be so
diligent as in Canluum, but crossing the Bridge of Sunrise,
amid tides of wagons and carts and people mounted and
afoot flowing both ways, still took some little while.

Once inside the first wall, Lan wasted no time drawing
rein, out of the way of the heavy-laden merchants' wagons
lumbering past. Even with Edeyn waiting, he had never
been so glad to see any place in his life. By the letter of
the law, they were not truly inside Chachin—the second,
higher, wall lay more than a hundred paces ahead, and the
third, still taller, as much beyond that—but he wanted to be
done with this Alys. Where in the Light had she found fleas
this early in the year? And blackflies! Blackflies should not
appear for another month! He was a mass of itching welts.
At least she had found no satisfaction in it. Of that, he was
certain.

"The pledge was protection to Chachin, and it has been
kept," he told the woman. "So long as you avoid the rougher

parts of the city, you are as safe on any street as if you had
a bodyguard of ten. So you may see to your affairs, and we
will see to ours. Keep your coin," he added coldly when
she reached for her purse. Irritation flared, for losing self-
control. Yet she offered insult atop insult.

Ryne immediately started going on about giving offense
to Aes Sedai and offering her smiling apologies and deep
bows from his saddle that had his bells ringing like alarm
gongs, while Bukama grumbled sourly about men with the
manners of pigs, with some justification. Alys herself gazed
at him, so near expressionless that she might even have
been what she claimed. A dangerous claim if untrue. And if
true . . . He especially wanted no part of her, then.

Whirling Cat Dancer, he galloped up the wide street
scattering people afoot and some mounted. Another time
that might have sparked duels. The *hadori* and the reputation that went with it certainly would not have held back
anyone but commoners. But he rode too fast to hear a cry
of challenge, dodging around sedan chairs and tradesmen's
high-wheeled carts and porters carrying loads on their
shoulder-poles, without slackening his pace. After the quiet
of the country, the rumble of iron-rimmed wheels on paving
stones and the cries of hawkers and shopkeepers seemed
raucous. The flutes of street musicians sounded strident.
The smells of roasted nuts and meat pies on vendors' barrows, the smells of cooking in the kitchens of dozens of
inns and hundreds of homes, blended into an unpleasant
stench after the clean air on the road. A hundred stables full
of horses added their own flavor.

Bukama and Ryne caught him up with the packhorse
before he was halfway up the mountain to the Aesdaishar
Palace and fell in to either side. If Edeyn was in Chachin,
she would be there. Wisely, Bukama and Ryne held their
silence. Bukama, at least, knew what he was about to face.
Entering the Blight would be much easier. Leaving the
Blight alive, at any rate. Any fool could ride into the Blight.
Was he a fool to come here?

The higher they climbed, the more slowly they moved.
There were fewer people in the streets high up, where tile-
roofed houses gave way to palaces and the homes of wealthy
merchants and bankers, their walls covered with bright
tiles, and the street musicians to liveried servants scurrying

on errands. Brightly lacquered coaches with House sigils on the doors replaced merchants' wagons and sedan chairs. A coach behind a team of four or six with plumes on their bridles took up a great deal of room, and most had half a dozen outriders as well as a pair of backmen clinging to the rear of the coach, all armed and armored and ready to dispute with anyone who tried brushing by too closely. In particular, with three roughly dressed men who tried. Ryne's yellow coat did not look so fine as it had in Canluum, and with Lan's second-best coat bloodstained, he was reduced to wearing his third, worn enough to make Bukama seem well dressed. Thought of the bloodstains brought other thoughts. He owed Alys a debt for her Healing, as well as for her torments, though in honor it was only the first he could repay. No. He had to get that odd little woman out of his head, although she seemed to have lodged herself inside his skull, somehow. It was Edeyn he needed to concentrate on. Edeyn and the most desperate fight of his life.

The Aesdaishar Palace filled the flattened mountaintop completely, an immense, shining structure of domes and high balconies covering fifty hides, a small city to itself, every surface shining in patterns of red and green. The great bronze gates, worked with the lacquered Red Horse, stood invitingly open beneath a red-tiled arch that led to the Visitor's Yard, but a dozen guards stepped out to bar the way when Lan and the others approached. The Red Horse was embroidered on the green tabards they wore over their breastplates, and their halberds bore red-and-green streamers. They were quite colorful, with their red helmets and breeches and their polished high green boots, but any man who served here was a veteran of more than a single battle, and they regarded the three new arrivals through the steel face-bars of their helmets with hard eyes.

Lan stepped down from the saddle and bowed, not too deeply, touching forehead, heart and sword hilt. "I am Lan Mandragoran," he said. Nothing more.

The guards' stiffness lessened at his name, but they did not give way immediately. A man could claim any name, after all. One of them went running off and returned in moments with a gray-haired officer who carried his red-plumed helmet on his hip. Jurad Shiman was a seasoned campaigner who had ridden with Lan in the south for a time, and his long face broke into a smile.

"Be welcome, al'Lan Mandragoran," he said, bowing much more deeply than he ever had for Lan on any previous visit. *"Tai'shar Malkier!"* Oh, yes; if Edeyn was not here now, she had been.

Leading his bay, Lan followed Jurad through the red arch onto the smooth paving stones of the Visitor's Yard feeling as though he should have his sword in hand and his armor on. The balconies of stone fretwork that overlooked the broad courtyard took on the aspect of archers' balconies to his eye. Ridiculous, of course. Those open balconies, like lace woven from stone, afforded little protection for archers. They were for watching new arrivals on grand occasions, not defense. No enemy had ever broken past the second ringwall, and should Trollocs ever make it this deep into the city, all was lost. Still, Edeyn might be here, and he could not shake the feeling of walking onto a battlefield.

Grooms in red-and-green livery with the Red Horse embroidered on the shoulders came running to take the horses, and more men and women to carry the contents of the packhorse's wicker hampers and show each man to rooms befitting his station. Worryingly, the *shatayan* of the palace herself led them. She was a stately, straight-backed woman in livery, graying hair worn in a thick roll on the nape of her neck. The silvered ring of keys at her belt proclaimed that Mistress Romera had charge of all the Palace servants, but a *shatayan* was more than a servant herself. Usually, only crowned rulers could look for a greeting at the gates from the *shatayan*. He was swimming in a sea of other people's expectations. Men had drowned in seas like that.

He went along to see Bukama's and Ryne's rooms, and express his delight in them to Mistress Romera, not because he expected them to be given anything unsuitable, but because it was necessary that he see to his men before himself. Ryne wore a sour expression, but surely he had not expected better than this small room in one of the palace's stone barracks, the same as Bukama. He had known well enough how things would be here. At least Ryne had a room to himself, a bannerman's room with a tiled stove built in beneath the bed. Ordinary soldiers slept ten to a room and, as Lan recalled, spent half their time in winter arguing over who got the beds nearest the fireplace.

Bukama settled in happily—well, happily for him; his scowl very nearly vanished—talking over pipes of tabac with a few men he had fought alongside, and Ryne seemed to recover himself quickly. At any rate, by the time Lan was led away, Ryne was asking among the soldiers whether there were any pretty girls among the serving maids and how he could go about getting his clothes cleaned and pressed. He cared almost as much about his appearance, especially in front of women, young or old, as he did about women themselves. Perhaps it had been the thought of appearing in travel-stained garb in front of the *shatayan* and the serving women that had soured him.

To Lan's great relief, he was not given a visiting king's apartments despite the *shatayan*'s escort. His three rooms were spacious, with silk tapestries on the blue walls and a broad cornice worked in stylized mountains rimming the high ceilings, and the substantial furniture was simply carved with only a little gilding. The bedchamber had a small balcony overlooking one of the palace gardens and had a bed with a feather mattress wide enough to accommodate four or five. It was all entirely suitable to his station, and he thanked Mistress Romera perhaps a little more profusely than he should have, because she smiled, her hazel eyes crinkling.

"No one can know what the future may hold, my Lord," she said, "but we know who you are." And then she offered him a small curtsy before leaving. A curtsy. Remarkable. Whatever she said, the *shatayan* had her expectations of the future, too.

Along with the rooms, he acquired two square-faced serving women, Anya and Esne, who began placing his meager belongings in the wardrobe, and a lanky young fellow named Bulen, to run errands, who gaped at Lan's helmet and breast- and backplates as he set them on the black-lacquered rack beside the door, though he must have seen the like many times, here.

"Is Her Majesty in residence?" Lan asked politely.

"No, my Lord," Anya replied, frowning at his blood-stained coat and setting it aside with a sigh. The gray-haired one of the pair, she might be Esne's mother, he thought. It was not the sight of blood that made her sigh—she would be accustomed to that—but the difficulty of cleaning the coat. With luck, he would receive it back both cleaned and mended. As well as it could be, anyway. "Queen Ethenielle is making a progress through the heartland."

"And Prince Brys?" He knew the answer to that—Ethenielle and Brys Consort could be out of the city at the same time only during wartime—yet there were forms to be followed.

Bulen's jaw dropped open at the suggestion the Prince Consort might be absent, but an errand boy could not be expected to know all the usages of the court yet. Anya would not have been placed to serve Lan if she were not fully conversant, though. "Oh, yes, my Lord," she said. Lifting the black-stained shirt, she shook her head before laying the garment aside. Not with the coat. Apparently, the shirt was a lost cause. She was shaking her head over most of his garments, even those she put into the wardrobe. Most of them had seen hard use.

"Are any notables visiting?" He had been itching to ask that as badly as he did from flea and blackfly bites.

Anya and Esne exchanged looks. "Only one of true note, my Lord," Anya replied. She folded a shirt and laid it in the wardrobe, making him wait. "The Lady Edeyn Arrel." The two women smiled at one another, looking even more alike. Of course they had known from the start what he was trying to find out, but they had no call to go around grinning over it like idiots.

While Bulen gave his boots a much-needed blacking, Lan washed himself from head to toe at the washstand rather than waiting for a bathtub to be brought, and dabbed an ointment that Anya sent Esne for onto his welts, but he let the women dress him. Just because they were servants was no reason to insult them. He had one white silk shirt that did not show too much wear, a pair of tight black silk breeches that showed almost none, and a good black silk coat embroidered along the sleeves with golden bloodroses among their hooked thorns. Bloodroses for loss and remembrance. Fitting. His boots had taken on a gleam he had never expected Bulen to achieve. He was armored as well as he could be. With a weapon in hand, there was little he feared, but Edeyn's weapons would not be steel. He had

small experience in the kind of battle he needed to fight
now.

Giving Anya and Esne each a silver mark, and Bulen a
silver penny—Mistress Romera would have been outraged
to be offered coin, but a visitor's servants expected something on the first day and on the last—he sent the boy to
make sure the stables had followed his instructions about
Cat Dancer and set the women in the corridor to guard his
door. Then he sat down to wait. His meetings with Edeyn
must be public, with as many people around as possible. In
private, all advantage belonged to a man's *carneira*.

He found himself wondering where Alys had gone, what
she had wanted with him and the others, and tried to shake
her out of his head. Even absent, the woman was a cockle-
burr down the back of his neck. A tall silver pitcher of tea
sat on one of the carved side tables, doubtless flavored with
berries and mint, and another of wine, but he ignored them.
He was not thirsty, and he needed a clear head and focus for
Edeyn. Waiting, he assumed the *ko'di* and sat wrapped in
emotionless emptiness. It was always better to go into battle
without emotion.

In a shockingly short time, Anya reentered, carefully
closing the door behind her. "My Lord, the Lady Edeyn
sends a request for your presence in her chambers." Her
tone was very neutral, her face as blank as an Aes Sedai's.

"Tell her messenger I have not yet recovered from my
journey," he said.

Anya seemed disappointed with that answer as she curtsied.

Courtesy demanded he be given time for that recovery,
as much as he required, but in less than half an hour by the
gilded ball-clock on the mantel over the fireplace, Anya
entered again carrying a letter sealed with a crouching lioness impressed in blue wax. A crouching lioness ready to
spring. Edeyn's personal sigil, and worthy of her. He broke
it reluctantly. The letter was very short.

Come to me, sweetling. Come to me now.

There was no signature, but he would have needed none
had the sealing wax been blank. Her elaborate hand remained as familiar to him as his own far plainer. The letter

was very like Edeyn. Commanding. Edeyn had been born to be a queen, and knew it.

He consigned the page to the flames in the fireplace. There was no seeming about Anya's disappointment this time. Light, the woman had been placed to serve him, but Edeyn had an ally in her if she knew it. Very likely, Edeyn did. She had a way of learning anything that might be of use to her.

No more summonses came from Edeyn, but as the ball-clock chimed three times for the hour, Mistress Romera appeared.

"My Lord," she said formally, "are you rested enough to be received by the Prince Consort?" At last.

It was an honor to be conducted by her personally, but outsiders needed a guide to find their way anywhere in the Palace. He had been there many times and still lost himself upon occasion. His sword remained on the lacquered rack by the door. It would do him no good here, and would insult Brys besides, indicating he thought he needed to protect himself. Which he did, only not with steel.

He expected a private meeting first, but Mistress Romera took him to a large formal hall with a dome painted like the sky in the center of the high ceiling, its base supported by thin, fluted white columns, and the hall was full of people and a murmur of conversation that died as his arrival was noticed. Soft-footed servants in livery moved through the crowd offering spiced wine to Kandori lords and ladies in silks embroidered with House sigils, and to folk in fine woolens worked with the sigils of the more important guilds. And to others, too. Lan saw men in long coats wearing the *hadori,* men he knew had not worn it these ten years or more. Women with hair still cut at the shoulders and higher wore the small dot of the *ki'sain* painted on their foreheads. They bowed at his appearance, and made deep curtsies, those men and women who had decided to remember Malkier. They watched the *shatayan* present him to Brys like hawks watching a field mouse. Or like hawks awaiting a signal to take wing. Perhaps he never should have come here. Too late for that decision now. The only way was forward, whatever lay at the end.

Prince Brys was a stocky, rough-hewn man in his middle years who appeared more suited to armor than to his gold-worked green silks, though in truth he was accustomed to either. Brys was Ethenielle's Swordbearer, the general of her armies, as well as her consort, and he had not come by the office through marrying Ethenielle. Brys owned a strong reputation as a general. He caught Lan's shoulders, refusing to allow him to bow.

"None of that from the man who twice saved my life in the Blight, Lan." He laughed.

"And twice you saved mine," Lan said. "Honors are even."

"That's as may be, that's as may be. But your coming seems to have rubbed some of your luck off on Diryk. He fell from a balcony this morning, a good fifty feet to the paving stones, without breaking a bone." He motioned to his second son, a handsome dark-eyed boy of eight in a coat like his. The child came forward. A large bruise marred the side of his head, and he moved with the stiffness of other bruises, yet he made a formal bow spoiled only somewhat by a wide grin. "He should be at his lessons," Brys confided, "but he was so eager to meet you, he'd have forgotten his letters and cut himself on a sword." Frowning, the boy protested that he would never cut himself.

Lan returned the lad's bow with equal formality, but the last shreds of protocol vanished from the boy in an instant.

"They say you've fought Aiel in the south and on the Shienaran marches, my Lord," he said. "Is that true? Are they really ten feet tall? Do they really veil their faces before they kill? And eat their dead? Is the White Tower really taller than a mountain?"

"Give the man a chance to answer, Diryk," Brys said, mock outrage spoiled by amused laughter. The boy blushed in embarrassment, but still managed an affectionate smile for his father, who ruffled his hair with a quick hand.

"Recall what it is like to be eight, Brys," Lan said. "Let the boy show his excitement." For himself, at eight he had been learning the *ko'di* and what he would face when he first entered the Blight. Beginning to learn how to kill with hands and feet. Let Diryk have a happier childhood before he had to think too closely on death.

Freed, Diryk unleashed another torrent of questions, though he did wait for answers this time. Given a chance, the boy would have drained him dry about the Aiel, and the wonders of the great cities in the south like Tar Valon and Far

Madding. Likely, he would not have believed Chachin was as big as either of those. At last, his father put an end to it.

"Lord Mandragoran will fill your head to your heart's content later," Brys told the boy. "There is someone else he must meet now. Off with you to Mistress Tuval and your books."

Lan thought everyone in the room was holding their breath in anticipation as Brys escorted him across the red-and-white floor tiles.

Edeyn was exactly as he remembered. Oh, ten years older, with touches of white streaking her temples and a few fine lines at the corners of her eyes, but those large dark eyes gripped him. Her *ki'sain* was still the white of a widow, and her hair still hung in black waves below her waist. She wore a red silk gown in the Domani style, clinging and little short of sheer. She was beautiful, but even she could do nothing here. He made his bow calmly.

For a moment she merely looked at him, cool and considering. "It would have been . . . easier had you come to me," she murmured, seeming not to care whether Brys heard. And then, shockingly, she knelt gracefully and took his hands in hers. "Beneath the Light," she announced in a strong, clear voice, "I, Edeyn ti Gemallen Arrel, pledge fealty to al'Lan Mandragoran, Lord of the Seven Towers, Lord of the Lakes, the true Blade of Malkier. May he sever the Shadow!" Even Brys looked startled. A moment of silence held while she kissed Lan's fingers; then cheers erupted on every side. Cries of "The Golden Crane!" and even "Kandor rides with Malkier!"

The sound freed him to pull his hands loose, to lift her to her feet. "My Lady," he said quietly, but in a tight voice, "there is no King of Malkier. The Great Lords have not cast the rods."

She put a hand over his lips. A warm hand. "Three of the surviving five are in this room, Lan. Shall we ask them how they will cast? What must be, will be." And then she faded back into the crowd of those who wanted to cluster around him, congratulate him, pledge fealty on the spot had he let them.

Brys rescued him, drawing him off to a long, stone-railed walk above a two-hundred-foot drop to the roofs below. It was known as a place Brys went to be private, and no one followed. Only one door let onto it, no window overlooked it, and no sound from the Palace intruded.

"Had I known she intended that," the older man said as they walked up and down, hands clasped behind their backs, "I would never have given her welcome. If you wish it, I'll let her know that welcome is withdrawn. Don't look at me that way, man. I know enough of Malkieri customs not to insult her. She has you neatly nailed into a box I know you would never choose for yourself." Brys knew less than he thought he did. However delicate the words, withdrawing the welcome would be a deadly insult.

"'Even the mountains will be worn down with time,'" Lan quoted. He was unsure whether he could avoid leading men in to the Blight, now. Unsure that he wanted to avoid it. All of those men and women remembering Malkier. Malkier deserved remembrance. But at what price?

"What will you do?" A simple question simply stated, yet very hard to answer.

"I do not know," Lan replied. She had won only a skirmish, but he felt stunned at the ease of it. A formidable opponent, the woman who wore part of his soul in her hair.

For the rest they spoke quietly of hunting and bandits and whether this past year's flare-up in the Blight might die down soon. Brys regretted withdrawing his army from the war against the Aiel, but there had been no alternative. They talked of the rumors about a man who could channel—every tale had him in a different place; Brys thought it another jak o'the mists and Lan agreed—and of the Aes Sedai who seemed to be everywhere, for what reason no one knew. Ethenielle had written him that in a village along her progression two sisters had caught a woman pretending to be Aes Sedai. The woman could channel, but that did her no good. The two real Aes Sedai flogged her squealing through the village, making her confess her crime to every last man and woman who lived there. Then one of the sisters carried her off to Tar Valon for her true punishment, whatever that might be. Lan found himself hoping that Alys had not lied about being Aes Sedai, though he could not think why he should care.

He hoped to avoid Edeyn the rest of the day, too, but when he was guided back to his rooms—by a serving man, this time—she was there, waiting languorously in one of the gilded chairs in the sitting room. His servants were no-where to be seen. It seemed Anya truly was Edeyn's ally.

"You are no longer beautiful, I fear, sweetling," she said when he came in. "I think you may even be ugly when you are older. But I always enjoyed your eyes more than your face." Her smile became sultry. "And your hands."

He stopped still gripping the door handle. "My Lady, not two hours gone you swore—" She cut him off.

"And I will obey my king. But as the saying goes, a king is not a king, alone with his *carneira*." She laughed, a smoky laugh. Enjoying her power over him. "I brought your *daori*. Bring it to me."

Unwillingly, his eyes followed hers to a flat lacquered box on a small table beside the door. Lifting the hinged lid took as much effort as lifting a boulder. Coiled inside lay a long cord woven of hair. He could recall every moment of the morning after their first night, when she took him to the women's quarters of the Royal Palace in Fal Moran and let ladies and serving women watch as she cut his hair at his shoulders. She even told them what it signified. The women had all been amused, making jokes as he sat at Edeyn's feet to weave the *daori* for her. Edeyn kept custom, but in her own way. The hair felt soft and supple; she must have had it rubbed with lotions every day.

Crossing the floor slowly, he knelt before her and held out his *daori* stretched between his hands. "In token of what I owe to you, Edeyn, always and forever." If his voice did not hold the fervor of that first morning, surely she understood.

She did not take the cord. Instead, she studied him, a lion-ess studying a fawn. "I knew you had not been gone so long as to forget our ways," she said finally. "Come."

Rising, she grasped his wrist and drew him to the doors to the balcony overlooking the garden ten paces below. Two servants were pouring water from buckets onto chosen plants, and a young woman was strolling along a slate path in a blue dress as bright as any of the early flowers that grew beneath the trees.

"My daughter, Iselle." For a moment, pride and affection warmed Edeyn's voice. "Do you remember her? She is sev-enteen, now. She hasn't chosen her *carneira*, yet." Young men were chosen by their *carneira*; young women chose theirs. "But I think it time she married anyway."

He vaguely recalled a child who always had servants running, the blossom of her mother's heart, but his head had been full of Edeyn, then. Light, the woman filled his head now, just as the scent of her perfume filled his nose. The scent of her. "She is as beautiful as her mother, I am sure," he said politely. He twisted the *daori* in his hands. She had too much advantage as long as he held it, all advantage, but she had to take it from him. "Edeyn, we must talk." She ignored that.

"Time you were married, too, sweetling. Since none of your female relatives is alive, it is up to me to arrange." She smiled warmly toward the girl below, a loving mother's smile.

He gasped at what she seemed to be suggesting. At first he could not believe. "*Iselle?*" he said hoarsely. "*Your* daughter?" She might keep custom in her own way, but this was scandalous. "I'll not be reined into something so shameful, Edeyn. Not by you, or by this." He shook the *daori* at her, but she only looked at it and smiled.

"Of course you won't be reined, sweetling. You are a man, not a boy. Yet you do keep custom," she mused, running a finger along the cord of hair quivering between his hands. "Perhaps we do need to talk."

But it was to the bed that she led him. At least he would regain some lost ground there, whether or not she took the *daori* from his hands. He was a man, not a fawn, however much the lioness she was. He was not surprised when she told him he could lay it aside to help her undress, though. Edeyn would never give up all of her advantage. Not until she presented his *daori* to his bride on his wedding day. And he could see no way to stop that bride being Iselle.

CHAPTER

23

The Evening Star

Moiraine allowed herself a small smile as Lan's friends galloped after him. If he wanted to be away from her so quickly, then she had made some impression. A deeper one had to wait. So he thought she needed to avoid the rougher parts of Chachin, did he? The way she handled those bandits should have taught him better.

Putting him out of her mind, she went in search of exactly those rougher quarters. When she and Siuan had been allowed a trip into Tar Valon as Accepted, the common rooms Siuan liked to visit were always in that sort of area. Their food and wine were cheap, and they were unlikely to be frequented by Aes Sedai who would surely have disapproved of Accepted having a cup of wine in such a place. Besides, Siuan said she felt more comfortable in those inns than at the better establishments where Moiraine would have preferred to eat. Besides, tightfisted as Siuan was, she certainly would have sought out a room at the cheapest inn to be found.

Moiraine rode through the crowded streets until she found a place inside the first ringwall where there were no sedan chairs or street musicians and the rare pushbarrow vendors had no patrons and faces without hope of having any soon. The stone buildings lining the narrow street had a shabby appearance that belied their brightly tiled roofs, cracked paint on doors and window frames where there was any paint, dirty windows with broken panes. Ragged children ran laughing and playing, but children played and laughed in the direst surroundings. Shopkeepers with cudgels stood guard over the goods displayed on tables in front of their shops and eyed the passersby as though considering every one of them capable of theft. Maybe some of those folk were, in their worn, patched woolens, scuttling along with head down or swaggering with defiant scowls. A poor woman might easily be tempted into theft when she had nothing. Moiraine's fur-lined cloak and silk riding dress drew furtive glances, and so did Arrow. There was not another horse on the street.

As she dismounted in front of the first inn she came to, a dusty-appearing place called The Ruffled Goose, a slat-ribbed yellow dog growled at her, hackles standing, till she flicked it with a fine flow of Air and sent it yelping down the street. Of more concern was a tall young woman in a much-darned red dress that had faded in patches of different shades. She was pretending to search for a stone in her shoe while eyeing Arrow sideways. A covetous gaze, that. There were no hitching posts or rings here. Letting the reins hang free, which would tell Arrow not to move, Moiraine wove hobbles of Air for the mare's forefeet and a ward around her that would warn if anyone tried to move the animal. That one, she held on to rather than tying off.

The dim common room of The Ruffled Goose bore out the exterior. The floor was covered with what might have been sawdust once, but now appeared to be congealed mud. The air stank of stale tabac smoke and sour ale, and something that seemed to be scorching in the kitchen. The patrons huddled over their mugs at the small tables, rough-faced men in rough coats, lifted their heads in surprise at her entrance. The innkeeper proved to be a lean, leathery fellow in a stained gray coat with his narrow face cast in a permanent leer, as villainous in appearance as any of those bandits on the high road had been.

"Do you have a Tairen woman staying here?" she asked. "A young Tairen woman with blue eyes?"

"This place isn't for the likes of you, my Lady," he muttered, rubbing a wiry hand across his stubbly cheek. He might have rearranged some dirt. "Come, let me show you to something more fit."

He started for the door, but she laid a hand on his sleeve.

Lightly. Some of the stains on his coat appeared to be encrusted food, and up close, he smelled as though he had not washed in weeks. "The Tairen woman."

"I've never seen a blue-eyed Tairen. Please, my Lady. I know a fine inn, a grand place, only two streets over."

The ward she had set on Arrow tingled against her skin. "Thank you, no," she told the innkeeper, and hurried outside.

The woman in the faded red dress was trying to lead Arrow away, tugging at the reins and growing increasingly frustrated at the mare's tiny mincing steps.

"I would abandon that notion if I were you," Moiraine said loudly. "The penalty for horse-theft is flogging if the horse is recovered, and worse if not." Every Accepted was required to become acquainted with the more common laws of the different nations.

The young woman spun, mouth dropping open. Apparently she had believed she had more time before Moiraine came out. Surprise vanished quickly, though, and she straightened her back and laid a hand on her long-bladed belt knife. "I suppose you think you can make me," she said, contemptuously eyeing Moiraine up and down.

It would have been a pleasure to send the woman off with a few stripes across her back, but doing so might well have revealed who she was. A number of passersby, men and women and children, had stopped to watch. Not to interfere; just to see the outcome. "I will if I must," Moiraine said calmly, coolly.

The young woman frowned, licking her lips and fingering the hilt of her knife. Abruptly, she flung down Arrow's reins. "Keep her then! Truth is, she isn't worth stealing." Turning her back, she strode away shooting defiant glares in every direction.

Temper flared in Moiraine, and she channeled Air, striking the woman a hard blow across the bottom. A very hard blow. With a shriek, the woman leaped at least a foot in the air. Gripping her knife hilt, she spun about, scowling and searching for who had hit her, but there was no one closer than two paces, and people were looking at her in open puzzlement. She started off again, rubbing herself with both hands.

Moiraine gave a small nod of satisfaction. Perhaps in

the future the would-be horsethief would know not to insult another woman's horse. Her satisfaction did not last long.

At the second inn on the street, The Blind Pig, a round-faced, squinting woman in a long apron that might have once been white cackled that she had no Tairens in her rooms. Every word out of her mouth came with a shrill laugh. "Best you be off, girl," she said as well. "My trade will have a pretty tender like you for dinner if you don't scurry away quick." Tilting her head back, she roared with laughter that her customers echoed.

At The Silver Penny, the last inn on the street, the innkeeper was a beautiful woman in her middle years, not too overly tall, with a joyous smile and glossy black hair worn in a thick braid that started atop her head. Wonder of wonders, Nedare Satarov's brown woolen dress was neat, clean and well cut, and her common-room floor was freshly swept. Her patrons were rough-faced men and hard-eyed women, but the smells from the kitchen promised something tolerable.

"Why, yes, my Lady," she said, "I do have a Tairen woman of that description staying here. She's gone out just now. Why don't you have a seat and some nice spiced wine while you wait for her." She held out a wooden mug she had been carrying when she first approached. The mug gave off the sweet smell of fresh spices.

"Thank you," Moiraine said, returning the woman's smile with one just as bright. What luck to find Siuan so fast. But her hand stopped just short of the mug. Something had altered in Mistress Satarov's expression. Just by a hair, but there was definitely a slight air of anticipation about her now. And she had been carrying the mug when she approached. Moiraine had not seen a sign of wine in the first two inns. No one in this part of the city could afford wine. Spices could cover many other tastes.

Embracing the Source, she wove Spirit in one of the Blue's secret weaves and touched the innkeeper with it. Slight anticipation became definite unease. "Are you certain the young woman meets my description exactly?" she asked, and tightened the weave a fraction. Sweat appeared on Mistress Satarov's forehead. "Are you absolutely certain?" Another tightening, and a edge of fear appeared in the woman's eyes.

"Come to think, she doesn't have blue eyes at that. And . . . And she left this morning, come to think."

"How many unwary visitors have you fed wine?" Moiraine asked coldly. "How many women? Do you leave them alive? Or simply wishing they were dead?"

"I. . . . I don't know what you're talking about. If you'll excuse me, I. . . ."

"Drink," Moiraine commanded, tightening the weave to just short of panic. Trembling, Mistress Satarov was unable to break free from her gaze. "Drink it all."

Still staring into Moiraine's eyes, the woman raised the mug unsteadily to her mouth, and her throat worked convulsively as she swallowed. Abruptly, her eyes widened as she realized what she was doing, and with a cry she flung the mug away in a spray of wine. Moiraine released the weave, but that did not lessen Mistress Satarov's fear. The woman's face contorted with terror as she gazed around her common room. Hoisting her skirts above her knees, she began running toward the kitchens, perhaps the stairs at the back of the room, yet in three paces she was staggering from side to side, and in three more she collapsed to the floor as though her bones had melted, her stockinged legs exposed to the thigh. Silk stockings. The woman had made a tidy profit from her vile trade. She waved her arms as though seeking to crawl, but there was no strength in them.

Some of the men and women at the tables looked at Moiraine in wonderment, doubtless amazed that she was not the one lying on the floor, but most seemed to be studying Mistress Satarov's futile attempts to claw her way along. A wiry man with a long scar down his face gained a slow smile that never touched his eyes. A heavyset fellow with a blacksmith's shoulders licked his lips. By twos and threes women began hurrying out into the street, many shrinking back from Moiraine as they passed her. Some of the men went, too. She joined the exodus without looking back. Sometimes justice came from other than laws or swords.

That was how the rest of her day went, finding the scattered districts where people's clothes were worn and patched and everyone went afoot. In Chachin, a matter of five streets could take you from the homes and shops of craftsmen who were at least moderately prosperous to squalid poverty and back again. Rulers always tried to do something about those in need, if they were good and decent rulers, and she had heard that Ethenielle was considered generous, yet every time one man was lifted from penury, another seemed to fall into it. That might not be fair, but it was the way of the world. The frustration of it was another reason she wanted to avoid the Sun Throne.

She asked in common rooms filled with drunken shouts and laughter and in grim ones where the men and women at the tables seemed to want only to drown their troubles in drink, but no one admitted to seeing a blue-eyed young Tairen woman. Three more times she was offered wine under suspicious circumstances, but she did not repeat what she had done to Mistress Satarov. Not that she was not tempted, but word of that sort of thing would spread. Once might be dismissed as rumor; four was something else again. Any Blue hearing about that would certainly suspect another Blue was in the city. She disliked thinking that a Blue sister could really be Black, but any sister at all could be, and she needed to remain hidden as long as she could manage.

Twice she was attacked by pairs of men who seized Arrow's bridle and tried to claw her from the saddle. Had there been more, she might have had to reveal herself, but the fear-inducing weave at full strength sent them dashing away through the crowds in mindless panic. Onlookers stared at the running men in amazement, obviously wondering why strong men intent on stealing a horse should suddenly flee, yet unless there was a wilder among them, no one was any the wiser. No fewer than seven more times someone tried to steal Arrow while she was inside an inn. Once it was a pack of children she scattered with a shout, another time half a dozen young men who thought they could ignore her, until she sent them leaping and yelping their way down the street under a flurry of Air-woven switches. It was not that Chachin was any more lawless than other cities, but she was in places where silk clothing and a fur-lined cloak and a fine horse were simply signs that she was ripe for plucking. Had she lost Arrow there, a magistrate might well have said it was her own fault. There was nothing for it but to grit her teeth and move on. Cold daylight began to settle toward yet another icy night.

She was walking Arrow through lengthening shadows, eyeing darknesses that moved suspiciously in an alley and thinking that she would have to give up for today, when Siuan came bustling up from behind.

"I thought you might look down here when you came," Siuan said, taking her elbow to hurry her along. She was wearing the same blue wool riding dress. Moiraine doubted she had even considered spending some of the coin Moiraine had given her on another. "I've been haunting these regions looking for you. Let's get inside before we freeze." Siuan eyed those shadows in the alley, too, and absently fingered her belt knife, as if using the Power could not deal with any ten of them. Well, not without revealing themselves. Perhaps it was best to move quickly. "Not the quarter for you, Moiraine. There are fellows around here would bloody well have you for dinner before you knew you were in the pot. Are you laughing or choking?"

"Both," Moiraine replied with some difficulty. How often today had she heard some variation on her being something to be cooked and eaten if she was not careful? She had to stop and hug the other woman. "Oh, Siuan, it is so good to see your face. Where are you staying? Somewhere that serves fish, I suppose. May I at least hope the beds lack fleas and lice?"

"Maybe it isn't what you're used to," Siuan replied, "but a sound roof to keep off rain is really all you need. And there are no sisters there, so you can chase fleas and lice to your heart's content. But we'd better hurry if we want to reach it before full dark."

Moiraine sighed. And hurried. After dark was not a good time to be out near the sorts of places Siuan favored.

Siuan, it turned out, had a room at a most respectable inn called The Evening Star, three sprawling stories of stone that catered to merchants of middling rank, especially women unwilling to be bothered by noise or rough sorts in the spacious common room. A pair of bull-shouldered fellows, leaning against blue-painted columns as they kept watch on the front door, made sure there was none of that. In truth, they were the only men in the room. A good many of the tables were taken by women, most in well-cut but plain woolens with only a brooch or earrings for jewelry and two with the chains of the Kandori Merchants' Guild looping across their bosoms, though three in bright Domani dresses, discussing something heatedly if in low voices, wore tall chain-necklaces of gold that covered their entire necks. A gray-haired woman plying her hammers on a dulcimer was striking a quiet yet merry tune, and the smells from the kitchens spoke of lamb roasting, not fish.

The innkeeper, Ailene Tolvina, was a lean woman with an air of brooking little nonsense, in a gray dress embroidered with a sprinkling of blue flowers on the shoulders. She had no rooms free, but she made no objection to Moiraine joining Siuan. "So long as the extra for two is paid," she added, holding out a hand. Silks and fur were insufficient to bring curtsies from Mistress Tolvina.

"I can chase fleas to my heart's content?" Moiraine said, hanging her cloak on a peg in Siuan's small room on the top floor. At least it was warm, with a stove built under the not-very-wide bed, and tidy. Siuan was never untidy. "I am surprised you are staying here." The "extra" had been a silver penny, which meant Siuan must be paying two.

"You'll just have to call the fleas first. Why surprised?" Siuan settled cross-legged on the bed, yet she all but bounced. She seemed invigorated since Canluum. A goal always made Siuan bubble with enthusiasm.

Moiraine did not answer the question. They were going to be sharing that bed, and Siuan knew exactly which ticklish spots could reduce her to helpless laughter and pleading. "What have you learned?"

"A great deal and nothing. I've had a time, Moiraine, I tell you. That fool horse nearly beat me to death getting here. The Creator made people to walk or go by boat, not be bounced around. I suppose the Sahera woman wasn't the one, or you'd be jumping like a ladyfish in spring. I found Ines Demain almost right off, but not where *I* can reach her. She's a new widow, but she did have a son, for sure. Named him Rahien because she saw the dawn come up over Dragonmount. Talk of the streets. Everybody thinks it a fool reason to name a child."

Moiraine pushed down a momentary thrill. Seeing dawn

over the mountain did not mean the child had been born on it. There was no chair or stool, nor room for one, so she sat on the end of the bed, wrapping her arms around her knees. "If you have found Ines and her son, Siuan, why is she out of reach?"

"She's in the bloody Aesdaishar Palace, that's why." Siuan could have gained entry easily as Aes Sedai, but otherwise only if the Palace was hiring servants.

The Aesdaishar Palace. "We will take care of that in the morning," Moiraine sighed. It meant risk, yet the Lady Ines had to be questioned. No woman Moiraine had found yet had been able to *see* Dragonmount when her child was born. "Have you seen any sign of . . . of the Black Ajah?" She *had* to get used to saying that name.

Siuan frowned at her lap and fingered her divided skirt. "This is a strange city, Moiraine," she said finally. "Lamps in the streets, and women who fight duels, even if they do deny it, and more gossip than ten men full of ale could spew. Some of it is interesting." She leaned forward to put a hand on Moiraine's knee. "Everybody's talking about a young blacksmith who died of a broken back a couple of nights ago. Nobody expected much of him, but this last month or so he turned into quite a speaker. Convinced his guild to take up money for the poor who've come into the city, afraid of the bandits, folks not connected to a guild or House."

"Siuan, what under the Light—?"

"Just listen, Moiraine. He collected a lot of silver himself, and it seems he was on his way to the guild house to turn in six or eight bags of it when he was killed. Fool was carrying it all by himself. The point is, there wasn't a bloody coin of it taken, Moiraine. And he didn't have a mark on him, aside from his broken back."

They shared a long look; then Moiraine shook her head. "I cannot see how to tie that to Meilyn or Tamra. A blacksmith? Siuan, we can go mad thinking we see Black sisters everywhere."

"We can die from thinking they aren't there," Siuan replied. "Well. Maybe we can be silverpike in the nets instead of grunters. Just remember silverpike go to the fish-market, too. What do you have in mind about this Lady Ines?"

Moiraine told her. Siuan did not like it, and this time

it took most of the night to make her see sense. In truth, Moiraine almost wished Siuan would talk her into trying something else. But Lady Ines had seen dawn over Dragonmount. At least Ethenielle's Aes Sedai advisor was with her in the south.

CHAPTER
24

Making Use of Invisibility

Siuan started up again while they were dressing the next morning. She disliked being argued out of anything, particularly when she thought herself in the right. And she usually did think herself in the right. "I don't like you taking all the risks," she muttered, pulling a blue wool dress over her head. She had brought a change, as it turned out, and she had been near to snippy in pointing out that Moiraine was the one with only a single dress to her name.

"I will not *be* taking all the risks," Moiraine said, suppressing a sigh. They had gone over this and over it last night. "You must take as many as I. Will you help me with these buttons?"

Siuan turned her around by the shoulders almost roughly and attacked the two rows of small mother-of-pearl buttons that ran down her back. "Don't be a gudgeon," she grumbled, tugging at the dress much more fiercely than was necessary. "If this works as you say it will, nobody will notice me. You'll have all sails set, the sweeps out, and banners flying. I say there has to be a better way, and we're going to sit down and talk it over till you see the right of it."

Moiraine did sigh then. A bear with a sore tooth would have been better company. Even that fellow Lan! Doing up Siuan's buttons in turn, she tried distracting the other woman by telling her how much the cut of her dress molded her hips and bosom. Well, for a little more than distraction. Siuan deserved a bit of snippiness back.

"It does attract men's eyes," Siuan replied. And giggled! She even gave her hips a twitch! Moiraine thought she might spend the whole day sighing.

When they went down, with their cloaks folded over their arms, the common room was nearly full of merchants chatting over breakfast, still all women. The two Kandori, one with three chains across her chest, the other with two, were eating hurriedly and beaming like women who foresaw a prosperous day ahead. Some had done business the night before, it seemed. One slender woman in dark gray was eyeing her plump, complacent companion with the sickly expression of someone who had been brought near financial ruin. The three Domani picked at their plates, pushing the food around with their forks; by their tight eyes and pallid faces, they were all nursing sore heads from too much drink.

"A big breakfast, and then we can talk," Siuan said, going on tiptoe to scan the room for an empty table. "The kitchens here make a fine breakfast."

"Rolls that we can eat on the way," Moiraine said firmly, and hurried toward Mistress Tolvina, who was giving instructions to a serving girl in a snowy apron with a blue border. The only way to win an argument with Siuan was to sweep her along. If you let up for an instant, you would find yourself the one being swept.

"Good morning, Mistress Tolvina," she said as the innkeeper turned from the waiting girl. "We wish to hire two of your men to escort us for a few hours this morning." The pair watching the door this morning were different from those who had been on duty last night, though just as large.

The lean woman's eyebrows rose slightly, increasing her no-nonsense air. Again, there was no curtsy, though Moiraine had used the Power to make sure her dress looked fresh from the laundress. "Why? If you've gotten yourself engaged in a duel, I'll have no part of it. A fool thing, these whip-duels and the like, and I'll not abet you. You'd just come back lashed bloody, in any case. I certainly doubt you've ever fought before."

Moiraine bit her tongue. Siuan said the innkeeper had all sorts of rules, from locking the outside doors at midnight to no male visitors in rooms, and enforced them strictly, but she would not have spoken so had she known they were Aes Sedai. "I wish to visit a banker," she said once she could trust herself to speak. Getting them thrown out of Siuan's room would not be a disaster, but it would be inconvenient.

They had a great deal to do today. "A good and reputable banker. Do you know of one nearby?"

As it happened, Mistress Tolvina did, the one she herself used, and for that purpose, she was willing to have two of her "watchers," as she called them, rousted from their rooms over the stable—for an amount Moiraine was sure at least doubled their daily wage. She paid at once, though. Objecting would only waste time, and might drive the price up. Ailene Tolvina did not look like a woman who bargained. Soon enough, she and Siuan were sitting facing each other in a large sedan chair borne by four wiry men who hardly looked strong enough to bear the weight, though they trotted up the crowded streets much more easily than the pair of tall men who escorted the chair carrying long, brass-studded cudgels.

"This isn't going to work," Siuan muttered between gnaws at a large, crusty roll. "If you think we need more money, all right. Though you do fling it around, Moiraine. But, burn me, this scheme of yours will never work. We'll be netted right away. They'll probably send for a sister. If there isn't one there already. I tell you, we have to find another way."

Moiraine pretended to be too busy eating her own roll, still warm from the oven, to answer. Besides, she was hungry. If they encountered another Aes Sedai. . . . That was a chasm they would have to cross when they came to it. She told herself the flutter in her belly was hunger, not fear. But you could think a lie. Her plan had to work. There *was* no other way.

As in Tar Valon, the bank resembled a small palace, this one glittering in the morning sunlight like the real palaces farther up the mountain, with golden tiles on every wall and two tall white domes. The doorman who bowed them inside wore a dark red coat embroidered on the cuffs with silver bees, and the footmen short black coats that exposed their bottoms in their tight breeches. Moiraine's dress with the slashes of Cairhienin nobility on the front was enough to get them an interview with the banker herself rather than an underling, in a quiet, wood-paneled room with silvered stand-lamps and small lines of gilding on the furniture.

Kamile Noallin was a lovely slim woman in her middle years, with graying hair worn in four long braids and stern, questioning eyes. Kandor was a long way from Cairhien, after all, and from Tar Valon. Still, she had no call to use an enlarging glass to study Ilain Dormaile's seal at the bottom of Moiraine's letter-of-rights. At least the letter itself was only a little blurred from its immersion in that pond. It was not the largest she carried, yet even so it produced an imposing pile of gold in ten leather pouches stacked on the banker's writing table, even after the steep discount for the distance between the two banks.

"You have bodyguards, I hope." Mistress Noallin murmured politely. Large quantities of gold tended to bring courtesy.

"Is Chachin so lawless two women are not safe by daylight?" Moiraine asked her coolly. An enlarging glass! "I think our business is done."

A pair of very large footmen carried the purses outside and placed them on the floor of the sedan chair, looking relieved at the sight of Mistress Tolvina's two "watchers" with their cudgels. The bearers hoisted the extra weight effortlessly, it seemed.

"Even that blacksmith must have staggered, loaded down like a mule," Siuan muttered, toeing the purses piled between them. "Who could have broken his back that way? Fish guts! Whatever the reason, Moiraine, it must be the Black Ajah."

The bearers could hear that clearly, but they trotted along without faltering, ignorant of what the words Black Ajah meant, likely ignorant of what an Ajah was, for that matter. On the other hand, an imposing woman gliding by with ivory combs in her hair gave a start, then hiked her skirts to her knees and ran, leaving her two gaping servants to scramble after her through the crowd.

Moiraine directed a reproving look at Siuan. They could not depend on others' ignorance for protection. Siuan flushed slightly, yet her blue eyes were defiant.

The Evening Star had a small strongroom where merchants could store their coin safely, those who did not keep strongboxes in their rooms, but placing most of the gold there did not bring any curtsies from Mistress Tolvina, even after Moiraine gave her a gold crown for her troubles. No doubt she had seen too many merchants lose everything to be impressed just because someone had coin at the moment.

"The best seamstress in Chachin would be Silene Dorelmin," she said in answer to Moiraine's question, "but she's very dear, or so I hear. Very dear." Moiraine took back one of the fat purses, though it dragged her belt down on one side when she tied the strings. That blacksmith *must* have staggered! No, Siuan was seeing jak o'the mists, that was all.

Silene proved to be a slim woman with a haughty air and a cool voice, in a shimmering blue dress with a neckline cut to show most of her cleavage. The garment barely clung to her shoulders! Moiraine did not worry over being pressed into that sort of dress, though. She intended to violate nearly every rule of propriety between a woman and her seamstress. She tolerated the measuring, since there was no way to hasten it, but Silene's eyes narrowed at the speed with which she chose fabrics and colors. For a moment it seemed she would refuse to sew what Siuan needed, but Moiraine calmly said she would pay twice the usual rate. The woman's eyes went almost to slits at the mention of price, yet she nodded. And Moiraine knew she would get what she wanted. Here, at least.

"I want them tomorrow," she said. "Put all of your seamstresses to work."

Silene's eyes did not narrow at that. They widened, flashing with anger. Her voice became icy. "Impossible. At the end of the month, perhaps. Perhaps later. If I can find time at all. A great many ladies have ordered new gowns. The King of Malkier is visiting the Aesdaishar Palace."

"The last King of Malkier died twenty-five years ago, Silene." Taking up the fat purse, Moiraine upended it over the table in the measuring room, spilling out thirty gold crowns. She was ordering more than three dresses, but while silk was as expensive in Chachin as in Tar Valon, the sewing was much less, and that was the largest expense in a dress.

Silene eyed the fat coins greedily, and her eyes positively shone when she was told there would be as much again when the dresses were done.

"But I will keep six coins from the second thirty for each day it takes." Suddenly it seemed that the dresses could be finished sooner than a month after all. Much sooner.

"You should have your dresses made like what that skinny trull was wearing," Siuan said as they climbed back into the sedan chair. "Ready to fall off. You might as well enjoy men looking at you if you're going to lay your fool head on the chopping block."

Moiraine performed a novice exercise, imaging herself a rosebud in stillness, opening to the sun. Thankfully, it brought calm. Though holding on to it around Siuan could prove trying. She would crack a tooth if she kept grinding them. "There is no other way, Siuan." The day was more than half gone, and much remained to be done. "Do you think Mistress Tolvina will hire out one of her strongarms for more than a few hours?" The King of *Malkier*? Light! The woman must have thought her a complete fool!

At midmorning two days after Moiraine arrived in Chachin, a yellow-lacquered carriage behind a team of four matched grays, driven by a fellow with shoulders like a bull, arrived at the Aesdaishar Palace, with two mares tied behind, a fine-necked bay and a lanky gray. The Lady Moiraine Damodred, colored slashes marching from the high neck of her dark blue gown to below her knees, was received with all due honor, by an upper servant with silvery keys embroidered behind the Red Horse on his shoulder. The name of House Damodred was known, of course, if not hers, and with Laman dead, any Damodred might ascend to the Sun Throne if another House did not seize it. They could not know how she hoped for that.

She was given suitable apartments, three spacious rooms with silk tapestries on the flower-carved wall panels and a marble-railed balcony looking north across the city toward higher, snowcapped peaks, and assigned servants, two maids and an errand boy, who rushed about unpacking the lady's brass-bound chests and pouring hot rose-scented water for the lady to wash. No one but the servants so much as glanced at Suki, the Lady Moiraine's maid.

"All right," Siuan muttered when the servants finally left them alone in the sitting room, "I admit I'm invisible in this." Her dark gray dress was fine wool, entirely plain except for collar and cuffs banded in Damodred colors. "You, though, stand out like a High Lord pulling oar. Light, I nearly swallowed my tongue when you asked if there were any sisters in the Palace. I'm so nervous I'm starting to get light-headed. It feels hard to breathe."

"It is the altitude," Moiraine told her. "You will get used

to it. Any visitor would ask about Aes Sedai; you could see, the servants never blinked." She had held her breath, however, until she heard the answer. One sister would have changed everything. "I do not know why I must keep telling you. A royal palace is not an inn; 'You may call me Lady Alys' would satisfy no one, here. That is fact, not opinion. I must be myself. Suppose you make use of that invisibility and see what you can learn about the Lady Ines. I would be pleased if we leave as soon as possible."

Tomorrow, that would be, without causing insult and talk. Siuan was right. Every eye in the palace would be on the outland noblewoman from the House that had started the Aiel War. Any Aes Sedai who came to the Aesdaishar would hear of her immediately, and any Aes Sedai who passed through Chachin might well come. And if this Gorthanes was still trying to find her, word of Moiraine Damodred in the Aesdaishar Palace would reach his ears all too soon. In her experience, palaces were riper for assassination than highways were. Siuan was right; she was standing on a pedestal like a target, and without a clue as to who might be an archer. Tomorrow, early.

Siuan slipped out, but returned quickly with bad news. The Lady Ines was in seclusion, mourning her husband. "He fell over dead in his breakfast porridge ten days ago," she reported, dropping onto a sitting-room chair and hanging an arm over the back. Lessons in deportment were something else forgotten once the shawl was hers. "A much older man, but it seems she loved him. She's been given ten rooms and a garden on the south side of the palace; her husband was a close friend to Prince Brys." Ines would remain to herself a full month, seeing no one but close family. Her servants only came out when absolutely necessary.

"She will see an Aes Sedai," Moiraine sighed. Not even a woman in mourning would refuse to see a sister.

Siuan bolted to her feet. "Are you mad? The Lady Moiraine Damodred attracts enough attention. Moiraine Damodred Aes Sedai might as well send out riders! I thought the idea was to be gone before anyone outside the Palace knows we were here!"

One of the serving women, a plump gray-haired woman named Aiko, came in just then, to announce that the *shatayan* had arrived to escort Moiraine to Prince Brys, and was plainly startled to find Suki standing over her mistress and stabbing a finger at her.

"Tell the *shatayan* I will come to her," Moiraine said calmly, and as soon as the wide-eyed woman curtsied and backed out, she rose to put herself on a more equal footing, hard enough with Siuan even when one had all the advantage. "What else do you suggest? Remaining almost two weeks till she comes out will be as bad, and you cannot befriend her servants if they are secluded with her."

"They may only come out for errands, Moiraine, but I think I can get myself invited inside."

Moiraine started to say that might take as long as the other, but Siuan took her firmly by the shoulders and turned her around, eyeing her up and down critically. "A lady's maid is supposed to make sure her mistress is properly dressed," she said, and gave Moiraine a push toward the door. "Go. The *shatayan* is waiting for you. And with any luck, a young footman named Cal is waiting for Suki."

CHAPTER
25

An Answer

The *shatayan* indeed was waiting, a tall handsome woman, wrapped in dignity and frosty at being made to wait. Her hazel eyes could have chilled wine. Any queen who got on the wrong side of a *shatayan* was a fool, so Moiraine made herself pleasant as the woman escorted her through the halls. She thought she made some progress in melting that frost, but it was difficult to concentrate. A young footman? She did not know whether Siuan had ever been with a man, but surely she would not just to reach Ines' servants! Not a *footman*!

Statues and tapestries lined the hallways, most surprising for what she knew of the Borderlands. Marble carvings of women with flowers or children playing, silk weavings of fields of flowers and nobles in gardens and only a few hunting scenes, without a single battle shown anywhere. At intervals along the halls arched windows looked down into many more gardens than she expected, too, and flagged courtyards, some with a splashing marble fountain. In one of those, she saw something that pushed questions about Siuan and a footman to the back of her mind.

It was a simple courtyard, without fountain or columned walk, and men stood in rows along the walls watching two others, stripped to the waist and fighting with wooden practice swords. Ryne and Bukama. It was fighting, if in practice; blows landed on flesh hard enough for her to hear the thuds. All landed by Ryne. She would have to avoid them, and Lan, if he was there, too. He had not bothered to hide his doubts, and he might raise questions she did not dare have asked. Was she Moiraine or Alys? Worse, was she

Aes Sedai or a wilder pretending? Questions that would be discussed in the streets by the next night, for any sister to hear, and that last was one any sister would investigate. Fortunately, three wandering soldiers would hardly be present anywhere she was.

Prince Brys, a solid, green-eyed man, greeted her intimately in a large room paneled red and gold. Two of the Prince's married sisters were present with their husbands, and one of Ethenielle's with hers, the men in muted silks, the women in bright colors belted high beneath their breasts and embroidered down the arms and along the hems of their skirts. Liveried servants offered sweetmeats and nuts. Moiraine thought she might get a sore neck from looking up; the shortest of the women was taller than Siuan, and they all stood very straight. Their necks would have bent a little for a sister, men's and women's alike, but they knew themselves the equals of the Lady Moiraine.

The talk ranged from music and the best musicians among the nobles at court to the rigors of travel, from whether to credit rumors of a man who could channel to why so many Aes Sedai seemed to be about, and Moiraine found it difficult to maintain the expected light wittiness. She cared little for music and less for whoever played the instruments; in Cairhien, musicians were hired and forgotten. Everyone knew that travel was arduous, with no assurance of beds or decent food at the end of the day's twenty or thirty miles, and that was when the weather was good. Obviously some of the sisters were about because of rumors about the man, and others to tighten ties that might have loosened during the Aiel War, to make sure thrones and Houses understood they were still expected to meet their obligations to the Tower, both public and private. If an Aes Sedai had not come to the Aesdaishar yet, one soon would, reason enough for her to make heavy going of idle chat. That and thinking about other reasons for sisters to be wandering. The men put a good face on it, but she thought the women found her particularly dull.

When Brys's children were brought in, Moiraine felt a great relief. Having his children introduced to her was a sign of acceptance to his household, but more, it signaled the end of the audience. The eldest son, Antol, was in the south with Ethenielle as heir, leaving a lovely green-eyed girl of twelve named Jarene to lead in her sister and four brothers, formally aligned by age, though in truth the two youngest boys were still in skirts and carried by nursemaids. Stifling her impatience to find out what Siuan had learned, Moiraine complimented the children on their behavior, encouraged them at their lessons. They must think her as dull as their elders did. Something a little less flat.

"And how did you earn your bruises, my Lord Diryk?" she asked, hardly listening to the boy's soberly delivered story of a fall. Until. . . .

"My father says it was Lan's luck I wasn't killed, my Lady," Diryk said, brightening out of his formality. "Lan is the King of Malkier, and the luckiest man in the world, and the best swordsman. Except for my father, of course."

"The King of Malkier?" Moiraine said, blinking. Diryk nodded vigorously and began explaining in a rush of words about Lan's exploits in the Blight and the Malkieri who had come to the Aesdaishar to follow him, until his father motioned him to silence.

"Lan is a king if he wishes it, my Lady," Brys said. A very odd thing to say, and his doubtful tone made it odder. "He keeps much to his rooms," Brys sounded troubled about that, too, "but you will meet him before you—My Lady, are you well?"

"Not very," she told him. She had hoped for another meeting with Lan Mandragoran, planned for it, but not here! Her stomach was trying to twist into knots. "I myself may keep to my rooms for a few days, if you will forgive me."

He would, of course, and everyone was full of regret at missing her company and sympathy for the strain traveling must have put on her. Though she did hear one of the women murmur that southlanders must be very delicate.

A pale-haired young woman in green-and-red was waiting to show Moiraine back to her rooms. Elis bobbed a curtsy every time she spoke, which meant she bobbed quite often in the beginning. She had been told of Moiraine's "faintness," and she asked every twenty paces whether Moiraine wished to sit and catch her breath, or have cool damp cloths brought to her rooms, or hot bricks for her feet, or smelling salts, or a dozen more sure cures for "a light head," until Moiraine curtly told her to be quiet. The fool girl led on in silence, face blank.

Moiraine cared not a whit whether the woman was offended. All she wanted right then was to find Siuan with good news. With the boy in her arms, born on Dragonmount, and his mother packed to travel would be best of all. Most of all, though, she wanted herself out of the halls before she ran into Lan Mandragoran.

Worrying about him, she rounded a corner behind the serving girl and came face-to-face with Merean, blue-fringed shawl looped over her arms. The *shatayan* herself was guiding Merean, and behind the motherly-looking sister came a train of servants, one woman carrying her red riding gloves, another her fur-trimmed cloak, a third her dark velvet hat. Pairs of men bore wicker pack hampers that could have been carried by one, and others had arms full of flowers. An Aes Sedai received more honor than a mere lady, however high her House.

Merean's eyes narrowed at the sight of Moiraine. "A surprise to see you here," she said slowly. "By your dress, I take it you've given over your disguise? But no. Still no ring, I see."

Moiraine was so startled at the woman's sudden appearance that she hardly heard what Merean said. "Are you alone?" she blurted.

For a moment Merean's eyes became slits. "Larelle decided to go her own way. South, I believe. More, I don't know."

"It was Cadsuane, I was thinking of," Moiraine said, blinking in surprise. The more she had thought about Cadsuane, the more she had become convinced the woman must be Black Ajah. What surprised her was Larelle. Larelle had seemed bent on reaching Chachin, and without delay. Of course, plans could change, but suddenly Moiraine realized something that should have been obvious. Black sisters could lie. It was impossible—the Oaths *could* not be broken!—yet it had to be.

Merean moved close to Moiraine, and when Moiraine took a step back, she followed. Moiraine held herself erect, but she still came no higher than the other woman's chin. "Are you so eager to see Cadsuane?" Merean said, looking down at her. Her voice was pleasant, her smooth face comforting, but her eyes were cold iron. "The last I saw her, she said that next time she met you, she'd spank your bottom till you couldn't sit for a week. She'll do it, too."

Abruptly glancing at the servants, she seemed to realize they were not alone. The iron faded, but it did not disappear. "Cadsuane was right, you know. A young woman who thinks she knows more than she does can land herself in very deep trouble. I suggest you be very still and very quiet until we can talk." Her gesture for the *shatayan* to lead on was peremptory, and the dignified woman leaped to obey. A king or queen might find themselves in a *shatayan*'s bad graces, but never an Aes Sedai.

Moiraine stared after Merean until she vanished around a corner far down the corridor. Everything Merean had just said could have come from one of Tamra's chosen. Black sisters could lie. Had Larelle changed her mind about Chachin? Or was she dead somewhere, like Tamra and the others? Suddenly she realized she was smoothing her skirts. Stilling her hands was easy, but she could not stop herself trembling faintly.

Elis was staring at her with her mouth open. "You're Aes Sedai, too!" the woman squeaked, then gave a jump, taking Moiraine's wince for a grimace. "You must be in disguise," she said breathlessly. "I won't say a word to anyone, Aes Sedai. I swear, by the Light and my father's grave!" As if every person behind Merean had not heard everything she had. They would not hold their tongues.

"Take me to Lan Mandragoran's apartments," Moiraine told her. What was true at sunrise could change by noon, and so could what was necessary. She took the Great Serpent ring from her pouch and put it on her right hand. Sometimes, you had to gamble.

After a long walk, mercifully in silence, Elis rapped at a red door and announced to the gray-haired woman who opened it that the Lady Moiraine Damodred Aes Sedai wished to speak with King al'Lan Mandragoran. The woman had added her own touches to what Moiraine told her. King, indeed! Shockingly, the reply came back that Lord Mandragoran had no wish to speak with any Aes Sedai. The gray-haired woman looked scandalized, but closed the door firmly.

Elis stared at Moiraine wide-eyed. "I can show my Lady Aes Sedai to her own rooms now," she said uncertainly, "if—" She squeaked when Moiraine pushed open the door and went in.

The gray-haired serving woman and a younger leaped

up from where they had been sitting, apparently darning shirts. A bony young man scrambled awkwardly to his feet beside the fireplace, looking to the women for instruction. They simply stared at Moiraine until she raised a questioning eyebrow. Then the gray-haired woman pointed to one of the two doors leading deeper into the apartments.

The door she pointed to led to a sitting room much like Moiraine's own, but all of the gilded chairs had been moved back against the walls and the flowered carpets rolled up. Shirtless, Lan was practicing the sword in the cleared area. A small golden locket swung at his neck as he moved, his blade a blur. Sweat covered him. And the wounds she had Healed him of had been replaced by. . . . Claw marks from some wild animal on his back? Or marks left by a woman. Could this cold man actually inspire such passion in a woman that she would. . . . She felt her cheeks heating at the image that popped into her head. Let him have as many women as he wished, so long as he did what she wished.

He spun gracefully out of the forms to face her, the point of his sword grounding on the floor tiles. He still did not quite meet her gaze, in that strange way he and Bukama had. His hair hung damply, clinging to his face despite the leather cord, but he was not breathing hard.

"You," he growled. "So you are Aes Sedai *and* a Damodred today. I've no time for your games, Cairhienin. I am waiting for someone." Cold blue eyes flickered to the door behind her. Oddly, what appeared to be a cord woven of hair was tied around the inner handle in an elaborate knot. "She will not be pleased to find another woman here."

"Your lady love need have no fear of me," Moiraine told him dryly. "For one thing, you are much too tall, and for another, I prefer men with at least a modicum of charm. And manners. I came for your help. There was a pledge made, and held since the War of the Hundred Years, that Malkier would ride when the White Tower called. I *am* Aes Sedai, and I call you!"

"You know the hills are high, but not how they lie," he muttered as if quoting some Malkieri saying. Stalking across the room away from her, he snatched up his scabbard and sheathed the sword forcefully. "I'll give you your help, if you can answer a question. I've asked Aes Sedai over the years, but they wriggled away from answering like vipers. If you are Aes Sedai, answer it."

"If I know the answer, I will." She would not tell him again that she was what she was, but she embraced *saidar,* and moved one of the gilded chairs out into the middle of the floor. She could not have lifted the thing with her hands, yet it floated easily on flows of Air, and would have had it been twice as heavy. Sitting, she rested her hands on crossed knees where the golden serpent on her finger was plain. The taller person had an advantage when both stood, but someone standing must feel they were being judged by someone sitting, especially an Aes Sedai.

He did not seem to feel anything of the kind. For the first time since she had met him, he met her eyes directly, and his stare was blue ice. "When Malkier died," he said in tones of quiet steel, "Shienar and Arafel sent men. They could not stop the flood of Trollocs and Myrddraal, yet they came. Men rode from Kandor, and even Saldaea. They came too late, but they came." Blue ice became blue fire. His voice did not change, but his knuckles grew white gripping his sword. "For nine hundred years we rode when the White Tower called, but where was the Tower when Malkier died? If you are Aes Sedai, answer me that!"

Moiraine hesitated. The answer he wanted was Sealed to the Tower, taught to Accepted in history lessons yet forbidden to any except initiates of the Tower. But what was another penance alongside what she faced? "Over a hundred sisters were ordered to Malkier," she said more calmly than she felt. By everything she had been taught, she should *ask* a penance for what she had told him already. "Even Aes Sedai cannot fly, however. They were too late." By the time the first had arrived, the armies of Malkier were already broken by endless hordes of Shadowspawn, the people fleeing or dead. The death of Malkier had been hard and blood-soaked, and fast. "That was before I was born, but I regret it deeply. And I regret that the Tower decided to keep their effort secret." Better that the Tower be thought to have done nothing than to have it known Aes Sedai had tried and failed. Failure was a blow to stature, and mystery an armor the Tower needed. Aes Sedai had reasons of their own for what they did, and for what they did not do, and those reasons were known only to Aes Sedai. "That is as much answer as I can give. More than I should have, more than any other sister ever will, I think. Will it suffice?"

For a time he simply looked at her, fire slowly fading to ice once more. His eyes fell away. "Almost, I can believe," he muttered finally, without saying what he almost believed. He gave a bitter laugh. "What help can I give you?"

Moiraine frowned. She very much wanted time alone with this man, to bring him to heel, but that had to wait. She very much hoped he was not a Darkfriend. "There is another sister in the Palace. Merean Redhill. I need to know where she goes, what she does, who she meets." He blinked, but did not ask the obvious questions. Perhaps he knew he would get no answers, but his silence was still pleasing.

"I have been keeping to my rooms the past few days," he said, looking at the door again. "I do not know how much watching I can do."

In spite of herself, she sniffed. The man promised help, then looked anxiously for his lady. Perhaps he was not what she had thought. But he was who she had. "Not you," she told him. Her visit here would be known throughout the Aesdaishar soon, if it was not already, and if he was noticed spying on Merean. . . . That could be disaster even if the woman was as innocent as a babe. "I thought you might ask one of the Malkieri I understand have gathered here to follow you. Someone with a sharp eye and a close tongue. This must be done in utter secrecy."

"No one follows me," he said sharply. Glancing at the door once more, he suddenly seemed weary. He did not slump, but he moved to the fireplace and propped his sword beside it with the care of a tired man. Standing with his back to her, he said, "I will ask Bukama and Ryne to watch her, but I cannot promise for them. That is all I can do for you."

She stifled a vexed sound. Whether it was all he could do or all he would, she had no leverage to force him. "Bukama," she said. "Only him." Going by how he had behaved around her, Ryne would be too busy gaping at Merean to see or hear anything. That was if he did not confess what he was doing the moment Merean looked at him. "And do not tell him why."

His head whipped around, but after a moment he nodded.

And again he did not ask the questions most people would have. Telling him how to get word to her, by notes passed to her maid Suki, she prayed she was not making a grave mistake.

Back in her own rooms, she discovered just how quickly news had spread. In the sitting room, Siuan was offering a tray of sweetmeats to a tall, full-mouthed young woman in pale green silk, little older than a girl, with black hair that fell well below her hips and a small blue dot painted on her forehead about where the stone of Moiraine's *kesiera* hung. Siuan's face was smooth, but her voice was tight as she made introductions. The Lady Iselle quickly showed why.

"Everyone in the Palace is saying you are Aes Sedai," she said, eyeing Moiraine doubtfully. She did not rise, much less curtsy, or even incline her head. "If that is so, I need your assistance. I wish to go to the White Tower. My mother wants me to marry. I would not mind Lan as my *carneira* if Mother were not already his, but when I marry, I think it will be one of my Warders. I will be Green Ajah." She frowned faintly at Siuan. "Don't hover, girl. Stand over there until you are needed." Siuan took up a stance by the fireplace, back stiff and arms folded beneath her breasts. No real servant would have stood so—or frowned so—but Iselle no longer noticed her. "Do sit down, Moiraine," she went on with a smile, "and I will tell you what I need of you. If you *are* Aes Sedai, of course."

Moiraine stared. Invited to take a chair in her own sitting room. This silly child was certainly a suitable match for Lan when it came to arrogance. Her *carneira*? That meant "first" in the Old Tongue, and plainly something else here. Not what it seemed to, of course; even these Malkieri could not be that peculiar! Sitting, she said dryly, "Choosing your Ajah should at least wait until I test you to see whether there is any point in sending you to the Tower. A few minutes will determine whether you can learn to channel, and your potential strength if you—" The girl blithely broke in.

"Oh, I was tested years ago. The Aes Sedai said I would be very strong. I told her I was fifteen, but she learned the truth. I don't see why I could not go to the Tower at twelve if I wanted. Mother was furious. She has always said I was to be Queen of Malkier one day, but that means marrying Lan, which I would not want even if Mother weren't his *carneira*. When you tell her you are taking me to the Tower, she will have to listen. Everyone knows that Aes Sedai take any woman they want for training, and no one can stop them." That full mouth pursed. "You *are* Aes Sedai, aren't you?"

Moiraine performed the rosebud exercise. "If you want to go to Tar Valon, then go. I certainly do not have time to escort you. You will find sisters there about whom you can have no doubts. Suki, will you show the Lady Iselle out? No doubt she does not wish to delay in setting off before her mother catches her."

The chit was all indignation, of course, but Moiraine wanted only to see the back of her, and Siuan very nearly pushed her out into the corridor protesting every step of the way. Moiraine felt Siuan embrace the Source, and the protests cut off with a sharp yelp.

"That one," Siuan said as she came back dusting her hands, "won't last a month if she can equal Cadsuane."

"Sierin herself can toss her from the top of the Tower for all I care," Moiraine snapped. "Did you learn anything?"

"Well, I learned that young Cal knows how to kiss, and aside from that, I came up with a bucket of bilgewater." Siuan scowled suddenly. "Why are you looking at me that way? I only kissed him, Moiraine. Have you kissed a pretty man since young Cormanes the night before you left for the Tower? Well, it's been as long for me, too long, and Cal is *very* pretty."

"That is all very well," Moiraine said briskly. Light, how long since she had thought of Cormanes? He had been beautiful.

Surprisingly, learning that Moiraine had approached Lan upset Siuan more than Merean's appearance.

"Skin me and salt me if you don't take idiot risks, Moiraine. A man who claims the throne of a dead country is nine kinds of fool. He could be flapping his tongue about you right this minute to anybody who'll bloody listen! If Merean learns you're having her watched. . . . Burn me!"

"He is many kinds of fool, Siuan, but I do not think he ever 'flaps his tongue.' Besides, 'you cannot win if you will not risk a copper,' as you always tell me your father used to say. We have no choice but to take risks. With Merean here, time may be running out. You must reach the Lady Ines as quickly as you can."

"I'll do what I can," Siuan muttered, and stalked out squaring her shoulders as if for a struggle. But she was smoothing her skirt over her hips, too. Moiraine hoped matters were not going to proceed beyond kissing. Siuan's business if it did, but that sort of thing was foolish. Especially with a footman!

Night had long since fallen and she was trying to read by lamplight when Siuan returned. Moiraine set her book aside; she had been staring at the same page for the past hour. This time, Siuan did have news, delivered while digging through her woolen dresses and shifts.

For one thing, she had been approached on her way back to Moiraine's rooms by "a gristly old stork" who asked if she was Suki, then told her Merean had spent almost the entire day with Prince Brys before retiring to her apartments for the night. No clue there to anything. More importantly, Siuan had been able to bring up Rahien in casual conversation with Cal. The footman had not been with the Lady Ines when the boy was born, but he did know the day, one day after the Aiel began their retreat from Tar Valon. Moiraine and Siuan shared a long look over that. One day after Gitara Moroso had made her Foretelling of the Dragon's Rebirth and dropped dead from the shock of it. Dawn over the mountain, and born during the ten days before that sudden thaw.

"Anyway," Siuan went on, beginning to make a bundle of clothes and stockings, "I led Cal to believe I'd been dismissed from your service for spilling wine on your dress, and he's offered me a bed with the Lady Ines' servants. He thinks he might be able to get me a place with his lady." She snorted with amusement, then caught Moiraine's eyes and snorted again, more roughly. "It isn't *his* bloody bed, Moiraine. And if it was, well, he has a gentle manner and the prettiest brown eyes you've ever seen. One of these days, you're going to find yourself ready to do more than dream about some man, and I hope I'm there to see it!"

"Do not talk nonsense," Moiraine told her. The task in front of them was too important to spare thoughts for men. In the way Siuan meant, at least. Merean had spent all day with Brys? Without going near Lady Ines? One of Tamra's chosen or Black Ajah, that made no sense, and it went beyond credibility to believe Merean was not one or the other. She was missing something, and that worried her. What she did not know could kill her. Worse, it could kill the Dragon Reborn in his cradle.

CHAPTER 26

When to Surrender

Lan slipped through the corridors of the Aesdaishar
alone, using every bit of the skill he had learned in the
Blight, taking care not to round a corner until he was
certain the hallway ahead was empty. Wrapped in the *ko'di*,
he could almost feel it whenever someone entered the corridor behind him, feel the beginning of another presence and
duck out of sight through an open door or an archway before
whoever it was could see him. He might have been a ghost.

Anya and Esne took Edeyn's commands ahead of his,
now, as though they believed that some part of Malkieri
ways. She might have told them it was. Bulen remained
loyal, he believed so, but he expected that anyone in the Aesdaishar wearing livery would tell Edeyn where to find him.
He thought he knew where he was, now. Despite those previous visits, without a guide he had gotten lost twice since
leaving his rooms, and only a feel for direction let him find
himself again. He felt a fool for wearing his sword. Steel
was no use in this battle. But he felt naked without it, and naked was one thing he could not afford to be against Edeyn.

A flicker of movement made him flatten himself against
the wall behind a statue of a woman clad in clouds, her
arms full of flowers. Just in time. Two women came out of
the crossing corridor ahead, pausing in close conversation.
Iselle and the Aes Sedai, Merean. He was as still as the
stone he hid behind. It was motion that attracted eyes.

He did not like skulking, but while Edeyn was untying
the knot in his *daori* that had kept him penned for two days
she had made it clear that she intended to announce his marriage to Iselle soon. Bukama had been right. Edeyn used his

daori like reins. By custom, most of her power over him would end once Iselle had the cord of his hair among her keepsakes, no longer any more than a token of the past, yet he was certain Edeyn would use Iselle herself in its place. And Iselle would cooperate. He doubted that she had the strength to stand against her mother openly. The only thing to do when faced by an opponent you could not defeat was run, unless your death could serve some greater purpose, and he very much wanted to run. Only Bukama held him here. Bukama and a dream.

At a sharp gesture from Merean, Iselle nodded eagerly and hurried back the way they had come. For a moment Merean watched her go, face unreadable in Aes Sedai serenity. Then, surprisingly, she followed, gliding along the green floor tiles in a way that made Iselle look awkward.

Lan did not waste time wondering what Merean was up to, any more than he had in wondering why Moiraine wanted her watched. A man could go mad trying to puzzle out Aes Sedai. Which Moiraine really must be, or Merean would have her howling up and down the corridors. Waiting long enough for the pair to move well out of sight again, he slipped quietly to the corner and peeked. They were both gone, so he hurried on. Aes Sedai were no concern of his today. He had to talk to Bukama. About dreams.

Running would end Edeyn's schemes of marriage. If he avoided her long enough, she would find another husband for Iselle. Running would end Edeyn's dream of reclaiming Malkier; her support would fade like mist under a noon sun once people learned he was gone. Running would end many dreams. The man who had carried an infant tied to his back had a right to dreams, though. Duty was a mountain, but it had to be carried.

Ahead lay a long flight of broad, stone-railed stairs. He turned to start down, and suddenly he was falling. He just had time to go limp, and then he was bouncing from step to step, tumbling head over heels, landing on the tiled floor at the bottom with a crash that drove the last remaining air from his lungs. Spots shimmered in front of his eyes. He struggled to breathe, to push himself up.

Servants appeared from nowhere, helping him to his feet, all exclaiming over his luck in not killing himself in such a fall, asking whether he wanted to see one of the Aes Sedai for

Healing. Frowning dizzily up the stairway, he murmured replies, anything in hope of making them go away. He thought he might be as bruised as he had ever been in his life, but bruises went away, and the last thing he wanted at that moment was a sister. Most men would have fought that fall and been lucky to end with half their bones broken. Something had jerked his ankles up there. Something had hit him between the shoulders. There was only one thing it could have been, however little sense it made. He would have known had anyone been close enough to touch him physically. An Aes Sedai had tried to kill him with the Power.

"Lord Mandragoran!" A stocky man in the green coat of a palace guard skidded to a halt and nearly fell over trying to bow while still moving. "We've been looking for you everywhere, my Lord!" he panted. "It's your man, Bukama! Come quickly, my Lord! He may still be alive!"

Cursing, Lan ran behind the guard, shouting for the man to go faster, but he was too late. Too late for the man who had carried an infant. Too late for dreams.

Guards crowding a narrow passage just off one of the practice yards squeezed back to let Lan through. Bukama lay facedown, blood pooled around his mouth, the plain wooden hilt of a dagger rising from the dark stain on the back of his coat. His staring eyes looked surprised. Kneeling, Lan closed those eyes and murmured a prayer for the last embrace of the mother to welcome Bukama home.

"Who found him?" he asked, but he barely heard the jumbled replies about who and where and what. He hoped Bukama was reborn in a world where the Golden Crane flew on the wind, and the Seven Towers stood unbroken, and the Thousand Lakes shone like a necklace beneath the sun. How could he have let anyone get close enough to do this? Bukama could *feel* steel being unsheathed near him. Only one thing was sure. Bukama was dead because Lan had tangled him in an Aes Sedai's schemes.

Rising, he began to run again. Not away from anything, though. Toward someone. And he did not care who saw him.

The muffled crash of the door in the anteroom and outraged shouts from the serving women lifted Moiraine from the cushioned armchair where she had been waiting. For anything but this. Embracing *saidar,* she started from the sitting room, but before she reached the door, it swung open. Lan shook off the liveried women clinging to his arms, shut the door in their faces, and put his back to it, meeting Moiraine's startled gaze. Purpling bruises marred his angular face, and he moved as if he had been beaten. From outside came silence. Whatever he intended, they would be sure she could handle it.

Absurdly, she found herself fingering her belt knife. With the Power she could wrap him up like a child, however large he was, and yet. . . . He did not glare. There certainly was no fire in those eyes. She wanted to step back. No fire, but death seared cold. That black coat suited him with its cruel thorns and stark golden blossoms.

"Bukama is dead with a knife in his heart," he said calmly, "and not an hour gone, someone tried to kill me with the One Power. At first I thought it must be Merean, but the last I saw of her, she was trailing after Iselle, and unless she saw me and wanted to lull me, she had no time. Few see me when I do not want to be seen, and I don't think she did. That leaves you."

Moiraine winced, and only in part for the certainty in his tone. She should have known the fool girl would go straight to Merean. "You would be surprised how little escapes a sister," she told him. Especially if the sister was filled with *saidar.* "Perhaps I should not have asked Bukama to watch Merean. She is very dangerous." The woman *was* Black Ajah; she was certain of that, now. Sisters might make painful examples of people caught snooping, but they did not kill them. But what to do about her? Certainty was not proof, surely not proof that would stand up before the Amyrlin Seat. And if Sierin herself was Black. . . . Not a worry she could do anything about now. What was the woman doing wasting any time at all with Iselle? "If you care for the girl, I suggest you find her as quickly as possible and keep her away from Merean."

Lan grunted. "All Aes Sedai are dangerous. Iselle is safe enough for the moment; I saw her on my way here, hurrying somewhere with Brys and Diryk. Why did Bukama die, Aes Sedai? What did I snare him in for you?"

Moiraine flung up a hand for silence, and a tiny part of her was surprised when he obeyed. The rest of her thought furiously. Merean with Iselle. Iselle with Brys and Diryk. Merean had tried to kill Lan. Suddenly she saw a pattern, perfect in every line; it made no sense, but she did not doubt it was real.

"Diryk told me you are the luckiest man in the world," she said, leaning toward Lan intently, "and for his sake, I hope he was right. Where would Brys go for absolute privacy? Somewhere he would not be seen or heard." It would have to be a place he felt comfortable, yet isolated.

"There is a walk on the west side of the Palace," Lan said slowly. Then his voice quickened. "If there is danger to Brys, I must rouse the guards." He was already turning, hand on the door handle.

"No!" she said. She still held the Power, and she prepared a weave of Air to seize him if necessary. "Prince Brys will not appreciate having his guards burst in if Merean is simply talking to him."

"And if she is not talking?" he demanded.

"Then there is not enough time for rousing the guards, if they would come. We have no proof of anything against her, Lan. Suspicions against the word of an Aes Sedai." His head jerked angrily, and he growled something about Aes Sedai that she deliberately did not hear. She would have had to make him smart for it, and there was no time. "Take me to this walk, Lan. Let Aes Sedai deal with Aes Sedai. And let us hurry." If Merean did any talking, Moiraine did not expect her to talk for long.

Hurry Lan surely did, long legs flashing as he ran. All she could do was gather her skirts high and run after him, ignoring the stares and murmurs of servants and others in the corridors at her exposure of stockinged legs, thanking the Light that the man did not outpace her. She let the Power fill her as she ran, till sweetness and joy bordered pain in their intensity, and tried to plan what she would do, what she could do, against a woman considerably stronger than she, a woman who had been Aes Sedai more than a hundred years before her own great-grandmother was born. She wished she were not so afraid. She wished Siuan were with her.

The mad dash led through glittering state chambers, along statuary-lined hallways, and suddenly they were into the open, the sounds of the Palace left behind, on a long stone-railed walk twenty paces wide with a vista across the city roofs far below. A cold wind blew like a storm, tugging at her skirts. Merean was there, surrounded by the glow of *saidar,* and Brys and Diryk, standing by the rail, twisting futilely against bonds and gags of Air. Iselle was frowning at the Prince and his son, and surprisingly, further down the walk stood a glowering Ryne, his arms folded across his chest. So he *was* a Darkfriend.

". . . and I could hardly bring Lord Diryk to you without his father," Iselle was saying petulantly. "I *did* make sure no one knows, but why—?"

Weaving a shield of Spirit, Moiraine hurled it at Merean with every shred of the Power in her, hoping against hope to cut the woman off from the Source. The shield struck and splintered. Merean was too strong, drawing too near her capacity.

She knew she had caught the Blue sister—the Black sister—by surprise, but Merean did not even blink. "You did well enough killing the spy, Ryne," she said calmly as she wove a gag of Air to stop up Iselle's mouth and bonds that held the girl stiff and wide-eyed. "See if you can make certain of the younger one this time. You did say you are a better swordsman."

Everything seemed to happen at once. Ryne rushed forward, scowling, the bells in his braids chiming. Lan barely got his own sword out in time to meet him. And before the first clash of steel on steel, Merean struck at Moiraine with the same weave she herself had used, but stronger. In horror Moiraine realized that Merean might have sufficient strength remaining to shield her even while she was embracing as much of *saidar* as she could. Frantically she struck out with Air and Fire, and Merean grunted as the severed flows snapped back into her. In the brief interval, Moiraine tried to slice the flows holding Diryk and the others, but before her weave touched Merean's, Merean sliced hers instead, and this time Merean's attempted shield actually touched her before she could cut it. Moiraine's stomach tried to tie itself in a knot.

"You appear too often, Moiraine," Merean said as though they were simply chatting. She looked as if there were no more to it, serene and motherly, not in the slightest perturbed. "I fear I must ask you how, and why." Moiraine just managed to sever a weave of Fire that would have burned off her clothes and perhaps most of her skin, and Merean smiled, a mother amused at the mischief young women get up to. "Don't worry, child. I'll Heal you to answer my questions. And answer, you will. Out here, no one will hear your screams."

If Moiraine had had any lingering doubts that Merean was Black Ajah, that weave of Fire would have ended them. In the next moments she had more proof, weavings that made sparks dance on her dress and her hair rise, weavings that had her gasping for air that was no longer there, weavings she could not recognize yet surely would have left her broken and bleeding if they settled around her, if she had failed to cut them. . . .

When she could, she tried again and again to cut the bonds holding Diryk and the others, to shield Merean, even to knock her unconscious. She knew she fought for her life—she would die if the other woman won, now or after Merean's questioning—but she never considered that loophole in the Oaths that held her. She had questions of her own for the woman, and the fate of the world might rest on the answers. Unfortunately, most of what she could do was defend herself, and that always on the brink. Her stomach *was* in a knot, and trying to make another. Holding three people bound, Merean was still a match for her, and maybe more. If only Lan could distract the woman.

A hasty glance showed how unlikely that was. Lan and Ryne danced the forms, gracefully flowing from one to another, their blades like whirlwinds, but if there was a hair between their abilities, it rested with Ryne. Blood fanned down the side of Lan's face.

Grimly, Moiraine bore down, not even sparing the bit of concentration necessary to ignore the cold. Shivering, she struck at Merean, defended herself and struck again, defended and struck. If she could manage to wear the woman down, or. . . .

"This is taking too long, don't you think, child?" Merean said. Diryk floated into the air, struggling against the bonds he could not see as he drifted over the railing. Brys's head twisted, following his son, and his mouth worked around his unseen gag.

"No!" Moiraine screamed. Desperately, she flung out flows of Air to drag the boy back to safety. Merean slashed them even as she released her own hold on him. Wailing, Diryk fell, and white light exploded in Moiraine's head.

Groggily she opened her eyes, the boy's fading shriek

still echoing in her mind. She was on her back on the stone walk, her head spinning. Until that cleared, she had as much chance of embracing *saidar* as a cat did of singing. Not that it made any difference, now. She could see the shield Merean was holding on her, and even a weaker woman could maintain a shield once in place. She tried to rise, fell back, managed to push up on an elbow.

Only moments had passed. Lan and Ryne still danced their deadly dance to the clash of steel. Brys was rigid for more than his bonds, staring at Merean with such implacable hate it seemed he might break free on the strength of his rage. Iselle was trembling, snuffling and weeping and staring wide-eyed at where the boy had fallen. Diryk. Moiraine made herself think the boy's name, flinched to recall his grinning enthusiasm. Only moments.

"You will hold a little longer for me, I think," Merean said, turning away from her. Brys rose above the walk. The stocky man's face never changed, never stopped staring hatred at Merean.

Moiraine struggled to her knees. She could not channel. She had no courage left, no strength. Only determination. Brys floated over the railing. Moiraine tottered to her feet. Determination. That look of pure hate etched on his face, Brys fell, never making a sound. This had to end. Iselle lifted into the air, writhing frantically, throat working in an effort to scream past her gag. It had to end now! Stumbling, Moiraine drove her belt knife into Merean's back to the hilt, blood spurting over her hands.

They fell to the paving stones together, the glow around Merean vanishing as she died, the shield on Moiraine vanishing. Iselle screamed, swaying where Merean's bonds had let her drop, atop the stone railing. Pushing herself to move, Moiraine scrambled across Merean's corpse, seized one of Iselle's flailing hands in hers just as the girl's slippers slid off into open air.

The jolt pulled Moiraine belly-down across the railing, staring down at the girl held by her blood-slick grip above a drop that seemed to go on forever. It was all Moiraine could do to hold them where they were, teetering. If she tried to pull the girl up, they would both go over. Iselle's face was contorted, her mouth a rictus. Her hand slipped in Moiraine's grasp. Forcing herself to calm, Moiraine reached for the Source and failed. Staring down at those distant rooftops did not help her whirling head. Again she tried, but it was like trying to scoop up water with spread fingers. She *would* save one of the three, though, if the most useless of them. Fighting dizziness, she strove for *saidar*. And Iselle's hand slid out of her bloody fingers. All Moiraine could do was watch her fall, shrieking a long, dwindling cry, hand still stretched up as if she believed someone might yet save her.

An arm pulled Moiraine away from the railing.

"Never watch a death you don't have to," Lan said, setting her on her feet. His right arm hung at his side, a long slash laying open the blood-soaked sleeve and the flesh beneath, and he had other injuries besides the gash on his scalp that still trickled red down his face. Ryne lay on his back ten paces away, staring at the sky in sightless surprise. "A black day," Lan muttered. "As black as ever I've seen."

"A moment," she told him, her voice unsteady. "I am too dizzy to walk far, yet." Her knees wavered as she walked to Merean's body. There would be no answers. The Black Ajah would remain hidden. Bending, she withdrew her belt knife from the woman's back and cleaned it on the traitor's skirts.

"You are a cool one, Aes Sedai," Lan said flatly.

"As cool as I must be," she told him. Diryk's scream rang in her ears. Iselle's face dwindled below her. As in the test for the shawl, all her calm was outward show, but she clung to it tightly. Let go for an instant, and she would be on her knees weeping. Howling with grief. "It seems Ryne was wrong as well as a Darkfriend. You were better than he."

Lan shook his head slightly. "He was better. But he thought I was finished, with only one arm. He never understood. You surrender after you're dead."

Moiraine nodded. Surrender after you are dead. Yes.

It took a little while for her head to clear enough that she could embrace the Source again, and she had to put up with Lan's anxiety to let the *shatayan* know that Brys and Diryk were dead before word came that their bodies had been found on the rooftops. Understandably, he seemed less eager to inform the Lady Edeyn of her daughter's death. Moiraine was anxious about time, too, if not for the same reasons. She should have been able to save the girl. That death lay on her as much as on Merean.

She Healed Lan as soon as she was able, and he gasped in shock as the complex weaves of Spirit, Air and Water knit up his wounds, flesh writhing together into unscarred wholeness, but she felt no satisfaction that he finally showed himself mortal. He was weak afterward, drained by Healing atop his fight, weak enough to catch his breath leaning on the stone rail. He would run nowhere for a while. She had to make sure he knew what to say. And she had other plans for him.

Carefully she floated Merean's body over that rail on flows of Air, and down a little, close to the stone of the mountain. Flows of Fire, and flame enveloped the Black sister, flame so hot there was no smoke, only a thick shimmering in the air, and the occasional crack of a splitting rock.

"What are you—?" Lan began, then changed it to "Why?"

She let herself feel the rising heat, currents of air fit for a furnace. "There is no proof she was Black Ajah, only that she was Aes Sedai." She winced at her slip. The White Tower needed its armor of secrecy again, more than it had when Malkier died, but she could not tell him that. Not yet. But he did not so much as blink at mention of the Black Ajah. Perhaps he was ignorant of it, but she would not wager on it. The man was as self-contained as any sister. "I cannot lie about what happened here, but I can be silent. Will you be silent, or will you do the Shadow's work?"

"You are a very hard woman," he said finally. That was the only answer he gave, but it was enough.

"I am as hard as I must be," she told him. Diryk's scream. Iselle's face. There was still Ryne's body to dispose of, and the blood on the floorstones, on their clothing. As hard as she must be.

EPILOGUE

Next dawn found the Aesdaishar in mourning, white banners flying from every prominence, the servants with long white cloths tied to their arms. Rumors in the city already talked of portents that had foretold the deaths, comets in the night, fires in the sky. People had a way of folding what they saw into what they knew and what they wanted to believe. The disappearance of a simple soldier, and even of an Aes Sedai, escaped notice alongside bone-deep grief that had strong men weeping in the corridors.

Returning from destroying Merean's belongings—after searching in vain for any clue to other Black sisters—Moiraine stepped aside for Edeyn Arrel, who glided down the hallway in a white gown, her hair cut raggedly short. Whispers said she intended to retire from the world. Moiraine thought she already had. The woman's staring eyes looked haggard and old. In a way, they looked much as her daughter's did, in Moiraine's mind, full of despair and the knowledge of death coming soon.

When she entered her apartments, Siuan leaped up from a chair in the sitting room. It seemed weeks since Moiraine had seen her. "You look like you reached into the bait well and found a fangfish," she growled. "Well, it's no surprise. I always hated mourning when I knew the people. Anyway, we can go whenever you're ready. Rahien was born in a farmhouse almost two miles from Dragonmount. Merean hasn't been near him, as of this morning. I don't suppose she'll harm him on suspicion even if she is Black."

Not the one. Somehow, Moiraine had almost expected

that. "Merean will not harm anyone ever again, Siuan. Put that mind of yours to a puzzle for me." Settling in a chair, she began with the end, and hurried through despite Siuan's gasps and demands for more detail. It was almost like living it again. Getting to what had led her to that confrontation was a relief. "She wanted Diryk dead most of all, Siuan; she killed him first. And she tried to kill Lan."

"That's mad," Siuan growled. "What links an eight-year-old boy to a coldhearted lionfish like Lan?"

"Luck. Diryk survived a fall that should have killed him, and everyone says Lan is the luckiest man alive or the Blight would have killed him years ago. It makes a pattern, but the pattern looks crazy to me. Maybe your blacksmith is even part of it. And Josef Najima, back in Canluum, for all I know. He was lucky, too. Puzzle it out for me if you can. I think it is important, but I cannot see how."

Siuan strode back and forth across the room, kicking her skirt and rubbing her chin, muttering about "men with luck" and "the blacksmith rose suddenly" and other things Moiraine could not make out. Suddenly she stopped dead and said, "She never went near Rahien, Moiraine. The Black Ajah knows the Dragon was Reborn, but they don't bloody know *when*! Maybe Tamra managed to keep it back, or maybe they were too rough and she died before they could pry it out of her. That has to be it!" Her eagerness turned to horror. "Light! They're killing any man or boy who *might* be able to channel! Oh, burn me, thousands could die, Moiraine. Tens of thousands."

It did make a terrible sense. Men who could channel seldom knew what they were doing, at least in the beginning. At first, they often just seemed to be lucky. Events favored them, and frequently, like the blacksmith, they rose to prominence with unexpected suddenness. Siuan was right. The Black Ajah had begun a slaughter.

"But they do not know to look for a baby," Moiraine said. As hard as she had to be. "An infant will show no signs. We have more time than we thought. Not enough to be careless, though. Any sister can be Black. I think Cadsuane is. They know others are looking. If one of Tamra's searchers locates the boy and they find her with him, or if they decide to question one of them instead of killing her as soon as it is convenient. . . ." Siuan was staring at her. "We still have the task," Moiraine told her.

"I know," Siuan said slowly. "I just never thought. . . . Well, when there's work to do, you haul nets or gut fish." That lacked her usual force, though. "We can be on our way to Arafel before noon."

"You go back to the Tower," Moiraine said. Together, they could search no faster than one could alone, and if they had to be apart, what better place for Siuan than working for Cetalia Delarme, seeing the reports of all the Blue Ajah eyes-and-ears? While Moiraine hunted for the boy, Siuan could learn what was happening in every land, and knowing what she was looking for, she could spot any sign of the Black Ajah or the Dragon Reborn. Siuan truly could see sense when it was pointed out to her, though it took some effort this time, and when she agreed, she did it with a poor grace.

"Cetalia will use me to caulk drafts for running off without leave," she grumbled. "Burn me! Hung out on a drying rack in the Tower! I'll be lucky if she doesn't have me birched! Moiraine, the politics are enough to make you sweat buckets in midwinter! I hate it!" But she was already pawing through the trunks to see what she could take with her for the ride back to Tar Valon. "I suppose you warned that fellow Lan. Seems to me, he deserves it, much good it'll do him. I heard he rode out an hour ago, heading for the Blight, and if that doesn't kill him—Where are you going?"

"I have unfinished business with the man," Moiraine said over her shoulder. She had made a decision about him the first day she knew him, if he turned out not to be a Darkfriend, and she intended to keep it.

In the stable where Arrow was kept, silver marks tossed like pennies got the mare saddled and bridled almost while the coins were still in air, and she scrambled onto the animal's back without a care that her skirts pushed up to bare her legs above the knee. Digging her heels in, she galloped out of the Aesdaishar and north through the city, making people leap aside and once setting Arrow to leap cleanly over an empty wagon with a driver too slow to move out of her way. She left a tumult of shouts and shaken fists behind.

On the road north from the city, she slowed enough to ask wagon drivers heading the other way whether they had seen a Malkieri on a bay stallion, and was more than a little relieved the first time she got a "yes." The man could have gone in fifty directions after crossing the moat bridge. And with an hour's lead. . . . She would catch him if she had to follow him into the Blight!

"A Malkieri?" The skinny merchant in a dark blue cloak looked startled. "Well, my guards told me there's one up there. Dangerous fellows, those Malkieri." Twisting on his wagon seat, he pointed to a grassy hill a hundred paces off the road. Two horses stood in plain sight at the crest, one a packhorse, and the thin smoke of a fire curled into the breeze.

Lan barely looked up when she dismounted. Kneeling beside the remains of a small fire, he was stirring the ashes with a long twig. Strangely, the smell of burned hair hung in the air. "I had hoped you were done with me," he said.

"Not quite yet," she told him. "Burning your future? It will sorrow a great many, I think, when you die in the Blight."

"Burning my past," he said, rising. "Burning memories. A nation. The Golden Crane will fly no more." He started to kick dirt over the ashes, then hesitated and bent to scoop up damp soil and pour it out of his hands almost formally. "No one will sorrow for me when I die, because those who would are dead already. Besides, all men die."

"Only fools choose to die before they must. I want you to be my Warder, Lan Mandragoran."

He stared at her unblinking, then shook his head. "I should have known it would be that. I have a war to fight, Aes Sedai, and no desire to help you weave White Tower webs. Find another."

"I fight the same war as you, against the Shadow. Merean was Black Ajah." She told him all of it, from Gitara's Foretelling in the presence of the Amyrlin Seat and two Accepted to what she and Siuan had reasoned out, the deaths of Tamra's searchers, every last bit. For another man, she would have left most unsaid, but there were few secrets between Warder and Aes Sedai. For another man, she might have softened it, but she did not believe hidden enemies frightened him, not even when they were Aes Sedai. "You said you burned your past. Let the past have its ashes. This is the same war, Lan. The most important battle yet in that war. And this one, you can win."

For a long time he stood staring north, toward the Blight. She did not know what she would do if he refused. She had told him more than she should have anyone but her bonded Warder.

Suddenly he turned, sword flashing out, and for an instant she thought he meant to attack her. Instead he sank to his knees, the sword lying bare across his hands. "By my mother's name, I will draw as you say 'draw' and sheathe as you say 'sheathe.' By my mother's name, I will come as you say 'come' and go as you say 'go.'" He kissed the blade and looked up at her expectantly. On his knees, he made any king on a throne look meek. She would have to teach him some humility for his own sake. And for a pond's sake.

"There is a little more," she said, laying hands on his head.

The weave of Spirit was one of the most intricate known to Aes Sedai. It wove around him, settled into him, vanished. Suddenly she was aware of him, in the way that Aes Sedai were of their Warders. His emotions were a small knot in the back of her head, all steely hard determination, sharp as his blade's edge. She knew the muted pain of old injuries, tamped down and ignored. She would be able to draw on his strength at need, to find him however far away he was. They were bonded.

He rose smoothly, sheathing his sword, studying her. "Men who weren't there call it the Battle of the Shining Walls," he said abruptly. "Men who were, call it the Blood Snow. No more. They know it was a battle. On the morning of the first day, I led nearly five hundred men. Kandori, Saldaeans, Domani. By evening on the third day, half were dead or wounded. Had I made different choices, some of those dead would be alive. And others would be dead in their places. In war, you say a prayer for your dead and ride on, because there is always another fight over the next horizon. Say a prayer for the dead, Moiraine Sedai, and ride on."

Startled, she came close to gaping. She had forgotten that the bond's flow worked both ways. He knew her emotions, too, and apparently could make out hers far better than she could his. After a moment, she nodded, though she did not know how many prayers it would take to clear her mind.

Handing her Arrow's reins, he said, "Where do we ride first?"

"Back to Chachin," she admitted. "And then Arafel, and...." So few names remained that were easy to find. "The world, if need be. We win this battle, or the world dies."

Side by side they rode down the hill and turned south. Behind them the sky rumbled and turned black, another late storm rolling down from the Blight.

About the Author

Robert Jordan was born in 1948 in Charleston, South Carolina. He taught himself to read when he was four with the incidental aid of a twelve-years-older brother, and was tackling Mark Twain and Jules Verne by five. He was a graduate of the Citadel, the Military College of South Carolina, with a degree in physics. He served two tours in Vietnam with the U.S. Army; among his decorations are the Distinguished Flying Cross with bronze oak leaf cluster, the Bronze Star with "V" and bronze oak leaf cluster, and two Vietnamese Gallantry Crosses with Palm. A history buff, he also wrote dance and theater criticism. He enjoyed the outdoor sports of hunting, fishing, and sailing, and the indoor sports of poker, chess, pool, and pipe collecting. He began writing in 1977 and continued until his death on September 16, 2007.